love's true colors

Krista,

I'm so glad we had the chance to know one another! Thank you for your friendship over these past two years — and I pray God will bless your wedding & marriage! I hope you enjoy my novel!

Love,

T. E. PRICE

Ark House Press
PO Box 1722, Port Orchard, WA 98366 USA
PO Box 1321, Mona Vale NSW 1660 Australia
PO Box 318 334, West Harbour, Auckland 0661 New Zealand
arkhousepress.com

All Scripture quotations, unless otherwise indicated, are taken from the HOLY BIBLE, NEW INTERNATIONAL VERSION®. NIV®. Copyright ©1973, 1978, 1984 by International Bible Society. Used by permission of Zondervan. All rights reserved.

Cataloguing in Publication Data:
Title: Love's True Colors
ISBN: 9780994596826 (pbk.)
Subjects: Fiction
Other Authors/Contributors: Price, Tiffany

Printed and bound in the United Kingdom
Design and layout by initiateagency.com

The paper in this book is FSC Certified. FSC promotes environmentally responsible, socially beneficial and economically viable management of the world's forests.

MIX
Paper from responsible sources
FSC
www.fsc.org
FSC® C011217

contents

a note to my readers

This story of love is not necessarily a pretty one. There have been so many hardships endured over the years, and those hardships are explicitly expressed throughout this novel based on my life. What I hope you discover is that although romance is compelling, it is nothing compared to the discovery of Christ's love for us. I have made some poor decisions in life, but I have undeniably discovered that God's love is the most precious, healing, and fulfilling power known to human kind, and that love has been revealed directly to me. My prayer is that as you read this novel, you will extend grace while ultimately realizing that Christ took all of my sins, the sins that nailed him to a cross, and He died so that I might live. The beauty of Christ's gift to me became mine when I expressed faith in my resurrected Lord and Savior, and I – an undeserving sinner – was accepted by God because of what Christ did on the cross for me. "For God so loved the world that he gave his one and only Son, that whoever believes in him shall not perish but have eternal life" John 3:16.

acknowledgements

I want to thank my mom, Dr. Mary-Lynn Chambers, for the endless hours spent editing my work and exploring the story line with me. You believed in my dream to cultivate my love story into a novel from the moment I suggested it, and you were willing to assist me every step of the way. I also want to give a big thank you to my dad, Bob Chambers, for always refocusing my vision for this novel on the opportunity to share the Gospel with those who need to hear it the most, and for reminding me that doing God's work is not always easy, but it is always worth the hardships. Thank you to my sisters who were an inspiration; April and Chanelle are my best friends, and they have stuck with me through thick and thin. Another thank you goes to my extended family, the McRae clan, and my closest friends for being there for me when I needed them the most. Finally, I thank God for making this novel possible. My relationship with Christ is the ultimate reason why I wanted to share my love story with the hope of making real the true revelation of love – God's undeniable love for us, His children.

dedication

To my husband, thank you for loving me unconditionally, championing my work, and ultimately making this love story possible through your commitment to honor God in our relationship. I love being your wife – you are my soulmate and my one true love. Thank you for your willingness to endure all the hardships over the years in order to make our marriage what it is today.

prologue

I'm Tessa McRae – here is what I know about love…

Love is unexpected, unexplainable, and unpredictable. Love is not always fair, and it's never a perfect fairytale. At times, love is a choice, but often it can be an unrelenting, repetitive stab to the heart. Love can be beneficial, or it can be an inescapable curse. Love can part the heavens, or shatter your world. Love can keep you rooted, or make you do unfathomable things. Love is defined in many ways, but those who know love know its bite.

Love is capable of surprises. A smile from a certain someone can set love in motion. A coo from the infant in your arms can fill a hurting heart. Mended family relationships can provide a home full of warmth. Patience from God can reveal a grace unknown. Love can be accompanied by many joys. Yet, if love is so wonderful, why does it cause so much pain?

I don't have all the answers, who knows, maybe one day I will. What I do know is that my view on love is seen through my eyes and my experiences. Love has pieced together my story filled with disappointments, with surprises, with hurt, and with hope, and it is a story worth telling because it is a tale of discovery. This is my story, revealing the true colors of love, and it starts when I was just 16…

chapter one

(March, 2006)

I roll down my window and let the breeze blow through my long, sandy brown hair. The fresh air offers a welcome contrast to my slightly warm face as the hot, North Carolina sun insists on burning through the occasional cloud that attempts to conceal it. We drive by a field of freshly cut grass on our way into town, and I take in the scent of spring as I close my eyes and listen to the radio play J Lo's latest song.

Rachel is driving. She received her license a week ago, and we have been driving her new 2005, 4-door red Nissan in and out of town many times since she proudly pulled away from the DMV. Honestly, I was shocked that she passed her test. Rachel is my best friend, and I think she has several useful talents; unfortunately, driving is not one of them. I am quickly reminded of this as she yanks the steering wheel to the right, dodging a black object that is heading straight for her front, left tire. I grab for my seat belt that has yet to be strapped over my body and hold on tight as she comes dangerously close to the graveled edge of the country road.

"Whoa," Rachel half snickers as she attempts to regain control of her new car. "Did you see what was in the middle of the road? I think it was a dog, poor thing."

Slightly traumatized, I try to force out a few words as my adrenaline from the near miss begins to subside. "Yeah Rach, you have to be careful out here," I squeak through a constricted throat, while trying to ignore the beating of my heart still pounding loudly in my ears. Of course, what do I know? Between my athletic schedule and the remaining hours of Drivers Ed, I still have a couple of months before I can take my test. Although I am looking forward to joining the newly licensed, I am not eager to take my mother's clunky old van to the DMV and complete the tedious, yet effortless task of navigating through the few traffic lights, three point turns, and one way streets that our small town has to offer.

Risking a side glance at Rachel, I try to inconspicuously put on my seat belt without her catching the movement that visibly reveals my lack of confidence in her driving. Thankfully, she is distracted by unrolling her window and letting her slightly flushed cheeks feel the breeze; clearly she is flustered from the object in the road and by her decision to put our lives at risk in order to dodge it.

Watching Rachel's long, dark hair sway in the breeze as she places her designer shades on her gorgeous face, I am reminded of how inferior I feel sitting next to this stunning Brazilian who decided to befriend me four years ago. Her perfectly manicured fingernails, flawless bronze face beautifully framed by her flowing bangs, and her outfits pieced together perfectly makes her an ideal candidate for the front page of Cosmo Magazine. Even after our potentially life threatening near miss just behind us, Rachel is calm and collected. That is always her demeanor. Rachel displays a sense of confidence and control no matter what the circumstance. Envious of her mannerisms, I secretly try to mimic them when she isn't around, but the truth remains - Rachel and I are polar opposites.

She is sexy, I am fun. She is strong willed, I am prone to let people walk all over me. She is dominant, I am submissive. She never leaves the house without fully applying make-up, I am content with a touch of cover up and a dash of mascara. She is a cheerleader, I am an athlete. She has a naturally dark complexion, I struggle to keep a base tan between regular visits to the tanning salon. She has beautiful, shiny, flowing hair, I have naturally curly hair that requires constant use of the straightener. She is loved by all men, I am barely noticed by them. She is flawless, I am flawed. However, no matter the differences, we are best friends.

The harsh curb of our city's most popular fast food joint, Sonic, jolts me out of my self-commiserating thoughts. The rows of angled parking spots all lined with their own menu and speaker to order, makes this place a favorite for all new drivers who are pleased to be sitting behind the wheel.

"Whatcha want Tessa? I'll treat you seeing as you grabbed the bill last night at Smoothie King," says Rachel, jovially.

"Not sure yet," I say slowly. I had plenty of time to meditate on what would help cool me off on this unusually warm Saturday afternoon in March, but I got distracted on our trip here. "Just pull up to the menu and I'll take a look."

However, I don't get a chance to filter through the options that Sonic has to offer because I spot Destiny who is parked beside us. "Rach, look, there's Destiny," I whisper, nodding at the brand new Mustang parked uncomfortably close to our vehicle. The convertible is black and shiny, offering a blinding reminder of my family's financial circumstances and the fact that my two choices of vehicles to eventually parade around in when I get my license are either my mother's unsightly van or my father's little, beat-up, black truck. My hope is to save enough babysitting money to buy my own car, but for the time being, I am content with being the permanent passenger in Rachel's appealing new Nissan.

"Ah, figures she would have the top down," Rachel sighs quietly as she steals a glance up to the sun roof she has in place – the second option to the convertible her dad refused to buy. Rachel adores anything that will draw extra attention to the ever present sexy image that she most elegantly portrays. She is the classy type, Destiny is not.

"I strongly dislike that girl!" I hiss between clenched teeth. "You know last volleyball season she actually tried to trip me underneath the net as I raced to set a ball that was poorly passed. The ref didn't see, but I was sure to utter a piece of my mind loud enough for her to catch bits and pieces of it."

"Yeah, she is in my Spanish class. I'm not a big fan of her either; she is always friendly, but she is two faced, and I know she bashes me every chance she gets," Rachel says with an air of indifference. However, Rachel doesn't have to play against her. Knowing that our two high schools are rivals and have been for over 40 years only heightens my dislike towards Destiny.

"She is a catalyst for drama on the court as well," I spit out as Destiny glances towards our car and immediately picks up her cell phone. She is probably texting all her friends regarding our whereabouts. She is detestable.

The waiter drops off a large ice cream at Destiny's window. I smirk at the reason why she carries a little extra weight in her stomach. I'm unfortunately aware of her physique because of the many times she needlessly lifted her volleyball jersey to wipe her sweat-less face during a game. Then there were all those times when she paraded around the court in her spandex shorts, which were purposefully pulled up to display the lower curves of her enormous bottom. My butt commands a significant amount of attention, but it is nothing compared to Destiny's. She certainly knows how to draw all the high school boys to our rival matches.

"I wouldn't stress about her Tessa. She may be attractive, but half the time she is trying to decide whether she likes boys or girls and the other half of her time she spends smothering cover up all over the visible parts of her ghostly body to mask her hickeys." Rachel laughs as she continues, "Girls don't tend to like me anyway, so I'm not too worried about Destiny. Let's order, this heat is clouding my thoughts and making me talk badly about people I don't necessarily care for."

After I give my order to Rachel, I watch her press the intercom button that connects our voice to the readily available waiter standing inside the small yellow building perched at the end of the angled cars. Rachel clears her throat before communicating our beverage order with her seductive voice; this is the voice she uses tirelessly when ordering from a male.

"A large sweet tea and a medium blueberry slushy please," she reels off as the waiter tells us our total and promises to be out with our two drinks in no time. Her provocative voice has undoubtedly peaked his interest. This is evident through his willingness to deliver our drinks swiftly to our car window. I'm confident that his only job is to take the orders, not to carry them to the vehicles.

"Here you are ladies," says the attractive waiter who was moments before just a voice over the intercom. He hands Rachel the drinks, and she shoves my slushy at me without even glancing in my direction, then pays the waiter.

"Thanks," she says flirtatiously, "it's a scorching day and we were eager to cool off; where else to get an ice cold beverage but Sonic?" she giggles. The Mustang beside us pulls loudly into the thin traffic of our town's busiest road, distracting Rachel for a second. Her diverted gaze momentarily allows the attention of the waiter to drift off of Rachel and let his eyes briefly linger on me before deciding that my Lady Bruins volleyball t-shirt and torn jean shorts were not worthy of wasting valuable time that could be spent feasting his eyes on Rachel. They talk for a bit longer as I reflect on how Rachel nonchalantly tosses her hair over her shoulder, curls one tanned leg under the other and sips her drink periodically between bouts of fake laughter and fanning her bare neck. This action easily directs the waiter's gaze down to a perfect, birds-eye view of her cleavage, revealing only a small portion of her huge breasts hidden mysteriously inside her Banana Republic tank top.

"3344," I barely hear her say as she repeats the last four digits of her cell phone number for the waiter, who is scribbling on the receipt before he rushes back to his responsibilities with a promise to text her after his shift ends. This is a normal scene for us. Rachel flirts, I sit awkwardly on the side lines trying not to reveal my interest in examining her many tactics that I will eventually use at my school, the one setting I don't share with Rachel.

Neither one of us has a boyfriend. Actually, I don't have a boyfriend and Rachel has many boyfriends, none of whom she is willing to go steady with, for then she would have to drop all the others. One of the many things I love about Rachel is that she can be found sharing a kiss with a guy behind a cracked door or in an almost empty room, but she never commits to anything more. I'm sure this has left many of the guys frustrated, faced with a challenge they are devoted to pursue, but she has no interest in sacrificing her virginity for fleeting pleasure.

Considering Rachel's most recent flirtatious conversations, I reflect on the fact that I have never had a steady boyfriend, although at the young age of 16 what is to be expected? However, I did have a few prospects at my high school. I play three sports a year and spend most of my weekends with Rachel; there isn't much room for anything or anyone else, not that I wouldn't be interested in creating some space in my schedule if the right guy came along.

"I think your family is coming over for dinner tonight," Rachel states with the slightest hint of a smile still lingering from the scene a few moments earlier.

"Yeah, my mom mentioned that while dropping me off at your place last night. I was tired after track practice, so I was only half listening to her. What time are we supposed to be coming over?" Our families, the McRaes and the Herns, spend almost every Saturday evening together. Our mothers are best friends, our fathers are best friends, and our sisters (both older and younger) in both families are best friends. Together, each family of five has created an inseparable bond with the other since we were introduced at our church over four years ago.

"5:30 I believe," says Rachel, "but you know our mothers, they are probably sipping red wine in our lounge, while enjoying the sun shining in through those big windows my mom is so proud of. I am sure she is pointing out to your mom our newly planted garden next to the pool as they laugh about this past week's events."

It is 4:00, and Rachel is probably correct. "Well, we better hurry home and figure out what is so comical about their day-to-day activities that they have to meet early to discuss them," I smirk. The truth is, I love the dynamics of our family's friendship with the Herns; we have what most wish for with blood relatives.

Rachel lets out a hearty laugh as she steps on the gas and turns up the radio. We spend most of the trip back to her place singing along to the popular tunes of our one, and only one, hit station.

Pulling onto Santa Monica Drive, Rachel turns the volume down on the radio and begins to roll up our windows. We both know that if Mr. Hern catches us having a great time driving "recklessly" with loud music and no care in the world, he will be skeptical about future trips into town, or anywhere for that matter. "Safety comes first," he warns, unfailingly, every time we head out in Rachel's car.

I bend down to collect the contents of my purse that are strewn across the floor of the passenger's side, an inevitable result from the many sharp curves Rachel has taken without slowing down to the recommended speed. However, movement out of the corner of my eye distracts me from completing this tedious task.

Off to one side, on a large cement drive, is an amazingly built, shirtless, highly attractive blonde dribbling a basketball athletically toward the hoop that is suspended from a pole firmly positioned beside the drive. I realize his driveway is only a few houses down from the Herns. At this point, my eyes are so fixed on the guy that I don't even care to see the outcome of his shot. However, I happen to notice the ball effortlessly slips through the hoop as this mysterious male picks it up, hikes up his sagging athletic mesh shorts and dribbles to the outskirts of his driveway with ease.

"Who is that?" I inquire as my head turns with the car's movement so that I can continue to gaze on the show that I am so eager to watch, not caring if he happens to catch sight of my slightly gaping mouth and transfixed eyes.

"Oh, that's Mason Pierce. He goes to my high school, he's in our year too. I'm surprised you haven't seen him out here before. Then again, I'm told he spends all his extra time on the baseball diamond behind Bojangles with his dad. Someone said they saw his dad pitching to him, and Mason didn't even have a catcher's chest protector on. They said it's actually really dangerous because if he blocks a pitch just right, it could stop his heart, and his dad wasn't throwing gently either. But I guess that's Mason for you, he's willing to take whatever risk possible to advance his sporting career," she concludes as she throws her Nissan into park, swings open her car door and grabs our two empty Sonic cups from the center consol.

"Gosh, he is gorgeous!! He has never asked for your number in the three years you've been going to high school together?" I ask, hoping against all hope that he hasn't shown any interest in my stunning best friend.

"Well, we have Algebra together this semester, but we have only chatted a few times, and that's usually because I ask for his help. I did discover that he was held back in elementary school though, which is shocking because he has one of the highest grade point averages in our graduating class. But Tessa, you know I like my men to be at least 6'3, Mason's baseball roster says he's only 5'10 – not tall enough for me," she reels off absent-mindedly, completely oblivious at this point to my obvious interest in the guy.

He looks perfect to me; just the right height with an athletic, broad build, gorgeously shaped face, and nice bulging biceps – every girl's dream! I think as I hastily grab for my purse and it's belongings before closing my door with an extra humph in a lousy attempt to alert Mason's attention to my existence.

"Is he dating anyone?" I ask Rachel eagerly. She pauses on the white stone stairs leading up to her house, understanding dawning on her face as she raises one eyebrow and cocks her head to the side.

"No," she contemplates, "but Destiny showed some interest in him a couple of months back. I heard Mason hung out with her a little here and there, but that was mostly because he was already at their house spending time with her older brother who plays on the team with him. He's never really been interested in hooking up with girls Tessa, I honestly think his obsession with baseball is too strong to let a girl interfere."

I speed up the stairs behind my best friend and step through their front door, but not before stealing another glimpse at this Mason character. "I want you to introduce me to him Rach," I say earnestly, as I swing the front door closed behind me.

"Heelloooo!" I hear two women call out warmly from the lounge as we walk through the dinning room and throw our personal belongings down on the table. I had not noticed my mother's van in the driveway as we had pulled in. I was distracted with the athletic, half naked model shooting hoops a couple of houses away.

"Hi Mom," Rachel and I both say simultaneously, but we avoid the sunny lounge as I grab Rachel by the arm and drag her down the high ceilinged hallway to the bathroom. I slam the door closed, turn quickly to the large mirror and examine myself, seeing if I can hastily improve anything before walking 300 yards to meet the guy who has so dramatically captured my interest.

"You can't honestly mean that you want to meet him now Tessa," Rachel says with disdain as her eyebrows furrow, creating a wrinkle at the bridge of her nose.

"Yes, I do," I say with enthusiasm, as I grab her stick of mascara and apply it to both eyes, then quickly pinch my cheeks right above my cheek bone - all in an effort to bring some color to my face. Luckily, the open car window and blue slushy I sucked back on our way home have collectively kept the beads of sweat from sticking to my forehead and upper lip. Flashing my pearly whites at the mirror, I notice that I still have a hint of blue at the edge of my gums and teeth. Cursing my drink preference, I clutch onto Rachel and together we move to the front door, once again avoiding our moms.

"Be back in a bit!" Rachel calls out to our mothers, "I guess," she adds, for my benefit, as we step out into the sunshine. I turn to see if Mason is still visible. He is!

With emotions landing me somewhere between excited and anxious, I explain, "Okay, we are going to walk by casually, and you are going to 'notice' him, then strike up a conversation. Quickly, after you exchange greetings, you are going to introduce me and say some really great things about my personality; don't lie, but make me look really fantastic!" I say energetically, as we start in his direction. I run my tongue across my teeth remembering that I should probably just share a shy smile, thanks to the lingering blue tint.

"Alright, I will," Rachel complies, "but you have to calm down a little. Mason is not the type to be enthusiastic under any circumstances. He doesn't talk much to begin with, but his whole persona is pretty modest, and I don't think he'll find your buoyancy appealing." I notice a slight hint of a grin spread across her face, and I know she is taking joy in my sudden spark of interest.

I look up as we advance closer to the greeting that I'm positive will change my life in an instant, but to my dismay, I see Mason grab his basketball and start to make his way inside. My heart sinks. I fight the sudden temptation to run and catch him before he enters through his front door, but I see the chance of him falling in love with me at first glance dwindle with every step he takes. I hear the door slam behind him, a sound that echoes in my heart and forces me to reckon with the sharp feeling of disappointment that creeps into my optimism and rapidly drains me of it.

"Huh, guess that was short lived," Rachel says with an underlying tone of discontent that I'm sure was more for my sake then hers. "You know, a lot of people at my school think Mason is a cocky prick, but I think he's just shy," she reassures me.

Whatever his reason for abandoning his basketball drills on this gorgeous afternoon, I'm sure it wasn't the weather or his sudden lack of interest in the sport. We continue walking past his house in silence, our arms linked and our heads bowed, watching our shoes slap the pavement beneath us.

"I could always introduce you next week or something. I know where he hangs out, and we have a lot of mutual friends. We could 'accidentally' bump into him, and I am sure the greeting you were hoping for will be just as exciting," she says to me with anticipation filling her voice.

"Yeah, that would be cool," I respond, knowing that my tone is void of all the enthusiasm it had contained only moments before. About half way down the road we turn around to head back to the Herns, walking in silence, not feeling the need to converse. My thoughts, filled with self-doubt, seem to repeat themselves in the same rhythmic pattern as my steps. *Am I not pretty enough? Did he catch a glimpse of me and shudder at the thought that I might be interested in striking up a conversation? Was he disgusted by my appearance and desperate to escape the greeting that was inching closer?* My thoughts circulate through my mind and heart as we pass his house again on our way back. For some reason, I have a nagging feeling that this isn't the end of my efforts to meet Mason. Maybe I feel this way because of the reassurance Rachel had given me a few houses back. Lifting up a mindless, silent prayer that I had not just lost my one opportunity to meet this guy, the desperation to get introduced to Mason continues to grow stronger. Unaware of the reasoning behind my emotions, I take one last fleeting glance at the driveway that offered so much hope only minutes before. Sighing loudly, I shrug my shoulders in an attempt to leave behind my disappointment on the front stoop. Then, with a step inside, I ready myself for an evening with my family and the Herns as I slowly click the handle of the front door closed behind me.

chapter two

(March, 2006)

"We are not letting our Friday night go to waste; quick, pack an overnight bag and get your mom to drop you off at my place as soon as possible! I have a surprise for you tonight, then we are going to Max's bonfire party out in South Hermon!" Rachel announces vibrantly over the phone. I fill my lungs slowly with air, utilizing the long pause to collect some energy before responding. It's not that I lack excitement over Rachel's plan; it's just that between my honors chemistry class this morning and track practice this afternoon, I feel exhausted. Confident that I can rejuvenate myself with a hot shower and some of my mom's pot roast, which is currently filling our modest home with a mouth watering aroma, I clear my throat, preparing to embrace Rachel's enthusiasm and match it with my own.

"Wow, that sounds like a fun night – I'm in! Let me jump in the shower and eat, I'll be over at your place in two hours, tops!" I say, allowing my faux keenness towards the nights' events slightly lift my spirits.

"Alright, sounds great! See you then!" Rachel says with more emphasis in her voice than she is prone to using.

"Okay, bye," I respond, then add hastily, "Oh, Rach," but she has already hung up. As I place my cordless phone back on its base, so that the battery can charge while I'm gone, I am reminded of my frustration towards my family's finances and the fact that I am still without a personal cell phone, but I ignore it as I consider the surprise that Rachel hinted at during the beginning of our conversation. I contemplate the many possibilities and half consider calling her back in an attempt to draw out some details. However, accustomed to my best friend's tendency to enthuse over the smallest gesture, I figure she probably just picked up a pack of Reese's Cups for me at the gas station while filling up her car. Then again, my rumbling stomach may be causing me to jump to that conclusion.

Peeling my sticky practice clothes off of my aching body, I move slowly to the shower and turn on the hot water. "Amber!" I yell. "What did you do with my body wash!?" I allow my anger to drench every word that I scream at my older sister, who unfailingly shows zero concern for my personal belongings. I can hear all 100 pounds of her tiny body stomp from her bedroom and swing open the bathroom door. Without a word, she opens the cupboard below the sink and slams it shut. I jump as I hear the thud of the large bottle hit the bottom of the bath tub and scowl at my sister's detestable mannerisms. Although Amber's new relationship with her boyfriend, Shane, has helped to ease some of her hostility, she still finds moments to express the aggressive side of her personality. Expecting to hear the bathroom door slam behind her, I pull back the curtain only to see the door standing wide open, providing a cool breeze and a room void of privacy for me to shower in. I shake my head in disbelief; although, I know I shouldn't be shocked by Amber's animosity toward me. She has been antagonistic and moody since the day she hit puberty. My hopes of mending our relationship wilted a long time ago. Now that she is completing her final year of her associates at the local community college, I have concluded that our relationship will only be agreeable at best. Cursing my laziness to shut the door, I decide to endure the cool breeze as I continue my shower.

Trying to ignore Amber's attempt to dampen my mood, I blow dry my hair, straighten it and take an unusually long time to apply my make up. Standing back, I reflect on what I see in the full length mirror. Although I spend a lot of time criticizing most of my features, I revel in what I do like about my body and face. I have a slender neck, toned arms, and a flat stomach. I wouldn't mind if my breasts were a bit larger, but they are perky and sit high on my chest, elongating my torso that leads to my lower half, where I find my build to be more athletic. The make up on my heart shaped face highlights my hazel eyes, high cheekbones, and nicely shaped lips. Overall, I don't have much to complain about, although I know I am no match to Rachel's beauty.

I throw on my favorite pair of dark jeans, a loose, hunter green sweater that hangs casually off one shoulder and my black boots, a knock off of the popular brand that were a Christmas present from my parents. Following the delicious scent of dinner, I obnoxiously hit my overnight bag on every other step as I make my way to the kitchen. Secretly, I am hoping to irritate Amber who is still locked away in her bedroom next to mine, at the top of the stairs.

"Hi love," my dad greets me as we meet in the kitchen. He is just getting home from what I assume to be a long day at the church office. He kisses the top of my head, then, lacking his usual bouncing energy, lethargically makes his way toward the recliner. I hate his decision to continue pastoring in the church after all the pain we went through two years ago, but he loves the Lord and he is committed to doing God's work, no matter the price. I will never understand why a family chooses to endure the pain and heartache of church politics only to be rewarded with a measly check at the end of each month. However, I respect my dad, and I know, beyond a shadow of a doubt, that he takes joy in his chosen line of work, even if it does exhaust him at times.

I grab a plate and start to pile a healthy amount of roast beef, potatoes, and carrots onto it. Reaching for the gravy, my mom walks into the kitchen and raises one eyebrow, "We aren't going to eat as a family tonight?" she asks, her tone hinting towards her displeasure at my premature ingestion of food.

"It's Friday night, and I promised Rachel I would be at her house in thirty minutes," I respond as I shove in the food that my mom spent all day preparing. "On that note, would you mind driving me?" I request, throwing in a meat and carrot speckled smile so that my mother would not be utterly offended at my request.

She glances at my father wistfully, hoping that maybe he would be more willing to drive me than she was, but his eyes are already closed and he is breathing deeply while laid back in his favorite recliner. With her eyes on my dad, I watch her frustration subside as the corners of her mouth slowly bloom into a small grin, revealing the 25 years of love and admiration my parents have for each other. "Okay, let's go in the next five, I want to let him sleep a little before we eat. He's had a hard week at work, he can use a little rest," she says, nodding towards my dad who confirms her statement with a quiet snore and a twitch of his leg.

"Hi Tess! Whoa, you look good," my younger sister, Chantel, says, examining me head to toe as she walks from her bottom floor bedroom to the kitchen. Chantel never fails to compliment others when the opportunity presents itself, even though she is more beautiful than most people I know. Actually both of my sisters are beautiful, and thinner than I am, but Chantel is kind and humble, unlike our grumpy older sister.

"Thanks hun," I say adoringly as I pull her in for a hug, while swallowing the last remnants of the meal I just inhaled. "If you're staying around here tonight be careful of Amber, she is in rare form," I add.

Chantel giggles, and I know it won't be long before she knocks on Amber's door to see if there is anything she can do to help Amber's pessimism towards life subside. "Love you! And don't let her ruin your night," I warn my naïve, 14 year old sister as I rush out of the back door, duffle bag swung over my shoulder.

My mom turns to me as we walk down the back steps, "Your little sister has been a peacekeeper since the day your dad named her in that memorable French hospital," she says with pride as we hop into the van and reverse down the driveway. All three of us were born and raised in Canada. My dad worked in Quebec, where he enjoyed using his French. He wanted his last daughter's name to reflect the love he has for the French language, and my mother had surprisingly agreed, despite her struggles with speaking the French language. We spend the rest of the trip to the Herns exchanging stories and memories of my childhood, formed in the country my family still takes great pride in.

"Thanks Mrs. McRae!" Rachel calls out to my mother as I jump out of my mom's van and join Rachel in her Nissan. My mother waves in response while inching the van back slowly through the gate that guards the entrance to the Hern's property.

"Alright, where to?" I question, as I inhale the familiar scent of Rachel's leather seats. I glance down at the dashboard that illuminates the interior as my best friend shifts into reverse. It is only 8:34, and I know Rachel likes to be fashionably late, especially to parties.

"The bowling alley," Rachel says, allowing a little of her revulsion for the place escape with her statement.

"What? You hate it there, and I'm not exactly in the mood to bowl at the moment. Today, our psychotic coach had us running 100 yard dashes, one after the other. He finally decided to give me a break after I lost .8 seconds from my time during the ninth round of all-out sprinting," I say, massaging my tense leg muscles full of lactic acid that rendered me incapable of moving only hours earlier.

"We are not going to the bowling alley for me, it's for you."

"Um, what exactly does that entail, Rach? Like I said, I don't think my legs can endure much more exercise today."

"You'll see," my best friend mysteriously responds with a

smile dancing across her gorgeous face. At this point, I am reminded of the surprise she mentioned in our phone call, and suddenly I am bombarding her with questions; but she refuses to tell me anything as she continues driving.

Prancing up to the bowling alley, I am giddy with anticipation. I comically announce to Rachel, "I can guarantee that I have never been this eager to spend an evening in a smoky haze, or with the company of toothless, old men, who are the usual patrons at the alley." We make our way up the steps to one of the only places in town still open after 11pm. I grab hold of the door and enter the building, pausing briefly to let Rachel step in behind me before I let it swing shut.

Then, my heart stops. I freeze in place and feel the tips of my fingers go numb with shock. Mason Pierce is sitting 20 feet inside the door, with his back facing my now trembling body, quietly watching a group of rambunctious high school boys bowl.

Rachel senses my anxiety and links her arm through mine in an effort to reassure me while escorting me to the greeting I was so desperate for last weekend. My mind is still reeling from the unexpected surprise that my best friend planned. I shake my head quickly, continue forward, and squeeze my hands together, hoping to steady them before I make my first impression. Rachel walks confidently up to the group with me at her side and calls, "Hey guys!" The group of boys quickly turn in response to Rachel's flirtatious voice. I see half of them almost drooling at the sight of her as they all exchange genuinely pleased greetings. I recognize a few of the group members from previous parties and make an effort to keep my eyes fixed on them as I wave, while avoiding, for as long as possible, turning to face Mason.

"Hi Mason, not bowling tonight?" I hear Rachel ask behind me. I am still too shaky to turn. However, he doesn't even get the chance to respond before I feel myself getting whipped around by my friend. I am suddenly standing face to face with the introduction I've been hopelessly anticipating.

"This is my bestie, Tessa," she says as I smile shyly, still too nervous to risk a greeting of my own.

Mason looks at me briefly, and my breath is cut short as our eyes meet. He has the most beautiful, crystal blue eyes, and his face is more gorgeous up close than what I thought when we drove by him the other day.

"What's up," he quietly murmurs as he looks back to his group of friends, not bothering to hold my gaze.

"Tessa is a Bruin," Rachel jokingly states with disgust as one of Mason's teammates, Braden, abandons his interest in the game and slinks a casual arm around Rachel's shoulder.

I know it's my turn to carry on the conversation now that Rachel has suddenly become preoccupied, and the silence sends me grasping for anything to fill it. "Rachel didn't explain that well," I attempt. "I play volleyball, basketball and run track against your school, and obviously you're aware of our rivalry," I finish, pointing to his Pirates baseball t-shirt that reveals a logo matching Braden's sweatshirt. Turning slightly to clarify what I had observed moments ago on Braden's upper half, I notice that Braden has whisked Rachel out of my sight.

"Yeah," is Mason's only response, still refusing to take his eyes off of his friends, who are now laughing loudly, we sit quietly for a few awkward moments before I make my last attempt at conversing with this sexy, distracted guy seated beside me.

Looking around I ask, "Any idea where Rachel is?" I am trying to make my concern for my friend's disappearance obvious; although, if he were willing to offer a lengthy response, I would not be so distressed about her current location.

"No," he quietly answers, while turning briefly to glance in the other direction, as if trying to help ease the awkwardness.

"Right, well I should probably find her," I verbalize, acting as if she needed my presence more then I needed hers. I saunter to the next room with my chest held high and my arms swinging confidently beside my body in case he is watching me walk away. I spot Rachel giggling next to Braden as he returns his bowling shoes, obviously deciding that his evening would be better spent by Rachel's side rather than with his buddies.

"Hi guys," I greet. "Rach, I need to use the bathroom, wanna come with?"

We walk casually to the restroom where I repeat, verbatim, my uneventful conversation with Mason. Although I discuss my apprehension regarding an attempt at another chat with Mason, I confide in Rachel my strong attraction to him and my desperate desire for him to reciprocate my feelings. We emerge minutes later from the bathroom, giggling fictitiously to disguise our topic of conversation shared in the privacy of the bowling alley's single-stall, ladies room.

The next hour passes with cordial conversations, occasional sport stories, and inconspicuous side glances in Mason's direction, who does not show much interest toward interacting with the group; although he sporadically engages when someone nudges him jokingly or when others look to him for approval after sharing another baseball story.

"Alright boys, we have to go," Rachel says, glancing down at her expensive wrist watch. "We are heading to Max's party for a bit," she adds, gingerly. I am sure this comment was made to enlighten Braden of her whereabouts for the remainder of the night.

As I mentally predict, he responds on cue, "Yeah we're heading there tonight too. We just have to stop off at Mason's and pick up the booze."

"Great, see you there," Rachel responds, throwing in a flashy smile and dainty wave. I slip out of the door behind her and deeply inhale the cool, crisp, fresh air, realizing how tense my body has been.

I close my door and melt into the car's luxurious seat. Throwing my head back and closing my eyes, I pray that Mason stole a side glance or two in my direction, although I know the probability of that is low. "He is perfect, Rach. How is it that I can be so attracted to a guy who will barely look at me, let alone give me the time of day?" I question while I open my eyes and shake my head, hoping the butterflies in my stomach would stop.

"I warned you, Mason is shy and he honestly doesn't talk much. You saw him with his friends - he barely managed to produce a grin in the last hour. That's just how he is."

"But he is so cool. I noticed how most of the guys in the group either glanced at him or Braden for approval with each story or joke."

"Yeah, well, they're both the captains for the team. Actually, if you want to hear Mason communicate or get passionate about something, you should come to one of his games this week. He's like Dr. Jekyll and Mr. Hyde; on the field he is loud and dominant, but everywhere else he is quiet and reserved."

"Hmm," I contemplate, "maybe I can make it to a game." My schedule is usually busy, but our only track meet this week is on Wednesday, and our coach is bound to give us a day off with the way we've been training lately.

As we drive out to South Hermon, Rachel fills the time by sharing her attraction towards Braden and the many flirtatious scenes they have shared since the start of the semester. I nod at appropriate moments, although I am barely listening – my mind is focused, unequivocally, on Mason.

We park the car on the dark road and make our way up the long driveway to the densely populated party. After pouring a double shot of vodka into my cranberry juice, I park it in a camping chair staged comfortably close to the huge fire pit at Max's. In between conversations with familiar people, I reflect on the fact that the crowd is made up of at least three high schools. I ponder the distance that a lot of people had to travel to make it to this event; there are probably three or four counties represented in the large group of high school students gathered around the fire. Sipping my drink and laughing with the many drunks who make their way from one convening group to the next, my attention is drawn immediately to the group of rowdy boys who strut up to the scene; Mason is leading the pack. I watch, incredulously, as one person after the next rushes to greet Mason. Obviously, the guy has made a name for himself, and I am wondering why it has taken me so long to find out about him. All of a sudden, I am abruptly jolted from behind. My chair nearly topples over as I reach out to steady myself. While trying to avoid spilling my drink all over my jeans, Braden leans on my chair and slurs an apology - he is drunk.

"Oh, Tessa, my bad," he laughs, hoarsely. Clearly the group has been yelling in drunken competition with one another on the way over here; that is the only explanation as to why his voice is suddenly raspy.

"No worries," I say with contempt, although he is too obliterated to detect my scorn.

"You know," he drawls, "I talked with Mason about you on the way here. He says you're super hot."

My mouth suddenly goes dry. I part my lips to answer, but words refuse to come. Quickly lifting my drink, I gulp fiercely in an attempt to mask my astonishment and delight. However, Braden must have seen my eyes widen with interest because he continues. "Yeah, I bet he would date you if he wasn't playing baseball – the guy loves the game, ya know," Braden says, using the back of his hand to wipe his mouth free of beer from his last, long drag on the bottle.

"Is he drinking tonight?" I ask Braden, wishing with all my might that the alcohol might allow some of the walls Mason undoubtedly builds to fall. I was preparing to rise from my chair in order to attempt another conversation with Mason when Braden responds.

"Are you kidding?!" he says, with a little too much enthusiasm for my taste. "We're in season! Mason won't touch alcohol or anything else for that matter. He says it slows him down on the field, and he isn't willing to take that risk. It's a lucky thing for us though because he is our designated driver, that is, until the last game of the season." He attempts to clink his beer bottle against my plastic cup, as if celebrating the fact that Mason is sober. "Cheers!" he says with a sloppy smile, but I am not celebrating with him; I am convinced that Mason would be more willing to engage in conversation with me if he were drunk.

Out of the corner of my eye I see Rachel approaching. "Uhh, Tessa, we have to go. My mom just called and she wants us home in 30 minutes. It will take us every bit of 25 to get back to my place – sorry," she says, to both me and Braden, as I tip my drink back and drain it before tossing my red solo cup in the huge trash bin placed conveniently beside my chair.

I stand quickly and watch the ground below me teeter a bit, probably due to a combination of my hasty ascent and the amount of alcohol I just consumed. We walk back to the car as I explain my conversation with Braden. Before climbing in, I glance back hoping to catch one last glimpse of Mason, but he is out of sight.

On the trip back to the Herns, I attempt to examine my emotions. Feeling overjoyed at the fact that Mason did find me attractive, I am forced to face my irritation toward his love for baseball. Braden claims that if he wasn't playing the sport, that Mason might be interested in dating me. Does that mean that we can see each other in between seasons, or does his involvement with any team have to be completely over to consider a relationship? And when do the ties with the sport end? I'm sure he takes his training so seriously because of his intentions to be recruited.

These thoughts swirl through my mind as I trudge up the front stairs to the Hern's house, make my way to Rachel's bedroom and lay my head down on the pillow that is on my side of Rachel's king size bed. Although I am half expecting the alcohol to depress my central nervous system and provide deep, sound sleep, instead I spend the night tossing and turning; thoughts and images of Mason come and go as the hours creep by.

The bright morning light shines through the adjacent window, and I awake with a slight headache and a deep feeling of agitation as I reflect on my unsatisfying sleep. I turn to where Rachel slept beside me, expecting to see her curled up in a ball, oblivious to the world, but she is not sleeping. Instead, she is sitting up in the bed, a look of fear spread across her face as her cell phone shakes slightly in her trembling hands.

"Tessa, Mason's been in a car accident."

chapter three

(April, 2006)

The beautiful orange and pink sunset has captured my attention as my family and I ride silently in the van to the Hern's house for dinner. It is unusual for the five of us to be so quiet, so I take advantage of the serenity that the sunset and silence offer and let my mind wander easily to Mason.

It had been exactly two weeks since his accident. I remember back to the Saturday morning when Rachel and I were shocked out of our sleepy slumber with the news. We had washed up quickly and threw on clothes before scrambling down to Mason's house where Braden and a couple of his friends stayed the night. They all had slept soundly and awoke only to find Mason's bed empty. Braden explained to us that Mason had dropped the group off at the end of Santa Monica Drive, given them the house key and went back to the party to pick up another car full of people. "That's the kind of guy Mason is," Braden said. "He is willing to sacrifice a night of sleep just to be sure that everyone who needs a sober driver has one." Braden paused to shake his head before moving forward with the story. "As fate would have it, Mason was on his own when he fell asleep at the wheel and flipped his Jeep twice before toppling it into a ditch. Luckily the ambulance staff recognized him and called his dad." At this point, Braden turned to me to clarify, "Mason's mom used to work at the hospital," he said as an aside. He glanced at the floor, cleared his throat and struggled to continue, "Anyway, he stayed the night in the hospital. He has a lot of bumps and bruises, a gash over his left eye where his head hit the steering wheel, but..." Braden's jaw line bulged while he clenched and unclenched his teeth. "But, he tore some pretty important ligaments in his throwing shoulder and the doctor told him that his baseball season is over. He could schedule reconstructive surgery, but the recovery time would be at least a year." Fraught with his emotions, Braden excused himself from our presence. Rachel and I were left alone in Mason's living room to contemplate the radical events that had taken place while we were sleeping. I was not sure what Rachel was thinking, but my thoughts were bouncing between the agony that I'm sure Mason was battling, and the possibilities that may be available now that Mason couldn't play baseball. Although it was selfish of me, I couldn't help but think that maybe the information Braden shared with me at the party might be a possibility now that the car accident had rendered Mason's baseball career suspended.

The driver's side window squeaks loudly, quickly bringing me back to reality as my dad raises his window cutting off the breeze that was keeping me cool. "We are here, wake up McRae clan," my dad says cheerily as he cranks our rickety van into the Hern's driveway. I am glad to see him share his usual enthusiasm for life again, now that the busyness of his church schedule has decreased, at least for the weekend. As we walk into the house, we all exchange our normal joyful greetings, full of hugs and laughter, then we head in different directions. Our mothers make for the kitchen, our fathers grab a seat in the lounge, our older sisters slink upstairs, and the younger ones race to a bedroom down the hall. Attempting to find some privacy of our own, Rachel and I make our way to the outside deck. We roll our jeans up to our knees and swing our legs into the warm water of their heated, in-ground, salt water pool that the Herns had installed a couple of summers ago.

"Well, how is he?" I ask. Rachel and I have spent most nights over the last two weeks on the phone talking about Mason. Rachel has continually updated me on his progress since the accident, and I share my many emotions on the topic. It's hard not to discuss him when he has filled my thoughts and dreams since I first spotted him playing basketball a month ago.

"He's recovering," she sighs. "He came back to school this week, but he's been even more reserved than normal. I think he is pretty devastated about the outcome of the accident. His arm isn't in a sling yet, but I overheard him telling Braden at lunch today that he will be having surgery as soon as finals are over."

"Wow, that was quick," I mutter disappointedly, knowing that I should be showing excitement for Mason's return to the sport he loves.

Rachel looks at me knowingly, as if she predicted the complicated thoughts that are muddled in my mind. "You know," she starts, "he still has a year before he can play again. His physical therapy will start a month after the surgery, so technically, he can't even play his senior year. He discussed his plans with Braden earlier this week – he wants to join a summer league as soon as he is cleared from his physical therapist, and he hopes to get recruited there. Although, his chances of this are slim, because Braden told me that most scouts look for potential recruits during their senior seasons."

I look down at our feet swinging slowly side by side in the pool water. My heart is torn, I want Mason to be involved with baseball, but not if it means that he won't have any time for me. "So, he is definitely not calling it quits for good then," I state. Rachel shakes her head in response, confirming my fears. Mason may not ever be ready for a relationship. If he has the next year and a half of his baseball career planned out perfectly, the chances of him allowing a girl to interfere are unlikely.

"Dinner's ready," I hear my mother call through the open kitchen window. Rachel gracefully withdraws her feet from the water and tiptoes over to the wicker chest that holds all the towels underneath the cabana. She takes one out, dries off her legs, and tosses the towel to me just as I pull my feet from the water.

We walk to the kitchen and grab a plate from the counter, preparing to fill it with the many food choices displayed beautifully in front of us. My dad blesses the food before the other five girls begin digging into the dishes that line the counter. I wait patiently to make my way through the options, half of my attention focused on the food, while the other half considers Mason's current circumstances.

Mrs. Hern slips in beside me, kisses the top of my head and runs her hand affectionately through my hair. "You look tired," she says as she observes my sullen face.

"Yeah, I've been thinking a lot about Mason and his car accident," I respond, pointing over my shoulder in the direction of his house to help indicate which Mason I was referring to.

"It's awful," she whispers, "the boy's been through enough, what with his family's circumstances and all."

The tongs in my right hand, which are full of my favorite goat cheese, strawberry and almond salad, stop midway to my plate as I turn to Mrs. Hern, preparing to ask about Mason and his family; however, our conversation is cut short by Chantel's exasperated scream.

"Mrs. Hern, I'm so sorry," Chantel yells from the lounge, "I accidentally spilled my grape juice on your white carpet!" My mother kicks it into high gear, grabs a rag from the sink and rushes to the site of the spill where Chantel has burst into sobs. Mrs. Hern follows my mom into the lounge and comforts Chantel, while reassuring her that the spill is not worth the tears, she bends to assist in the clean up.

Dinner consists of many conversations regarding the new events that our church is planning to implement over the summer. My dad shares some exciting information about the changes that they are making, but I manage to disengage, like I often do when they bring up church stuff. It seems that everyone in the group is excited over the events, but I remain somewhat indifferent.

* * *

The night ends as my parents call out a goodbye from the front hall, leaving all six girls curled up on the comfy, L-shaped couch for a sleep over. We waste the next couple of hours hiding under our blankets in order to avoid from the horrific movie images displayed across the big T.V. screen.

The next morning is spent lounging around the house comfortably in our pajamas. Rachel's phone buzzes loudly from it's charging outlet in the kitchen, indicating a text message. She rolls off the couch and saunters towards the illuminated phone as I follow her into the kitchen, pour another cup of coffee and curl up on the stool beside her.

"Party at Mason's tonight," she announces excitedly as she turns to catch sight of my reaction.

Thrilled, I begin to consider the clothing I chose to pack for the quiet and uneventful weekend I was anticipating. "What am I going to wear?" I ask, frantically. Although we are the same height, my bottom half is larger then Rachel's and her top half is larger then mine.

"We can easily find something for you to wear between my closet, my sisters' closets, and the overnight bags that both your sisters packed," she resolves. However, I immediately eliminate Amber's clothing from my options. Our parents banned us from borrowing each other's clothes due to the amount of arguments that flourished in the past year concerning our outfit dilemmas.

We spent the rest of the afternoon filtering through the piles of clothes from one bedroom to the next. I finally decide on a black and purple patterned tube top that clings attractively to my fit frame, low rise jean shorts that elongate my short, athletic legs, and a pair of casual flip-flops that finish off my outfit, giving it a look of easy summertime living.

Between a quick dinner, showers, hair, and make up, Rachel and I become a bit frenzied as we glance at the glowing clock on the stove and gather our purses before racing out of the front door. It is 10:00 pm and our curfew is 12:30. Luckily we only have a few hundred yards to travel. We walk excitedly, noticing the few people scattered across Mason's front lawn as they turn into familiar faces.

"What took you so long?" Braden shouts over the loud music that was playing through the sound system as we make our way into Mason's luxurious home. "You guys are only a couple of houses down, right?"

Rachel smiles and teasingly shoves Braden, "It takes a while to perfect this, ya know," she says flirtatiously, running a hand up and down her body in a show case manner.

"I highly doubt that," Braden responds, his eyes following her hand, but lingering a little longer on her partially exposed chest. "Come on," he continues, "let's get you ladies a drink."

We both follow him to the kitchen and I catch a quick glimpse of Mason in the game room grinning at one of his teammates who is dancing foolishly in front of a large group. Mason pulls his beer up to his lips and takes a swig. My stomach flips with excitement as I catch up quickly to Rachel and pour myself a drink. Rachel asks me a question as she hands me the margarita mix, but I nod without even hearing what she said. Between Pretty Ricky's voice booming through the speakers and contemplating the conversation I was going to start with Mason, I don't understand Rachel, nor do I care to.

"I'll be in the other room," I turn and say loudly to Rachel, but she just smiles and waves in my direction while getting pulled into the living room by Braden.

I pick up my pre-mixed margarita, take a couple of big gulps, and confidently make my way to the game room, where I saw Mason only minutes before. However, as I mosey into the room and scan it quickly, I see that Mason is no longer there. Confused, I pop my head out of the room, glance in both directions and continue down the hall to the living room, where I hope to find the only guy I'm looking forward to interacting with tonight.

My search for Mason is put on hold as someone leaves the bathroom at the exact moment I cross in front of the doorway. I hear a vaguely familiar voice cuss under his breath and apologize as I look at the beer dripping down my leg. The sticky substance clearly came from the bottle held in the hand of this stranger who collided with me in the dimly lit hallway. I look up, preparing to respond with fury, but my heart is instantly caught in my throat as I stare blankly into the gorgeous, blue eyes of Mason Pierce. "Let me help you with that," he says as he bends down and runs his hand up my leg, trying to clean the mess he just made.

My whole body shivers with excitement at the touch of Mason's hand, and I take a quick sip of my drink, desperate for the alcohol to suppress my butterflies and create a response worthy of his attention. He stands up slowly and wipes his beer covered hand on his jeans. As he lifts his head, the gash above his left eye comes into view, and I reflect on how well it is healing.

"Thanks, you didn't have to wipe up the beer," I say, pleased at how fortunate I was to get the host of the party cornered, alone and slightly drunk, in a romantically lit hallway.

"Oh hey, Tessa, right?" he says, focusing on my face in the muted light.

"Yeah, we met at the bowling alley a couple of weeks ago," I remind him, although I pray that he hasn't forgotten. "I'm sorry to hear about your accident. Glad that the damage wasn't too drastic though," I add, as I use my gaze to indicate the gash on his forehead.

"If you think this is bad, you should see my Jeep," Mason responds, brushing his fingers gently across his visible wound, then reaching for his right shoulder. I'm sure it is easier to discuss his vehicle rather than his career-ending injury that I know must dominate his thoughts.

"I'm sorry to hear that," I say, but quickly move the conversation forward as I watch some of the alcohol-induced optimism fade slowly from his face. "I saw a Trail Blazer in your driveway last night when we passed your house on the way to the Herns. It seems like your accident allowed for a vehicle upgrade," I add with a small grin.

"The Blazer's pretty great," he says as he drains the last few gulps of his beer. Desperate to keep him all to myself, I spur on the conversation before he has a chance to leave the hall and make his way to the kitchen for another drink.

"So, are you going to prom next weekend?" I ask hastily, as I see him turn for a moment in the direction of the kitchen. Thankfully, he decides against moving as he leans against the wall to answer me.

"No, not this year," he responds. "A girl on the volleyball team asked me to go, but our season doesn't end till two weeks after the event, so I decided against it." Then he adds with a shrug, "I figure I will probably make an appearance my senior year."

Resentment causes my face to flush a little, figuring that the girl who invited him to prom was probably Destiny. Luckily, the hallway is too dark for him to notice the new color I feel burn my cheeks as I continue. "Oh gotcha, yeah I decided not to go to mine either. I was going with a friend, but he got a girl friend two months ago and asked if he could take her instead," I say, pausing long enough to take a sip from my drink. "I didn't have a dress yet, and we hadn't decided on any details, so I just thought it was best to skip out on the fun this year and make up for it next year," I laugh in an effort to cover up my embarrassment surrounding the situation. The truth is, I want to go, but I don't have anyone to go with.

Mason chuckles as he shares, "Yeah Rachel is going to our prom with a senior from the basketball team. Braden is pissed that he didn't ask her first." We both laugh together as I finish the last few sips of my margarita. At this point, I accept the fact that we will have to leave the privacy of this wonderful hallway and head to the crowded kitchen to refill our beverages.

"Want another?" Mason asks, pointing to my empty cup.

I look down as if I didn't notice that I was finished with it, "Sure," I say as I follow him into the kitchen. Half expecting him to grab another beer and abandon my side, he surprises me by taking my empty cup and filling it up with another margarita before opening the fridge and taking a long drag from his new bottle.

We hear a burst of laughter erupt from the living room and decide to make our way to the apparently comical scene. As we walk through the entrance we catch the last line of Braden's baseball story as the crowd gathered around him laughs heartily at the joke that we missed.

"Mason, come tell everyone about that time that I got caught in a run down between second and third base - in our game against Hillside last year," Braden calls out loudly over the group, while laughing and gesturing towards Mason. However, Braden is oblivious to the look of despair that is spreading across Mason's face.

The heartache that I witnessed in Mason's features a split second earlier is now gone as he shakes his head, smiles and responds, "I think you got it covered man." He was excellent at hiding his emotions from the crowd, but his fleeting look of sorrow didn't evade my eyes. He takes another gulp of his beer and turns to me, "Wanna go outside?" he asks.

"Yeah, that sounds great," I say, as I glance in Rachel's direction, but she is distracted by the new story that Braden is proudly sharing with the crowd.

While welcoming the comfortable outdoor temperature, Mason and I talk about school, courses that we like, subjects that we do exceptionally well in and our extracurricular activities that lie outside of sports. He asks me where I live and I explain the simple way to navigate to my house. Since it is located on a well-known road in our small town, he assures me that he knows the exact location. I ask him if he has always lived in this town, and he tells me that, apart from a year in Massachusetts, he was born and raised here. We both talk so much that our drinks are still half full when Rachel comes out of the front door and motions to me. I glance down at my watch and realize that we are three minutes past our curfew, "Oh wow," I exclaim, surprised at how quickly the time has passed, "I have to go. We are a bit late for our curfew."

"Wait," he responds, then shifts his weight from one foot to the other as if trying to regain his confidence, "Can I have your number?" he asks.

My heart thuds loudly in my chest as he takes out his cell phone, and I recite the seven digits to my home line. "I should warn you, that's my house number," I say, as I blush with embarrassment. "I don't have a cell phone, and I won't be home until Sunday night," I add hastily as Rachel comes up and basically drags me from his front lawn.

"Okay, I'll give you a call then," he calls out casually while waving goodbye. He returns his cell phone to his pocket as I wave back and turn in the direction of the Hern's home, with my drink still in my hand.

Rachel looks at me, clearly impressed, "Whoa, you two must have hit it off tonight!" she says excitedly, obviously expecting me to the match her buoyancy.

I finish my margarita and wait a couple of paces before I respond reluctantly, "Yeah, we spent the whole night together, but he was drunk. He probably won't even remember that we talked, let alone his promise to call me Sunday night."

We quietly open the front door to the Herns, hoping that we don't draw attention to our tardiness. "Don't be so cynical Tessa, you never know," Rachel says in a hushed voice, while taking my empty cup from me and tossing it in the trash. We make our way to her bedroom and go through our usual nightly routine before climbing into bed. "I'm setting the alarm for 9:00 am so we have some time to get ready before church in the morning," she says to me as she turns off the lamp on her nightstand.

"That's fine," I respond, thinking that Rachel will undoubtedly take more time to get ready than I will - she always does. I roll over and try to focus my attention on the wonderful night I had just spent with Mason, while avoiding my sneaking suspicion that he won't remember our flirtatious conversations when he wakes up tomorrow morning.

* * *

It's Sunday evening and I am curled up into a ball as I gawk over the side of my bed at the mound of chemistry homework piled high on the floor next to me. I have just spent the last two hours preparing for a test in the morning. I glance at the phone that is sitting in its base on the other side of my bedroom. Mason promised to call me tonight and it is already 9:15. Although chemistry has kept me busy, my subconscious has been focused on the phone that I keep praying will ring. I turn off my lamp and stare for a long time at the little red light that indicates the charge of my cordless phone. My pain grows deeper with each passing minute that Mason refuses to call. The silence of my room is a steady reminder of my confirmed fear that Mason has totally forgotten about our time together Saturday night. I refuse to let any tears fall for a guy who I barely know, as I turn over and drift off to sleep.

Monday was an eventful day, and I didn't have a lot of time to dwell on Mason between my chemistry test, my other classes, laughing at lunch with my friends, and training hard during track practice. After dinner, I take out my chemistry book again and climb into bed. My hair is damp from my shower, and my stomach is full from another delicious meal; both the shower and the food provide a new sense of clarity as I flip through the many pages of my homework packet. I finished most of the equations at lunch with a little help from Bianca, my intelligent teammate who has competed with me on the volleyball court for 3 consecutive years, but I am still struggling with question 27. I make for the phone to call up Bianca and ask for assistance, but I notice that it is not charging in its base. Leaning forward and feeling underneath my pillow for it, I reflect on my relationship with Bianca, thankful that our different skin color has not put a wedge between our friendship and team camaraderie. Due to the missing phone, I decide that the question can wait till the morning. So, I throw my books over the side of my bed, then glance up at my mom, who has just stuck her head in my room.

"Can I come in?" she asks. I nod as she walks towards me with my phone pressed to her shoulder in an effort to conceal her voice from the mouth piece. "Tessa," she continues, "there is a Mason Pierce on the phone for you."

chapter four

(April, 2006 – June, 2006)

My mind is racing and my heart is thudding loudly in my chest. I bring the phone up to my ear. This is the fourth night in a row that Mason has called to talk; and now, confident that my nerves should be used to the exhilaration, I offer my greeting to the guy who has challenged my composure every night since he first called on Monday evening.

"Hi Mason," I say with more confidence than I feel. My hands shake a little, but I grin thinking how thankful I am that he can't see my fluster.

"Hey, how was chemistry today?" he starts the conversation with ease, and I notice that Mason has become more comfortable on the phone. Monday night I rambled on and on about nothing, really. I was nervous, and I wanted to fill all potentially awkward pauses and silences with my voice. I wished that he would offer opinions and stories of his own, but he seemed content to simply listen. Although we didn't hang up till half past one in the morning, I figured that, because the conversation was only one sided, he might not be interested in repeating the episode. However, much to my relief, he called again Tuesday night; and every night since.

I sigh in response as I begin complaining, "The teacher is horrible, she tried to write a new equation on the board and explain it, but I had to ask Bianca how to solve it properly." I snicker in vain at my circumstances, then continue, "I have to take my end of course, state test in a little over two weeks. I really don't know if I'm going to pass this class."

"You'll do fine," Mason responds. It's easy for him to say,

with a 4.1 GPA and ranking sixth out of 123 students in his class, he sails through all his courses effortlessly.

"Thanks, but I am kind of concerned," I sigh, "and it doesn't help that my normal sleep schedule has been a bit off this week." I grin and reach over to my nightstand to turn off my lamp. It is getting late, I don't want my parents to see the light on in my bedroom and discover that I'm still on the phone.

Mason responds quickly, "If it's too late, I can let you go. I don't want to be the reason you fail this class."

"No," I reassure him, "it's fine! I did my studying right after practice today so that I could have some time to chat tonight."

"Okay good," I hear him say with what sounds like relief. I smile, convinced that he is enjoying our late night phone calls as much as I am. Mason goes on to tell me about his conversation with his coach today. He discusses the details surrounding his surgery that is scheduled for mid-June. Last night he voluntarily shared some facts about his accident and his anger regarding the shoulder injury. He got choked up a few times, but quickly recovered with a joke. I can still hear the pain etched in his voice though, and I know falling asleep at the wheel will be an action that he regrets for the rest of his life.

We talk for a while about what the doctors are saying and how long it will be before he starts his physical therapy. I am glad that he is willing to share these details with me, although I wonder why he is pouring out his emotions on the phone to a recent acquaintance instead of talking them out with either of his parents.

I glance up at my clock that is sitting on the other side of my bedroom. It's 11:11 and although my superstition may be stupid, I half wish, half pray that Mason will be mine forever. I have made the same wish at the same time every night that we have spent on the phone. I find it ironic that I always look up at the exact time that will allow for wishes to come true, if made within the minute of 11:11, or so the tale goes. Mason coughs, bringing me back to our conversation.

"Mason, if you don't mind me asking, why are you so willing to share these details with me?" I pause, "I mean, if it were me, I would want to talk out these circumstances with my parents before sharing them with someone outside of my family."

Mason was silent for a second, as if contemplating exactly how he wanted to answer my question. "Well," he starts, "my parents aren't really around to discuss these things with me." He pauses, obviously waiting for my response, but I stay silent, hoping that he will share more about his family's circumstances. Mason clears his throat and continues, "My parents split up a little over two years ago. My mom couldn't seem to handle the pressure of the lawyers, so she flew back to Canada to avoid all the attention and has been living there with my Nanny ever since." I hear papers crumpling in the background, and I imagine he is fiddling with something to distract him from his sorrow, which is evident in his words. "And my dad," he continues, "he's been traveling a lot more for work. He didn't used to, but he accepted a new position that takes him away for weeks at a time." He stops to regain his composure, then finishes, "I think the split was hard on both of them and everything in the house, including me, reminds them of the 21 years they spent together."

I begin slowly, hoping not to push the subject too much, "Do you have any siblings?" I ask.

"I have a sister," he shares, "but she started her first year at UNC Wilmington right before they split. Lexi wasn't around to witness the repercussions of it all, although I know she has to cope with her own pain surrounding the whole ordeal." The tone of his voice tells me how much he respects and loves his older sister.

"I'm sorry to hear all this," I say. Sensing that he has told me all he is willing to share at the moment, I change the conversation over to my family. I explain to him that my parents are still happily married and that I get along really well with my dad, but not so much with my mom. I share the many stories that I have growing up in a happy home and how my relationship with my sisters has changed with age. We talk for a long time about family, and I surprise myself when I switch gears to discuss religion. Mason explains that his mom is Catholic and his dad is Agnostic. He tells me that he isn't sure what he believes. After his comments, I share with him my Christian upbringing.

"It seems a bit funny to be discussing these things over the phone," I say, shaking my head, but not willing to end the discussion. I continue to tell him how I feel about church and God, but only sharing little details from my past. I refuse to hint towards any of the facts surrounding the horrific scene that has forever changed my view on church since that rainy Sunday two years ago.

I pause, mid sentence, listening intently to a small dinging noise in the background. "What is that sound?" I ask Mason.

"I'm not sure," Mason says quickly, just as the sound cuts short, "but please continue, I like hearing about your childhood, even if it has a lot to do with church."

I laugh and pick up where I left off, disregarding the noise. I talk about the many nights my sisters and I spent in the church nursery when we were very little, as my dad ran different events in the auditorium. My mom would leave the auditorium to come and check on us regularly, accepting that this was the life they were called to when my dad became a pastor. Mason laughs for all the right punch lines, but he doesn't interrupt with his own accounts, he just allows me to continue with one story after the next. Bright lights shine through the blinds of my bedroom window that faces the busy road, distracting me momentarily from my childhood stories.

"That's weird," I say, "I think a car just pulled into our driveway." I glance at the clock that is blinking 1:28 am and resolve that it must just be someone who needed a convenient place to turn around, but then Mason responds sheepishly.

"I figured that you were right when you said it seemed silly to be talking about such important things over the phone, so I decided to come see you."

My heart catches in my throat and my legs begin to shake. Mason drove to see me! My nervous excitement suddenly turns into horror as I look down at my pajamas and catch a glimpse in my bedroom mirror of my tousled hair. I silently race to the bathroom to do something with myself while still holding onto the phone.

"Okay," I say, trying to sound nonchalant, "just park at the end of my driveway and turn off your headlights, I'll be down in a sec."

Hastily, I throw my hair up into a messy bun, slip my glasses onto my face, and fill my mouth with Listerine. Swishing it around for a bit, I allow the burn of the mouthwash to distract me from my trembling body. As I exchange my pajamas for sweatpants and a t-shirt, I wonder how Mason figured out where I lived. Then, I quickly remember giving him directions the night of his party, and I am suddenly impressed at his ability to recollect such detail, especially when drinking, as I quietly tiptoe out of the back door.

I make my way down our long driveway to where Mason is leaning confidently on his Blazer. I steady my walk, trying to mask my tightly wound nerves that threaten, with each step, to reveal themselves through my thick sweatpants that I have purposefully put on to hide my visibly quivering legs.

I smile at him as I get close to where he is standing and attempt an icebreaker, "Wow, I didn't think you would…" but my sentence is cut short as Mason slips his hand around the back of my neck and gently pulls my face towards his. He pauses long enough to look into my eyes, seeing if I am willing to embrace what is to come next. Then, detecting my anticipation, he places his other hand on my hip and tenderly presses his lips against mine.

My head is spinning with delight as my lips meet his, and we sink into the most amazing kiss I have ever had. At first, I find that I am leading, but he quickly takes the reigns from me as he moves closer and presses his muscular body against mine, stealing away my confidence one swift move at a time. The kiss continues as he holds me firmly, but delicately; his thumb tenderly rubs against my cheek and down my neck.

Mason ends the kiss just as my legs experience their worst quivering episode yet. I am desperate to sit and allow my mind time to catch up with the actions that just whisked me away from reality, but Mason holds my gaze, and I can't bring myself to move out of his embrace, even if my trembling has become noticeable.

"I'm sorry," he begins, "it's just that I have been desperate to do that since I met you in the bowling alley." He releases me and looks down at my driveway, revealing his shyness, which he was willing to put aside for our kiss moments before. I try to answer him, but I can't seem to find the appropriate words that will enable me to express my pleasure without unmasking my nerves. He doesn't seem to notice my struggle as he makes his way back to his Blazer. "I'll let you get some rest, hope I didn't intrude," he says as he opens up his car door and lifts one leg to get in.

"Wait!" I manage to say, "Do you want to come over for dinner tomorrow night?" I ask hopefully, praying that our sudden kiss hasn't placed an invisible wedge between us.

He smiles, "Yeah that would be great. Should I come for around 6?" I nod before he starts up his car and backs out of the driveway. My fingers run the length of my lips as I recount the pleasurable event over and over again in my mind while making my way back up to my bedroom. I have trouble sleeping that night, thanks to Mason's kiss, and the eagerness I feel towards the upcoming evening where I will introduce the most amazing guy I have ever met to my family.

* * *

It's Friday evening, and I am pacing back and fourth in my bedroom, moving frantically between my dresser and closet trying to come up with an appropriate outfit for the night. I got off the phone with Rachel a couple of minutes ago and she wished me luck. She was getting her hair done preparing for prom that evening, and, although she didn't have much time to spare, she wanted to catch up with me before her big event. Mason is probably on his way to my house, and although my hair and make-up are in place, I take another glance in the mirror, hoping to impress him while making up for last night's sweat-pants and hair-tied appearance. I decide on a pair of loose fitting khaki shorts and a light pink tank top that tastefully falls low in the front, revealing just a little cleavage; I only have a little to show, anyway.

I rush downstairs and start nervously barking orders to my family. "Don't bombard him with questions, mom," I begin. "Mason doesn't talk much; remember, it took him nearly a month to even talk to me. And Dad," I beg, "please don't ask Mason to bless the food before dinner. That would make him very uncomfortable." My dad laughs in response to my request, confirming the possibility that he may attempt something of the sort, but he pulls me in for a hug and kisses the top of my head in an effort to reassure me. I turn to Amber and hesitate, Shane is seated next to her on the couch and I don't want him to feel uncomfortable, but I continue anyway, "Amber, try to pretend that you don't hate me tonight, I want Mason to think that you have a heart and that it is capable of loving." Amber snorts and reaches up to rub Shane's thick red hair, which is nicely trimmed thanks to his career in the Army. She uses this action to signify that their relationship proves she's capable of loving, but she doesn't start an argument, and I see that as an instant improvement to most of our conversations.

"Tessa, everything is going to be great!" Chantel says with enthusiasm. "You look beautiful, and we all promise to be on our best behavior." She smiles and opens her mouth to continue with her compliments, but a knock on the door alerts all of our attention to the greeting for which my family has been properly prepped.

As nervous as I was, the evening went well. We all laughed in between mouthfuls of the delicious meal that we shared on our back deck. We took turns recounting the many details of our recent activities, and when Mason was asked about his day, he explained some interesting things that happened at school. Although I saw his foot anxiously tapping the patio underneath the glass table for most of dinner, Mason exuded confidence with every word he shared. My family handled the evening well, and they even left us alone to watch a movie later that night.

"I hope that wasn't too nerve wracking," I turn to him and say as we leave my family in the living room while making our way down the hall to the T.V. room.

"No, that was great," Mason says with fervor. "You really do have a nice family, even if you knock heads with your mom and Amber every once in a while." We both laugh, then he continues, "Besides, tonight wasn't nearly as nerve wracking as last night was." He smiles a little, and I assume it is in remembrance of the kiss we shared less the 24 hours ago.

"Yeah, you caught me a little off guard, but I'm glad you made a move," I reassure him, as I bend down to look through our DVD collection in the book case beside our ancient T.V. that never fails to mortify me. However, Mason is not focused on our outdated Sony, his gaze is fixed on me. I smile shyly and motion for him to come help me choose a movie.

"You know," he continues, as he moves his eyes from my face to the book shelf, "last night was my first kiss," he refuses to take his eyes off our movie collection as I disregard the options and turn to study him, trying to determine if he is joking or not.

I hesitate, "Do you mean first kiss with me, or first kiss ever?" I ask, positive that with the amount of confidence he displayed the night before, it couldn't have been his first experience ever.

"Ever," he responds, as his ears turn pink with embarrassment, proving his statement true, although I could have sworn that he was lying.

"Well done," I commend, "my first kiss paled in comparison to that." My cheeks flush due to the shameful statement I just offered. My mind is reeling from this newly discovered information; Mason was 17 and had never kissed a girl before last night. However, on top of just now finding this out, I wonder what possessed me to share my previous kissing experiences. I didn't want to think about the many kisses from my past, so instead I focus my attention on grabbing the chosen disc and shoving it into the DVD player.

We spend the rest of the night together, nestled in each other's arms and watching the movie in silence. Surprisingly, we are not uncomfortable. The information that we shared with one another before the movie started should have made us slightly awkward, but it doesn't.

After the movie, I walk Mason out to his car and he kisses me again. The feelings I experienced the night before come flooding back as I steady myself. After our final goodbye, he climbs into his car and promises to give me a call tomorrow.

* * *

May quickly turns into June as I juggle passing my finals, getting my license, and receiving late night phone calls from Mason. Before I know it, my 17th birthday is only a couple of days away. Mason and I don't have a lot of time to spend together, although we see each other occasionally. He has been working on finishing his end of course tests and putting together the details for his surgery that is coming up on the 14th. When he asked me out on our first official date for this upcoming Friday night, I was too ecstatic to withhold my elation from my family, and now, the night of our first date is finally here.

"When is Mason picking you up?" my mom asks as she rounds the corner and finds me squirming with anticipation in front of the window, desperate to see him turn into our driveway.

"Any second now," I exclaim, sneaking a glance at the hallway mirror to check one last time if my outfit was just as appealing as I hoped it would be. I have chosen a tight fitting, tan, lace skirt and a loose flowing, white top for our date and finished the outfit off with a pair of heels that accentuated my calves. "He is taking me to The White Horse," I say, eagerly awaiting my visit to the most expensive restaurant in town.

"Very nice," my mom offers, "you're certainly dressed for the occasion," she says as she runs her eyes approvingly over my outfit. "Don't forget," she continues, "your grandparents are coming in tonight for your birthday this weekend. They are driving straight from the cottage. They just called to tell me that they crossed the boarder into the States about eight hours ago and they should be here within the next two hours or so. I don't know what our plans are for tonight, but I would like you to see them before they go to bed, so don't be too late."

"I'll try," I promise, "but I'm not cutting our first date short when it comes down to it." I pause, giving her a chance to scold me, but then I see Mason pull into the driveway, and I lunge for the front door. "He's here! See you later tonight."

Mason looks dashing, and treats me like a princess all night. I keep sharing with him how delicious the food is, and I secretly smile when I overhear him telling the waiter that it is my birthday. Although I am a bit embarrassed when the staff comes out singing a little birthday tune as they hand me a small bowl of vanilla ice cream, Mason and I laugh at the whole event while making our way through the crowded parking lot to his car. We slip into our seats while I reflect on how delightful the evening has been.

"I hope you don't mind if we swing by my place before I drop you off at your house tonight," Mason says. "I have to let my dog out, he's been cooped up all evening, and I don't want to have a mess to clean up when I get home."

I turn to him in the driver's seat and respond, "That's fine, isn't your dad home though?" I ask.

"No, he got called out for the week about an hour before I picked you up," Mason says as he shakes his head slowly and focuses intently on the road ahead of him; clearly he has an opinion, but he is unwilling to share it. I think back to a conversation that I had with my parents about a week ago. They expressed their apprehension regarding Mason basically living alone, and told me that the two of us should not be found in his house unaccompanied, lest any "temptations" arise. I disregard their command as we make our way to Mason's house; what they don't know won't hurt them.

We pull into Mason's driveway. When he unlocks the front door, his black lab, George, comes bounding through the entrance and rushes to the front lawn. "No, George, let's go to the backyard," Mason calls to his beloved pet. George obeys and leaps back into the house after Mason. As George follows Mason to the sliding glass door, they leave me waiting patiently in the front room.

I reflect on how wonderful the evening has been and how quickly I seem to be falling for this guy when a knock on the door startles me out of my thoughts. I reluctantly open the front door, and I immediately regret the decision as I stare into the stern and disappointed face of my mother.

"We were driving back from the Herns and saw Mason's car in the driveway, you two are alone, aren't you?" I open my mouth to rebut her statement, but the look on my face gives me away before I even have the chance to lie. "We are taking you home," my mom tells me. "Your grandparents are in the car, and they don't need to know that Mason's dad isn't here," she continues. "Please give them a warm welcome, we just had a nice visit with the Herns, and I would hate for you to ruin it." She turns to make her way back to the car as she firmly states over her shoulder, "I'm giving you two minutes to say goodbye."

I close the door without saying a word, just as Mason and George make their way back into the room. I fake a big smile and laugh before I say, "Sorry about that, my mom was just coming home from the Herns and saw that we were here, she has offered to take me home," I say with optimism, as if I'm excited about the prospect, "that way you don't have to use your gas to get all the way out to my house and back." I feel like crying, but I smile instead, intent on letting Mason know how wonderful the evening was, that is, up until about a minute ago when my mom ruined it.

"Uh, okay," he begins, "but I really don't mind taking you back myself." He looks like he is going to continue, but I cut him off before he does, desperate to keep my spirits high and mask my anger and frustration toward my mom.

"It's fine," I insist, "this is much easier, anyway. Thanks for an amazing night," I say quickly as I plant a short kiss on his lips, and make my way for the door.

"Yeah, I had fun," he says just as I open the front door and turn to smile. "I'll call you later," he finishes as he waves with an unsettled look on his face. I nod and leave before I allow my emotions to get the better of me in front of him.

Although it's my birthday weekend, I spend the next two days sobbing behind closed doors convincing myself that Mason won't want to be with me when he finds out that my parents have such strict rules surrounding our relationship. I refuse to engage in much conversation with my mom, after all, it is her fault that things ended awkwardly on our first date, and her fault that Mason and I will never find ourselves in an official relationship. My anger toward my parents heightens with each of Mason's phone calls that I refuse to take; I have convinced myself that I need to end things with Mason, but every opportunity that presents itself sends me dashing back to my bedroom racked with new sobs of pain. He has so much freedom, so why would he want a girl's parents holding him accountable for every move he makes. *He doesn't want this*, I conclude, and although it breaks my heart, I know I have to extricate him before his whole world gets turned upside down.

On Sunday, Rachel drives me home from church. For the first part of our ride she tolerates my misery as I explain my painful plans with Mason. "Tessa, I have never seen you cry like this over a guy," she says, as we make our way up to my bedroom. "Your birthday party is in an hour, and you look like hell." She sighs as I crawl onto my bed and start sobbing again. "Why don't you just tell Mason what you're thinking and let him make the decision?" she asks. "After all, he is half of the equation here, and it's not entirely fair for you to make this arrangement without discussing it with him first."

"Let's be realistic," I respond through sobs, "he won't want me when he finds out what my family is like. He doesn't understand our Christian values, and I don't expect him to understand, this early in the game." Just then the phone rings. Rachel picks it up and says hello to Mason. Although I can't hear what he is saying, I know that he is questioning why I haven't taken one of his calls since our date Friday night.

"Um, I think Tessa should explain something to you," Rachel says before she shoves the phone at me. Although I don't want to take it, I know I have to face this eventually. I pull the phone up to my ear and explain to Mason all that happened Friday night and the reason that I left his house in such a hurry. I don't hold back my tears as I tell him that I think we should just end things to save us both the trouble.

After listening to all that I had to say, I hear Mason take in a deep breath before he responds, "I think I need a while to decide what would be best," he states. "I'll call you back in a bit." He says goodbye and we both hang up. I fall to pieces all over again, knowing that there is no chance of this working out in my favor. Rachel lays down beside me on my small twin bed as we listen to our two family's bustle around the kitchen a floor below us, preparing for a birthday party that I don't want, even if it does only consist of close friends and family. I roll over to face the wall that my bed is edged against, and Rachel places a hand on my shoulder in an effort to comfort me as my tears continue to fall. My sobs are the only sound that breaks the silence as time creeps closer and closer to the party that I dread attending. We hear a knock on my door, and I feel Rachel get up to open it. I know it will be my mother, asking me to wipe my tears and come downstairs to entertain my guests. My mom loves me and she wants the best for me, but she has very little patience for the tears I have been shedding the past couple of days. She thinks I've determined my future with my actions. I had explained the reasons why we were home alone at Mason's on Friday night and assured my parents that nothing had happened, but they pointed out the blatant fact that I had broken one of their rules.

I listen to the door handle turn with my back to the intruder, but in place of my mothers' voice, I hear Mason's. "I had some time to think about it on my way over here," he says as I whip away from the wall and quickly swing my legs over the side of my bed. Now that I am facing him, I try to wipe away my tears. Rachel has left the door cracked on her way out; she knows we need our privacy. My face is red and blotchy, but that doesn't stop Mason, "I figure, if I have to endure a second set of parents and some strict rules, it would be a small price to pay to have you as my girlfriend." I sniffle and stare at him, his words confuse me as they are slowly communicated, contradicting all my predictions for our future. "So," he continues, "What do you say – will you officially be my girlfriend?" I wipe my tear stained cheeks and smile widely, without a word I rush into his arms and offer a long, satisfying kiss as my affirmative response.

chapter five

(August, 2006 – August, 2007)

The evening is cool and crisp, preparing North Carolina for the beautiful fall season that will change the colors of the leaves and the humidity in the air. Mason and I have just come home from a dinner date. We are lingering outside his empty house, leaning against his car parked in his driveway, listening to the radio and putting off our goodbyes.

I stare into Mason's eyes and smile. "I have just had the best summer of my life, thanks to you," I say, while thinking back on the time we have spent together. Between trips to the beach, his birthday in July, and plenty of dates, we have remained inseparable. I reflect on how much more confident I am since Mason and I started dating, convinced that my newfound security is derived from all the compliments and attentiveness Mason has offered in the past two months.

"Yes, apart from my surgery, this has been a pretty fantastic summer," he responds with a chuckle. His arm is now out of a sling, and his physical therapist has cleared him for some lower body exercise, along with a few moves that will strengthen his shoulder. I glance in the direction of the Hern's home, knowing that I should head that way in the next couple of minutes for Rachel's birthday party, but I am desperate to spend every remaining second with Mason.

A familiar tune drifts out of his open car window. "Oh, turn this song up," I request. Mason opens the driver's side door, leans across the steering wheel and turns up the volume on his radio. One of Mason's qualities that endears my parents to him is that he listens to oldies. Although I don't appreciate this about my boyfriend as much as I should, there are a few songs that I do like. I begin to sing along with the Lennon Sisters' rendition of *Tonight You Belong to Me*.

Following along with the rhythm, I start to sway my head from side to side, singing with an amusing smirk as I provide Mason with an entertaining performance. *"Way down by the stream, how sweet it will seem, once more just to dream in the moonlight. I know you belong to somebody new, but tonight, you belong to me."* I sing, as I shift my weight from one foot to the other while he smiles endearingly at me in return. The song comes to the end as I make a special effort to sing the last verse with extra enthusiasm, *"My honey, I know, with the dawn that you will be gone, but tonight, you belong to me; just a little old me!"* I end the song with a curtsey. While laughing together, Mason leans toward me and grabs my waist, drawing me into his embrace. We stand intertwined as our laughing subsides, and he holds me close to his body, his bent head comes to a rest on my shoulder.

The silent moment is broken as Mason whispers in my ear, "dawn or day, I will never be gone." I pull away from his hold to meet his eyes, thankful for his promise because I know that I want to spend the rest of my life with him. He moves his hands from around my waist and rests them on both sides of my face. Pulling me in, he presses his lips to mine and passionately kisses me.

We chat in each other's arms for another five minutes or so before I decide that it is time to go to Rachel's. "I'm sorry Mason, but I really do have to go now. Rachel will want me there early for her party," I sigh, unwilling to withdraw from his side, but knowing that I have no choice.

"Tell me why I can't come with you again?" Mason asks with a bit of irritation laced in his question. I had explained to him over dinner how upset Rachel has been lately due to the lack of attention I am giving her. She is happy that Mason and I are enjoying our time together; however, she keeps pointing out that

I have been replacing my nights and weekends that I usually spend with her for time with Mason.

"Mason, please, let's not get into this again," I start. "Rachel needs to feel important, and I know I have been neglecting her lately. It will mean a lot for me to dedicate this night to her and her only." I sigh as I watch Mason's face, etched with frustration, turn from me. Although I don't like getting into arguments with him, at least I can accept that this one is surrounding time that Mason wants to spend with me – I can't complain about that. "I'll see you later," I promise as I quickly kiss his cheek and turn to walk down his driveway. Behind me, I hear him take his keys out of the ignition and slam his car door shut in an effort to communicate his anger without using words. I cringe, but I know if I turn around and try to resolve the dilemma, I will be late to Rachel's, then I will have another argument to face with her.

Rachel's birthday celebration is terrific. Although it is only a few close families enjoying music and finger food beside the pool, Rachel and I reconnect as I try to give her my undivided attention for the whole evening. While Rachel opens her presents under the cabana, I steal a glance at Mason's house. Wondering what he is doing and how he is filling his time. Distracted for a moment, I contemplate his reaction to my evening spent with Rachel. I know it is going to be difficult to balance my time between Rachel and Mason, but I need to help them recognize that they both have to accept that my hours need to be shared.

My attention is drawn back to the pool party as Rachel swoons over her new Vera Wang perfume that I spent most of my summer babysitting money on for her birthday present.

I smile at Rachel, "You are welcome!" I say, glad that my present made my best friend happy. It's hard to buy for Rachel since she already has everything!

The party draws to an end while Rachel walks a few of the guests to the front hall. My parents have driven off, leaving me to spend the night. Knowing that Rachel will take a while to say goodbye to everyone, I slip out the backyard gate, unnoticed, and quickly make my way down to Mason's house. I figure that I will knock on the door and see what he is up to, hoping that our argument hasn't left him upset for the last couple of hours. However, as I walk up his front stoop, I spot a guy jogging down Santa Monica and realize that it's Mason. I sit on the antique bench perched on his front porch and wait for him to approach. He is sweaty, and I can tell that his jog was meant for more than just exercise; he is clearly using the run as a means to release some frustration. He sits down on the bench beside me and takes off his shirt, using it to wipe his face free from sweat.

"I'm sorry…" I start, but before I can continue, Mason cuts me off.

"It was good that you spent some time with Rachel tonight," he says. "I haven't been sharing you well lately, and I don't want her to feel ignored." He takes the shirt and swings it around the back of his neck. Hanging onto both sides of the garment, he stands up and faces me while he leans on the porch railing. He looks like an athletic masterpiece standing in front of me with his exposed six-pack and bulging biceps. "It's just that, I get jealous," he continues, "and I think," he looks down at the long white boards that run the length of his porch, averting his eyes from mine, obviously struggling to share his thoughts. He clears his throat and corrects himself, "Actually I know…that I love you."

Silence fills the front stoop as my eyes widen in wonder. Waiting for him to return my gaze and witness the bliss that has filled my heart, I see that he is too embarrassed to look up. I stand with reverence and reach for his bent arm, "Mason, I love you too," I say as a tear silently rolls down my cheek. His eyes meet mine and a shy grin causes his lips to part. He uses one hand to drop his shirt from his neck and the other to pull me into his arms. I don't care that he is sleek with sweat; I return his kiss with fervor, knowing that, although he is my first love, he will remain my only love.

* * *

October is here, and the loud sirens from the ambulance that is racing down our busy road echo through my open bedroom window and jolt me from my sleep. I glance at my clock, realizing that I have overslept, but before hustling out of bed, I say a little prayer for the person who needs the urgent assistance of the medical team that just drove by my house. My family often prays when they hear an ambulance; however, the action seems to have gained more importance since we moved to this small town and are now familiar with most of the people who live in the area. I sit up in bed and stretch both arms above my head. As I quickly get ready for school, anticipation fills my thoughts. Our volleyball season has been pretty successful, leading us to tonight's match. Bianca and I are co-captains for the varsity team, and we have fulfilled our senior goal of making it to the third round of the state playoffs. Bianca is a talented defensive specialist, which was developed in the off season while playing for a club team in Virginia. However, aside from the fact that my parents can't afford club ball, I still consider myself to be an equal team asset. Together, we have led the team to tonight's match against our rivals - Destiny's team. Mason has promised to be there, but he hasn't hinted towards which side of the bleachers he will be sitting. Although he likes to honor his high school, he also wants to support me, even if it means defeating the Pirates.

I grab an apple for breakfast, swing my heavy backpack onto one shoulder and make my way to my car. Although it isn't pretty, I spent all my savings on my silver, Ford Escort. The car is a tiny, stick shift, but it is good on gas. Although it isn't luxurious, like Rachel's Nissan or Mason's Blazer, it gets me from point A to point B in one piece. Sporting one of my many Lady Bruin's volleyball t-shirts, I eagerly make my way in through the front doors of my high school. Even though I am about five minutes late, I still expect to be enthusiastically greeted by my teacher and classmates all wishing me good luck on our match tonight; instead, I enter my chemistry class, and I am greeted by grim faces.

"Tessa, can you step outside for a moment?" my teacher asks. I nod and close the door behind me. Waiting impatiently in the hallway, I decide that she has blown my tardiness a little out of proportion. My teacher exits the classroom and turns to face me. "I thought you would already know, seeing as it happened just down the street from you," she starts, "but Bianca was in a pretty serious car accident on her way to school this morning." Thinking back to the ambulance sirens that woke me, I drop my backpack, and I pin my body against the wall as anguish rips through me. My teacher continues, "She has broken her leg in many places and her upper body is badly bruised from the head-on collision. She will be staying in the hospital for a while, but one thing's for sure – she won't be competing with you on the court tonight." The rest of the day is a blur as the whole school talks about the seriousness of Bianca's accident and whether she will ever play again.

Our pregame warm-ups come to an end as a member of our opposing team approaches the microphone and shares some kind words concerning Bianca's absence from our match that is minutes from beginning. Tears stain my face while we are asked to take a moment of silence for Bianca's sake before the national anthem blares through the speakers in our rival's gym. When the song is over, I wipe my face and turn to my team, giving them the best pep-talk I can manage without succumbing to any more of my grief. "The Pirates are a talented team," I say, "but if we pull together and work with one another, I believe we stand a chance – even if we are short a teammate." We take our positions on the court, and the match begins with a jump serve from the opposing team. Although we battle many plays and the score of each set is close, we end the second set with two losses. Our matches are always played in sets to 25 points, and the best three out of five sets wins the match. Knowing that we are two sets down from our biggest rivals, I gather the girls together for a motivational speech that ends with excessive passion, "We can do this team! Don't let the Pirates get the better of us! If you are not willing to get this win for yourselves, do it for Bianca who couldn't be with us tonight!" The girls on the team nod with growing enthusiasm as we make our way to our positions. I know that I am more confident on the court then off, but I like that I can use my tenacity to drive my team forward. I glance at Mason, who had decided to sit with my parents on the Bruin's bleachers, probably because he knows how difficult today has been for me. He winks at me, and I smile back for a moment; but my gaze returns to the court, and my grin fades as I make eye contact with Destiny on the other side of the net. I can't deny that she is a talented player, but her sportsmanship is terrible. After almost every point that her team loses, she prances to the ref and makes some excuse as to why their call was unfair. The next two sets end in our favor, and we are now faced with the fifth and final set of our match. The ref calls the two opposing captains back for a final coin toss. Destiny and I face each other with disdain. I can tell by her facial expressions that she dislikes me almost as much as I dislike her. The coin is tossed and lands on tails, which is the opposite of what Destiny called. With a burst of exhilaration, I request to take the first serve.

We go back to our opposite sides of the net, and I draw my fellow Bruins together. "Great job on those last two sets, team; we really have them where we want them! We have the first serve, and if we can manage to ace them early on, we can end this match with a victory," I announce as the girls look at me and grin, eager to move forward to the fourth round of the state playoffs. "Just remember," I warn, "this set only goes to 15, so we have to start out on top." We break away and the few members of our team who sit the bench, cheer us on, giving us a rejuvenated sense of optimism. The game goes back and forth with every point, and after many rallies, our efforts are about to come to an end. The score is 13 to 14 and we are down one point. "Don't let up!" I call to the girls as I turn to face the net. I use my hands behind my back to call the next play. We have the serve, which puts us in an excellent position. The ball sails over the net and is returned to our side with a hard hit, our defense picks it up, and I am positioned perfectly to set up our best hitter with the play that I called moments before. The swing is strong, but much to my chagrin, the Pirate's defensive player takes a dive, keeping the play alive. The set has been made, and the Pirate's tall middle player goes up for a hit. The ball is driven to the floor on our side, straight to the left back position, where Bianca usually plays. I watch in horror as her substitute fails to pick up the play, and the Pirates scream in shouts of victory as the match comes to an end, 13 to 15.

I stay in the locker room 30 minutes after the rest of the team has left it empty, crying alone with shame and frustration at the outcome of the last volleyball match of my high school career. Bianca should have been by my side through this match, and I'm confident that, if she was, the outcome of tonight's game would have been different. My thoughts are interrupted as my coach quietly enters the locker room and makes her way to the wooden bench where I am sitting. "Tessa," she whispers, "you had a terrific season – it's going to be impossible to replace you next year." She hugs me and continues, "However, on the bright side, there is a coach from Callan University waiting outside, asking to talk to you." I lift my puffy, red eyes to my coach, replacing my anguish with a glint of hope as I wipe my face, collect my things and make my way out of the locker room.

"Tessa McRae, is it?" the woman in front of me asks. I

nod and she continues, "Great display of volleyball tonight, I thoroughly enjoyed watching the match." She shakes my hand and introduces herself, "I'm Pam Greenly, head coach at Callan University, a Division II school here in North Carolina. I would like to invite you to our recruiting try-out on January 6th." Without saying much, I accept the invitation and exchange contact information with the coach. Mason watches me from 30 feet away with one eyebrow raised, sharing his excitement for this new prospect. After saying goodbye to Coach Greenly, I make my way to Mason and my family to explain what just happened. After my parents congratulate me on a game well-played, Mason assures my mom that he doesn't mind driving me home; I know he wants to hear more details about my feelings surrounding this potential recruit.

Mason takes my gym bag from me as we make our way to the gym exit, but when we enter into the cold night air, Destiny, who had been waiting outside the doors, purposefully crosses our path. "Good job tonight, Tessa, you guys fought hard," she states with a victorious smirk on her face. She pauses, obviously waiting for my response, but a nod is all I am willing to offer in reply. "Well," she continues as she makes her way to her Mustang, "guess we'll be seeing each other soon." She gets in her car and squeals away from the parking lot.

"What do you think that means?" I ask Mason, hoping that she isn't interested in taking up basketball and meeting me on the court again in the upcoming season. "I certainly don't want to see her again, although I know it is a small town, and you can't avoid people you don't like."

"Yeah, not sure," he deliberates, "maybe she knows about Braden's party this weekend and intends to make an appearance." We forget about her comment as we make our way to his car, discussing the many highlights and regrets of my last high school volleyball match.

* * *

It's the night before Callan's recruiting try-out, and Mason and I are sitting on the loveseat in my living room; I know I should be getting some sleep, but I've been waiting for months to have this conversation. Mason takes my hand and squeezes it in his own. "Okay," he says, "I'm ready to make this decision." We have spent the last few months discussing, arguing and even viciously fighting about what a Christian faith entails. Mason has attended many church services with me, but has fought the idea of a personal relationship with Jesus Christ. We just spent the last two hours talking about accepting Christ and what that means, and although he has been hostile in the past towards the gospel, he seems to be coming to terms with the fact that he needs a higher power present in his life.

"What have you decided?" I ask with anticipation. The slight smile appearing on his face gives me the answer – he wants to become a Christian! Although it is obvious to everyone my fluctuating commitment to church, my belief in Christ has never failed, despite the pain and anger that I occasionally revisit surrounding my thoughts on church politics. I thank God we are at a good church now. I know I need to surrender my resentment towards our last church, but forgiveness is a lot easier said than done. I cast my negative thoughts aside and smile with excitement in response to Mason's grin.

"That's excellent," I proclaim, as I indicate to Mason our need to pray. Mason verbalizes his need for Jesus and asks to be forgiven of his sins. With my head bowed, I smile at every word Mason shares with his new Lord and Savior. Mason finishes his prayer, and we cling to each other as we settle into our familiar cuddling position on the couch. I know that I should run upstairs and announce to my parents Mason's decision to adopt our faith as his own, but I don't want to ruin this moment by interrupting it. After a while, Mason kisses the top of my head and mentions that I should get some sleep. I walk him to the back door and kiss him goodnight.

Later that night, I am almost too ecstatic to fall asleep. I reflect on the progression that Mason and I have made as a couple since he told me he loved me that wonderful, August night. Together, in the past several months, we have attended church, talked about Jesus, complained about family, discussed potential universities, shared our future intentions surrounding our relationship, taken romantic walks, watched many movies, and expressed our love through sexual encounters, which, have always ended before giving into the temptation to have sex, thanks to my commitment to God's will for us. In our relationship, we have experienced a lot, and I am convinced that I love him more now then when I first told him I did. Somehow, in the midst of all my thoughts, I manage to drift off to sleep, knowing that I need some rest before I give it my best at Callan's try-out tomorrow.

My mom drives me to Callan's campus, which is only a little over an hour from our home. On the way, we discuss Mason's new found faith and revel in the decision that he has made for himself. I knew that our relationship couldn't continue if he didn't understand and accept what Jesus did for him on the cross, but luckily, we never had to discuss breaking up because of it. Our conversation leads to Amber and Shane's recent engagement, and I share with my mom my desire to get engaged to Mason several years down the road. For the remainder of the trip, I allow my mind to drift to what a marriage with Mason would look like, now that I know our Christian beliefs are of the same accord.

My spirits are high as my mom drops me off with my equipment bag at the entrance of the huge university gym. I make my way through the front doors and take a seat alongside the many other girls who are there for the try-out. After slipping on my knee pads and ankle braces, I stand up and start stretching. I glance around at the girls who are doing their own personal stretches, getting ready for the tasks that await. Grinning to myself, I reflect on how thrilled I am to be considered for a position on this team; however, my face immediately contorts with disgust as I watch the gym door open and see Destiny enter. Anger shoots through me as I recall our last encounter. She knew I was going to be here. Clearly, Coach Greenly had a chat with Destiny before I left the Pirate's visiting locker room, one thing's for sure – I do not want to be teammates with Destiny!

Coach Greenly makes her way into the gym and the group of girls introduce themselves, each reciting their name and hometown. There are girls from all over the country represented in this gym, and I am grateful to be a part of the group. We spend the next two hours scrimmaging before Coach Greenly pulls us, one-by-one, into her office to discuss our roles on the team.

"Tessa," Coach Greenly's voice rings out from her office. I make my way into the small room off of the gym and shut the door behind me. "Well, I really liked what I saw on the court today, and I am willing to offer you a partial scholarship for this upcoming season." We go over details, and she explains that she wants me to pursue a defensive position rather than setting. Internally, I accept the new challenge of learning a different position, and she promises to be in touch. On the way home, I offer the news to my mom and together we weigh the pro's and con's of going to Callan University, rather than going to some of my other top choices. While I was in the gym, my mom had taken advantage of the two hour window by visiting admissions. After talking with a counselor, the two had determined that, between athletic and academic scholarships, I can get a free ride to Callan for all four years. My decision is made by the time we pull into our driveway; I am going to be a Callan University Athlete as of August 2007, even if it means playing on the same team as Destiny.

* * *

My freshman essentials are mostly packed, and although my parents are short on money, they went out and surprised me with a whole new bed set for my dorm room, which will be beautifully decorated as of tomorrow. I finish folding some clothes into a box and glance at Mason who is lounging comfortably on my twin bed.

"I can't believe you're leaving for college tomorrow," he says with excitement, although I know he is upset that he doesn't have the opportunity to leave our small town as well. Mason accepted a walk on position with ECSU's baseball team; not his number one choice, but with his shoulder just returning to health, he couldn't expect much more.

"I know," I say, taking a break from my packing and sitting on my bed beside him. "However," I continue, "our universities are only about an hour apart and our seasons don't coincide. You'll be able to come watch some games, and we can see each other on the weekends when we don't have tournaments." I smile at him as I bend down to kiss him. We both know that we won't be far away from each other, but we have spent the last year together, and any adjustment from that is bound to be difficult.

"I love you," he responds, as I make my way back to packing, "and I'm glad that you'll be rooming with Rachel." Rachel had applied to almost every school in California. She had been desperate to return ever since they moved from San Diego to our sleepy town over five years ago, but her grades kept her from being considered, so she settled for Callan. I know she is excited to cheer on the university's squad, and although it isn't California, she is eager to be going to school with me.

"Yeah, she will be joining me on campus in two weeks," I say excitedly, "but I heard pre-season is going to be grueling; I'm not sure how much help I will be when she comes to move in." We laugh as I stretch the duck tape along the top of the last box that I will be taking with me. I stack it in the corner of my room with the other boxes and make my way back to Mason's side.

"Oh, I saw Bianca today," I say. "She stopped by on her way into town to wish me luck and say one last goodbye." I sigh as my face falls with sorrow; I am going to miss her presence on my new team. Cringing at the thought of her limp, caused by her car accident, I battle my grief for her circumstances while considering her plan to study at the local university and live with her parents, instead of pursing a position on a collegiate volleyball team.

I glance at the clock to determine how much longer we have together before our midnight curfew; it's 11:11. Plopping down beside Mason, I consider whether I should share the significance of the numbers on the clock; however, due to the delicate state of my emotions, I decide against it. His voice breaks the silence. In a playful manner, he quietly sings a verse to our song, *"My honey I know, by the dawn that you will be gone, but tonight, you belong to me."* Although he is trying to offer a sweet relief, the words shatter my last hope of containing my emotions as I drop my face into my hand and sob. Mason takes me into his arms and holds me while I fall apart. Neither one of us says anything. I know he understands my grief, and I sense that he doesn't want to talk about it, afraid that he might cry as well. Eventually, I turn to face him, and he brushes my hair back from my face. "I really am going to miss you," I say, trying to hold back my tears as I express my thoughts, "and I know that we didn't always see each other during the week, but we will see even less of each other this year." I give into my anguish and begin sobbing even harder, mourning the time that Mason and I will spend away from each other this coming year.

Mason lifts my face to his and smiles at me. "As long as you don't let those college boys persuade you differently, our relationship will only grow stronger while we are apart," he says. We both kind of snicker at the idea, but I detect a hint of unrelenting fear expressed in Mason's statement.

"I could never let another guy come between us," I promise.

Mason leans over and kisses my forehead. We spend our remaining time together laughing and joking about the few guys at my high school who consistently spoke negatively about Mason, hoping to alter my adoration for him. Lying side by side, we gaze into each others faces, making the most of every minute together while listening to my parents shuffling around in their bedroom across the hall. I know that we are not supposed to be lying on the bed together, but I am prepared to face their reprimands if either one of my parents poke their head through my open, bedroom door. After Mason kisses me goodnight, he turns to leave my room, but his hand pauses for a moment on my light switch as he looks back in my direction. "I love you, Tessa," he says, and I see a tear fall. He turns out the light quickly, hoping to hide his pain. "I love you too," I reply, "see you soon." He closes the door behind him, leaving me alone and crushed. Suffering with the difficulty of saying goodbye to Mason, even if it's only for a short while, I cling to my pillow for comfort and cry myself to sleep.

chapter six

(October, 2007 – December, 2007)

Aware of each breath that escapes into the cool, October morning air, I throw my keys into my backpack and shift the weight onto my shoulder. The leaves have begun to fall from the trees that fill our university's park, creating a colorful maze for me to crunch through as I make my way to my early morning Psychology class. I pull the sleeves of my volleyball sweatshirt down over my balled up fists in an attempt to help warm my fingers. Luckily, our campus is small and the walk from my dorm room to the Guilder building, where my class meets, is a short one.

Settling into a seat toward the front of the classroom, I take out my textbook and shake my head at the unreasonable price I paid for it; however, I was warned in freshman orientation about the next four years of textbook expenses. My professor makes her way to the front of the room just as I flip open my notebook, ready to copy down the lecture notes for today's class. I have enjoyed listening to the lectures that Dr. Pickner prepares; she engages her students as we discuss relevant topics and she encourages the class to ask questions about the material. I have enjoyed just about everything surrounding my recent introduction to university life. The classes are intriguing, the students are friendly, and our volleyball team has experienced a successful season so far, despite my disdain for Destiny. I take a moment to reflect on our season that is coming to a close, but we still have our homecoming game tonight, and our practices leading up to this match have been promising.

"Good morning," Dr. Pickner starts, "I hope you all have had a productive week and that you're getting geared up for the homecoming festivities this weekend." I see a group of girls to my right giggle in response and two boys from the soccer team high five each other; clearly they all have big plans for the eventful weekend. "Alright, alright," Dr. Pickner continues, "please turn to chapter 9. Today we will be examining the contrast between Maslow's Hierarchy of Needs and Freud's Psychosexual Stages of Development in terms of dating relationships."

The lecture goes by quickly, given the subject material and the interest of the students who are verbalizing the conclusions that they have drawn from the text. I usually don't ask questions in any of my classes, but since I detect the lesson coming to a close, I force myself to raise my hand.

Dr. Pickner nods in my direction and the question I have been contemplating for most of the hour long lesson comes blurting out; "What do you make of relationships that begin in high school, and what does the text say in references to the longevity of them?"

Dr. Pickner shakes her head and half snickers before offering her response. "You know," she sighs, "I get that question every year I teach this freshman course. Students may start university clinging to a relationship that was developed in high school, but the character changes that an individual undergoes during their university term almost always separates the two instead of bringing them closer together. In simpler terms, high school relationships never last." She glances down at her watch, "That's all for today, please be safe this weekend."

As I watch Dr. Pickner turn toward the front board, my face burns with anger. Although I like my professor and I respect her lectures, I do not agree with her answer to my question. My heart quickly fills with fear for the future while I determine to prove this theory wrong. I know that Mason and I will both change in the next few years, but that doesn't mean that we won't be good for each other because of it. Still flustered, I mindlessly reach for my notebook and shove it into my backpack.

My textbook falls off my desk with a thud, and I startle at the sound. As I lean over my desk to see where my textbook landed, I hear a voice from behind me, "I can get that for you." I turn in response, hoping that my face isn't a blatant reflection of my anger toward my professor's last statement. A fairly attractive guy leans down to pick up my textbook and hands it to me with a smile. "I'm Tripp, by the way," he continues, not allowing me time to express my thanks for his kind gesture.

"I'm Tessa," I respond, bowing my head and focusing my attention on zipping up my backpack. As I stand up from my seat, I steal a glance at Tripp, and I notice his striking green eyes are still fixed on mine. Tripp grabs my backpack from the floor and hands it to me, his exposed bicep flexes in response to the weight, and I'm immediately taken aback by his toned build.

"You play on the team?" Tripp asks, while pointing to my sweatshirt. I nod, still recovering from my anger. I avoid Tripp's gaze as I swing my backpack over my shoulder. The encounter has left me feeling awkward, so I make my way to the door, hoping to avoid further conversation. From behind I hear, "I think I saw you a couple of times in the cafeteria during pre-season. I am the quarterback for the football team, so I came in the same time you did."

At this point, I am a bit irritated at Tripp's attempt to continue the conversation, so I turn in his direction and offer a quick comment as I continue walking backwards toward the door, "Well, good luck tomorrow in your homecoming game. I have to get to my next class, which is on the other side of campus. It was nice to meet you." I offer a feeble smile as he drops his gaze. He glances toward the nearest exit as he runs his hand through his short brown hair. It's obvious that he is catching on to my subtle rejection. One corner of his mouth turns up in a respectful smile as he looks back at me and responds, "Thanks, it was good to meet you too." He takes off in the opposite direction, and I slump my shoulders, momentarily regretting my shortness with him as I push my way through the door. Dismissing Tripp, I return to my thoughts concerning the transition of high school relationships, and quicken my pace as I commit my future to Mason, no matter what our relationship is bound to face.

The team's warm-up music blares in our large gym as my teammates and I make our way through our pre-game routine. Shuffling distractedly to my back row position, my eyes dart from my coach to the front doors of the gym, hoping to catch a glimpse of my family, who promised to be at this match. Mason regretfully informed me that he couldn't make it tonight; unfortunately, some of his baseball responsibilities are interfering. Suddenly, a swift movement from a teammate brings me back to the task at hand, and I quickly realize that I am next in line to make a pass. Coach Greenly swings hard at me, preparing me for hits that I will undoubtedly see throughout the game tonight. I read the rotation of the ball and line myself up for a perfect pass to the target. Coach half smiles in response, and I make my way to the back of the line, pleased with her approving grin. I glance at the door and happen to notice Tripp making his way through the entrance. I am pretty sure I have never seen him at any of our matches before; however, this is the homecoming game and our attendance is bound to be higher than normal. Tripp quickly finds me on the court and meets my gaze. He smiles in my direction, but turns to make his way up the bleachers before my facial features have a chance to respond. Briefly watching him climb the steps, I notice that he is relatively attractive and carries himself with confidence and ease. However, my thoughts are quickly drawn away from him as I catch a glimpse of my parents entering the gym. I am excited to see them, but my heart lurches as I see Mason walk in behind them. His surprise visit to watch my match is exactly what I needed after Psych class this morning. I grin widely in his direction and offer an enthusiastic wave when his eyes find mine. I wish I could run into his arms, but realistically, I know that won't be possible until after the match. My warm-up continues to go well as I allow my delight in Mason's attendance to inspire me.

"Nice warm-up Tessa," Coach Greenly compliments as our two senior captains rejoin the team after the coin toss. "I'm going to have you start this match, you will begin with the first serve." She turns from me before I can give a response and my heart leaps with joy and nervous anticipation. This is the first university match I have ever started in, and as I make my way out to the court with the rest of the starting line-up, butterflies fill my stomach. Yet, there is also a sense of relief that Coach Greenly believes in my ability, and this gives me confidence.

My best match ever played comes to a close as we celebrate the victory. Our opposing team was talented, but we battled through it. I know that although I have played in several matches already this season, being a part of the starting line-up helped boost my confidence for this particular game, and it showed on the court. After Coach Greenly's short and sweet closing speech, I make my way over to my family in the bleachers. Mason meets me on the bottom step, and I fall into his arms, thankful that he made the game tonight a priority and is able to share in my jubilance for my best performance on the court yet.

"I can't believe you're here," I say into his chest. My excitement is muffled by his embrace, but I know he detects my enthusiasm because he squeezes me tighter and kisses the top of my head in response.

Thrilled to have my parents, sisters, Rachel and Mason all at the match, we make plans to go out for dinner once I change out of my uniform. Mason, who drove separately, pulls me aside to discuss the plans for the night.

"Tessa, unfortunately I can't go out to dinner tonight," Mason sighs with frustration. "Our coach made us sign a contract that we will be home by 10 pm the night before our game, and we have a fall season, double header tomorrow."

I smile in an attempt to mask my disappointment, "I understand," I respond, "I'm just glad that you were able to come to my match. When will I see you next?" I ask, hoping that baseball won't interfere too much with future plans to spend time together.

"Well, I was thinking that we could go visit Lexi in Wilmington the weekend after next – What do you say?"

"That sounds terrific!" I state with delight. "Oh gosh, I'm nervous about meeting your sister for the first time! However, it works out perfectly with our volleyball schedule - we have that Saturday free." I smile at the idea of spending some one-on-one time with Mason. I have missed him so much these past two months, and I know that a weekend getaway will be the perfect prescription for my lonely heart.

"Great, I'll pick you up after practice Friday afternoon, and we will head out straight from here." He wraps his hands around the sides of my face and kisses me before turning to leave the gym. As I watch him exit, I fight the temptation to pout. Instead, I allow my eagerness for our upcoming trip to keep my spirits high. I turn to Rachel, who is talking with my family, and promise them a five minute visit to the locker room before heading to the restaurant.

* * *

Lexi pours me another glass of wine and carries it over to the couch where I've been comfortably lounging the past hour since we arrived at her adorable little one-bedroom house in Wilmington. This is my first introduction to Mason's sister, and I am pleasantly surprised at how inviting and friendly she is. Mason makes his way down the small hall from Lexi's bedroom back to the open layout of her kitchen, dining area and living room.

"Did you get everything from the car?" Lexi asks as she makes her way back to the fridge and pops open another can of beer for Mason.

"Yeah, we are good to go," Mason reassures his sister. Lexi hands Mason his beer and hugs him again. I reflect on how great Mason's relationship is with his older sister, and I revel in the fact that things between Amber and I have improved since I moved out. Our interactions with each other have been significantly more pleasant, which is surprising considering the amount of stress Amber is under with her wedding only two months away.

"Well, the bedroom's all yours for the night." Lexi says, grabbing her glass of wine and plopping down on the couch. She pats the soft fabric of the empty cushion between us and says, "You wouldn't believe how comfortable the couch is. I'm looking forward to a good night sleep on it!"

I laugh in response as I take the first sip from my second glass of wine. I conclude that I should slow down, but I don't want to look like a pansy in front of Lexi; first impressions are lasting impressions. So, in an attempt to keep up with her drinking, I decide to follow in her wake.

As the night continues, we laugh at childhood stories that Lexi shares about the fond memories she has growing up in what appeared to be a typical happy family. Mason is grinning, but he is not fully engaged in the trip down memory lane that Lexi is insisting upon. I wonder if maybe the stories of his fairytale upbringing are painful given the current circumstances of the family's dynamics, but Lexi doesn't seem to notice Mason's hesitation regarding it all; instead, she refills her wine glass a few more times and persists in sharing more details. Mason hasn't consumed much alcohol since he became a Christian several months back. We both know that drunkenness is a sin, but it doesn't seem to stop either of us from accepting yet another drink from Lexi. By the end of the night, my cheeks are flushed and my limbs are numb. My judgment seems to be skewed, and I notice that Mason is also feeling the effects, although he is more capable of hiding them.

"Well," Lexi says as she clinks her empty glass down on the coffee table. With a slight slur of her words, she continues, "I think I'll head out to one of my friend's parties down the street. Shouldn't be gone for more than an hour or so, but it will give the two of you some time alone." She sighs as she slowly gets up from the couch and bends down to grab her purse near the front door. "And don't worry," she adds, "I won't be driving anywhere tonight, the party is walking distance." She takes out her keys and jingles them in front of her chest, "I'll lock up behind me," she promises, then throws a comment over her shoulder, "and don't do anything I wouldn't do." With a wink and a wave, she is out the door, slamming it behind her, leaving Mason and I drunk and alone together.

"Wow, it's 12:30 already," Mason states, while staring at his wrist watch. "Funny how time flies when you're enjoying good company."

"Your sister is great," I add with a smile, "I have to admit, I was a bit nervous to meet her, but she's been very welcoming since the minute I walked in."

Mason laughs and shakes his head, "Yeah, that's Lexi for you; she's always up for a good time, and as long as you don't cross her, she's as friendly as can be!"

Laughing, I glance at my almost empty glass of wine that seemed bottomless when Lexi was around. I take the last two gulps back to back, and place the empty glass on the coffee table next to Lexi's. Yawning, I stand up slowly from the couch and decide to get ready for bed. Trying to fix my eyes on Mason, I realize that the images in front of me are blurred, and I conclude that the last few drinks are definitely catching up with me.

I make my way past Mason, who is sitting in the lounge chair next to the hallway; however, my short journey toward Lexi's bedroom comes to a halt as Mason sticks out his arm and catches my hip in his hand. Using his grip to turn my body toward him, he looks up at me longingly as he slowly runs his hand around my hip and down toward the small crevice where my leg meets my backside. My body tingles in response to his movements, and I allow him to pull me tenderly on top of him, moving my body over the mold of his muscular frame. He looks me in the eyes, and my slightly numb body becomes fully aware of his intentional hand placements. I lower my lips to his and kiss him passionately in response. Mason slides his hands up my legs that have fallen easily around his body, then, placing one hand firmly on my lower back, he lifts his other hand affectionately to the base of my neck. In one swift move, Mason stands from the chair and my legs wrap tightly around his torso, both of us desperate to keep tight in our embrace. He holds my body close to his as he delicately lowers me to the soft, plush carpet, seductively kissing my neck the whole way down. Once my body sinks onto the floor, I turn my head and close my eyes, enjoying the slow movement of his lips as they climb from the side of my neck up to my ear. He sweeps a few strands of my hair away from my temple, then drops his hand to the base of my neck again. The brush of his fingers leave a tingling sensation in their trail. Moving his hand upward, he cradles my head and pulls my face toward his. Softly pressing his lips against mine, I allow the kiss to whisk me away as my hands find the hem of his shirt, and I begin lifting the material up to his shoulders. He backs away from my face and allows me to remove his shirt from his toned upper torso. As he hovers half naked above me, I know that my love and desire for him, combined with our alcohol consumption and a house void of company, led us down this path. Our eyes meet, and I realize that there is no turning back. The visible desperation in our gaze communicates to the other our willingness to put aside any moral obligations for what is to come next. So, for the first time, we give into 18 months of resistance as we intertwine our bodies together, sealing ourselves in an embrace that we know is only meant for marriage.

*　*　*

The fall has slipped away, and the winter chill has settled in, covering the ground with frost for the morning of Amber's wedding day. The brisk outdoor temperature keeps the bridal party indoors for most of the morning as we take care of last minute details before Amber puts on her wedding dress. I knew this day was coming a long time ago, but I am shocked at how quickly the engagement flew by. My green bridesmaids dress is hanging on the doorframe of my bedroom, and I am standing in the hallway, glancing back and forth from my room to Amber's. The color of the dress is perfect, given that the wedding is so close to Christmas, and Amber was kind enough to choose a flattering style. Reflecting on how Shane's mellow personality has helped Amber to gain a more mature perspective on life, I'm glad that the last two weeks I've spent home for Christmas break have been enjoyable between me and my older sister. The miles between us these past few months have helped move us toward a more reasonable sister relationship, and a small tear escapes from the corner of my eye as I reflect on the rough years of our past. Now, looking into her nearly empty bedroom, I curse the many opportunities that I gladly let pass to better our relationship. Just then, Amber walks up behind me, and I quickly wipe my cheek while lowering my gaze to the floor in embarrassment. I pray that she is too distracted to see my pain; however, to my great surprise, my older sister wraps both of her arms around me in an awkward hug.

"I know things haven't always been great between us Tess," she says, "but I'm glad that you're standing up as a bridesmaid for me today, and I promise to make a better effort with our friendship in the future."

I crumble at her words and let the emotions of this day, which signifies change in our family dynamic, overcome my composure. Marriage is a positive thing, and I know that I am eager to accept Shane into the family, but it doesn't alter the fact that things are going to be different from here on out. "Thanks," I squeak, as I try to regain my composure, "I love you Amber, and I am excited for your future." Amber smiles in response and tells me she loves me too, and just as quickly as the moment came, it is gone. My mom, who is bounding up the stairs, interrupts us and encourages everyone to get into their dresses.

The ceremony is beautiful and the weather turns out to be perfect. Between wedding party pictures, toasts, bouquet and garter tosses, and cutting the cake, I am eager to finally get to the dance floor. Mason takes my hand and guides me to the center of the crowd as Nat "King" Cole's song, L-O-V-E comes on. We sway together in perfect rhythm as I sink deeper into the arms of the man that I love so much.

"I love winter weddings," I say into Mason's ear. "There is just something about the warm feeling that you get when you are with loved ones on such an important day, and all of it falling so close to Christmas."

Mason leans his head back so he can look into my eyes, "Maybe we will get married in the winter," he offers with a smile, then pulls me back in close as my forehead rests on his shoulder.

"I would love that," I say. "We could spend our first Christmas together shortly after our honeymoon, and every Christmas after that, for the rest of our lives."

Mason leans his head against mine. "I want to spend the rest of my life with you Tessa," he whispers in my ear. I smile as we remain silent for the duration of the song, swaying in unison to the familiar tune and enjoying the simplicity of one another's embrace.

As Amber and Shane drive off, I sigh and turn back to Mason. "I can only guess what their plans are for tonight, huh?" Realizing the seriousness of my comment, I laugh, attempting to lighten the mood. On the way back from Lexi's, Mason and I had a lengthy discussion regarding our choice the night before, and although we both agreed that it was a pleasurable experience, we decided that it wasn't wise and that it shouldn't happen again.

Mason glances at me and changes the topic, "That dress looks terrific on you," he compliments, as his eyes run the length of my body.

"Thanks," I reply, "but I feel like it's uncomfortably tight. It wasn't this snug when I went to my final fitting a couple months ago." I shrug and pull on the elastic material wrapped tightly around my midsection, desperate to create some wiggle room. "Who knows, maybe I've put on some extra weight since our volleyball season ended."

"You look great to me," Mason retorts, and he takes my hand in his, leading me back into the warmth of the reception hall.

* * *

A sharp pain in my abdomen causes me to wake with a start. I roll over in my bed and wrap both of my arms around my stomach, concerned about the pain, but immediately realizing that it must be that time of the month. My menstrual cycle has never been very consistent, but I hate when it comes in the middle of the night. Contemplating getting out of bed and making sure I haven't leaked through my new pajama pants that I got for Christmas yesterday morning, my midsection contracts with a second sharp pain that sends me doubling over. My mind starts racing, my menstrual cramps have never been this painful, and the state of my pain is quickly reaching excruciating levels.

I lean over the side of my bed, wondering if I can actually make it to the bathroom. Pulling back the covers, I look down at the bed and shudder at the sight of my sheets. My breath starts to come up short, but I manage to scream for my mother; the sound of my screeching voice sounds as if it's coming from another person.

My mom rushes into my room and immediately sees the mess.

The look of fear that fills her face as her eyes take in the scene sends me reeling and confused about the severe throbs that I am struggling with.

My mother hurries to the side of the bed and grabs my arm, "Tessa, we need to get you to the bathroom."

By now, the cramping is so ruthless that I can't respond. I let her lead me the short distance from my bedroom to the bathroom. She holds on tight to my arm, but she is struggling underneath my weight, for I have lost the ability to walk upright. Clutching my stomach, I finally make it to the bathroom where my mom removes my blood soaked pants and seats me on the toilet. As soon as I sit, the room goes blurry, and I am convinced I am going to faint.

"Mom," I murmur, "…blacking out," is all I can manage to say. Something cold touches my face, and for a split second I wonder if it's a soaked washcloth, but the pain in my abdomen is all I can manage to focus on. A wave of nausea hits, and I immediately grab for the trashcan. Aware that all my food from Christmas dinner the night before is about to come up, it's almost as if I am watching everything from above; however, my sharp stabs of pain keep me rooted in reality.

"Tessa, your face is white as a ghost," my mother says to me, "I think I need to get some medicine from the cabinet downstairs." Her words work their way into my brain, but it sounds as if she's a hundred yards away, shouting down a long corridor, the sound reverberating off the walls and barely reaching my ears.

I gasp for words, worried that she is going to leave me alone to fend for myself in this terrible state, "No… don't… leave." I struggle to say, and I know my mother is torn between getting medication for my pain and leaving her daughter to momentarily take care of herself.

Obviously deciding to hold off going downstairs, she moves to the shower and turns on the water. "Do you think you can sit under the shower? You could use the heat, your whole body is shaking." I nod in response, and she helps me off the toilet. I am shocked that the action of standing has helped me gain some clarity instead of lose it, but I immediately drop to my knees as the most excruciating pain I have ever felt rips through my abdomen. I scream in response and clutch my lower torso. Somehow, I find myself sitting in the tub, with the water from the shower pouring down over my body, but I am ignorant as to how I got here.

The pain continues to shoot through my stomach, causing my muscles to react, as if trying to take on some of the unbearable stabs that my abdomen can't seem to handle. I am not sure how long this pain continues, but I know that I scream through the entirety of it; unable to produce tears, I rock back and fourth in a fetal position on the floor of the tub. Then, almost as quickly as the pain came, it stops. I extend my body down the length of the tub, and try to catch my breath. I notice that my mom has left the bathroom, but I am unsure if she is rummaging through the cabinet, or just wanting to give me some privacy. My mind is racing trying to discern what is happening to my body; however, I only get about 45 seconds of rest before I am slung back into the agonizing pain again; this pattern repeats several times, and it seems that just as I am able to catch my breath, my body begins contracting again.

The harsh stabs of pain eventually ease; however, I feel another wave of nausea hitting. I stand, trying to climb out of the tub and get to the toilet, which is the most appropriate place for me to get sick. My legs wobble a little underneath me, and I look down to see if they are visibly shaking as I climb over the edge of the tub; however, as I step one foot onto the bathmat, the sight of what falls from between my legs causes me to vomit on the bathroom floor. I stare at the mass that my body has expelled, and the tears that the fierce pain prohibited me to cry before, now come retching out as realization hits - I have just had a miscarriage.

chapter seven

(August, 2008 – September, 2008)

Momentarily distracted from helping Rachel pack her dorm room necessities, I turn to my best friend who is moving her clothes from her huge walk-in closet at her parent's house to a box sitting on top of her king size bed.

"I dunno Rach, it's just been a weird summer," I sigh as I reflect on the change that Mason and I have experienced in our relationship. "He barely touches me anymore, and when we kiss, he just gives me a peck." I shake my head, trying to wrap my mind around what it is that has made me so undesirable these past few months as I look out of the window, waiting for Mason to pull in the driveway and pick me up for a dinner date.

Rachel grabs another handbag and gingerly places it into the box, "Well," she starts, "do you think it has something to do with your miscarriage?"

The miscarriage caused some tension with my parents, given the fact that their questions lead to the conclusion that Mason and I had messed up, but I didn't predict that it would change things between me and Mason. My mind wanders back to the afternoon when I shared with Mason the unbearable details surrounding the event. He wasn't there to experience the tragedy with me, so he had a lot of trouble understanding the pain, both emotional and physical, that I dealt with that terrible morning. He is a guy, and the idea of losing a baby was a blessing in disguise. We would have faced the future head-strong if I had remained pregnant, but Mason still views the miscarriage as a lucky opportunity to continue our relationship with more wisdom and without extra baggage. I, on the other hand, still struggle with the loss of our child.

Understanding sinks in as I lay back on Rachel's bed. "Wow," I say, while shaking my head, "that all makes sense. He isn't touching or kissing me intimately because of the night we had sex and how it ended up in a miscarriage." Although I want to cry, I slam my fist into the mattress instead. "It's obvious he is withdrawing from me! He doesn't want a repeat episode, so I guess he is avoiding getting too close."

Rachel leans over to give my hand a squeeze, then she returns to her packing, allowing me time to grapple with my frustration. Although Mason showed nothing but love and adoration the afternoon I told him about the miscarriage, he has shown little of those emotions since. As I push off the bed and begin to pace, I angrily acknowledge that he still loves me, but most of the time he's hiding it, especially when it comes to the sexual side of our relationship. "I don't care what exciting news Mason plans on sharing with me over dinner!" I huff. "When he picks me up in a couple minutes, I'm gunna tell him how angry I am that our relationship has become so loveless!"

"Tessa, you may want to take it easy on him," Rachel advises. "In reality, he probably doesn't realize that he has been withdrawing from you." She shrugs, trying to make light of the conversation. "He doesn't want to experience another pregnancy, so he is putting up parameters to help avoid any temptations."

It is easy for Rachel to speak into the situation; she isn't dealing with my current predicament. I appreciate her counsel, but the way Mason and I have been interacting lately makes me feel like a fat, ugly wife who is battling a dying marriage of 30 plus years with her uninterested husband because he fails to see her as attractive.

Headlights flash through the window announcing Mason's arrival. I say a quick goodbye to Rachel as I grab my purse at the base of her bed and thump my feet angrily down the Hern's hallway to the front door.

"Hey, babe," Mason greets as I pull the passenger side door closed and yank the seatbelt over my body. He leans across the center consol and plants a kiss on my cheek. Immediately my anger toward him starts to melt away as I consider what Rachel said earlier while reflecting on the signs that evidence his persistent love for me. I turn to him and smile, and although I want to share my epiphany with him, I remember that he has good news to share with me, and I decide not to ruin the evening.

We settle into the booth of a popular restaurant in our little city and listen to the band play some jazz tunes as we order. After the waitress takes away our menus, Mason reaches across the table for my hand as a shy smile spreads across his face. "So," he begins, "you know how I have been seeking recruitment from other universities this summer?" I nod slowly in response. "Well, I've been praying about it a lot lately, and…" he pauses, giving me time to contemplate his prayer life and how his relationship with Christ has progressed. "I got a call from Callan University this afternoon and they have given me an offer." My eyes widen at his words, "I'm going to university with you!"

My heart fills with joy, and I gasp as my hands fly to my face. I didn't even know he was considering Callan, and I am overjoyed at the prospect of being on the same campus with him. I begin chattering about all we can do together on campus having quickly dismissed the topic I wanted to address earlier. I am immediately convinced that having him at Callan with me will change the way we have been interacting together lately. We eat dinner and drive back to my parents, ending the lovely evening cuddled up, close and comfortable on the couch. Sitting here, tangled in the arms of the man I love, I know that our relationship is going to be just fine, and I lay my head on his shoulder, resting in the fact that the passion we have for each other will reignite the moment he moves onto the campus.

Mason and I walk back from the cafeteria to his dorm room, hand in hand. He has been on campus for a little over two weeks now, and although I have introduced him to many of my friends, he's still trying to get settled in. Mason takes out his keys and opens his door. His roommate Lucas, a tall, gangly brunette from South Carolina, who happens to be the new pitcher for the baseball team, is sitting in his computer chair in front of his 46" flat screen T.V., playing a video game. I like Lucas. He is easy going and considerate, especially when it comes to sharing a room with Mason. Their friendship has developed quickly in a short time, and I foresee their rooming situation being a good fit for both of them.

"Hey man," Lucas says as he pauses the game and turns in our direction, his long shaggy hair flopping to one side of his face in the process, "anything good in the cafe tonight?"

"Nah, not really," Mason responds, "you're better off grabbing some fast food in town." I nod, affirming Mason's remarks, and without skipping a beat, Lucas turns off the T.V. and grabs his wallet and keys.

"Be back in a bit," he says, just before the door closes behind him, leaving us alone. I've enjoyed having Mason on campus with me, but between our roommates and athletic schedules, we haven't had much time to ourselves.

"Ah, some time alone with my favorite man," I say jokingly, as I crawl onto Mason's bed and pat the spot on the mattress beside me. Happy that I don't have my parents poking their head through my bedroom door every so often to hold us accountable, my heart skips a couple of beats at the idea of having Mason to myself for a bit. Although he sits down on the bed next to me, I notice that he intentionally keeps a few inches between us. I shake my head and decide that the conversation I contemplated bringing up a few weeks earlier needs to be discussed.

"Mason," I sigh, "you've been distant for months now. I thought that things were going to change when you moved onto the campus with me, but you still seem withdrawn. Is everything ok?"

Mason quickly picks up the remote on his bedside table and starts fiddling with the object. This action frustrates me as I reflect on the fact that before the miscarriage, we didn't seem to have any issues communicating our thoughts to one another. I pull the remote from his hands and toss it behind me as I turn to face him directly, my eyes pleading with him to share his thoughts.

"Tess," he hesitates, "…it's just that, well…" he shrugs his shoulders as he lifts his eyes to mine, and I witness the struggle that he is dealing with while he searches for the right words to say. "I love you, but we made a bad choice several months ago, and I don't want to make the same mistake again. We dealt with the consequences, but we should learn from our past and make wiser choices because of it."

His words confirm my fears, and I am torn as to how I should respond. He has a point - our decision led to an unplanned pregnancy, which led to a painful miscarriage - but it doesn't mean that our relationship should lack intimacy because of it. I huff a little before trying to explain my side of the dilemma, "Yes, I know, but that doesn't mean you should avoid being passionate with me altogether. Girls like me need to be desired, and lately I feel like I fall short of your expectations. I feel like there must be something wrong with my appearance, which is the only logical reason why a guy your age isn't attracted to his girlfriend." I drop my head, a little embarrassed and slightly worried that maybe I'm right - that he isn't attracted to me anymore.

"No, you are beautiful," he assures me, "but every time I think our kissing is getting too passionate, I am reminded of what happened and how upset your parents were about it and how the Bible insists that I don't act on my sexual impulses, and..." he drops his head into his hands for a moment, then lifts it again to meet my eyes, "and, I just don't know how to handle it all."

A frustrated tear escapes as I bark in response. "So, what are we going to do about it, then? It's not like we are going to get married in the next year or two; it's going to be a long time before we get married, Mason. Does that mean this is how our relationship will stay until then? Because I can't handle this!" My anger surrounding the whole ordeal increases, and I begin spilling hot tears of rage as I struggle with the idea of a long term relationship void of passion.

Mason matches a little of my anger as he retorts, "Well, I'm certainly not going to ignore all the details of our past for a little pleasure, Tessa!" He gets up from the bed and stands in front of me, "You act like all of this is easy for me to deal with! Well, it's not, I just want to honor God and your parents with my actions, and I haven't exactly figured out how to manage the expectations of everyone in this situation."

Immediately, I allow my disdain for my parents and their strict rules to create a new level of anger inside me. "Mason!!" I yell, "To hell with my parents' rules, if you haven't noticed, THEY AREN'T HERE!"

"Yeah," Mason whispers, "but God is." With defiance, I wipe my face and stand. I refuse to look up as my fury toward God increases. I lunge for my keys, which are sitting on Mason's dresser pressed against the wall on the other side of the room. Although Mason is quiet, I know he is aware of my anger evident in my actions. I snatch my keys and stomp toward the door.

"Well," I say, pausing at the door, "maybe a break will help us gain some perspective." My eyes find a rip in the carpet near the opening of the door, and I fix my gaze on that instead of the negative reaction I suspect to be evident on Mason's face. "I'll talk to you in a couple of weeks Mason, maybe by then you will have figured out what is important to you," and without another word, I leave the room, unwilling to witness the impact that my decision has had on Mason.

* * *

Apart from class and volleyball practice, I've spent the last week in bed, clinging tightly to a box of tissues and attempting to sleep away my sorrow. Mason hasn't called. He hasn't made any attempt to converse with me on campus, and although we don't have any classes together, he knows my schedule and is clearly avoiding crossing my path. I know that my last words implied that I would talk to him in a couple of weeks, but I expected him to beat me to it. Brushing aside my long, wet hair, I hang up my towel to dry. I consider going to the cafe for a late dinner, but decide against it; my bed looks much too inviting.

Just as I make my way to my side of the room, ready to crawl into the sweet embrace of my cotton sheets, Rachel jiggles her key in the door and swings it wide open. "Oh, no you don't!" she starts, as she catches the tail end of my slow trudge toward my bed. "Tessa, I'm taking you out to a party tonight. Come on, it will be like old times when we were in high school," she says enthusiastically, until she catches a glimpse of my face. "You want to talk about it?" she asks. I shrug, trying to determine how much I am willing to share. "He hasn't called, has he?" she continues, although she knows the answer.

"I just don't get it, Rach." I start to cry again, an action that Rachel has become quite accustomed to in the past week. "I announced our break-up hoping that Mason would realize what he is missing out on and come racing back to me; however, he hasn't so much as glanced in my direction since I shut his dorm door." I reach for the box of tissues and continue, "He wasn't showing me any physical attention, and I thought if I broke-up with him for a couple of weeks that he would come to the conclusion that I was right. We don't have to have sex to have intimacy, but the break-up has placed an even larger wedge between us." My words spill out as I pat my cheeks dry, "I love him so much, and I want him to show me some attention, not completely forget about me!"

I know there is nothing more to be said, so I surrender to Rachel's plan and slowly start getting ready for the party. During the search for an outfit, I wonder if Mason's silence is more about his commitment to God rather than his lack of commitment to me. This thought plagues me as I finish getting ready, then I move to make an assessment before my full length mirror. I have pulled on a pair of ripped jean shorts and a yellow, backless halter top, taking advantage of the few days we have left of summer weather. My hair is thrown up into a messy bun, and my make-up has managed to cover my earlier tears.

We walk the short distance to the party happening at Katie's house. Since Katie is the setter for our volleyball team, I know most of my teammates will be there. However, I am hopeful that Destiny continues with her pattern of avoiding these parties. I feel warmly welcomed as the door opens to Katie's off campus house where she lives year round. "Tessa, I'm so glad you're here," Katie pulls her long curly blonde hair over to one shoulder as she closes the door behind me. Katie is cute, and everyone on campus is drawn to her bubbly personality, making her house a popular destination on a Thursday night. "Let's get you a drink, help wipe that sullen look off your face," Katie giggles as she skips to her kitchen and starts rummaging through her fridge. "Wine, wine, wine - it's always the answer, my love!" she reaches for a cup from the stack on the counter and starts pouring the newly opened bottle, but I take the Chardonnay out of her grip and tip the bottle back to my lips instead. Katie laughs, "Welcome to the party, hun – go hard, or go home!" She slings one arm around my shoulder and places the cup back on the counter.

The party is a hit, as always, and before long her place is

crawling with university students. I am about half way through the bottle of Chardonnay, and although the alcohol has blurred my vision, it has also helped to lift my spirits. Thankful that I left our room a few hours earlier, I am surprised when Rachel catches my eye from across the room, indicating that she wants to head home. I look at my watch in surprise, then remember her big exam in the morning. I know she needs to leave; however, I want to stay, so I convince her that I am fine to walk home alone. Rachel takes my word for it, but still looks a little unsure as she gives me one last glance before she weaves through Katie's crowded living room to the front door. "I'll be back in like an hour or so," I yell in Rachel's direction over the loud music. She glances back at me and gives me the thumbs-up in reply. I wait till she is out of sight before tipping the bottle back again, not wanting to give her any reason to worry if I happen to come back a little later than promised. I look to the front door to confirm that Rachel is no longer in sight, and in place of Rachel, I see Tripp. He is smiling at me, and my heart starts to beat a little faster as he ambles to my side.

"Hey, Tessa," he greets, "having a good time?" He laughs while pointing to the bottle in my hand, I offer a shy smile in return. "You see," he continues, "everyone else at the party is drinking from red solo cups – somehow, I think you missed the memo." I look around in response to his hand gesture, desperate for something to distract me from his attractive grin and shining green eyes. We both laugh as I shrug my shoulders and raise the bottle in a toast like fashion.

"You know what they say," I add jokingly, "when in Rome…" I am not entirely sure what that comment means, but uneasiness washes over me as I realize that I am enjoying the conversation and Tripp's attentiveness. The alcohol burns my throat and muddles my thoughts that are bouncing back and forth between Mason and Tripp, but I continue drinking anyway as Tripp and I discuss how our sports' seasons are progressing. Somehow, the conversation lands on Mason and me. "Are you dating that guy I see you with on campus?" He raises one eyebrow, waiting for my answer.

I lift the bottle to my lips again, buying time to consider my response to his question. Technically, no, I am not dating Mason, but the break was to draw Mason closer, not drive him away, like it seems to have done. "Ummm," I start, "no, we are not dating." I take another swig and avoid his gaze, but his hand slips nonchalantly to my exposed lower back and his proximity causes my eyes to find his, unsure of how I want to handle his touch. Tripp's smile penetrates my discomfort, and I grin back, surprising myself as I welcome the touch of another guy. I move closer to his muscular chest, suddenly desperate to experience the warmth. The conversation continues as I lean into his arm, nodding when it's appropriate, for the alcohol has turned my words into jumbled slurs, and I don't want to reveal its effects. Eventually, Tripp lowers his lips to my ear. "Do you want to get out of here?" he asks. "We could go back to my dorm room, my roommate left early for the weekend." Uncertain of what my heart actually wants, I mindlessly nod my head and trail behind Tripp toward the front door.

* * *

In the pre-dawn darkness, I stumble into my room, accidentally dropping my keys on the floor. The commotion wakes Rachel up, and she immediately turns on her study lamp beside her bed.

"Gosh, Tessa," she groans while glancing at her alarm clock, "there's no way you're just getting home from the party now. Where have you been?" She wipes her eyes, trying to adjust to the newly introduced light.

Although I was still drunk, realization of my terrible decision to follow Tripp back to his dorm hit while he was in the bathroom, and I slipped out of his room, tip-toeing down the hall and back to my own corridor. I didn't expect Rachel to wake up when I entered the room, but knowing that I will eventually tell her about the poor choice I just made, I decide to spill the beans as I close the door behind me, "I followed Tripp back to his dorm," I blurt out, ripping my clothes off in anger and pulling on my pajamas.

"Oh my gosh!" she says, sitting up in her bed. "What happened? Oh Tessa, please tell me you didn't have sex with him."

I cringe at her comment, "No, off course we didn't," I state, "I'm not that stupid." But I sigh, aware of just how stupid I really am, given that I want to be with Mason, but temporarily chose the attention of Tripp as an alternative. "I don't want to talk about it," I mumble, and I end the conversation as I sway over to her night stand, turn off her lamp, and climb into my bed.

* * *

The next day, Tripp catches me on campus and asks me where I went. I explain that it was best for me to stay in my own room and manage to hold back tears as I battle the deep regret I feel. Although Mason has yet to talk to me since I broke things off last week, I know that he will come around eventually, and the decision I made to follow Tripp back to his room only helps to reaffirm my desperate desire to be Mason's girlfriend, whether or not he chooses to embrace my need for intimacy.

"Listen, Tripp," I start, "if we could just keep last night confidential, I would really appreciate it." I shift my weight from one foot to the other, desperate for the awkward moment to pass. I know it's important that Mason never finds out about what happened.

"Yeah, yeah," Tripp responds, "no worries." He turns his head in the opposite direction, "Well, I need to get to the Guilder building, see you later," and without another word, he turns and walks off. Immediately fighting a rush of nausea, I turn toward my dorm.

* * *

The unfinished food sitting cold on my lunch tray holds no appeal as I push it away and ponder last week's encounter with Tripp. Actually, food and fun have held little interest for me lately. I have been struggling with the fact that Mason has yet to talk to me since we broke-up two weeks ago, and now, as I stare down at my food, I'm wondering if I will ever be able to enjoy a meal again.

"Hey," a voice sounds from behind me. I swivel quickly in the booth as I recognize Mason's voice. I look up at him and fiercely fight the desire to burst into tears in the middle of the campus cafeteria. "Can I sit?" he asks, pointing to the empty bench on the opposite side of my table. I nod, nervous that my voice will quiver if I speak.

"Listen," he starts, as he scoots into the seat across from me, "I know it's been a while since we have talked, but I wasn't sure how to handle our last discussion." He clears his throat then continues, "I dialed your number a couple of times, but hung up before it rang. I considered visiting your dorm, but I wasn't sure how I wanted to address our issues." He swallows, "However, even though I'm still confused as to how I should handle the situation, the fact remains - I really miss you, Tessa."

I smile in response as a tear escapes down my cheek, "Oh gosh Mason, I miss you too. Just forget what I said last time we talked, I don't care about that whole physical thing, I just want to be with you." Mason gets up and walks around the table, sliding next to me in the booth. He tenderly kisses me, then sheepishly pulls away, aware that a make-out session might create an unwanted scene in a public location.

Staring into my eyes, he affectionately strokes the side of my face. "Then let's not let anything come between us, again," he says. I drop my head to his chest and allow him to hold my trembling body. Knowing that I will never let anything (or anyone) come between us ever again, the guilt of last week's terrible decision weighs down on me heavily. Yet, I am unwilling to share the details of it all and watch my last chance at happiness with Mason pass. So, desperate to cling to the relationship that Mason and I had before our break two weeks ago, I bury my guilt and meet his gaze, firmly deciding to take my secret to the grave.

chapter eight

(April, 2009)

Huffing and puffing angrily down the long road that leads from our university's gym back to my dorm room, I swing my gym bag over my shoulder and grab for my phone to call Mason and complain about our spring season.

"Hey," I say quickly, "where are you? I need to vent."

I wait for Mason's response before I suggest that we meet in the university park, a central location that will allow me to enjoy some fresh air while I relay to Mason the ugly details of the frustrating scene that just happened in the gym. I hang up the phone and wipe my sweaty forehead, thankful that the late night breeze will help cool off my body, and hopefully my anger, by the time I make it to the park.

"Hi Tess," Mason greets, "what's going on? You sounded pretty upset on the phone." We both plop down in the two-seater tree swing. I angrily throw my gym bag on the ground beside the dirt, sling my head back, and let out a groan.

"Our spring season is a disaster," I start to unravel. "Destiny and I don't get along, we lost some really essential seniors this year, and Coach Greenly is being ridiculous." I breath in deeply, rest my head on the wooden back support and close my eyes for a moment, allowing my mind to get caught up in the swaying of the swing instead of my disdain for what is happening with the volleyball team.

Mason places a hand on my bare leg. His action provides comfort as my body begins to unwind. I'm convinced that he is on my side no matter what, and I rest in the fact that as I begin to share with him the details surrounding the spat that just broke out in the gym, he will assure me that I had good reason to react the way I did. I pick my head up and begin, "Destiny and I got into a fight." I don't wait for him to respond before continuing, "I made a diving play in the back row and really hurt my hip, which is all worth it if we get the point in the end, but instead of playing hard, Destiny didn't put any effort into getting the ball over the net." I push a few strands of hair away from my eyes. "So I laid into her, I told her that she never honors my efforts and that she always has an excuse for why the play didn't work out!" My jaw flexes in contempt, "We argued for a few seconds, but I was yelling so loud that I didn't really hear what Destiny was saying in return. Then our coach intervened. She told me that I was being unreasonable and that I was reading into Destiny's actions more than I needed to." Pausing for a moment to take a breath, I kick at the dirt as our bodies swing forward. "Coach Greenly still doesn't understand our history, and she says that I see a lot of Destiny's actions as personal, when they are just errors unrelated to our past." I pick my feet up and cross them Indian style on the seat, knowing that Mason has enough power behind his push to keep the swing swaying without my help.

"What was the outcome?" Mason asks.

"We have an early morning work-out because of my accusations." I shake my head and lower it, staring at my upper thighs where my spandex meet my bare legs. "Coach Greenly says team chemistry is important, and that if I don't let go of my anger toward my teammate, then the whole team will have 6 am work-outs until I understand how destructive my resentment is for the whole team." I feel guilt rise as my thoughts focus on my amazing teammates, minus Destiny, who now have to get up excessively early tomorrow morning thanks to my actions. Bringing my knees up to my chest, I wrap my arms around my shins, hugging my legs closer to my body and dropping my forehead onto them. "I'm upset with Coach Greenly – I think she sided with Destiny, without seeing my point of view at all." My voice is muffled thanks to my huddled body, yet I continue anyway, "I am angry that I made a big deal about it though - and now we have an added work-out to our already busy schedule. All my teammates have to wake up early and participate thanks to how I reacted." I lift my head up, reaching the conclusion that I should get some sleep before our 6 am work-out in the morning, so I ask Mason what time it is.

Mason pulls his cell phone from his pocket to check, "It's 10:43 babe." Slightly distracted, he adds, "Just a sec, I need to check this message from Lucas." The cell phone's glow casts a bright light on Mason's face, allowing me to see his features fall in confusion as he reads Lucas's text. "Tessa," he says slowly, "what is this about?" He turns the cell phone in my direction, and my heart plummets as I read the words that Lucas wrote to my boyfriend. My heart starts to race while I fight the urge to vomit. My forehead quickly becomes soaked with perspiration as I read the line over and over again, knowing that even if I wanted to lie about it, my face tells Mason that the text is true – I did follow Tripp back to his room.

I burst into tears as Mason shoots out of the swing and I follow, realizing that our conversation about volleyball has quickly turned into a much more heightened and real dilemma. Mason slams his phone down and it shatters the moment it meets the harsh cement of the nearby park path. Furious, Mason insists on visiting Tripp. I beg against it, explaining to him that the night happened months ago and that it was my fault. Turning his back to me, Mason kicks the swing out of frustration while I sag to the grass, my legs unwilling to hold my body thanks to the weight of my guilt and self-hatred. Ignoring my tears, Mason snatches my phone from my gym bag and finds Tripp's number. I shudder at every word he yells into the phone once Tripp answers. I don't know what Tripp's response is, but Mason's face twists with rage, and I conclude that Tripp's retort is unkind. With tears streaming down my face, I plead with Mason to forgive me, but Mason refuses to respond to my desperation as he paces in front of me.

Looking for a way to release his anger, Mason picks up my gym bag and throws it at a nearby tree. I don't have anything breakable in the bag, but I crawl over to where it lands anyway. Realizing that his actions are much too aggressive, Mason slowly and more calmly steps in my direction, tosses my cell phone on top of my gym bag, and slides down the trunk opposite me. We both find ourselves sitting silently across from each other. My body feels like it is going to shut down. Between my strenuous practice, my anger from the fight with Destiny, the time of night, and the agony over the discovery regarding Tripp, my mind is dizzied from exhaustion as I try to determine where Mason and I will go from here.

I hear a low, cracking voice break the silence, "Why?" Mason asks. Even though it's only one word, I detect that his emotions have shifted from blinding anger to agonizing pain.

Confident that I have shed all the tears my body could possibly produce for one night, I surprise myself when I am hit with the need to sob. It takes a while before I answer, knowing that I cannot justify my actions with Tripp – I was wrong, and there was no way of getting around it. "There is no justifiable reason," I start, trying to gain control of my quivering voice. "I was selfish, and I wanted attention. I was drunk and upset that you hadn't called since our break-up. I was stupid." I humbly lift my head and look at him, hoping that he is considering showing me some mercy; however, the vision that catches my eye will haunt my dreams forever. Mason has his head bowed in his hands and his body is shaking from his silent sobs. The man that I have known to overcome the pain of his parents' divorce with a shake of his head, or disregard the tragedy of his car accident with a witty joke, is now sobbing, an action that I have never witnessed, and it's me who has driven him to this point. Not his family. Not his shoulder injury. Me.

The minutes tick by slowly, leading us into the early hours of the morning, and I am painfully aware of the agonizingly long silence. Mason periodically breaks the silence with a question, and I answer, sparing him the gruesome details of my terrible decision, while I allow him time to mull over my responses. I don't know where the conversation is leading us, but I know that I love him with all of my heart, and I am willing to give him as long as he needs to work through this.

Eventually, the questions stop. I stand slowly from the tree that has held me up for the majority of the night, and notice for the first time that my backside is aching from the hours spent on the hard ground. Reaching down for my phone, I flip it open and glance at the numbers on the screen, "It's 2:36," I tell Mason. He nods, but refuses to look up at me. Having heard his change of tone in the last several attempts at conversing, I determine that it is safe for me to move closer to him. So, although a little hesitant, I sit on the ground next to him, his back still leaning against the tree trunk. "Mason, I can't even begin to tell you how sorry I am," I offer, knowing that I have apologized numerous times over the past few hours, even though my apologies can't erase my actions. We sit quietly for a few moments before he responds.

"I know, Tess," he begins, still unable to look at me. "I understand what you faced that night and…" he pauses, "and, I forgive you for your actions." My heart fills with relief at his words. I am unwilling to smile, given the dynamics of the night, but I slowly move closer to him, wanting to offer my gratitude for his willingness to extend unwarranted grace. However, instead of opening up his arms to me, he puts out a hand and places it gently on my shoulder, stopping me from moving toward his embrace. "I can't," he says, "I'm sorry Tessa, but I just can't - it's over." He slowly drops his hand and shifts his weight onto his feet, and without looking back, he walks away, leaving me alone on the ground, my arm tingling in response to his last touch. The pieces of his shattered cell phone surround me, providing a vivid reminder of my actions and a perfect image of what my heart must resemble, and once again my tears begin to flow.

chapter nine

(May, 2009)

If I thought the two week break that Mason and I took back in the fall was difficult, I was wrong. The pain I am experiencing since Mason ended our relationship three weeks ago is much more extreme - it's excruciating. I roll over in my bed, unwilling to open my eyes thanks to the bright morning sun shining in through our open window. Rachel and I like a cool breeze during the night, but now I'm cursing the idea. I used to love the sun, a morning like this would have been spectacular several weeks ago, but now I hate it, and I doubt I will ever enjoy sunlight again. Squinting, I roll out of bed, slip on some shoes, and grab my pack of cigarettes on my dresser. Quickly, I throw on my thin gray jacket, which luckily has a lighter in the pocket, and grab my keys before making my way to the nearest exit of our dorm building.

Rachel doesn't approve of my smoking; however, she is in her last Friday morning class at the moment, probably where I should be. I used to secretly smoke a lot when I was 14 and 15, but I gave it up when Mason came around. He made it very clear that he didn't like me to smoke; however, he isn't around to complain about it now. In the last three weeks, my body has become dependent on the nicotine, and it's the one thing I look forward to anymore. Of course, I have no idea what I'm going to do when I move back in with my parents tomorrow. They certainly won't approve of it, even though it's legal for me to smoke now.

I plop down on the cement step leading up to the back entrance of our dorm building. Some students have already started packing up for the summer. Our campus requires us to be out by midnight on Sunday. Most are looking forward to moving back home; however, I shake my head in disgust at the thought of returning to our small little town for the summer. I put out my cigarette and consider going inside to fill up more of my boxes, but given the demands of those actions, I decide against it and light up another.

Suddenly, Rachel appears around the corner. "Oh Tessa, put that out," she says as soon as she sees me. "You are doing terrible things to your body!" Her suggestion falls on deaf ears as she sits down beside me. Her books cradled in one arm.

"How was class?" I ask.

"It was fine," Rachel responds. "We went over the answers to the exam we took earlier this week. I know you already got your final grade, but it still would have been helpful for you to have attended class this morning."

I roll my eyes, "Yeah, I'm not really worried about it." Rachel looks at me with concern, but we sit in silence for a few moments as I take my last few puffs. "Shall we go inside?" I ask, as I put out the cigarette.

Rachel gets up and puts her key in the door. "Tessa, I'm so concerned about your health," she sighs and looks me up and down as we enter into the building and walk down the long hall. "You have lost too much weight since Mason broke up with you."

I look down at my thin waist and my slightly wobbling legs; she does have a point, I haven't eaten much lately, and the nicotine has decreased my appetite and left me shaky. "Well, maybe it's better this way," I retort. "Maybe Mason will like how thin I've become and want me back."

"Tess, you know that the break-up had nothing to do with your weight," Rachel mutters. Although Rachel tries to reassure me, her words come crashing down as I remember vividly what the break-up was really over. I drop my head, and stand quietly behind my best friend as she opens the door to our dorm room stacked with half-packed boxes. "You know," she says, stopping in the doorway after glancing at my pain filled face. "Never mind," she murmurs, as she glances away. Although I feel like she had something important to tell me, I allow the comment to pass, since I know it pertains to Mason.

I walk in behind her, refusing to make eye contact; she didn't mean to hurt me with her last comment, but any conversation surrounding Mason hurts. I make for my cell phone that is sitting on my dresser. My heart lurches at the sight of a text from Mason. I have seen him at a distance on campus, but there has been no contact. I open the text:

Hi Tess, hope you are well. I am packing up my dorm room, and I have a pile of your things. Wondering if I can return them to you today? And maybe pick up some of my things?

Tears roll down my cheeks as I read the text over and over again. Something inside me thought that maybe he was texting me to tell me how much he missed me. To explain that he has forgiven me and wants me back. To express his sorrow since the night we broke up. But no, he just wants his things back. The treasures that I have kept from our relationship are scattered between my dorm room and my parents' house, but no matter the location, I want to keep his things forever.

About six months into our relationship, he gave me a stuffed animal that he had when he was a child. Corky is his name, and I have slept with him since Mason gave him to me. I look to my bed and see the fluffy tail sticking up from my rumpled sheets. I don't want to give him back. We laughed about me sleeping with a stuffed animal in my late teens, but I figured, if I couldn't cuddle up next to Mason every night, that this was the next best thing until we got married; and after marriage, we would give Corky to our first born. As I stare at Corky's tail, painful thoughts fill my mind. What if I return this keepsake and Mason gives it to his next girlfriend? Could Mason make plans with someone else besides me? I crawl into my bed and grab Corky, holding him close to my body for the last time as my tears stain my pillow. Then, reaching for my phone, my fingers shake as they move across the small keyboard, telling Mason that I will meet him in the parking lot of my dorm with his things in an hour.

* * *

The Blazer pulls up into the lot, and I reach down for the box of Mason's belongings that is sitting on the curb next to my feet. The box isn't heavy, but it is full of the many memories that Mason and I created in the past three years. I open up the passenger side door and slip into the seat beside Mason, while keeping my eyes on the box; I don't think my emotions can handle looking into the face of the man that I know I can never stop loving.

"Hi," Mason greets, and I can tell by his tone that this meeting is as hard on him as it is on me. "Here are your things, there are a few items of clothing, and some hair products, I think." He hands me a small box, and I place it on the floor in between my feet, unwilling to rummage through the items.

Still keeping my gaze averted from his face, I nod toward the box, "I have your things, but I actually need the box back to finish my packing." I clear my throat, desperate to hold back my tears. "It's mostly just clothes though," I say as I start to hand him gym shorts, t-shirts, and my favorite blue and gray Florida State Baseball sweatshirt of his. I fight the urge to cry as I empty the box and consider the irony of the action – it's as if I'm emptying my heart, one object at a time, leaving the most painful for last. By the time Mason tosses all his clothing in his back seat, the only thing left in the box is Corky. As I look down at the comfort object that has offered me relief from Mason's absence so many times, I can no longer hold back my tears.

I reach into the box and slowly remove Corky, handing the stuffed animal back to Mason as my tears start to flow. However, my arm remains extended, waiting for Mason to take Corky and without any emotion toss it into the back seat, just as he had done with the clothing. In the silence, I realize he isn't accepting the object. I look up to see what the issue is, and Mason's eyes are filled with tears. The image of his pain rips straight through my heart, and my tears turn into sobs. We sit there, not saying anything, just crying together. Mason more collected than I am as I set Corky between the two of us.

"You should keep him," Mason says as he tries to move the painful moment into a cordial conversation.

"I can't. He reminds me too much of what we used to have, Mason." I look out of the window as I try to reign in my sobs, "It would hurt me more than it would help."

Mason hesitantly moves Corky to the back seat. I hate the fact that it was my actions that split us apart, my actions that have resulted in this pain. For whatever reason, I don't get out of his car, and I don't feel that Mason is rushing me out either. We sit in silence for what seems like ages, both of us unwilling to look the other in the eye.

Eventually Mason speaks, "I'm staying with Lucas for the next little while." He clears his throat, gaining control over his quivering voice. "My dad is gone, and I don't want to go back to an empty house, so Lucas invited me to stay with his family in South Carolina." I nod in response, thankful that we won't be going back to our small town together. "His dad owns a golf course, so Lucas and I are going to work there." He drums his fingers on the steering wheel, and I feel like our time together is coming to a close.

"That will be a good opportunity for you to make some extra money," I respond. "I hope you have a good time." I mean every word I say, there is no need for me to wish terrible things for Mason's future. I reach for the door handle to get out, but

Mason catches my hand, and I allow him to hold my hand in his for a few moments.

"No matter what, I think you should know…" he pauses, contemplating his words. "… I wish the best for you." I feel like that wasn't what he wanted to say, but he kisses the back of my hand before releasing it, indicating his final farewell for the summer as the touch of his lips creates a painful lump in my throat.

I open the car door and watch my feet hit the pavement before turning back in his direction. "Yeah, you too," I say, as I grab my box of things from the floorboard and place it inside the empty box. Closing the car door, I turn to walk away, and my face contorts with pain evidenced in my silent sobs. Behind me I hear his car start up, and the tires crunch across the parking lot. Before I open the side door of our dorm building, I look back in the direction of the Blazer and watch the tail lights disappear. I shake my head and enter in the building angry with myself, but also with God, who stood-by and watched my relationship with Mason end this way.

* * *

"Well," Rachel says, glancing around our empty dorm room. "Guess this is goodbye for the summer." She places the departure sheet, complete with our signatures, on her dresser next to our dorm room keys. I pick up the only remaining box filled with a few pictures and decorations and follow Rachel out of the room. We close the door behind us and make our way down the long hall toward the parking lot. "What are your plans tonight?" Rachel asks.

I shift the box from one arm to the other as I remove my car keys from my pocket. "Well, I guess I'll unload everything at my parents," I say, "but to be honest, I really am not in the mood to spend time with them, they will only ask about what led to the break-up, and I don't want to talk about it." I sigh, thinking about my parents' curiosity surrounding Mason and me. They don't know the details, but they do know the break-up isn't something I wanted.

"Why don't you stay with me at my parents' tonight?" Rachel asks. "They just had the pool cleaned for the summer, and we can sneak some booze from my dad's cupboard - it'll be great." I accept Rachel's offer before getting into my tightly packed car. The ride home is only a little over an hour, and I know that my half-a-pack of cigarettes will be gone before I pull into my parents' driveway.

* * *

Rachel pours me a mixed drink that she concocted now that her parents are in bed. We sneak our cups up to the game room and sit back on the large comfy couch, turning on MTV and half watching some reality T.V. show between spotty conversations. I was happy to get my unpacking done right after dinner. I did end up spending some time with my parents, and my dad managed to slip in a pep-talk about placing my trust in God, no matter the circumstance. I felt like the conversation was heading toward Mason, so I explained that I was staying with Rachel and quickly packed an overnight bag before saying goodnight to my mom and dad.

"These shows are so stupid," I say with a laugh, then take another sip from my drink. We both snicker as the group of girls on the screen stumble into a house party and make a huge scene, thanks to their alcohol consumption. One of the guys at the party starts hitting on the girl, who I assume to be the main character of the whole show. Laughing in response to his terrible pick-up lines, I look at Rachel and expect to see her laughing also, but instead her head is lowered and she is fiddling with her empty cup.

"Rach, what's up?" I ask, noticing that there is something on her mind. She looks at her cup, then gets up from the couch in a rush of movement.

"I'm gunna get another drink, want one?" she asks me, still refusing to make eye contact.

"No, I want to know what's on your mind – obviously something is bothering you."

She shuffles her feet, looks longing at the staircase, then sighs loudly as she decides there is no way of getting around the conversation. She knows that her whole demeanor has peaked my interest and that I will keep prodding until I know what she is contemplating. "Tess…" she starts, "I wasn't sure if I wanted to tell you, and I tried to bring it up before, but I noticed how much pain you were dealing with concerning the break-up and thought better of it." She sits down beside me on the couch, and I turn toward her, my mind reeling at what she could possibly be struggling to tell me. "Do you remember that weekend in March when you went to Virginia for that Spring Athletic Leadership Conference?" I nod, remembering how I was asked to join Callan's Student Athletic Advisory Committee as a replacement for our senior captain who was graduating. "Well, the baseball boys had a party that weekend and Mason was there." I look at her, my brow furrowing in confusion. I remember Mason sharing with me over the phone that he was going to a party that night, so this wasn't new information. My head tilts skeptically to one side as Rachel continues, "I watched how excited the team was that Mason showed up, and they kept pouring him shots – let's just say, he was pretty drunk by midnight." She takes a slow, deep breath before going on, "I saw him disappear into the hallway with one of his teammates just as Destiny walked by. I went after him to suggest that he might want to go back to his dorm, given his state…" Rachel drops her gaze, and I notice that her legs are bouncing up and down nervously. "Mason didn't know I was behind him, and…" her face twists in discomfort.

"Well, I overheard him tell his teammate that if he didn't have a girlfriend, he would take Destiny home with him in a heartbeat."

I stare back at her blankly as my mind clears, trying to make sense of what Rachel was explaining. I sit silently for a few moments and let her story settle, until the realization of the whole situation hits, and I snap. "You mean to tell me that he wanted to sleep with Destiny?!" I feel the heat of my anger rise quickly to my face. "He wanted to take my worst enemy home with him for the night?! The one girl I hate most in the entire world?! The biggest slut on campus?! The teammate that I despise?!" I slam my cup on the coffee table, and stand enraged. After a few paces, my mind is made up, and I turn to race down the staircase. I grab my phone that is sitting on the kitchen counter and march to the back patio, closing the sliding glass door behind me. I quickly dial Mason's cell phone and angrily tap my foot waiting for him to pick up.

The moment I hear his voice, I explode. I yell at him without pause for roughly ten minutes, explaining to him what Rachel just told me and the fact that I am disgusted at his desire for Destiny. I reel off a list of things that I hate about Destiny and try to verbalize my disdain for the whole situation, although it is nearly impossible to communicate just how upset I am. Pausing to take a breath, I realize that my throat is hoarse due to my yelling, and I momentarily consider the neighbors who may have heard my wrath. My breathing clearly reflects my seething anger as Mason seizes his chance to defend himself.

"I don't even remember saying that - and if I did, I didn't mean it," I can tell that his temper is rising as I allow him more time to speak, hoping that he will adequately explain the mix up and give me reason not to hate him because of it. "Besides, clearly I wouldn't do that because I did have a girlfriend." He continues, with more angst, "You didn't exactly think that one through when you followed Tripp back to his room, did you?"

"We weren't dating when I did that, and you know how sorry

I am that it ever happened!" I retort, my emotions rising.

"Yeah Tess," he half laughs, "of course you're sorry, but that doesn't undo your mistake, does it?! The pain that you're feeling now surrounding my little comment is only a small dose of what I felt when I found out about you and Tripp! And I didn't act on my impulses – YOU DID!" He yells loudly into the phone, an action that Mason is rarely pushed to.

I slump down onto a lounge chair near the pool. My anger melts into pain, and I allow it to swallow me whole, "I just don't understand," I start, as tears flood down my face, "you wouldn't even let our kissing get too intimate, but you clearly didn't feel the same about Destiny." I shake my head and continue before he can respond. "I took a break from you because I wanted you to chase after me, and when I realized that you weren't doing that, I unfortunately found the attention that I was seeking from you in the arms of another guy." I sigh, "I was wrong for that Mason, but you were making me feel awful about it. You decided that it was over between us, but you never mentioned your feelings for Destiny, whether they were momentary or not." My anger starts to rise again as I think about the smug looks that Destiny has given me in the past – she must have known about Mason's lust for her, one way or another. "You wanted to take that slut home with you, and even if you didn't follow through with your desire, the concept hurts just as much – you know she is my worst enemy!" I am still crying, but my emotions seem to be confused, bouncing back and forth between furry and heartache.

"Well, maybe you deserve the pain that you're feeling right now," Mason says, definitively. I sense no remorse in his voice, and I immediately let my anger eclipse my sorrow.

"You are despicable," I spit with disdain. "This whole time you made me feel bad for what I did with Tripp, when you wanted to do the same with MY WORST ENEMY – whether you acted on it or not!" I clench my free fist, desperate to punch something so the physical pain will serve as a distraction. Furious, I offer my last remark, "I never want to talk to you again, Mason Pierce!" and without waiting for his response, I slam my phone down.

Laying down on the padded lounge chair, I curl up into a ball in the cool night air, wishing the tears could stop. I feel so rejected, Mason didn't want to put a hand on me, but the idea of putting his hands on Destiny didn't seem to bother him. He knows how much I hate her, and the whole time I complained about her, lustful thoughts probably skirted his mind. My heart sinks lower than I ever thought possible. I am so angry at him for his comment, yet I am still heartsick over my actions with Tripp. Contemplating the pain that I put Mason through, I am caught somewhere between guilt and contempt. I still love Mason, and I never wanted to hurt him, but after hearing about his desire for Destiny, I hope that he is dealing with some guilt of his own. After a few moments in the dark, I shake my head, wipe my cheeks, and try to bury it all. Instead of going back inside, I walk toward the fence to exit the backyard. Slowly, I make my way to my car and open the driver's side door. I reach in my center consol for the new pack of cigarettes that I bought on my drive over here. I light one up and inhale the object that I can count on to help calm my emotions. Staring at the warm glow, I decide that alcohol and nicotine are a much better comfort than God, and I push any thought of him away knowing that I am capable of dealing with my pain through other venues, rather than the help that he offers.

chapter ten

(July, 2009)

"They're here!" my mom yells from the bottom floor of our house. The arrival that we have been waiting for this grotesquely hot July day has finally come – Amber and Shane are here. The Army stationed them in Georgia not long after they got married, and they haven't had much free time to visit. However, they announced last week that they were coming to stay with us for a couple of days, and that they had a surprise to share. I dash out of my bedroom and accidentally bump into Chantel.

"Oops, sorry," I snicker, thinking how different that situation would have been if it were a couple of years ago and it was Amber with whom I had collided. Chantel recently moved into Amber's old room, and my parents made Chantel's bottom floor bedroom a guest room. I have to say, even though my friendship with Amber has continued to improve since her wedding day, it is a lot easier sharing a bathroom with my younger sister.

Chantel latches onto my arm as we race down the stairs together, "I can't wait to hear what their surprise is," she says with excitement.

We fly out of the back door where my parents are practically bouncing with excitement in the carport, while waiting for Shane and Amber to exit their car. They have driven 13 hours to get here, and I can't understand why they are sitting in their parked car when they could get out and stretch their legs. Then, the passenger door opens, and I see a little puppy leap from Amber's lap to run in our direction. Immediately, my younger sister squeals with delight and scrunches down so the puppy can jump into her arms and lick her face. My eyes move from the playful scene and rest on Shane and Amber, who are now making their way toward us. Amber is moving slowly, which I assume is due to the long trip spent cramped in the car. Shane grabs Amber's hand and holds it in his own as they approach the distracted members of my family, enamored with their puppy. Not me. My gaze is taking in the expression of love on Shane's face as he clings to Amber's hand. I swallow, hoping to suppress the sick feeling that is threatening to creep into my throat. My desperation for Mason's presence in this moment is unbearably depressing. I want Mason to hold my hand, to show me affection, to be by my side forever. Although it isn't fair, my face drops slightly as my parents greet my sister and brother-in-law. I know I shouldn't be angry or jealous at what Amber has with Shane, so I force a smile. While I hug them both, I notice a radiant happiness reflecting off Amber's face, and I try to let go of my negative emotions, glad to see my older sister so content with life.

"Your new puppy is so cute," Chantel exclaims as she scoops up the tiny blonde ball of fur and gives Amber and Shane a side hug, her eyes never leaving the puppy as she steps back and ruffles the curls near the dog's ears. "What's its name?"

"This is Sadie," Amber responds. "She is a cocker spaniel and a poodle mix. When I saw her in the pet store, I just couldn't resist," She laughs. "Luckily, Shane gave into my pleading." She looks up at Shane with gratitude, and he offers a genuine smile as he returns her gaze. The adoration between Amber and Shane reveals how much the two have matured in the time they have been married.

"So, this was your surprise, huh?" My dad asks, petting Sadie, who is panting happily in Chantel's arms.

"Well, actually," Shane starts, as he lets go of Amber's hand and wraps his arm around her shoulders, pulling her into a soft, loving embrace, "we have two surprises…"

"I'm pregnant!" Amber interrupts with a huge smile spread across her face. It takes a split second for my family to connect the dots, their eyes darting quickly between the happy couple's facial expressions and the gentle rounding of Amber's stomach that is slightly visible through her loose fitting shirt. As the news sinks in, they all start celebrating in one big eruption of cheers and hugging. I, on the other hand, feel my heart drop to the pit of my stomach. Amber has everything I ever wanted; marriage to a man she loves, an adorable puppy, and now a baby. This is what I could have had - this should have been my life with Mason.

* * *

"So, are you excited to be an Aunt?" Amber asks, as we arrange the plates on the dinner table. The rest of the family is outside playing with Sadie, but I didn't feel up to that, so I volunteered to set the table alongside Amber.

"I am very excited," I say with a slight smile, but Amber is quick to recognize my struggles.

"Tess, I'm sorry to hear about Mason," she sighs. "He is a good guy, and we all loved him, but I don't want to see you throw away all your happiness because of it. There are a lot of guys out there, and in the meantime, you just need to focus your attention on God."

I half laugh, "You've been talking to mom lately, haven't you?" I shake my head and wonder exactly how much information my mother has revealed to Amber.

Amber grabs the silverware and begins to place a set at each seat. "You know, mom's not so bad to talk to," she shrugs her shoulders as she makes her way around the table. "I know you guys had your differences during your teenage years, just like you and I did, but you've given me a chance, you should do the same for mom."

I nod, but don't offer any words. My mother and I are so much alike, which means we often butt heads when it comes to any conversation more serious than the weather. Yet, I have noticed a slight change since I moved back in for the summer. She doesn't coddle me as much; however, this could be due to my recent experiences. She is probably trying to give me some space, and I appreciate her efforts, now that I am considering them.

Amber clears her throat, and glances up at me, "So…" she starts with a little hesitation, "I haven't told the rest of the family, but I feel like you can keep a secret." She grins, and I can tell that she is trying to brighten my mood, "We have decided to name our little girl, Marley."

* * *

I crawl into bed, and the tears I have been holding back all evening come pouring out. My emotions are so strong, forcing me to face the reasons why I am shedding these tears. I am excited to be an aunt, and I am so proud that Shane and Amber are expanding their perfect little family, but I can't bury the pain I feel for having lost my child. Marley would have a cousin if I had remained pregnant, but more importantly, Mason wouldn't have left me. We would have been a happy little family, like Amber and Shane. Although our baby would have been born out of wedlock, we would have made it work. Mason and I would have been thrilled to be parents, and maybe we would have gotten a little puppy to add to our family. However, as much as I wish this were true of my life – it's not. I sob hard into my pillow, trying to smother the sound and keep it from Chantel's ears in the room next to me. I miss Mason so much, it actually causes physical pain in my heart. It was his birthday last week, and I thought about texting or calling him. However, he didn't contact me on my birthday, and the last conversation

I had with him, I told him I never wanted to talk to him again. I was angry at him and hurt at what he had done, but I still love him, and every part of my being wants to work out our differences and get back together.

"Tessa?" Chantel whispers into the pitch black room, clearly my sobs weren't as quiet as I wanted them to be. Chantel sighs loudly as I roll over in bed and wipe my cheeks. She can't see my face in the darkness, but I know she saw me at dinner. She must have witnessed my sorrow as we talked about the details of Amber's pregnancy. Without saying anything, she tiptoes to the side of my bed and curls up in the small space beside me. I roll back over to face the wall, unable to stop my tears. Chantel drapes one arm over me, and although she doesn't know all the details of the terrible break-up that Mason and I went through, she offers her condolences with her presence. We fall asleep together, lying side by side in my small twin bed.

The next day, we went shopping - just the girls. Shane took Sadie on his way to meet up with some of his old friends, and my dad had a long day ahead of him at the church office, so my mom drove me, Amber and Chantel to the mall in Virginia, our closest place to do any kind of significant shopping. We travel from store to store, looking at all the great summer clothes that are on display, and I buy a few summery shirts and a pair of white jean shorts that are frayed at the bottom. In the dressing room, my mother glances at the length of the shorts disapprovingly, but she doesn't say anything, and I appreciate her willingness to allow me some independence, even if I am still living under her roof for the summer. With shopping bags dangling from our hands, Amber suggests that we visit the food court for an early lunch, and we all laugh at her increased appetite, now that she is eating for two.

"I would like to visit Baby Gap after lunch," Amber explains through a mouthful of sushi. She can't eat raw fish, thanks to the pregnancy, but sushi is our family's all-time favorite food, so she is keen to settle for a couple of vegetable rolls for the next five months or so.

"Ohh baby clothes," Chantel coos. "I want to go with you! Little girls' clothes are the best!"

I lower my gaze to my plate, put down my chopsticks and reach for my cup of water. I tip the cup back, hoping for the moment to pass as I swig incessantly. Looking through an assortment of baby clothing would be too difficult.

My mom notices my sudden thirst, and understands my thoughts as if they were written on my forehead, "Yeah that sounds like fun for you two," she states. "However, I really need to stop in at the department store for some things. Tessa, would you mind accompany me?" I nod in response to her request, allowing my eyes to show my gratitude. My sisters don't notice the silent exchange between my mom and me as they fill their mouths with another piece from the roll. Although my mom does not approve of my actions that led to the miscarriage, I am glad that she doesn't try to rub it in my face by forcing me to revisit the emotional pain of the event.

After lunch, we pair up and part ways, deciding to meet back at the food court in an hour. My mother and I rarely get anytime together, just the two of us, and my heart beats a little faster at the idea of potentially deep conversation.

"So, how do you feel your summer is going so far?" she asks as we weave our way through the heavily populated hall.

"Umm," I start, wondering how I want this conversation to progress, "things are okay, I guess."

My mother nods and waits a couple of moments before responding, "I know that it's not easy for you, with Amber and Shane, but I am proud of your strength. You are handling things surprisingly well."

My heart swells at her words. The truth is, internally, I'm not handling things well. I am angry at God for my current circumstances, I am dreadfully missing Mason, and through it all, I have to once again face the despair of my miscarriage, now that my family is celebrating my older sister's pregnancy.

"Thanks," I mutter, "I just don't think I am handling it as I should be." I consider the fact that my mother and I have rarely had deep conversations since I reached my pre-teen years, but my desperation to talk with someone overwhelms me and I cave. "I miss Mason so much, Mom." I look down at my feet as they follow the pattern of the mall's tiles. "It was my fault that Mason broke up with me, but I am more angry with God than I am with myself, or Mason." Everything inside me is desperate for a cigarette, but my parents are still unaware that I smoke, and I can't exactly explain my need for nicotine at the moment, not with everything else I'm dealing with. "I love him, and I want nothing more than to be with him. However, he didn't even text me for my birthday – he obviously has moved on." I sigh, desperate for my last statement to be inaccurate, so I offer reasoning in his defense. "However, in all fairness, I did tell him that I never wanted to talk to him again during our last phone call." I glance up as a pair of shoes crosses my path, and a guy with a stubbly face and dirty blonde hair flashes a gorgeous smile at me. Although this attractive guy catches my attention for a split second, my gaze returns to the floor as I enter the department store, reflecting on the fact that my heart desires Mason, and Mason only.

"Maybe you should give him some time. Space might be the only thing he needs in order to realize that it's you he wants," my mom offers. "Besides, sometimes distance makes the heart grow fonder."

"I doubt that's the deal with us," I murmur. "He asked for his stuff back when we left campus; a guy that intends to get back together with his ex won't go to the trouble of retrieving his things from her."

Looking at me with a mother's love, she continues, "If that's the case, then I hope he realizes what he's missing." My mom smiles at me and winks, but I can't bring myself to smile back. She has no idea what I did to cause our break-up. My guilt and shame weigh down on me, but I am thankful I took the chance to share a little with my mom. Amber was right - my mom's not so bad to talk with, after all.

* * *

The remainder of our time with Shane, Amber and Sadie was great. We played games, talked about their future, rubbed Amber's baby bump, and took turns cuddling Sadie between her many bathroom breaks. This morning, they packed up hoping to take off shortly after an early lunch in order to get back to their home in Georgia a little after midnight. Shane will need some rest before his work week starts up again. While waving goodbye, I have mixed emotions watching them drive off. We probably won't see them until Amber delivers, considering Christmas was the last time we spent time with them before this visit. As I make my way back inside, my heart is heavy with the thought of Amber becoming a mother - unfortunately, I lost that opportunity a year and a half ago.

I keep myself busy for most of the afternoon, but I feel the house closing in around me. Rachel is on vacation with her family till next Monday, so I text Katie to see what she is up to. Maybe a visit would be possible, considering she lives only an hour down the road. My phone buzzes with her response:

Hey hott stuff! I'm so glad you got up with me – I'm actually having a party at my place tonight! My roommates are gone for the summer, and a bunch of my friends from Virginia Beach are coming down for it! Stay the night – you can sleep in my bed, I'll take one of the other rooms, it shouldn't be an issue! We have plenty of space in this two story house!

The opportunity to get out of the house for the night sounds great, and I grab it, excited for the distraction of an evening spent away from my family. "Hey Mom," I saunter into the kitchen, taking in the orange light of the setting sun that is shining in through the open window. "Katie, the blonde, curly headed setter for our volleyball team, is having a get together tonight at her place and has invited me to stay with her for the night."

My mom looks up from the sink full of dishes she is busy washing. "Okay, that sounds fine, but I would like you to be back for church in the morning."

I turn from my mom and roll my eyes as I take out my phone to text Katie. Although church and God are not on my priority list, I agree to the conditions. I'm sure I could put up a fight and get out of it for tomorrow, but it's easier to conform to my parents' desires than to create tension. I'll be at church tomorrow, but tonight I have every intention of getting wasted, and I smile at the thought of smoking all evening, lighting up whenever I feel like it, and not tiptoeing around my parents.

Finishing the last touch of my mascara, I stand back from the bathroom mirror and run my hands over the soft curls, staring at the outcome of a new hairstyle that Amber showed me during her visit. I make my way to my bedroom closet, and pull out some of the options from my mid-week shopping spree with my mom and sisters. I slip on my new white frayed shorts, and decide on a tight-fitting, light grey tank top that has a completely see-through back, thanks to the lace design. Choosing hoop earrings and a white watch to finish off the outfit, I cross my room to my full length mirror and revel at my reflection. My tanned skin offers a perfect contrast to the summery outfit, and my hazel eyes are popping from the specific make-up technique I used. I glance at my watch and decide I should probably head out. Slipping on my flip flops and grabbing my overnight bag, I make for my bedroom door, but stop halfway as my eyes meet a framed photo of me and Mason. The picture is a perfect reflection of what we used to have, I am wearing sweatpants, a sweatshirt, and no make up. He has on a long-sleeved t-shirt and a baseball cap. The attire is casual, enjoying the simplicity of being ourselves, completely transparent. I am curled in his lap, and he is holding me close while he sits comfortably in our living room recliner. My hood is up in the picture, so only a small portion of my face is visible, but I am smiling up at Mason with delight. He is grinning back down with nothing but affection in his eyes. The image takes me back to a time when I used to be happy, to a time when sitting around on a Saturday night in my sweats was enough, as long as I had Mason by my side. I shake my head, yank the frame from the wall, and bury it in the top drawer of my dresser. Those days are gone. Now, the only things that seem to bring me happiness anymore are skimpy outfits, excessive eye-liner, cigarettes and the thought of getting drunk.

* * *

"Hey! Wow, you look great!" Katie greets, as I walk into her house. "Just throw your things in my room at the top of the stairs, first door on the right. I'm sleeping in the bedroom down here tonight!"

I lob my overnight bag in through the bedroom door and skip down the stairs to the kitchen. Katie has already poured me a mixed drink from the many options that are displayed on the counter. She always knows how to throw a good party, and proves her hospitality skills with each one. Besides, her optimism tends to rub off on me. With a big smile, I take the drink from her.

"When is everyone arriving?" I ask.

"About 30 minutes," Katie states. "It's gunna be a packed house tonight, love! I have a lot of friends coming from Virginia Beach!" I nod, shifting my weight from one foot to the other as I take a large gulp of my drink. "But don't worry," Katie assures me, "everyone is really friendly, and I'll be sticking close by your side most of the night, introducing you to people and making sure your drink is always full!"

Within a few minutes, the guests start arriving, and the party takes off quickly. Various games are happening in different corners of Katie's large living room; card games, chugging games, and shot glass games are used to move the many guests to a state of excessive drunkenness. I join in, smiling at the unfamiliar faces of all the people, learning some names, but unable to remember them by my fourth drink. At several points in the night, the blaring music entices many of the guests to leave their game and dance to the beat of the various popular songs. During the commotion, people brush up against my elbow, causing me to spill my drink on the dark brown carpet. I join a group of girls for a lot of the dancing, but some guy creeps up behind me to dance, so I quickly decide to take a seat on the 1970's flower patterned couch, slightly cringing at the idea of getting close to any male tonight.

I get lost in the fun for hours, until I find myself stumbling across the living room toward the front of the house, accidentally bumping into several guys along the way who appear to be complimenting me. The floor tilts beneath me, and I try to communicate my need for sleep to Katie, who is standing near the open front door. My desperate slurs are not easily understood, but she laughs as she points to the stairs and tries to direct me to the bedroom. I fumble my empty cup and stare at it as it hits the doormat, wondering how that happened, but unable to do anything about it. I turn from Katie as she picks up my cup and returns to her conversation. I reach for the handrail at the base of the steps, but it keeps escaping my grasp. When I finally find it, I work hard to lift my heavy body slowly up the stairs, each foot feeling like it weighs 20 pounds, so I stop half way and slump my body against the wall for a rest. Eventually making it to the long second floor hallway, I collide with the closed bedroom door, and stop momentarily, holding onto the door handle for balance. I am not sure how many drinks I consumed tonight, but my head is spinning out of control, and I know my best bet is to sleep it off. Closing the door behind me with a bang, I collapse on the bed, my hair covering my face as I sink between the pillows. I tug at my shirt that refuses to pull loose, and decide I should get under the covers, but before I can do so, the room goes black.

* * *

My body shivers violently, waking me. I rub my eyes in confusion and try to adjust to the darkness. Turning my head slightly toward the window, I see that it's still dark outside. I grope for the covers, but my hand stops as it brushes past my waist - I don't have my shirt on. As I begin to roll my body, a sharp pain from between my bare legs shoots through me, and my breath catches in my lungs. My mind reels in confusion – why am I completely naked? Why am I in pain?

The covers twist underneath me, and I immediately jump from the movement I didn't cause. A small snore confirms my theory - there is someone else in the bed. Squinting, I start to make out shadows in the room, and I shudder at the sight of the guy sleeping soundly next to me. Who is this stranger? What is going on?

Understanding dawns, immediately sobering me. My mind works rapidly, visualizing images as they flash through my memory. Lips on my neck. Weight pressing down on my body. Me saying "no, no". These vague memories cause my throat to constrict, and I hold my breath, trying to silence my gasp and need to scream. I have to get out of here, now.

Slowly sliding off the bed, desperate to keep the stranger sleeping, my feet hit the floor, and I squat down feeling for my clothes, my hands shaking uncontrollably as my eyes brim with tears, making the search difficult. Finding them, I slip them on quickly and tiptoe to the corner of the room where my overnight bag is. My sweaty palm fumbles for the door handle in the dark, eventually grasping hold of it and sneaking out of the room. The hallway light is on, and the last sight I catch before closing the door is a thin face, framed by dark wiry hair, and a lean upper body visible from the sheet that is half slung across the stranger that took advantage of me – I flinch in horror at the momentary image that will forever be seared into my mind as I begin to shake all over. I try to quietly make my way down the hall, barely able to walk from the pain and panic that has taken over.

In my terror-filled departure, I struggle into the night air and drop my keys from my hands that can't stop shaking. Bending down, I ignore my physical pain and hastily grab the keys before rushing to my car. Starting the engine, the clock on my dash illuminates; it's 3:24 am. My trembling hands continue to be a hindrance as I try to shift into the right gear. I pull out of the driveway and watch the house disappear in my rear view mirror. Now, in the safety and silence of my familiar car, my sobs wrench my body. I hold tightly to the wheel, willing myself to drive on, even if my tears blind me. I disregard the dangerous act of driving in this emotional and mental state as I step on the gas, desperate to get as far away as possible from the nightmare I have left behind.

* * *

The hour drive was filled with angry words, pounding fists, revulsion and fear. All I want is a shower, and when I got home, I silently slip under the hot water, scrubbing hard to remove what happened. Crawling beneath my clean sheets, I feel so dirty. I curl up into a small ball – rocking – trying not to remember. Trying to escape with some sleep.

The sun announces the day is here, and I groan as I lay in bed, watching the clock from across my room advance, minute by minute, my desire to take another shower greater than my discernment to refuse. I am unclean. I am filthy. I am disgusting.

With these thoughts spinning in my mind, I am distracted when my mom pokes her head into my room. My mother shows her surprise to see me in my own bed, but she does not hesitate to try to get me up for church. My angry retort confirms that church is not an option this morning. I am sure she thinks it is because I am hung over and, although this is true, it's so much more. The house grows silent after everyone leaves for church, yet I continue to toss and turn for a couple of hours, trying to sleep, but unable to manage my tears or shame. Through bleary eyes, I glance once again at the clock and see that it's past noon. I am dreading the return of my family from church – I can't bear to have a conversation with any of them. Knowing they will arrive home soon, I lift my sore body slowly from my bed, and hobble to the shower where I hope I will be left alone.

With the hot water pounding down on my head, I drop on the floor of the bathtub, sobbing uncontrollably. The last time I was in this predicament, it was because of a miscarriage, now, it's because I've been raped. My mind flashes images from the previous night, and nausea overwhelms me; however, my body has nothing to throw up. There is no man in his right mind who will ever want me now, especially not Mason, although he isn't an option anyway. Rape and a miscarriage – I am used up. My body has been through too much in my 20 short years, and I realize that nobody would ever want to marry me given my history. My life is over, my future is obliterated, and my happiness is lost. I hate myself.

* * *

"May I come in?" my mom asks from the door I left slightly

ajar. I nod, my hair slung wildly across my pillow, still damp from the long shower I took this afternoon. It's evening now. My family indicated their concern all day regarding my odd behavior, especially when I skipped out on dinner. No doubt, my mother has come to see what is wrong, but I'm afraid if I tell her, she will hate me as much as I hate myself. "Tessa," she starts as she moves toward my bed, "What's going on? I'm worried about you."

I can't bring myself to answer. Tears roll silently down my cheeks and soak my pillow. I squeeze my eyes shut and desperately try to erase last night's event, but that's never going to happen. Fear of sexually transmitted diseases and another pregnancy have shaken me all day, and there is only one way to find out – I need to go to the doctor. Although I am desperate to keep this repulsive secret to myself, I decide that I am incapable of tackling the daunting situation alone.

"Mom," I squeak, through a broken voice. "There is something I need to tell you…"

chapter eleven

(July, 2009)

I hear a knock on the door just as I pull my sweatpants up around my waist. Monday mornings are never enjoyable, but this one is more excruciating then any other before it. I fight the urge to crawl back in bed and avoid all that is to come. With dread, I walk slowly to open my door, assuming I will see my mom on the other side. She made a doctor's appointment earlier this morning knowing how important it is to get looked at within 48 hours.

Cracking the door, I glance in my mom's direction. I can't look her in the eyes, not after what I told her last night. Her voice is gentle, "I picked this up, and I want you to take it." She slips a small packet into my free hand, then turns away slowly, "I'll give you a couple of minutes. I'm waiting in the car - we should leave soon for the doctor's." I flip the packet to the front side and see Plan B written across the top. Fear grips me once again as I consider my need for this Emergency Contraception. I'm sure many would turn up their nose at the idea of taking the morning after pill, but I'm thankful that my mother is supportive during this crisis. Turning the packet back over in my hand, I read the information given to the consumer. There are two pills to be taken at intervals starting immediately after unprotected sex, but still effective up to 120 hours. I grab my purse and make for the kitchen. Hastily filling a cup with water, I gulp down the first pill, and put the second inside my purse to take later, according to the directions. With a knot in my stomach, I slide into the passenger's seat of my mother's van, and we ride in silence to the doctor's office.

"Ms. McRae, what can we do for you?" The doctor enters the examining room, her white lab coat covering a steel blue blouse and black pants. I am slouching lifelessly on the patient's bed, a gown draped over my naked body while I stare at the stirrups awaiting me. I don't answer, I can't. Last night was difficult enough; I can't bear to talk about it again.

With concern etched on her face, the doctor looks up from my medical folder, her eyes darting between my mom and me as she waits for someone to respond. My mother, who is sitting in the corner of the large examining room, clears her throat to answer for me, "We need a rape kit done."

The last thing I want is to be touched, but the doctor insists, giving me no other option as I slip my feet into the stirrups, tears falling silently down my cheeks. For the next 15 minutes, I am violated all over again. The doctor takes swabs for different tests and offers her condolences as my body cramps in response to each new prod. She invites me to put my clothes back on in the far right corner of the room, behind a curtain draped for my privacy, which seems frivolous considering what I just went through. As I pull my clothes on, I strain to hear the whispered suggestions the doctor is giving to my mother.

"Although it is obvious that she took quite a few showers, we have drawn enough evidence to hold up in court. If that is something Tessa wants to pursue, please let our office know," the doctor states in a hushed tone. "Also, we advise all our patients in this situation to seek counseling. Here is a list of excellent psychologists in the area. I would suggest paying one of them a visit in the near future." The door clicks behind the doctor as she leaves my mother and me alone. I emerge from the changing space staring at the floor. My mom knows I heard the suggestions, but I am unwilling to offer a response at the moment. Right now, I am desperate to get back in the car, return to the comfort of my home and curl up in the safe confines of my bed.

* * *

It's Wednesday, the morning of my first counseling session. I have spent the last two days since my doctor's appointment in bed, only getting out for occasional visits to the bathroom and to get some food. My family has shown excessive concern, but my mother has reassured them that my sadness is coming from my break-up with Mason, who has still not spoken to me. However, I know that my mom is anxious about my seclusion, and I can tell she is eager for a reason to get me out of the house. Every time she tiptoes into my room, she suggests an activity that will compel me back into my normal routine, but I decline. There is nothing I want to do but sleep, yet it continues to escape me, especially in the loneliness of the late night hours when I desire it most.

After choosing another excessively baggy outfit, which will never attract male attention, I exit the back door and groan under the blazing sun. My mother drives me to the center of our small town where the office building of the psychologist is located. Although I can drive myself, I think my mother is worried that I will avoid the appointment and claim that I went, so she has decided to drive me instead. We park on Main Street, enter the brick building, and take a seat in the waiting room. I am skittish, jolting every time the main door opens, preparing to see someone I know walk in and immediately judge me for my need to see a therapist. My head is bowed when the doctor calls my name, and I follow her, leaving my mom in the waiting room.

"Hi Tessa, please take a seat." I walk through the corner door and into the cozy, little office of Dr. Kathleen R. Murray. Her degrees hang ostentatiously in large frames above her desk sitting immediately in front of me, giving off the intended sense of accomplishment. Dr. Murray follows me into the office, and her hand gestures toward two seats in the far corner of the room, away from her desk. I sink into the comfy, dark blue chair as Dr. Murray takes a seat across from me in a similar chair. A small, round table, just high enough for me to lean on, is tucked into the corner between the two chairs. A box of tissue is conveniently placed to the back side of the table, almost touching the wall. The office is decorated professionally with plush grey carpeting, a big mahogany desk, and a black rolling chair behind it. I glance over my left shoulder at the remaining corner. Dr. Murray obviously treats children as well, which is evident from the box of toys and the small yellow play rug sitting next to a chest high bookcase. Taking in my surroundings, I consider the well-placed table, creating a feel of a private seating arrangement, similar to a coffee shop. Apparently Dr. Murray wants her patients to talk to her as if they are talking to a friend that they have met for lunch or a latte. Although the office is small, Dr. Murray utilizes the space well. The front of the room is meant for paper work, and the back two corners split into areas designed to make both younger and older patients feel comfortable.

Dr. Murray clears her throat to indicate the start of our meeting. Her fingers flip through what I assume are my medical records sent over by my gynecologist, but after a few glances, she closes the folder, places it to the side of the table and takes out a notepad. "So, although you have seen my name," she points to the black name plate propped up at the front of her desk across the room, "I want to take the opportunity to properly introduce myself. I'm Dr. Murray."

I nod and offer a small, polite smile. Without hesitation, Dr. Murray dives right in, bringing the issue to the forefront of our conversation, allowing all the awkwardness of tiptoeing around the subject to fade as she addresses the rape. I went into this session expecting to keep all my thoughts and emotions to myself, not wanting to share my deepest feelings with a stranger. Yet, with her compassionate smiles and considerate replies,

Dr. Murray makes me feel at ease. I find that within a couple of minutes, I open up to her about the series of events that I remember from Saturday night, talking slowly to help control my emotions – it's too early in the meeting to be reaching for the tissues.

"I don't know why I just told you all that," I say after relaying the details of the horrific incident. "In fact, it was easier to tell you my terrible story than it was to tell my mother." Dr. Murray smiles in response. "Maybe," I pause for a moment, "it's because I don't know you, and I know you're not going to judge me. I mean, I know my mom doesn't judge me, but she will always know, and I can never escape that. On the other hand, you will always know, but unless I come back to see you, your knowledge won't haunt me at family gatherings, Christmases, birthdays…" I trail off. No matter how hard I try to control my emotions, my eyes grow heavy with moisture, and Dr. Murray tenderly nudges the box of tissues in my direction.

"Tessa," she starts, "what are some of the emotions that are causing you to cry right now?"

I sniffle as I give in and reach for a tissue. While wiping my eyes, my chin trembles from the pain that is plowing through me. "Well, I'm sad, lonely…" I take a few moments to sort out my emotions before coming to my final conclusion. "I'm disgusted with myself."

"Tell me why."

"I'm the one who put on skimpy clothing, trying to look seductive with heavy make-up, and perfect hair," I spit with disdain. "I'm the one who kept drinking and dancing in front of a crowd of people. I'm the one who passed out! I'm the one who couldn't defend myself! I'm the one who caused this!"

In horror, I drop my face into my hands. My tears turn into sobs - this is all my fault. I must have gotten this guy's attention at some point in the night, and he sought me out, thinking that I was inviting him. "Oh God," I whisper as I pick up my head and look to the door. My mom is still outside, we could leave and forget this ever happened. The walls of the small office begin to shrink, closing me in, "Why am I even here?" I question passionately. "Why did I get a rape kit? I did this to myself. I provoked the guy. I was asking for it. This is ALL MY FAULT!" My sobbing becomes heavier, as my self-hatred grows stronger with each passing statement.

"Tessa," Dr. Murray gently places a hand on my arm, trying to distract me from my disdain as my eyes dart for the door, desperate for an escape. "What I am about to say, you need to hear, and then I want you to repeat it." I take a few deep breaths, trying to reign in my sobs and calm my nerves, blinking several times as I focus in on her face. "This is not your fault." Dr. Murray looks deep into my eyes, her gaze softened by kindness, "I'm going to say it again - this is not your fault." She removes her hand from my arm, "Now I want you to say it," she invites.

"This is not my fault." I repeat, and as much as I want it to be true, a part of me doesn't believe it. "But what if it is?" I retort. "At one point he was kissing me, what if I kissed him back? I don't remember what happened, I only have a few flashes of images that I can recall." My hands start trembling, "Oh God, what if I invited him to lay in the bed with me?"

Dr. Murray returns to the notepad where she has been writing since we started, "You told me at the beginning of the meeting that you do remember saying 'no, no' - is this true?" I nod and rock slightly in my seat, sitting on my hands to help steady them. Dr. Murray continues with amicable authority, "Then it doesn't matter if you undressed yourself. You said no, and that is what you meant – therefore it is rape, regardless of what led up to it."

I shudder at the word rape, and my recoil reveals my disgust for the term. "Tessa," Dr. Murray says, having witnessed my expression of revulsion, "statistics prove that about one in six college age girls report rape. Although you may not know who else is a victim, you are one of many."

"No, it's not that," I whimper, addressing my reaction to Dr. Murray's previous statement, "it's just that…" I hesitate, "Well," I look down at the dark wood of the table, "I don't like using the word rape."

"We can call it something else. What would you rather I say?"

I think for a moment, *there is no other word that holds the same amount of power,* but I know I can't keep using that word throughout this entire meeting; in fact, I wonder if I will ever be able to bear the word again. "Can we just call it 'the mishap' please? Maybe I am a victim, but I can't stand that word."

"We can call it that," Dr. Murray complies. "But I want you to understand that this wasn't just an unfortunate accident, this was an attack by a man who took advantage of you - a defenseless girl. This was intentional."

With a short nod, my tense muscles start to relax and relief floods my mind as I experience a peace surrounding the idea of avoiding that horrible word. Dr. Murray continues to ask questions, while I discuss my emotions, digging deeper into my psyche as I slowly attempt to communicate the depth of my despair. Clearly, I need to talk about this, but I am thankful that I don't have to share the gruesome details with my mom, the only other person who knows about what happened to me.

Dr. Murray asks about previous relationships, and I tell her about Mason. I try my best to explain the love we had, although I feel like words are not strong enough to shed light on my heart's true feelings concerning our picture perfect past. Through tears, I share how our relationship came to an end and my reasons as to why Mason can never know about my mishap. If he found out, he would blame everything on me. I'm convinced he would throw my mistake with Tripp back in my face and use the mishap to prove my promiscuity, linking it all back to the reason why he broke up with me in the first place.

Dr. Murray listens with kind eyes, and when I feel like there is nothing more to say, she closes the notepad on her lap. With gentleness she concludes, "Well, we are coming to a close," I turn to look at the round, black and white clock hanging above her bookcase. "But, before you go," she continues, "there is one thing that I want to ask. Most of my patients who are in your shoes mention their anger, but you haven't. Do you feel angry, Tessa?"

"Yes," I say, expecting Dr. Murray to cut in, but she remains quiet, waiting for my explanation. "I am angry at myself for being so vulnerable, I am angry at God for not protecting me, and I am angry at Mason for breaking up with me. If Mason and I were still together, he would have been at that party with me, or we would have been in the safety of one of our homes."

Dr. Murray looks at my quizzically, "What about your offender, are you angry at him?"

I take a moment to reflect on my anger connected to the mishap. I have cursed God's name, developed a deep sense of self-loathing and resented Mason for the break-up, but I have never once been angry at the guy who took advantage of me. "No," I respond, "I don't know why, but I am angry at everyone except him."

Dr. Murray and I leave her office together. She pulls my mom aside in the empty waiting room and suggests that we make this Wednesday visit a weekly appointment, at least until I go back to school. My mom thanks her, and we leave, walking down the steps of the small office building in silence.

* * *

It's been nine days since I first met with Dr. Murray, and although this Friday dawned bright and beautiful, there is still a dark cloud hanging over my head. The entire day has been filled with sunshine and blue skies, but I have remained hidden in my bedroom. I plop down on the end of my bed and just stare out my window. My eyes take in the changing sky as the sun begins to set, but my mind is reflecting on the past week. I couldn't bring myself to go to Wednesday's counseling session – I just want to get on with life. The Herns came back from their vacation on Monday, and Rachel and I have chatted a few times since, but I have come up with an excuse every time she suggests we get together. I haven't recovered from my mishap of two weeks ago. I know that my best friend is very intuitive, so it won't take long for her to figure out something happened while she was away. The phone conversation that just ended with Rachel reminds me that I need to consider how things will be when I move back in with her for the fall term. Staring at my blue phone in my hand, I shake my head at the missed counseling session, deciding that maybe I do need more help if I am going to keep this a secret from the world. I know that I experienced some relief talking to Dr. Murray, but I used my family's lack of money as a good excuse to not keep my follow up appointment. However, that is no longer a viable reason, since yesterday when my mom was officially hired at the local university as an English professor. Her fulltime salary will undoubtedly give us the money to cover these visits. I sigh deeply in surrender at what I know to be the real reason I don't want to go – it is because of the ridiculous amount of effort it takes to get out of my bed, especially when I know I will have to talk to someone about the reason why I am living beneath my comforter. My battery beeps low on my cordless phone, and I cross my room to place it back on its base for charging. Just as I start to make my way back to my bed, my mom enters.

Closing the door behind her, she slowly approaches me with a plastic grocery bag. "I got this for you," she says, almost apologetically. Through the white plastic, I see the pink box of a first response home pregnancy test. About a week ago, I got a call from the doctor's office confirming all my STD tests had come back negative, which proved to be a huge relief. Yet, the possibility of being pregnant has weighed heavily on my mind, demanding my focus all week, even if I did take Plan B. A disquieting chill runs through my body as I take the bag from my mom. "Tess, we need to talk about it. I know you don't want to, but we need to discuss your mishap." I nod in response, grateful that my mother is willing to use the word I have requested. "If you're pregnant, we need to take this to court."

The bag drops from my grip to the floor, and I collapse on my knees beside it. My face cradled in my hands - I cry without restrain. I don't want to go to court. If I go to court, everyone will know what happened, including Mason. I will have to tell my ugly story to the world, yet I could barely tell it to my mother, whom I trust. I will have to create a case, and Mason will be there to watch it unfold. Maybe he will side with the defendant, sharing my history surrounding Tripp with the jury and confirming that this was all my fault, given my promiscuous past. What if I lose? What if the court decides that the guy will be acquitted because I provoked him someway, somehow? I can't go to court, I just can't.

Sending up a silent prayer for the first time in a long time, I beg God for a release from this mess. I ask him to give me a miscarriage if I am pregnant, just like he did with my first child. I plead with him to keep this thing from going to court, allowing me to hold on to this secret forever, never having to reveal the ugliness of it to anyone. I pray these things over and over in my mind, desperate for God to prove himself a loving Lord like the Bible says and save me from the disgrace of it all.

My mom kneels on the ground beside me, holding me while I sob. We stay like this for several minutes, but after I finally bow out of my silent cries to God, I request to be alone. She gets up to leave, and I hear her quietly sniff; she has been crying with me. Knowing that I will have my mother by my side, regardless of what happens, gives me a small sense of relief. She can help me through this, and I pray that God can too.

There on my knees, I take in the beauty of the sunset that is seeping in through my window and casting warm hues across my carpet. Eventually, I get up from my floor and glance at my bedroom door, thankful that my mom closed it behind her as she left me alone. I don't know if my dad and sister are home tonight, but I certainly don't want them seeing me curled up on my carpet, clinging pathetically to a pharmacy bag inadequately hiding a pregnancy test. I walk over to my dresser, searching for a place to hide the package until I unpack the test and directions tomorrow. As I push aside a pile of tops, preparing to shove the plastic bag underneath the clothing, I pull back a white t-shirt and see the framed photo of Mason and me that I shoved in the drawer only hours before my world completely crashed around me. The pain I feel ripping through my chest compresses my lungs, as if water has viciously filled the cavities. I feel more hopeless than I could ever imagine possible. Although the image of our happiness in the picture is now covered by the pregnancy test that will soon reveal the true extent of the physical damage from my mishap, I can't shake the pain it has evoked. I slam the drawer closed and hurl myself into the safety of my bed. I bury my head in my pillow and silently scream as I pound the mattress in an effort to fight my way out of this horrible mess. My clenched hands want to inflict pain that will somehow distract me from the agony I feel inside. My thrashing only serves to exhaust me as I finally find myself staring over the edge of my bed at my floor. For the moment, my tears have run dry. A stack of books on the bottom shelf of my bedside table catches my eye, and underneath all the paperbacks, I see the corner of my blue Bible. I'm not ready to do away with all my ungodly habits, like smoking and getting drunk, but during this time of desperation, I am starting to recognize my need to consider the contents of its pages.

Lord, I silently pray as I slowly sit up and place the Bible on my lap, *if you are there, and if you love me like you claim to, reveal yourself to me in this moment. I have never needed your presence more, but you know my heart better than anyone else. Please, forgive me of my sins, and fill this gaping hole with your Holy Spirit. Amen.*

Flipping open the Bible, I fumble through the pages. It has been a long time since I've encountered God, and I feel the distance from my Savior more than ever as I try to find the perfect passage to read. Two hours go by as I search through the pages - crying and praying - hoping something new will pull on my heart strings. Finally, I land on a bookmark that I must have left from my last devotional many months ago. After some reading, I look up at the clock and see that it's 12:18 am. I tear out a piece of paper from my journal and address it to my mother, who is sleeping soundly across the hall. She won't read my note till morning, but I want her to know what my heart is feeling:

> *Mom,*
> *Last night I felt God tugging at my heart. I wasn't sure where to read, so I decided to start where I last left off. I read Psalm 103. I want you to read it over too. God couldn't speak to me any clearer. I am literally in awe, its unbelievable how he leads me to the very passage that most pertains to my situation. God is good. I am putting this in his hands. I take the test this morning. Please pray. Thanks and I love you.*
> *Tessa*

chapter twelve

(July, 2009)

Waiting alone in Dr. Murray's office, I stare at the grey walls and silently commend myself for mustering the strength to make it to my therapy session. It took a fair amount of effort to get out of bed and travel here, but I have managed to do it — and I don't need my mother to accompany me this time.

"Sorry about that," Dr. Murray says as she enters the office and interrupts my thoughts. She hastily places some folders on her desk, picks up her notepad and makes her way to the corner of the room where her counseling chair awaits. "Tessa," she smiles as she settles into her seat, "I'm glad your back."

"Thanks," I half mumble, "in a strange way, I'm happy to be back too."

Dr. Murray ruffles through the notepad until she finds a blank page to begin her writing. Although her attention is momentarily focused on the lined pages, there is a demeanor about Dr. Murray that makes me feel comfortable, makes me feel like I am the most important person in the world to her, at least for the next hour. "Shall we get started then?" she asks with a warm smile. I nod in response. "I was sorry to see your cancelation last week - how have you been managing since our last visit?"

I don't necessarily want to talk about my mishap, although I suppose that is why I am here, so I shrug my shoulders and begin to share, "I've been better." My eyes drop to the grey carpet as I continue. "I took a pregnancy test this past weekend, and it came out negative. Those three minutes for the results to show up were the longest three minutes of my life, but when the lines on the test showed that it was negative, I was filled with relief. My period came last night, confirming that I am, in fact, not pregnant." I smooth my hand across the table that separates us and silently thank God yet again for working things out so that I won't have to go to court. "I got the results back from my gynecologist – I don't have any sexually transmitted diseases, and now I know I'm definitely not pregnant. Basically, it's like this mishap never actually happened, right?"

I look up from my moving hand to Dr. Murray who is absorbing my words with a sympathetic look on her face. She tilts her head slightly before she responds, "Regardless of the medical results, we both know the multitude of emotional difficulties that accompany such a traumatic event, Tessa."

As much as I want to forget about my mishap and move on, I confess that Dr. Murray has a point. However, I look to the box of tissues and feel my heart harden against the idea of crying about something that I barely remember and has failed to yield negative physical repercussions. "Well," I firmly state, "I don't want to talk about it anymore."

Dr. Murray nods slowly, she must understand what my heart is feeling, and the kindness in her eyes reveals her respect for my wishes. "Alright," she concurs, "let's talk about something else. Can you tell me about your childhood?"

My heart fills with bliss at her words – my childhood is something I can talk about without the feeling of depression hovering over me like a dark cloud. "Yes," I respond with a grin.

The next 30 minutes is spent explaining the wonderful experiences I had as a child. I tell Dr. Murray about my parents, and their obvious love for one another and for their children. Naturally, as we grew up, my sisters and I thought it was gross to watch them kiss goodbye as my father left for work, but there was never a question as to whether or not they loved each other. They would occasionally dance together in the kitchen when my dad got home from the church office, swaying step by step in the small space between the stove and the fridge. My sisters and I would creep around the corner and watch them giggle together as they slipped away to their own world for a few minutes. While we watched family movies together, my mother never failed to nuzzle into the closeness of my father's embrace. Then there were times when they had a little extra money and would go on a date night, leaving us with a babysitter.

"Even though we didn't have money," I clarify to Dr. Murray, "my parents always found a way to take us on family vacations." I smile at her as I share with her the details from the many trips we took. We made some good memories traveling in our small five seat Saturn as we crossed the Canadian border and toured the different states in America. We spent nights on a dude ranch in Texas, took a train ride to the top of Pikes Peak in Colorado, rode on horse back through the Palo Duro Canyon, stayed in Babe Ruth's bedroom at a Bed & Breakfast owned by his daughter in New Hampshire, soaked up the sun's rays in Virginia Beach, toured an alligator farm in Florida, played in the water parks of South Carolina, camped in the state parks of Georgia, enjoyed the luxury of an indoor swimming pool in Michigan, squinted against the bright lights of the streets in New York City, took in the beauty of Vermont, rode in a helicopter in Tennessee, taunted the gorillas at a zoo in Nebraska, rolled around in the colorful fall leaves in Connecticut, viewed Norman Rockwell's original works in Massachusetts, got stopped for speeding by a cop in Kansas, saw the arch in Missouri, stood before the Lincoln Memorial in D.C. and so much more that I know my retelling gave Dr. Murray insight into how thankful I am for my many experiences.

I begin to laugh as I launch into a story often told by my parents. "The best depiction of me and my sister's personalities surfaced during a trip to Disney." I shift in my chair as I move a stray hair off my face. "We were floated along a lazy river in an inner tube, and somehow my family got separated. It was probably an hour before my parents found each one of us. For my parents, it was a panic filled time, but now they can laugh as they explain each of our reactions when we were found and how our reactions were a perfect depiction of who we truly are." I laugh, "Amber was angry, shouting at my parents for having lost her. Chantel was sad, bursting into tears when she saw the familiar faces of our relieved parents. And I was complacent, traveling around the river in my own little world, experiencing independence for an hour. I had no idea that anything was wrong until I looked up and spotted my parents and a Disney World security guard standing on a bridge that arched over the lazy river. As I got closer, I could hear him confirming my safety over his radio."

"Well, the three of you seem to have very different personalities," Dr. Murray comments. "How were your relationships with each other growing up?"

"There were times when my sisters and I didn't get along," I explain. "Every so often I would bite the nose off of Chantel's Barbie, or give Amber's doll an unwarranted haircut, but the fact remains, my sisters were my best friends throughout my childhood." I groan, considering that statement, "Things did change with Amber when we hit our teenage years; however, we have worked through that stage." My voice lifts with slight excitement as I share, "And, I'm going to be an aunt soon as well - Amber is due in December." My eyes shift awkwardly around the room as I uncross my legs and try to get more comfortable. I don't want to talk about the conflicting sorrow I still feel toward Amber becoming a mother. That would open a whole new door for our counseling session, so I mentally dismiss the subject as I clear my throat, hoping that Dr. Murray has not witnessed the pain that my heart is experiencing. Dr. Murray breaks the silence when she asks, "What about the issues you experienced as a child? No one's childhood is perfect, Tessa. Is there something you remember struggling through?"

I examine my fingernails. I don't usually bite them, but right now seems like a good time to start. Chewing for a few moments, I contemplate the pain, both emotional and physical, I felt as a child. Dr. Murray is not going to let this question slip from her grasp, so I slowly move my hand away from my mouth, "Yes, I did struggle as a child, in a few areas."

"Would you mind sharing with me what these struggles were?"

I take one last fleeting glance at a couple of hang nails that I'm confident I produced, but I drop my hand onto the table as I decide to be completely transparent with Dr. Murray. "Well," I start, "I have Celiac Disease, and although a defective small intestine that can't digest gluten is more common now, it wasn't when I was diagnosed almost 20 years ago." I take some time to explain what my parents have told me concerning my first bout of symptoms. I was only a year old, just coming off breast milk, so I don't remember. However, the pictures in my family's photo albums reveal it all. My skin was white as a ghost, hanging off my bones. My hair that had been growing at one point started falling out. I had large, dark bags under my eyes, as if sleep was not a regular part of my routine. My belly protruded from my tiny frame like the African children you see on T.V. in ads that request donations to help feed the poor souls. And although all this was discomforting to my parents, they said the biggest concern was my behavior. Most children my age were learning to walk, talk, play, and dance. I, on the other hand, was sedentary, talked very little, and often struggled with the energy it took to regurgitate my meals.

"Doctor's visits became a regular part of my schedule," I explain. "Thank God for the Canadian health care system because we never would have been able to afford all those appointments in the States." Dr. Murray turns up the corner of her mouth in a small, but contemplative smile – she knows how much my hour with her once a week is costing my family. I move past the subject, "Most of the doctors told my parents that I was just a picky eater; that I would eventually get over it if they were just firm with me. So, just as my parents were advised, they tried tapping my hand as a discipline every time I threw up." I look down, knowing how heart breaking it is for my parents to reflect on such an awful time. "But the symptoms worsened, and my parents knew it had to be more than selective taste buds." I lift my gaze to where Dr. Murray is jotting down a few notes, but without waiting for her to pick up her head, I continue, "I guess my body was shutting down from lack of nutrients, and eventually the doctors started taking my symptoms seriously. They tested me for all sorts of things, one being Leukemia. The test came back negative, but that still meant that my sickness went undiagnosed."

I pause, allowing Dr. Murray to ask, "What happened after that?"

"My parents were at church, and one of the members suggested a new specialist that had just moved to the area. They booked an appointment with him that week, and sure enough – he took one look at me and suspected Celiac Disease."

"I presume he did some testing to confirm his theories?"

"Yes, they did a biopsy of my small intestine. Back then, they put patients to sleep as they fed a long tube down the esophagus. My parents stood by my bed the entire time and watched as I somehow woke up during the process. Natural instinct must have led me to grab for the tube, so my parents had to hold me down as I cried out of confusion and fear until the doctor put me to sleep again."

"But you don't remember that, do you?"

I shake my head, "I was only a couple of months away from turning two at that point. The biopsy confirmed that it was in fact Celiac, and the nice thing was that it could be controlled by simply changing my diet. I was put on display for the hospital to see. My mom said I stood in front of the doctors and nurses in a diaper so they could take notes on my symptoms, learning what Celiac Disease was and figuring out how to detect the signs early. Once it was all said and done, the doctor claimed that the timing of the appointment was nothing short of a miracle – my failure to thrive was critical. He sent us away with a list of around 125 items I could eat from the grocery store, and thanks to his guidance, my body returned to that of a normal toddler."

"Did your Celiac Disease affect you as you got older?"

I somewhat snicker at this question – how could something so drastic not affect a child? No one had heard of Celiac Disease, and finding gluten free food basically meant going to an expensive health food store or making it from scratch. "Being gluten free is nothing like it is today." I explain, and I take a few minutes to try to portray the difficulties of growing up with Celiac. There are so many things that I had to be careful of, when my sisters didn't. Because my symptoms were so severe, and my stomach was so sensitive, I followed a set of rules that naturally placed a wedge between me and my sisters, or anyone else with whom I was sharing a meal. My sisters would slurp their juice off the table if they spilled, but I couldn't. The chance of crumbs being left on the surface was too great, and my body wouldn't respond well if I swallowed even the smallest crumb of bread. So, I watched as my sisters made the slurping look like so much fun.

After our rounds on Halloween, I had to dump my candy on the floor as my parents filtered through it, taking out every delicious piece of candy and chocolate that contained gluten. My meals were made separate from the rest of my family, ostracizing me from the norm. Every birthday party I went to, I had to refuse a piece of cake, hoping that the other kids wouldn't ask questions as I beckoned the parent serving it to bend down so I could whisper my predicament into their ear. We had pizza day at my primary school once a month. The deliveries always smelled so delicious, and my mouth would water as I watched the rest of the class line up for a piece. I would look down to my Tupperware container holding my soggy homemade pizza that always smelled a little funny after sitting in my lunch bag for the morning. My mom wanted me to feel special, so she would make me pizza to eat alongside the rest of the students, but it was never the same. And no matter how we went about it, the other kids would always ask questions or whisper to their friends about my weird food.

Dr. Murray looks at me with a softened expression, "That must have been difficult."

"It was. I often felt like the oddball, whether it was because I had to turn down something to eat, or had my own separate meal." I shake my head as I remember a specific event when I decided to act out of rebellion. "There was this one time," I share, "my parents were having a dinner party, and they were serving bread rolls with the stew. Every one was eating the bread, so I took a whole roll and ate it too. My dad caught me at the tail end of my quick devour, and brought me up to my room. He kept asking me why I would do that to my body. I found that shrugging my shoulders wasn't getting me anywhere, so I told him that I just wanted to be like everyone else. I was told to stay in my room for the rest of the evening - I guess my dad knew what was coming. It wasn't long before I became extremely sick, running back and forth to the toilet all night and most of the next morning. My parents didn't want to punish me for eating bread, but they did want me to understand the repercussions of my decision." I laugh, "Let's just say it took the first heave of a long night of throwing up for me to understand the magnitude of my choice; I never made a decision like that again."

"So, there was Celiac Disease, but you mentioned earlier that there were a few areas in which you struggled." I see Dr. Murray glance at the clock behind me. We must have enough time left in the hour, because she asks, "What else did you experience?"

At this point I realize that I have already shared a big portion of insecurities deriving from my childhood, so I don't even hesitate to relay the issues surrounding my hearing. "When I was six, I remember having a conversation with my mom, who was in the shower at the time. I was standing beside the shower at the sink. She was trying to tell me something, but I couldn't hear what she was saying. I kept asking her to repeat herself, and finally my mom popped her head out of the shower. She asked me if I was trying to be funny, but I told her that the running water muffled her voice to the point where I couldn't understand her." I shake my head at the memory, "She took me to the doctors, they ran hearing tests and found problems in both my ears, so they put tubes in."

I continue to share with Dr. Murray what it was like during my childhood to have to wear wax every time I got in the water. The summers spent at my grandparents' cottage on the lake were fun, but at the same time agonizing. My sisters and cousins would run and jump off the end of the dock together, often times holding hands. However, I had to wait for the bright orange wax to be wedged into both my ears before jumping in. I wasn't a complainer, so I waited patiently while watching the rest of my family laugh and squeal in the water without me. When I finally did get to jump in, sometimes the wax would slip out from the impact of the water. I would kick my little legs as hard as I could to resurface quickly before my eardrums flooded, but often times it was inevitable. If I got water in my ear, the pain would ruin the fun, and I would climb up the ladder, wrap myself in a towel, and lay my head on one of my parents' laps, hoping for the water to drain and the pain to subside so I could rejoin the fun.

"As if having Celiac wasn't embarrassing enough," I say to Dr. Murray. "My sisters and I went to Pioneer Camp for two weeks every summer. My dad worked there, so we got to spend the latter week in Adventure Camp for free. My mom would talk with the kitchen staff the week leading up to it, explaining my Celiac and preparing meals that I could eat alongside my camp friends. As much as the staff made my meals look exactly like every one else's, there was nothing they could do about the bright orange wax that stood out like a sore thumb on the beach." I start drumming my fingers quietly on the table again, thinking back to the jokes that were thrown in my direction from the other campers. "Kids would laugh and point as my camp counselor would shove the wax into both my ears. One summer, my parents bought me a blue headband that I could put on myself, but that managed to draw more attention than the neon colored wax." I sigh, "But honestly, the taunting was nothing compared to the doctors' appointments and surgeries. Between getting tubes put in, having tubes removed, going through both those surgeries twice and raging ear infections in between, I still have trouble hearing - especially in my right ear. Every once in a while, I will go back to the doctor about it. He always tells me that I have a very bad infection and, even at my age, he suggests getting tubes put in again. However, after the last set of tubes left a hole in my eardrum, I'm done with it. I would rather live with the pain of an ongoing ear infection than go through another surgery."

Dr. Murray takes a moment to let this information sink in before asking, "Tessa, how do these things from your childhood make you feel?"

"Sometimes it made me sad," I say. "But aside from all the physical and emotional pain that both my Celiac and hearing brought on, I never questioned whether I was loved." I smile, thinking back to the number of times when my sisters would eat a doughnut or something and tell me it tasted disgusting, even though I knew it wasn't true. And although a lot of my cousins would jump in the water without me, occasionally one would stay back and wait till my wax was firmly in place, then take my hand and run off the end of the dock with me.

Something in the back of my mind is itching to be revealed, and it doesn't seem to matter how I attempt use my good memories to cover up my bad ones - the dominant word that sums up my difficult childhood memories surfaces, and I know I need to share it. "To tell you the truth, I struggled a lot with rejection."

Dr. Murray slowly nods her head, "I can imagine that would be the case." She sighs while looking at the clock, "We need to close, but before we say goodbye, can I ask if you felt that same sense of rejection during your teenage years?"

I think back to the changes that accompanied our move from Canada to North Carolina and all that I struggled through during my middle school years. However, my thoughts hone in on the awful situation from our last church and immediately feel a lump form in my throat, "Yes, I experienced the worst case of rejection alongside my family during my teenage years."

Dr. Murray stands from her chair, "I would really like to hear about that next time we meet. Same time, Wednesday next week?" I nod, then rise from my chair and follow her out of her office.

I thank Dr. Murray for her time as I leave the office building. While walking to my car, I ponder the rejection from my childhood and how it inevitably crept into my teenage years; thus explaining a lot of my actions. As I start the engine, I reflect on the last hour with Dr. Murray and conclude that my past has led to my current and constant fear of rejection. A shudder accompanies my epiphany, as if I have just been hit in the face with a mind-reeling dose of reality; this fear has driven my recent decisions, which led to my mishap, and now I'm left cleaning up the mess I made.

chapter thirteen

(August, 2009)

Standing in front of the foggy bathroom mirror, I wipe away the steam produced by my long Monday morning shower and stare back at my reflection. My mouth seems to droop slightly at the corners, the bags under my eyes are profound, and despite the fact that it's summer, my skin is white. I consider the amount of time spent indoors since the mishap and notice that the tan I had only weeks ago is now gone. I need to get out.

Throwing on a pair of shorts and a peach colored tank top, I shake my wet hair out once more before finding my flip flops and heading downstairs. "Good morning love," my dad greets from the kitchen. "Heading out?"

I force a smile, "Yeah, just going to enjoy some of this sun, I guess."

"You want to grab some breakfast before you leave?" he asks, but I shake my head in response as I make for the back door. "Okay, glad to see you're up and dressed for this gorgeous day," he adds jovially before the door closes behind me. I shudder slightly at my hasty and somewhat rude escape, but I don't want him to know that my reason for getting out this morning is mostly due to my desperate need for nicotine. My parents are still unaware of my smoking habit – somehow I have managed to conceal the evidence. I get in my car and pull out of the driveway, navigating a couple of miles down the road to the public picnic area that edges the river where I normally go for my smoke breaks.

I trudge through the long grass from the small parking area to the picnic table overlooking the water. The view is gorgeous, and the sun is bright. I slip my sunglasses off my head and over my eyes, take out a cigarette, light it, and lean back on the table as I close my eyes and tilt my head up toward the sun. I am thankful for the peace and tranquility this place offers. Many years earlier, the small beach that is an exposed part of the river bank would have been full of children splashing around, but the recent migration of alligators and growing population of copperhead snakes in the area has driven the children and their parents away. Now, the small sandy terrain is desolate, creating a quiet place for me to come and collect my thoughts.

As I puff away, I think back to last week's visit with Dr. Murray. I know that in two days time she will be asking questions about my teenage years, but I wonder how much I am willing to share with her. I look down at the cigarette resting between my fingers, and remember the first time I ever smoked. At the young age of 14, I went with a group of friends to a truck and tractor pull out in the middle of nowhere. The event was definitely not my idea of a good time, but I found ways to entertain myself as my country friends enjoyed the event. One of my friends bummed a couple of cigarettes and we lit them up together. I coughed through the first few of drags, but I liked the buzz that the nicotine gave me, and I knew from that moment, these cancer sticks had the potential to be an item of dependence – I was right.

That night proved to be the start of many bad habits I would continue to develop in my teenage years. Eventually, our group got tired of the tractor pull, and we drove off with a car full of boys to one of their houses nearby. They poured my friends and me a drink and invited us into the hot tub. My friends and I didn't have bathing suits, but we determined that our underwear would suffice. As I striped down to my undergarments, I watched the reaction of the boys and realized for the first time how much attention my nearly naked body commanded. From that point on, I knew what it took to finally fit in with the cool crowd.

Returning to the present, I shake my head as I recognize that night to be the spark of a rebellious streak in me. Since then, I have made unwise choices surrounding all three weak points – alcohol, nicotine, and boys. Many a night was spent with my friends getting drunk, smoking, and making out with some random guy. Although the alcohol assisted in several of my bad decisions, a fair amount of my mistakes were made sober, many of which were made here at this beach, before the alligators and snakes roamed the murky water. Rachel and I came out here with two guys late one night. We splashed around as we traveled deeper and deeper into the river. We split off into couples and spent the rest of the night kissing and flirting in the privacy of the moonlight. And although this happened quite a few times after, word eventually got back to my parents that I had been skinny dipping at the beach – thus began my years of grounding.

I half snicker as I light up another cigarette, thinking of those two years of my life I spent mostly grounded – a couple of weeks grounded, then a weekend or two off - the pattern repeated over and over. Sometimes it was because I was caught sneaking out, or trying to sneak back in after my curfew. Other times it was due to the rumors that were spread about me, many of them finding their way back to my parents. Occasionally, I had to credit my grounding to my desire to get the last word in during an argument with my mom. We did not get along during those years, and I couldn't resist talking back to her, even though Rachel would beg me to stop yelling as my mom increased my grounding one day at a time with each retort.

Word of my rebellious behavior inevitably made it back to my church, New Creations, where members felt the need to run to the head pastor, Max Gilliam, with each bout of new information. Growing up in a small town where my dad was the assistant pastor of a larger church had its privileges, but the downside came with tattling church members. If I was seen in a public location after 9 pm, the senior pastor would know about it by Sunday morning. Unlike my two sisters, I struggled during these years with the reputation that was supposed to accompany a pastor's daughter. Aside from my misbehavior, I did have some great experiences in church before it all hit the fan. I guess I should have seen the signs leading up to that terrible day, but I was completely blindsided.

Putting out my cigarette, I reach for the pack and my lighter. While walking back to my car, I consider the message I heard yesterday at our present church, Fair Havens, a place that has offered me and my family healing and acceptance. My dad started working at Fair Havens shortly before Mason and I began dating. During yesterday morning's message on forgiveness, I recognized that I still hold a grudge toward Max and the members of New Creations Church who ruthlessly ratted me out to him every other week.

As I get into my car, I hide the pack of cigarettes and reach for my lotion. Between smothering my hands with the scented cream, spraying down my body with my favorite perfume, and chewing a stick of gum, I have managed to keep my secret from my parents. I drive back to my home with the windows down, still contemplating my need to forgive quite a few people in my life.

* * *

"Alright, Tessa," Dr. Murray says a few minutes into our hour. "I thought we would start today's session in your pre-teen years, how does that sound?"

I nod and begin, knowing that Dr. Murray wants to understand everything that led up to the church crisis that our family faced. "We moved from Canada to North Carolina in 2000 when my dad accepted an Associate Pastoring position at New Creations Church." Just speaking the name of the church causes a sick feeling in my stomach, so I move on to a topic that is less painful. "When my sisters and I were finally enrolled in the school system, I found that school in the States was very different from what I was used to in Canada." I sigh, then continue, "The kids who had all grown up together since pre-school had trouble accepting someone who was so different, someone who was a foreigner to the ways of the sixth grade norm in the South."

Dr. Murray smiles, "I happen to know what you mean, in a way. I moved here from New York after completing my Doctorate, and the South certainly does life differently."

I laugh, thankful that Dr. Murray is familiar with my struggles, yet I know I need to examine my emotions as I relay the painful details of my middle school years. During my first few months, the other students laughed at me when I asked to go to the "washroom", a term that even the teacher didn't understand. They ostracized me for my clothing that was accepted when I was in Canada, but clearly wasn't part of the style in the South. They bullied me about my Canadian tendencies, and although some would try to help by encouraging me to adjust accordingly, I struggled with constant rejection and I couldn't seem to overcome it. Through it all, I wrestled with the new expectations that accompanied a move that I did not necessarily want.

"Naturally, I searched for a place where I was comfortable, where I could be accepted – New Creations' youth group was that place." With a grin, I continue, "It was ironic, because the youth pastor, Jacob Tunnel, was from Canada as well, and moved to the area shortly after we did." I tell Dr. Murray about the many great memories I had with Jacob leading the youth group. He was funny, filling our meetings with the persona of a stand-up comedian. He came up with great games and events that he advertised to the whole community – which led to the youth group growing tremendously. The Friday night group became my refuge, which is where I met Rachel shortly after I started attending. Jacob accepted everyone and anyone, whether you were a drug addict kicked out of your parents' house, or the Associate Pastor's well behaved kid.

"Jacob and his wife were great," I share with a smile. "They both encouraged me with my spiritual journey, and during that time, I learned a lot about what it meant to have a personal relationship with Jesus." I watch Dr. Murray shift slightly in her seat as her face twists with a hint of unease. Clearly she isn't a Christian, and I sense that this isn't a subject she can speak on professionally. I figure that she must have some experience with other patients wanting to talk about God, but somehow there is an air of apprehension attached to her demeanor. She isn't rude with her facial expressions – she probably doesn't mean to be this transparent about her lack of faith, but I can tell that she is ready for the subject to change, so I move on.

"But after a couple of years, Jacob announced they were moving back to Canada, and they were gone within three weeks of that announcement." I shake my head at the thought. The knowledge that I have now concerning New Creations Church and the ruthless ways of Max Gilliam answers all the questions that I had at the time of Jacob's move. However, we were just told that Jacob was accepting a position that he could not refuse. "After Jacob's move, the only other social setting I could depend on was my school." I tug on my shorts and adjust my position while thinking back to the beginning of high school, and the changes that I made in order to fit in with the popular crowd. I am not particularly proud of them, considering I often sacrificed my commitment to honor God. However, I will not deny that my high school years were significantly better than my experience being bullied and rejected in middle school.

"After making the JV volleyball team my freshman fall season, I was immediately accepted in the athlete circle. I played volleyball, basketball, and ran track during all four years of high school. Popularity automatically went hand-in-hand with my athleticism, and before I knew it, I was friends with the same people who bullied me through middle school." I explain to Dr. Murray the many memories I made with my new group of friends, who I never held a grudge against for laughing at me as I was trying to adjust to the drastic cultural changes that accompanied our move. Instead, I focused on the fun we shared at all the parties. Rachel and I would lie about our plans, weaving in and out of trouble when we sometimes got caught.

Dr. Murray asks about Rachel for the first time, and I shrug my shoulders as I try to explain our inseparable friendship. "We may not have gone to the same school, but we had the same group of friends. There were a few weekends that I can recall when we didn't spend time together – but only my grounding could keep us apart." My heart sinks at the way I have been avoiding Rachel. Her new summer course has kept her busy, and I confess that I was glad when she barely had time to hug me goodbye after church this past Sunday. I interrupt my reflection to confirm, "She is my best friend, and she has been there for me through it all."

Dr. Murray looks up from her notepad, "Was she there during the time your family went through that difficult stage you referenced in our last meeting?"

"Yes," I look down, "in fact, her family suffered through the event almost as much as my family did."

"Can you tell me what happened, Tessa?"

My heartache is evident on my face, "It all started when my dad accepted a job at New Creations Church." Pain and hatred fill my heart, and everything in me wants to act out of anger for what took place years ago. "When I found out the evil of the pastor and what he did to my dad, I questioned God. I hid in my room, away from my parents who had tried to explain why my dad's job had been terminated." I fight the threatening tears. This event was the ultimate act of rejection and betrayal in an environment I considered my safe haven, and my heart has yet to heal from it. "It was raining that Sunday…" I reach for a tissue, tearfully clinging to it as I recount the horror of that terrible time for my family.

* * *

I sit in the quiet of my car, trying to recover from the emotionally exhausting hour just spent sharing my church story with Dr. Murray. Somehow, it hurt more to relate the pain of betrayal inside the church than it did telling her about my mishap. However, I referenced God so often during the re-telling that I left Dr. Murray stumped regarding how to respond. I know I need someone who really understands, so I reach for my cell phone and dial Rachel.

"Rach," I whimper after she answers, "Why did Pastor Max have to cause so much pain? Why did he have to humiliate us the way he did?"

"I know Tessa, he hurt everyone," she responds, pausing for a moment, probably detecting the quivering in my voice. "How about you meet me at the waterfront park in ten minutes so we can talk about it? It's better not to discuss it around our families."

I agree. Tucking my cell phone back into my purse, I shift the car into first gear and drive the short distance to the park that sits in front of the museum, which overlooks our town's harbor. While the breeze blows through my open window, I recount the turn of events that happened at New Creations Church...

It was my sophomore year in high school. My father and mother went away one night, so I took advantage of their absence and had a small party at my house. My friends brought alcohol, and we poured the mixed drinks into mugs to conceal the content in case Amber decided to wander downstairs. By the time my friends left for the night, I was extremely drunk. Rachel and I slumped upstairs, and although we managed to hide our drunkenness from my sisters, we couldn't hide it from God. What happened later that weekend left me feeling like God was punishing me for all my poor choices.

Church had been awkward that fateful Sunday – a church meeting was called, my parents were crying, and I was confused. During a family conference after church, I discovered that things had been going from bad to worse. Pastor Max was angry that our family was such a bad testimony, and he didn't want the negative influence at his church anymore. He had a folder filled with examples of how I had shamed the church, and now my dad was without a job.

As I ran up to my room, I kicked my door shut and cursed God for allowing such a thing. My dad was a good man, the best. He had worked so hard for the church, and I didn't even know that he was experiencing issues with Max. Regardless of any arguments that may have taken place in the church office, he only spoke positively when discussing his job, which meant that getting fired came out of nowhere – I was blindsided.

Over the next couple of weeks, I discovered that Max had called elder meetings with my parents to discuss their rebellious teenager. Every rumor was examined, and he punished my parents for my actions.

During that Sunday morning message, Max had been preaching about grace. Yet, during the meeting that followed the service, he was shaming my family by openly firing my dad for the whole congregation to witness. My sisters and I didn't understand what was happening when the elders got up, and forced us to walk out of the church to never return. Without the slightest hint of sorrow in their hearts, they closed the doors behind us and locked my family out, leaving us standing hopelessly in the rain staring at the doors of a church that offered hope and a new future only five years before. That dark afternoon must have been a reflection of Max's heart, and the rain was God crying with us.

We discovered later that week that Max had shared with the congregation how my actions reflected on my dad and how my dad lacked control in his household - and that kind of man was not welcome or fit to pastor a church family. The Hern's knew the truth, and did not support Max, so they were ostracized too.

Max not only tried to ruin my father's name in the community, he refused to give him a good reference, and strategically fired him only two weeks before we received the final word on our immigration – basically ensuring that there was no way for us to work in the United States. However, my parents accepted the cruel actions of Max with grace and forgiveness, and assured us girls that God was not moving us from our little town. My parents went a year without income after the termination because we were not legally allowed to work in the United States. Many wonderful people supported us through that year, providing meals that would have been missed and helping with our mortgage payments, all during a time when deportation hovered over our heads. Thankfully, God quickly moved us into a church in the same town, and Fair Havens became a place where Pastor Sal celebrated that my dad was a man after God's heart.

We made it through that dark year, and God proved to be trustworthy, even in the midst of the mess that Max created. But the pain didn't stop there – we would often see members from New Creations Church in the grocery stores and restaurants of our small town. People that I used to trust and love scowled at me across the isles and over their menus. They believed every word that Max said about my family and me. In a way, he did ruin us – he ruined me. I have never been able to fully trust and rely on the church since that terrible day when we were escorted from the auditorium and humiliated in front of a congregation that Max manipulated. I begged my dad not to go back into ministry, but he replied that he was serving God, not a pastor. My dad might still be committed to church, but since that day, I made a decision to never get overly involved with another church again.

Rachel's car pulls into the lot beside mine, and we both emerge. We hug each other, and hold on for a bit. "Sorry, Rach – I guess I just needed to talk about it." I wipe my eyes, unwilling to tell her that I had just come from a counseling session that had sparked my current state of emotion.

"I know how you feel," she says as she releases me. We walk to the nearby swings and take a seat. "Sometimes I want to talk about what happened too, but my family has trouble bringing up the subject – Max hurt us bad."

I sigh as I consider the unreasonable measures Max took to ostracize my dad, even after he left the congregation. He demanded that the Hern's make a public apology to the congregation for being friends with the McRae's, as if to say that befriending our family was a sin and that New Creations Church deserved an apology for such an action. When Mr. and Mrs. Hern refused, he discharged them from the church, in a similar manner to the way he discharged us – publicly and humiliatingly.

"I just don't understand what would drive a man to be so cruel," I state. "What's worse is that he put on such a front. He made me believe I could trust and rely on him, but before I knew it, he threw me and my family out on the streets – waiting for the government to remove us from the country and do his dirty work for him."

Rachel responds, "Yeah, but look how God fought for you guys, for all of us. He continued to provide for your family financially, he found your dad a new job, presenting all of us with a new church – a church with a trustworthy pastor, and we are much better off not having to deal with the judgmental attitudes we faced from most of the congregation at New Creations."

"You know, I had a lot of fun in high school with you – and it's not like I've made many better decisions during college, but I still feel somewhat responsible for my dad getting fired." I shake my head as I consider this statement; it doesn't seem to matter how hard I fought rejection by conforming to the popular crowd, my decisions eventually led to my whole family getting rejected – not just me.

"It wasn't your fault, Tessa," Rachel reassures me, "Max was, and still is a man that is out to ruin families and lives – I'm just surprised the congregation still clings to his every last word as he continues to fire each new associate pastor, refusing to give them a good reference and somehow ensuring that they are left in the depths of despair." She looks down at her feet brushing the dirt beneath them. "I mean, look at the guy that replaced your dad, Tess. I can't remember his name, but he worked for the church only a little over a year, then he was fired and thrown out of the church to fend for himself. I mean, our families weathered much better than he did. His wife left him and took their kids, he gained a ridiculous amount of weight in his depression, and died a year later of a heart attack." I shudder at the memory, "That's just what Max does; he hires someone, disagrees with their theology or way of doing things, fires them, refuses to give a good reference, ruins their lives, and somehow manipulates the congregation into agreeing with his reasoning. We were all lucky to get out barely scathed!" Rachel concludes.

"Yeah, I suppose," I whisper. But the truth is, I didn't get out of New Creations Church barely scathed. Maybe it was the fact that Max publicly used my actions to blame my father for inadequately parenting his children, or that my weekend decisions caused a fair amount of commotion come Sunday morning, but I felt responsible for the pain that my family went through. I will forever be scarred from that awful day when Max unjustly threw us out of a church we loved and trusted.

I am moved out of my trance as Rachel releases her hand from the chain that holds her swing and reaches for my dangling hand, grasping it in a manner that convinces me of her capability to read my thoughts. "On the bright side," she says in a cheery tone, looking to change the topic, "I'm almost done with my online course, and we are both going back to campus to start our junior year in a little over a week!" I turn and smile at her, glad that my best friend is able to bring happiness and joy to each new chapter of my life. Rachel continues with a whimsical smile, "And when we get back on campus, we will have to figure out something fun for my upcoming birthday…"

chapter fourteen

(August, 2009)

Moving around our dorm room with my phone in my hand, I smile at the devious plans I am making. It is a few days past Rachel's birthday, and although we went out for a nice dinner together to celebrate, she has no idea that I have been collaborating with the men's soccer team to throw a surprise party at their place tonight. Most of the students are back on campus now because classes start on Monday. Earlier this week, as I exchanged secret texts with some of the soccer guys, we figured that Rachel's birthday was a perfect excuse to throw the first Saturday night party of the year.

Startled with movement from our dorm door, I quickly hide my phone as the door slams shut and Rachel slumps against it. Still in her cheerleading practice gear, she drops her head back and closes her eyes. "Rach, what's wrong?" I ask with concern.

"Practice was brutal tonight."

"Oh no, what happened?" I inquire, hoping that whatever went on during her late evening practice won't ruin what is to come for the night.

"We had to work muscles in our body that I didn't even know existed," she half mumbles. She points to her thin legs and lets out a small, self-indulgent whimper, still refusing to open her eyes. I laugh in response to her pain. Rachel has a great body, so I don't feel sorry for her when she occasionally has to work hard to look as good as she does in those tiny shorts.

My practice ended an hour before hers, giving me plenty of time to jump in the shower before Rachel's surprise party.

"Hey, there's a party tonight," I say, trying my best to sound nonchalant, yet hoping that Rachel will be up to going out. My stomach flutters with excitement knowing that she will be totally caught off guard when she is surprised that the party is thrown in her honor.

"Oh perfect, just what I wanted to hear – where is it?"

Relieved that her sore legs won't keep her confined to her bed tonight, I respond, "It's at the men's soccer house, lucky for you it is only a short walk." Most of the teams on campus have a house together, and the men's soccer house is located conveniently two streets behind our dorm room. Rachel snickers at my comment as she throws her duffle bag on her bed and begins to strip down for the shower. I pick up my hair dryer, knowing that I should finish getting ready if we want to get to the party at a reasonable time.

Once my hair is dry, I utilize Rachel's shower time to tie up a few loose ends for the party. My phone is still buzzing with the responses when Rachel walks into the room wrapped in a towel. Looking to distract Rachel from the messages I'm receiving, I turn on Lil' Wayne's most recent album and grab the half empty vodka bottle hidden in Rachel's underwear drawer. I make us both a vodka-tonic to drink while we get ready, then I watch carefully to make sure Rachel's back is turned before checking my phone.

The two of us lay out different outfit options in the midst of doing our hair and make-up. We will often share clothing back and forth, even though our body types are different, so we spend a while sifting through our over-stuffed closets. I debate on a tiny, form-fitting, gray and white cotton striped dress. Turning and twisting to examine myself in the mirror, I am caught off guard at the amount of weight I have lost over the summer. My stomach is as flat as ever and although my breasts have shrunk, my butt is still voluptuous and toned. When I arrived for pre-season, I decided that I needed to take a break with my smoking so that I would be able to keep up with the rest of the team during our workouts. Surprisingly, my appetite has yet to increase, even without the nicotine, and my weight is still dropping. Grabbing a small mirror to help assess my rear view, I am shocked at just how much skin I am showing. Although the dress looks good, I am unwilling to go to a house party dressed this seductively, given my most recent experience. So, I try on a few more options and finally decide on a pair of green dress shorts with small pockets in the back and a plain black top with a halter neckline.

Rachel wrestles with a couple of different clothing options, but based on my knowledge of the event, I convince her to wear a tight, high-waist coral skirt and a white tank-top; the outfit providing a perfect contrast to her thin, tanned body. I snatch my phone quickly and text the soccer guys, warning them that we will be arriving at the party in the next twenty minutes. Shoving my phone in my right back pocket, I finish off my outfit with a few pieces of subtle jewelry, still a bit wary that too much might attract some unwanted attention. Within an hour of Rachel's shower, we are dressed and grabbing for our keys as we make our way out the door. Together, we walk arm in arm down the long hallway of our dorm – outfits complementing both our body types, hair done, make-up perfect, and spirits high.

"SURPRISE!" everyone yells as we walk through the door. Above the large group that has gathered for the event hangs a banner that says 'Happy Birthday Rachel,' compliments of the cheerleading team. Rachel jumps, totally taken aback by the shouts and cheers. Immediately the group rushes to give her hugs and wish her a happy birthday. In all the commotion, I get separated from my best friend, but I am still able to see her glowing smile as everyone crowds around her, and I am thrilled that my surprise worked.

After a few minutes, I turn from the group and make for the kitchen, leaving the noise of excited voices and loud pumping music behind me. As I pour myself a drink in the quieter confines of the small space, I add only a little alcohol, aware of what happened last time I got drunk. After taking a sip of the sweet mixed drink, I draw in a slow, deep breath. This is the first time I have been to a party and drank since the mishap, and although counseling has helped me through my depression, I fight back the heavy emotions that are threatening to cloud my mind.

Dr Murray and I had one more meeting before I moved back on campus a couple of days ago. The session went well, offering closure to the details I revealed about my childhood, teenage years, removal from New Creations Church, and naturally, the mishap. My ongoing struggle with rejection clearly began in my childhood, continued in my teen-years, and climaxed with getting kicked out of church. It's clear now why I have been struggling with the rejection I feel from Mason, and how my horror from the mishap threatens permanent rejection that I fear is evident on my face.

No, I internally scold myself. *You have worked through so much this summer Tessa, don't let it all come back to haunt you. Relax, if you don't drink too much you will be safe here. Besides, no one is out to hurt you. Stop worrying. Be smart. Have fun. Let the past be the past – you have to move forward.* I take another sip of my drink and purposefully brighten with optimism, as if my silent resolution has provided strength to enjoy the rest of the night. With a slight lift of my shoulders, I straighten my posture and emerge from the empty kitchen ready to join the party.

* * *

The celebration is a hit, Rachel is clearly having a great time as people come and greet her, wishing her a happy birthday and throwing various compliments at her. The room is getting more and more crowded as students catch word of the party.

Before I know it, the air is too stuffy for me to handle, and I see a quick escape as a small path opens to the front door – without hesitation, I take it.

Practically throwing myself into the night air, I take a couple deep breaths and try to steady myself while my eyes squint against the bright porch light above my head. I look around at the many familiar faces scattered on the porch and in the front yard. Then, I suck in a startled breath as my gaze stops, making contact with the most beautiful, crystal blue eyes – Mason. My heart skips with emotion, bringing back flashing memories of our amazing three year relationship, the break-up, and the hurtful conversation that ended our contact for the summer. Mason doesn't break eye contact with me, and immediately I am fearful that he can detect the pain that I went through this summer, the pain from my mishap that I hope he never discovers. I smile briefly at him, aware that we have been holding each other's gaze for too long to pretend I didn't see him, then I quickly look down at my half empty cup.

My rapid heart rate and unsteady breathing caused by Mason's gaze has me wishing I never escaped the stuffy room. Looking up, I notice that Mason has left Lucas's side, and is now ambling his way through the crowd and up the stairs to where I am standing. I take a hurried sip from my drink, and, as his flawless features inch closer, I immediately recognize that I have been subconsciously searching for him all night.

"Uhh, hi," I offer my slightly awkward greeting to his approach.

Mason stands in front of me with an air of confidence that makes me weak in the knees. My heart thuds in my chest as I stand in the presence of the guy I am still in love with. He looks good; in fact, I don't think he has ever looked better. He must have spent most of his summer in a gym, because his arms and chest are bulging; his frame larger and more toned than it's ever been before. His tanned skin reveals that he spent many hours outside, then I remember he told me he would be working on Lucas's father's golf course in South Carolina. His blue t-shirt brings out the shocking color of his eyes, and although his fitted baseball cap is low on his forehead, it is incapable of shadowing his gorgeous gaze.

He offers a smile that melts my heart, "Hi Tess," he says. We stand in silence for a few moments.

"How was…" I start.

"You look good," he says at the same time. We pause, waiting for the other to finish their sentence, then we both half laugh at the awkwardness of the moment.

Mason starts again, "Listen, Tess – I'm sorry for what happened with Destiny." I think back to a few days ago when pre-season started. I had to grapple with her presence for the first time since learning about Mason's attraction to her. On top of fiercely disliking the girl, I noted that my added insecurities could easily put a damper on this volleyball season. Being around her is difficult, but I know that in the big scheme of things, including all I have dealt with over the summer, Mason's comment months ago was only a little bump in the road.

"I overreacted," I reply, "and I'm sorry for the way I hung up on you that night." Mason lifts the beer he is holding to his mouth and takes a swig. Desperate to move the conversation to a subject that's less weighty, I point to his beer, "At least you didn't spill your beer on me tonight, like you did the first party I went to at your house on Santa Monica."

We both laugh at the memory, "Yeah, I had a bit too much to drink that night," he says.

"You remembered to call me though - maybe not when you promised, but you did remember," I snicker.

Mason looks deep into my eyes for a split second, his facial expression a little too intense for the light conversation, "How could I forget." As a means of distraction, he reaches for his hat with his free hand and adjusts it a little on his forehead. He quietly clears his throat, "I thought about you a lot this summer," he continues, "and I think we should be friends." He shifts his weight from one foot to the other. "It wasn't right, not being able to call you, to wish you a happy birthday – we have been through too much to not be friends on this side of it all."

I nod. "I totally agree," I say with obvious relief, but I look down and fiddle with my drink, avoiding his stare and internally pleading that he will not be able to read my mind. I don't want to be just friends - I want to be his girlfriend. In fact, there is no one else in the world who makes me feel the way he does, and I know he is the only one I want to spend the rest of my life with – I want to be his wife. However, content with the idea of at least being friends for now, I lift my head and flash a smile.

We spend the next 45 minutes reflecting on the many memories we made while we were together. We laugh at the date we took down Main Street where my shoe somehow ended up floating in the water fountain. I remind him of the time we spent at his Aunt and Uncle's, when he accidentally walked in on his Aunt using the bathroom and how he has never been able to erase that terrible memory from his mind. Trying to forget that picture, he gets talking about the party at his place after our senior prom, when his buddy decided to put on a pair of Mason's childhood rollerblades and accidentally put a hole in the wall while skating across the living room. This leads to the Christmas mornings spent at my parent's home, when my sisters and I would try on all our new clothes at once.

"Amber and Shane are pregnant," I say with a grin. Not wanting to get caught up in the subject of my miscarriage, I add, "It's a girl."

"Wow," Mason says. "That's awesome, time sure does fly."

At Mason's comment, I think back to the significance of 11:11. As much as I wished and prayed that Mason and I would always be together, I could never have predicted that I would be the reason we would break-up. Deep in thought, I neglect to notice Mason studying me.

"What are you thinking about?" he asks.

"Oh nothing," I mumble, remembering how I never actually told him about the silly time thing. Then, with a half snicker, I conclude that there is no use keeping it a secret now, "It's just that, when we would spend hours on the phone - when you first started calling me…" I pause and look to Mason, raising one eyebrow curious whether or not he is following me – he nods, "Well, every night we were on the phone, I always happened to look at the clock at 11:11. I heard this myth that if you make a wish on 11:11, it will come true." I look down at my feet, slightly embarrassed, "Well, every night I wished that we would be together forever."

Mason doesn't say anything; instead, he shoves his free hand into the pocket of his khaki shorts and takes another drink from his almost empty beer bottle. "Well," he finally says, breaking the silence, "I'm just happy that we are friends now, Tessa."

I force a smile, not knowing what I expected him to say in response to my forward comment, but glad that he isn't shying away from our friendship. "Me too," I say.

"I'm going to grab another beer," Mason states, "I'll catch you later?"

"Yeah, for sure," I respond. Mason brushes past me and reaches for the front door. I watch him step into the dark, crowded room, but before the door closes behind him, I blink, desperate for my eyes to adjust to the dark backdrop so I can catch one more glimpse of him. He is perfect. The door slams shut, echoing the reality that slams into my mind and zeros in on my heart - he isn't mine anymore. I tip back the rest of my drink, digging deep into my psyche to find some optimism, just as Dr. Murray had suggested in our last meeting. As I finish the last drop, I find the silver lining to this ugly cloud called "friendship" – maybe he doesn't intend to date me, but he hasn't forgotten about me.

chapter fifteen

(September, 2009 – October, 2009)

Wiping the sweat from my brow, I take another large gulp of water from my squeeze bottle and look around the gym as my teammates drift toward the locker room. Without air conditioning, the September heat is taking its' toll, especially after what Coach Greenly just put us through in preparation for playing Barton tomorrow night. Feeling the effect of the heat, I grab my towel and dab the back of my neck with it.

"Tessa, could you join me in my office?" Coach Greenly calls from across the gym. Confused as to why I am being asked to a private meeting with my coach, I react to the pit that immediately forms in my stomach. Moving quickly, I enter her small office and close the door behind me. "Please, take a seat," my coach says, pointing to a chair across from her desk, while she drops onto her chair hidden behind her laptop and several stacks of papers.

After sitting down, I feel sweat starting to form again on my brow, but this time it's not because of the heat. "Is something wrong?" I inquire.

Coach Greenly closes a folder and sets it off to one side. "No, nothing's wrong – quite the opposite." I let out a quiet sigh of relief before she continues, "I've been looking at how much you have improved over the last couple of weeks, and I want you to know that I have decided to give you the libero position for this season."

My heart skips a beat at her words. I have been training hard in the off season to try to secure this back row defensive position, and although I may not respect every one of Coach Greenly's decisions, I am overjoyed with this one. "Oh wow!" I begin to offer my gratitude before she interrupts me.

"That's not all," my coach states matter-of-factly. "As you know, we have lost a lot of players this season. Some girls were not able to juggle the strain of the season and their academic responsibilities, and others have transferred." Coach Greenly raises one eyebrow to reveal her disdain for the loss our team has experienced. "But the fact remains," she continues, "Katie is our only senior, and I have always been a strong believer in dual leadership on the court."

My head tilts to the side, "Do you mean having two captains for the team instead of just one?" I ask.

"Yes," she replies, "and after considering a couple of the other juniors for the role of co-captain, I have concluded that you are the best fit."

My eyes pop in surprise as I try to contain my excitement. "I would love to be the co-captain for the team, Coach."

"Good," Coach Greenly leans back in her chair. "I have watched you during the preseason workouts, and I like the effort you have given. As you know, we have just joined a new conference, and I have every intention of becoming conference champions this year. I have watched how the team responds to you, and I see that you and Katie interact well together on the court. I believe that, given the amount of court time you will see with your Libero position and your innate ability to lead others, you will be a solid co-captain this season."

"Thanks Coach," I say, rewarding her words with a confident smile.

"Now, I will announce your leadership position to the rest of the team before the match tomorrow. Get some good rest tonight, the Barton Bulldogs may not be a part of our conference, but they are always good competition," She finishes. I nod, then get up to leave, "Oh and Tessa," I stop mid stride and turn back to her, "Don't forget, the team is wearing the blue jersey's tomorrow, so you need to bring your white one as the libero." Closing the door behind me, I let out a silent elated cheer of triumph as I skip across the empty gym to the locker room, thrilled that my fall semester has started out so well after such a lousy summer.

* * *

The minute hand seems to be moving slowly as I wait for my last class of the day to end. My growing anticipation for tonight's match has kept me on edge all day. On our way out of our dorm room this morning, Rachel promised that she would show up to our game after her evening practice. And I have discovered throughout the day that some of our teammates have managed to coerce several of the other athletes on campus to attend as well. My hope is that if we pack out the bleachers, the Bulldogs will be intimidated by our fans.

As soon as class ends, I race to the gym and get ready for the warm-up. I'm thrilled to see that the bleachers are filling quickly as Coach Greenly gathers our team together in front of our bench after the warm-up. "Well girls," she yells over the pumping music echoing throughout the gym, "tonight's match will not be an easy one. The Bulldogs have a few new recruits this year, and each girl seems to show a lot of potential, at least from what I saw during the warm-ups…" Our attention is momentarily pulled away from Coach Greenly's speech as a girl from Barton lets out a short cry of glee. We all pause to watch Barton's #2 player run to greet Callan's new tennis recruit who has just entered the gym. Her enthusiasm as she gives the Callan freshman a long hug has captured the attention of most in the gym. I turn to Katie standing beside me and quietly whisper, "Clearly they are long lost friends…typical freshmen."

I continue staring as the Barton player and the Callan tennis recruit make a big scene, shaking my head at their interaction before Coach Greenly's announcement jolts me back to her speech.

"...Tessa is going to be the team's co-captain this season." Most of the girls smile and pat my back while offering their congratulations. As I look around and smile back at my team, I notice Destiny turn from the huddle and roll her eyes – clearly she desired this position, which only gives me more joy as I celebrate my ability to beat her out of it. "Okay, starting line up for tonight..." Coach Greenly cuts the congratulatory remarks short before we make our way onto the court and line up for our roster introduction and the National Anthem.

Our announcer's booming voice echoes through the speakers, capturing the attention of our fans as he quickly introduces the Bulldogs. When he gets to the Barton player who created a scene a short while ago, I take special note of her introduction, "Jamie Forsythe, number two, a freshman from Greenville, North Carolina - Defensive Specialist." I look at the girl who steps out from the line; she is a cute, pale-skinned blonde, no taller than 5'1, and her short, pin straight hair is pulled back into a high ponytail – bobby pins scattered across her head to keep the strands out of her face. A single cheer from our bleachers tells me that her friend, regardless of being a Callan recruit, is a devoted one.

The announcer finishes introducing the Bulldogs and begins down our line with added enthusiasm. When he announces, "Tessa McRae, number nine," I step out of the line and offer a short wave toward the bleachers as the announcer continues with my hometown and ends with my starting position as libero. Although my contrasting jersey is an obvious indicator, I smile anyway, wishing that my family could be here for this moment, but enjoying the memory of their enthusiasm last night when I shared the exciting news. The announcer continues through my team's roster, but my attention is directed toward the back entrance as I see Mason and Lucas casually enter the gym and sit in the front row on the opposing side. My heart lurches at the sight of Mason, looking wildly attractive in his Callan Baseball t-shirt and mesh athletic shorts. We have exchanged friendly texts since our encounter a week ago, but I had no idea he was coming to the match tonight. My thoughts overflow with optimism as I face the flag for the National Anthem – *I am the co-captain for our team, my hard work has been rewarded with the libero position, and Mason is here to witness it all; apart from losing, what could go wrong?*

It doesn't take long for us to secure a win with the first two sets, but the third set doesn't seem to be going our way as we battle through hard hits and miscommunication between team members. Coach Greenly finally calls a time out, and we all move to the sidelines. Out of the corner of my eye, I notice Rachel walk in through the back entrance and throw her duffle bag down on the front row, only a couple of seats down from Mason. I smile at her and wave, and she waves back while settling in.

"Katie," my coach directs her attention toward our setter and head captain, "you have to establish more plays, communicate with the hitters so we can create some confusion for their tall middle blocker – she's killing us right now." Katie nods in response and takes another gulp of water. We make our way back out to the court, hoping to gain back some lost points. The opposing team has the serve, and I notice the Barton #2 player, Jamie, amble to the back row, her tiny body strutting confidently away from the Bulldog huddle. The announcer tosses the ball in Jamie's direction, but the ball bounces out of her reach. As I adjust my spandex shorts, I see the ball roll toward Mason's feet in the front row. Mason gets up from his seat, leans down for the ball, and tosses it to Jamie. My eyes narrow as I notice his lingering stare. She offers a flirtatious laugh and a quiet thanks before positioning herself for the serve. My stomach tightens at the exchange between my ex and the little blonde, but I don't have much time to dwell on it as the ref blows the whistle and Jamie's jump float serve comes sailing in my direction. I return the ball and line Katie up for a perfect set to Destiny. Although I can't stand the girl, I cheer along with the team as Destiny swings for the line and gets the point. We keep the serve for a couple of points, and before we know it, the Bulldogs have called a timeout, the score 18 – 21.

During the timeout, my eyes wander to Mason. Rachel, who is sitting only a couple of seats away from him has a troubled look plastered across her face – I wonder if she is catching bits and pieces of a conversation she knows I won't approve of. However, there is no room for distractions at this point in the game, so I go back onto the court and refocus my attention on winning. We continue to battle the set, gaining points more rapidly than the Bulldogs. The score is now 24 – 24, and I feel the stress knowing that our team must win by two. We have the serve, and the energy on our side of the court tells me that my team is as ready to win this game as I am. Our outside hitter has the serve and aces the Bulldogs - obviously they are flustered. After the ball is rolled again to our server, I ready myself for a return. I look to my coach and watch her point to the target, indicating that the serve should go to the back row position where Jamie is currently playing. The ball is tossed, and the hard, topspin serve sails right to the target. Jamie dives on the floor, but shanks the ball to the bleachers. My team shouts in victory as the match comes to a close, and I can't help but think that Jamie deserved it as I watch her get up from the floor struggling with defeat.

* * *

October is here, and the campus is pulsing with energy as we get ready for our homecoming weekend. Naturally, our volleyball team has a match scheduled for Friday night, but the real fun comes Saturday when we plan to cheer on the football team, then partake in waste-fest – a parade that bounces from house to house where we all enjoy the parties thrown by students that reside off-campus - a Callan homecoming tradition.

Rachel and I bought t-shirts and material paint for waste-fest this year. Now, with the t-shirts laid out on the floor of our dorm room, I start to get a little nervous, knowing that I cannot depend on my artistic ability to provide a decorated shirt worthy of attractive representation for the festivities.

"What's wrong?" Rachel asks, noticing my hesitation.

I groan, "I just don't know if I can make this paintbrush produce what I am mentally picturing."

Rachel laughs, "I will help if you need me to," she says. "Besides, it's Thursday night, if you don't like it, we can always go out and buy another t-shirt to decorate tomorrow morning – it should be dry by Saturday night." I'm not entirely sure why I am so worried about looking excessively fabulous for the parties, I suppose it's because I know Mason will be making his appearance. Rachel and I spend the next hour or so sharing paintbrushes and colors as we decorate our t-shirts to perfection.

"There," Rachel stands back from her t-shirt in full appreciation of her artwork. Her blue t-shirt has flowing letters spelling out 'Waste-Fest 2009' in a beautiful display of large elegant cursive – a perfect t-shirt for her.

"Ok, I'm almost done," I say, adding an apostrophe to the '09 of my t-shirt, waste-fest written in block letters tilting in every direction with alternating colors – an appropriate depiction of the potential mental state of many of the students come Saturday night. As I go to stand up, I am unaware that Rachel is behind me, hovering over my shoulder viewing my work. I feel the oozing of wet paint on the back of my neck and realize that I just backed up into Rachel's paintbrush. I reach to wipe away the mess when I notice Rachel giggling at my mistake. "So, you think that's funny?" I ask sarcastically.

Rachel bursts out in laughter, "More than funny – hilarious!"

As Rachel doubles over with laughter, I reach out and stroke my paintbrush across her forehead, leaving a bright streak in its track. Rachel immediately straightens as a shocked look spreads across her face. For a moment we stand, facing each other, the paintbrushes poised in each of our hands, and in a split second, the paint brushes become weapons as we attack each other in a bout of laughter and screams, the paint marking our skin and clothes.

With tears in my eyes from all the laughter, I glance at myself in our full length mirror and note the damage, "It's a good thing we put on old, cheap clothes – this paint is not gunna come out."

Rachel looks down at her ragged shorts, "I hate these shorts anyway," she says with a snort. "They are better off in the trash, I just hope the paint comes off our faces!" We collapse into a fit of hysterics again as we look at each other, glad that the attack didn't smear our waste-fest t-shirts drying on the floor between our two beds.

* * *

Thrilled that Saturday night has finally arrived, I wrap my towel tighter around my body and look in the mirror as I start to get ready for waste-fest tonight. While I apply my make-up, I reflect on the last 24 hours. We won our match last night. So far we only have two losses, and we are undefeated in the conference, although it's still too early in the season to predict our conference ranking as champions. The outcome of the season so far leaves me content with my ability to lead as a co-captain. Katie and I have inspired the team to accomplish some goals that have yet to be attained in any previous season, at least since I've been at Callan.

The football match this afternoon was intense. Rachel and I had a drink or two at a tailgating party thrown by the men's soccer team before the game. The alcohol assisted in the loud cheering of our gang as we flocked the bleachers for the kick-off. I watched Tripp make some great plays as his quarterbacking skills led the team to a victory. After the game, it started to drizzle a bit. I remember how I glanced around as the bleachers emptied, trying to find Mason. I figured that he must have been sitting on the other side, because I couldn't locate him, and I knew that he and Lucas wouldn't have missed the well attended athletic event.

Rachel enters the room, bringing me back to reality. "The girls down the hall just finished ironing on letters to their waste-fest t-shirts. They are good, but they aren't as awesome as ours," she swoons with pride as she glances down at the t-shirts lying on the floor.

"Sweet," I reply. "Hey, do you think I should just wear my hair curly tonight, since it's kinda raining and it's bound to get frizzy anyway?"

"Probably," she replies as she bends down to pick up our t-shirts. She gingerly runs a finger across the letters to check if they are dry. "Shirts are ready," she states with exhilaration.

After scrunching my hair with mousse, a little bit of gel, and a couple squirts of hairspray, I drop my towel, strap on a bra, and reach for my t-shirt. I pair the t-shirt with my low rise jeans, flaunting about an inch of my flat midriff. Pleased with the outcome of my appearance, even if my hair is curly, I cross the room toward my half-filled cup and take a sip. I turn back to Rachel to see what she has paired with her blue t-shirt, and I catch her swiveling in front of our full length mirror, trying to determine if her black mini-skirt will make-do for her outfit.

"Wow, you look good," I assure her as she twists back and forth.

"You don't think it's too much?" she asks.

Rachel always looks significantly hotter than anyone else at the Callan parties, "No, that outfit is perfect for you – besides, your t-shirt is written in cursive, I would expect nothing but a skirt to pair it with." Rachel turns from the mirror and smiles at me briefly before going to the sink to brush her teeth. Ready for the party festivities, Rachel and I walk to the end of the hall, where we told our fellow dorm hall residents to meet us. As we walk side by side I ask, "Have you seen Mason today?"

Rachel looks at me, a slight hint of uneasiness evident in her eyes, "No, I haven't."

I flinch, "It's just that I figured I would see him at the game today, but I couldn't find him."

"Did you text him?" she asks.

"No, I don't want to bother him," I reply. "We are friends and all, but I don't want to get obnoxious by contacting him too often."

Rachel nods, but the group of girls we are meeting up with cut the conversation short as they let out giddy squeals of delight at the sight of us. We all exchange compliments regarding each other's self-styled t-shirts while we exit the dorm building into the drizzling rain.

The first party we go to is at the soccer guys' house. Most of the guys haven't stopped drinking since the game, so the party is already in full motion when we arrive. Naturally, because we are traveling with a group of girls, we decide to bounce between the men's houses in close vicinity to each other, and the amount of attention our group receives makes our plans all worth it. The party is a blast, with people coming in and out of the house, and at one point I slink out while Rachel is distracted and bum a cigarette. I shouldn't be smoking since we are in season, but with all the withdrawal symptoms from the past few weeks, I conclude that I deserve at least one. Just as I put out my cigarette, Rachel, accompanied by our group, exits through the front door and tells me we are moving on to the next party, which is at the men's basketball house.

We walk up to the house, which is only a street over from the soccer guys, and it seems that the people attending this party don't mind the drizzle. There are many students scattered across the front lawn, but the girls and I scamper inside. The living room is dark and the loud hip-hop music is an immediate invitation to start dancing. Rachel is quickly whisked away by a senior basketball player. I know that my best friend is not complaining; the light skinned African American is attractive, talented, and towers over the crowd at 6'5. Rachel always loves basketball season; not only does she get to cheer indoors, where it is much warmer but she enjoys flirting with the players before and after the games. We spend a half hour dancing, but as the house continues to fill with bodies, the group of girls and I consider the stuffiness that accompanies this jam-packed room and decide it's time to move on. After dragging Rachel away, we head down the road to the baseball house.

"Rachel, do I look okay?" I whisper as we walk across the yard to the front door. "I think Mason will be here, and it was starting to get a little hot at the basketball house."

"Yeah, you look fine," Rachel responds. She isn't drunk yet, but she is well on her way, which leaves me worried that maybe her view of my appearance isn't entirely accurate. We walk into the baseball house, and with my head bowed, I weave between the partiers while heading for the bathroom.

Standing in front of the mirror, I am relieved to see that Rachel wasn't far off in her opinion earlier. The idea I had to wear my hair curly tonight was a good one. I run a finger under each eye, wiping away any running eyeliner, then scrunch my hair a little in the back, thankful that my natural curls haven't gotten too frizzy. Exiting the bathroom not long after occupying it, I make my way to the kitchen. "Jello-shots!" I hear someone yell from behind the fridge, and my friends and I meander over to take a couple. My head is buzzing, and grabbing a bottle from the fridge, I resolve that drinking water for a little while might be a wise choice, given that my mishap is still fresh in my memory.

"Come-on Tess," Rachel calls over her shoulder as she leaves the large kitchen. "They are playing beer pong in the other room." I follow her out of the kitchen to a screened-in patio. The table is long, and there are two players at each end; however, the patio is fairly spacious, and many of the students gather around to watch. I slink back in the corner, content with watching quietly and drinking my water. One of the baseball players who is competing on our side of the room picks up the ping pong ball and asks Rachel to kiss it for him for good luck. Rachel seductively blows a kiss in his direction, and the player smiles back at her. As he arches his elbow to shoot, Rachel turns and finds me in the corner, laughing as she pushes through the crowd to get to me.

"That guy always thinks I'm a good luck charm," she snickers as she slumps against the wall.

"I think he likes you," I comment. "He is really cute too, Rach, maybe you should be his lucky charm."

Rachel twists her face in disagreement, "He is too short."

Giggling at her remark, my thoughts slip back to Mason, "I haven't seen Mason yet," I say. "Maybe I missed him as I crossed the living room."

Rachel shrugs, but just as she does so, my eyes are drawn to the screen door in the opposite corner of the patio as it creaks open. My heart drops to my stomach as I see the gray and blue Florida State sweatshirt that I gave back to Mason months ago on a petite blonde. Bewilderment courses through me as the blonde turns toward me and I recognize her - Jamie Forsythe, the defensive specialist from Barton. I feel my lips part in confusion and horror as I watch Mason walk in behind her, followed by the Callan tennis player and Lucas. The two couples walk past the crowd on the patio and into the kitchen.

"Oh Tess," Rachel says quietly as she turns to me, having just seen what I saw. I can barely hear her talking as my mind races, trying to piece together the details that would explain why Jamie, who doesn't attend Callan, is here at this party and why she is wearing my favorite sweatshirt of Mason's. It doesn't take long for me to reach the tormenting conclusion that she must be here visiting that tennis player friend of hers. And, with the way Mason followed her onto the patio, it is evident that they have been in contact since Mason tossed her the ball a couple of weeks ago. Suddenly, I think I'm going to be sick.

I plow through the throng, desperate to get into the night air and allow my mind some clarity in an effort to understand these current circumstances. Rachel tails behind me. "Tessa, I'm so sorry! I should have seen this coming," she says as we escape from the closed in patio and walk the length of the side of the house to the front yard. "I heard him and Lucas talking about her at the volleyball game, I just didn't think Mason would ever make a move – given how shy he is."

"I need a cigarette," I state. Although my stomach hurts, I know that the nicotine will help calm my aching heart. Rachel witnesses my angst and marches quickly to the front porch to find what I need. As she returns, she knows now is not the time to scold me about my habits; instead, she stands by my side as I light up in silence.

Eventually my emotions settle, allowing my sorrow to turn into rage, "How could he?" I spit. "One, she is a volleyball player, he couldn't choose like a softball player or something? Two, she is a blonde, and a freshman! Three, she doesn't even live around here, what does he think he's going to do - visit her every other weekend, he didn't even do that for me while we were dating!" I seethe as I finish my last few drags on my cigarette, stomping it out in the dirt, trying to release some of my disdain with my action.

"I'm sorry, Tess," Rachel offers.

I clench my fists beside my rigid body, crushing the empty water bottle in my hand. "I mean, who does she think she is anyway? Is she at all aware of our past? Walking into this party wearing that sweatshirt - how dare she!" I kick the dirt again, appreciating the fact that it's just Rachel and me on this side of the yard. "Besides," I continue, "she looks like a wet dog in that oversized sweatshirt. Doesn't she know this is a party? Did she even look in the mirror before she came over here?"

"Her hair is really frizzy," Rachel says, doing her best to side with me.

I drop my head into my free hand. As much as I want to go on and on about Jamie's appearance, the fact remains – her petite frame, pale skin, and attractive features are all more than adequate competition for my physical appearance. It's no wonder she caught Mason's attention. Just as I pick up my head, I see Lucas saunter out toward us, a cigarette and a lighter in his hand.

"Hey guys," he greets.

"Um, who is Mason with?" I ask without bothering to offer a friendly greeting in return. I like Lucas, but at the moment my rage is too overpowering to produce a cordial hello.

"Uh, I'm going to leave you guys to it," Rachel says slowly, as she backs away and travels down the side of the house to the back patio stairs.

Lucas takes a long drag on his cigarette before answering, "That is Jamie, and she is really sweet, fun and pretty." I turn my head away from him, angered at his remark. "Listen Tessa," he continues, "I spent the whole summer with the guy, and this is the first girl that he has been interested in since you guys broke up. She has a shot at making him happy, and although they aren't dating yet, he really likes her."

I whip my head back around to address Lucas, "She's not the right girl for him Lucas - I am." With that said, I turn from the party and stomp down the road toward my dorm. On my way, I take out my cell and text Rachel, telling her that I've gone back to the room, promising that I'm fine and that she should enjoy the rest of the night. I put my cell phone back in my pocket just as the drizzle turns into pouring rain. I quicken my pace, eventually breaking into a run. Entering my dorm room, I slam the door behind me, throw the empty water bottle across the room, kick off my shoes and collapse onto my bed. Lying here alone, I finally allow myself to sob uncontrollably. With my wet hair splayed across my face, I cry out of pain for having lost Mason in the first place, but also because of his blatant desire to move on.

After about five minutes, I tearfully get up and cross the room to the sink. I look into the small mirror hanging above the faucet – mascara is running down my cheeks, my hair is tousled, and my skin is flushed. I splash some warm water on my face, then pat it dry with my towel. I move to my dresser drawers, but stop mid-way as I glance back at my reflection in the full-length mirror. Overwhelmed with anger and resentment, I rip my damp t-shirt off my body. Running a hand briefly across the letters that I worked so hard on, my stomach churns with disgust. I ball up the t-shirt and thrust it into the trash can, desperate to get rid of anything that will remind me of how this night has ended.

chapter sixteen

(November, 2009)

"Alright folks, that's all for today," Dr. Wolf concludes as he closes his textbook and begins to move the podium off to the side of the room. "Also, don't forget to read chapter 7 before we meet again for Friday's class." I wearily stretch my arms above my head, still desperate to wake up, even though it's 11 am. Yawning, I slowly reach for my backpack when I remember I am meeting Rachel at the Hawks Nest for coffee before lunch.

"Hi, sorry I'm a bit late," I say after I meander through the front doors of the student center and see Rachel sitting on the bench beside the campus mailboxes.

Rachel looks up from a handful of letters and flyers that she must have collected while waiting for me. "No worries, I only got here a few minutes ago." She tucks the mail into her large designer bag that she uses for text books and her laptop, then swings it over one shoulder. "Should we grab a seat in the café? It's bound to get crowded in there soon." I nod and follow her to the back right hand corner of the cavernous space.

"Black coffee, please," I request at the counter. The student worker turns from the register after scanning my card and pours the coffee from a fresh pot. Taking the steaming mug, I walk slowly to the two-seater table in the back that Rachel has reserved. I plop down in the seat across from her and rest my elbows on the table, hunched over my mug. "Sorry," I mumble, "I can't seem to wake up today."

"Didn't sleep well again last night, huh?" she asks. From the bags under my eyes and my lethargic saunter toward the table, she already knows my answer.

I look down at my coffee. "I can't stop thinking about them, Rach." Shaking my head, I take a second to blow at the rising steam. "He's obviously happy with her, it's evident through their Facebook pictures. He has already gone to Greenville to meet her family, and although his Facebook status still says he's single, that's bound to change any day now."

"Have you talked to him at all since you saw him at waste-fest?"

Thinking back to how I reacted with Lucas several weeks ago when he told me about Jamie, I have wondered if he shared our conversation with Mason. Lifting my mug up to my lips, I take a quick sip before answering. "No, I haven't. I'm angry at him and hurt that he could forget about me so easily." I take out a pack of sugar and dump it into my coffee that is ironically as bitter as my heart. "It's just that I didn't see this coming," I state. "He approached me at your surprise party, he told me that he missed me over the summer, and he requested that we remain friends. Now, he doesn't even care." Considering how his words lack merit, I exhale sharply, then tilt my mug for another sip.

"Well Tess, for starters, you have to stop stalking him on Facebook," Rachel takes a sip of her chai tea, then continues. "How about, instead of staying in our room tonight, filtering through all of Mason's Facebook pictures like I know you're going to do, you come with me to the softball house. They are having a low key party, given that it's Wednesday, and I bet it will be mostly girls who attend."

I half laugh, "Why is it that whenever I'm down, you always suggest a party?"

Rachel shrugs her shoulders with a slight grin on her face, "I dunno, parties always make me feel better. Plus, it will distract you, and let's face it – there isn't much else to do in this pathetic, sleepy town."

Raising my eyebrows in agreement, I take another sip from

my coffee. We talk about classes for a few minutes while we finish our drinks. As I drain the last mouthful, I reach for my backpack beside me and say, "Thanks for meeting me here." I point to the empty mug, "I really needed that. I have a long day ahead of me - a couple of work hours in the admissions office, then practice." I heave my bag over one shoulder, glad that the coffee has helped me to see this day as salvageable, at least until the caffeine wears off.

* * *

After practice, I throw on my sweats over my workout clothes and drive to the cafeteria for a quick dinner. With a full stomach, I enter my dorm room, expecting to see Rachel. Glancing around our empty room, I remove my key from the door and remember that her practice was scheduled to end late today. Knowing that I still have a decent amount of time before I should start getting ready for the party, I sink into my comfy computer chair and stare at the black screen of my laptop. In this moment, I know that I have a decision to make – am I going to spend the next hour looking at pictures of Mason and Jamie, struggling as I click from one tormenting photo to the next, or am I going to do something productive with my time?

Still contemplating, I turn slightly from my laptop and see my Bible sitting on the corner of my desk. Concluding that I should spend some time with God in substitution for time on Facebook, I reach for my Bible. Flipping through a couple of chapters to my bookmark, my sorrow for my current circumstance creeps deeper into my psyche. I quickly decide that if I am going to choose to read my devotional in my room, then I will eventually start crying - and at the moment, I am sick of crying. So, I take my Bible and a few of my study materials, shove them quickly into my backpack, and walk briskly to the library where I can do my reading in front of people who will unknowingly hold me accountable to keeping my tears at bay.

Entering in through the side door of the library, I remove my hood from my head as I bask in the heat of the building. Scanning the multitude of students working on the many computers, I decide to walk up to the second floor that might be a bit less occupied. With each step, I begin to regret my choice to study God's word in a public location, realizing the awkwardness that my Bible reading might produce if other students happen to walk by and see what I am up to. As I reach the top of the stairs, I see an empty table at the back of the room and stride toward it, hoping that none of the meandering students will sit there before I have the chance to claim it. Settling into the chair behind my chosen table, I position myself so that other students cannot see my reading materials, but they can see my face – just in case any unwanted tears during my time of reading and meditation try to escape.

I spend the next 30 minutes absorbing God's truth. I know that my relationship with my Lord and Savior is nowhere close to where it should be, but I rest in the direction it's going and the form it's beginning to take. As I read in Job, many things come to mind, and I pray through the several struggles that surge through my mind and heart. Eventually, I take out my journal, and just as Dr. Murray suggested during our last counseling session, I begin to write the many questions and emotions I am facing.

November 11ᵗʰ, 2009,

Three years spent with him. Lots of highs, lots of lows. Now, apart from vivid memories, a broken heart is all I have left. How do you fall out of love with someone? Is it a matter of time, or deep down, will I never stop loving him? What's the point of falling in love anyway? Clearly, the pain outweighs the pleasure, at least from what I've experienced. "It's better to have loved and lost, than never to have loved at all" – not true. I wish I had never fallen in love with him. Can or will I ever fall in love again? Why would I if it went so badly the first time?

Would I still be in love if Mason's shadow didn't follow me around campus? Why did God open up every door for him to come to Callan when he could have stayed where he was – away from me? It seems at every turn, I am reminded of him - when I drive by his dorm building, when I interact with one of his teammates, when I hear his name at a party, when I see the distant outline of his form across campus. Things would have been so much easier if he had not transferred here. By now, I would have forgotten about him, just as he has forgotten about me.

An episode of "Friends" came on a couple of nights ago. One of the actors was explaining his understanding of the term "soulmate" – that one person you search for your entire single life. I don't know if I believe in having a soulmate. Is there a person created just for me; my perfect match, or do two people just meet and happen to fall in love? If I do believe in soulmates, then how do I determine if the person I met was the right one for me, or if I was spending all my time with the wrong person while my soulmate was out there searching for me? Was Mason my soulmate, and I screwed it up? Is God separating me from Mason so I can find the right guy for me, or is he using this time to prepare us to get back together, thus appreciating each other more, thanks to the time spent apart? What is God doing?

* * *

"Come on, Tessa!" Rachel urges. "Just think of all the people who have started drinking without us," she adds a nonchalant giggle to her arbitrary statement. Clearly, I am not as excited to arrive at the party as she is, and this is evident as I lag behind her even with the softball house clearly in view. When we walk in the front door, I immediately notice that the party is small, which makes me curious as to whether Rachel was actually eager to get here, or if she was just wanting to inspire a little excitement in me. I grab a drink and sit in the navy blue recliner tucked into the corner of the small living room, adjacent to the kitchen. Although I don't know many of the softball girls very well, I exchange friendly greetings as people bounce back and forth from the drinking game happening in the kitchen to the hookah hose being passed around the living room.

The party seems very mellow and relaxed. Rachel is in the kitchen, but this doesn't bother me as I sit and interact with the few athletes that I do know, taking a hit from the hookah as it's passed in my direction. As the smoke muddles my brain, I am momentarily brought back to my time in God's word earlier this evening. Wondering why smoking and drinking are always something I turn to regardless of time spent with God, I pass on the hose as it circles its way around the group back to me.

Casually sipping my drink, I smile at Rachel who slinks into the living room, checking to make sure that I am having a good time. She flashes an "ok" hand sign, asking whether I'm happy. I give her the thumbs up sign in return, pleasantly surprised that her idea to get out tonight was actually a good one. The reggae music peacefully drifts through the speakers of the T.V. inviting me to sway back and forth with the rhythm. Looking down at my watch, I am astounded at how quickly two hours have passed – obviously I'm enjoying my time here.

Suddenly, the calm demeanor of the party is interrupted by the abrupt entrance of a loud group of guys – the baseball team. While watching one teammate after the next filter into the small living room, I prepare my heart to see Mason. When he finally appears, it doesn't matter how much I try to prep myself, my gut reels at the sight of him. He quickly scans the room, and his eyes settle on me. To my astonishment, he heads straight for the couch beside me, and plunks down onto the cushioned seat.

"What's-up Tessa?" he asks; he is drunk.

"Have you been drinking a bit?" I inquire, although the real question I want to ask is, "Why have you completely forgotten about our past and our history, and moved on to Jamie so quickly?" but I restrain myself.

"Yeah, the boys all got together after dinner and we started playing some drinking games," he says. "Thought we would go searching for a party, so here we are," he laughs, then pops open a can of beer from the six-pack he's carrying around with him.

I get lost in his eyes for a moment, even if he is drunk, there is an air about him that is collected and cool, and his conduct makes me miss him desperately. I clear my throat preparing to take advantage of his mental state, "I see that you have a new girlfriend."

His eyes avoid mine as his tone gets a little more serious. "Yeah, Lucas mentioned that he had a little talk with you." He takes another drink before adding, "And she isn't my girlfriend yet, I have decided to take it slow."

"Probably best," I spit out, "I mean, if things ended so badly with your first relationship, why would you want to run head first into the next one, right?"

"Tess," he starts, "come on, don't be that way." He sighs, then adds, "We had a good three years, and now I hope that we can be friends."

I shake my head in dismay, "But that's just the thing Mason, we did have a good three years, and I feel like you have completely forgotten about them now."

I can tell that Mason is trying to sober up for this conversation, but having trouble doing so as he continues, "I haven't forgotten - my memories of all our fun times are still there. When we were together, we were always laughing." He picks up his head to meet my gaze. "You were my best friend, which is why I still want to be friends with you now."

Nodding in return, I accept that friendship is all he is willing to extend at the moment; however, I try to direct the conversation to our past, hoping that if I can remind him of what we used to have, then he might show signs of hope for a future together. Our conversation moves to my family, and Mason changes gears as if he is reading my thoughts, "I met Jamie's family for the first time last weekend," he says. "They are great - really friendly, and they invited me back this weekend. I think I am going to drive there on Friday."

My face burns with jealousy as I ask, "What do you know about her though, Mason? I mean, is she even a Christian?"

Mason looks down at his can of beer. "I don't know what's important to me anymore, Tessa. Ever since we broke up, I have been struggling to make sense of this whole God thing. I spent the summer with Lucas, and he and his family aren't Christians. His parents have a happy marriage, Lucas and his brothers are good guys, I mean – how necessary is God?" He takes another gulp of his beer.

Aware that this conversation is not going how I wanted it to go, I change the topic. "How's Lexi?"

"She's good, working as a nurse now in Wilmington and enjoying it," he responds. We spend a little more time talking about his family. As he works his way through another couple of beers, he shares details from his dad's life and career, and I can tell that the subject stirs a little emotion in him. I reach out and put my hand on top of his as I offer my condolences for his fading relationship with his father, and to my delight, he doesn't pull back from my touch.

Detecting his fragile state, I decide to take further advantage of the situation. I quickly stage a scene as I look down at my watch and somewhat gasp, "Oh wow! I didn't realize it was this late – I have to get back to my room." Looking up at him, hoping that he doesn't see through my façade, I ask, "Will you walk me back?" Pleading with my eyes, I add, "Rachel is playing cards in the kitchen, and I don't want to disturb her."

Mason hesitates for a second, then agrees. Without saying anything to Rachel, I slip out of the front door and into the chilly night air with Mason close behind. We start walking in the direction of my dorm, and I take the opportunity to bring up our many inside jokes and silly antics we shared while we were dating. He smiles at some of my words, but doesn't offer any reply. As we near my dorm, I comically break out with a verse from our song, "*My honey I know, you belong to somebody new, but tonight you belong to me.*"

At this, Mason stops dead in his tracks. "What are you trying to do, Tessa?" he barks. "You are the one that hurt me, you are the one that caused our break-up, you are the one that kept that secret from me, breaking our trust!" His voice begins to rise as he gets more heated, and before I can offer a retort, he continues, "You broke my heart too, you know! I had a tough summer, dealing with it all! And now that I've found a little bit of happiness, are you trying to ruin it?" Mason turns away from me and begins to walk back down the road toward the party. After a few angry strides, he briefly turns back to yell, "You and I are done! There is nothing left between us Tessa, including our friendship – this whole thing is over!" and with that, he stomps off, shoving his hands deep in his pockets, his frustrated puffs of breath visibly marking his trail.

Reeling slightly from his outburst, I am thankful I am only a few strides away from my dorm hall. I fumble for my keys, recognizing that I should be crying at his remarks; however, my emotions are conflicting. As I enter my room, I sit down on my bed and examine my heart. His words were hurtful, and I should be devastated at what he just said, so why am I not falling apart? Then, the realization hits, and the corners of my mouth turn up in a faint grin when I stop to reflect on the one word that is holding me together right now - hope - he wouldn't have shown that degree of emotion if he didn't care.

chapter seventeen

(November, 2009)

Getting out of bed, I turn up the heat in our dorm room and reach for my phone. It is 11:45 am, and I smile as I consider last night's great sleep, leading me to awaken late this Saturday morning. Since my encounter with Mason a couple of nights ago, I have slept much better. Feeling at ease, I scroll through my contact list and text Rachel, who left yesterday with the cheerleading team for the football game in Chester County, Pennsylvania.

Good Luck!! I will be lonely this weekend without you, but I'm glad the football team has made it this far in the season! Cheer hard – crossing my fingers that we come out with another conference win!

I put down my phone and cross the room to our mini fridge. Taking out a yogurt, I peel the lid off and plop down at my desk. As I reach for a spoon, I glance up at my laptop screen while reflecting on Mason's comment that he would be traveling to see Jamie's family this weekend. I wonder if our encounter has made him think twice about his plans. Just to confirm, I run my finger across the touchpad of my laptop and open Facebook.

Ignoring my new notifications, I navigate to Mason's Facebook page. A pang of sadness stabs my heart as I stare at his profile picture – a picture of Mason and Jamie kissing. My thoughts go back to the first time Mason and I kissed during that surprise late night visit where we stole a moment at the end of my driveway. That moment became memorable as it led to the most perfect kiss I ever had. I remember Mason slowly drawing my face into his, gently holding the back of my neck as his lips met mine; exuding such confidence while exploring the exhilaration of his first kiss ever.

Something wet hits my finger and splashes across the touchpad. I reach up to touch my damp cheek, unaware that I had started crying – somehow, my mind knew to release tears without me commanding it. I rip my eyes from the image of Mason and Jamie, only to find something even more painful – Mason's relationship status has been changed from "single" to "in a relationship." My eyes flutter closed, unwilling to look at the screen in front of me while tears slip from beneath my eyelids, one at a time, falling from my face to the cold surface of the desk below. Slowly, I reach up and draw my laptop closed, the click echoes in my heart, and I exhale with an afflictive shake of my head – Mason has made his choice, and it's not me.

Defeated, I rise from my desk and crawl into my bed. Slowly, I curl my knees into my chest and lift my comforter to my chin, as if the aching of my heart has affected ever bone and muscle in my body. My empty gaze takes in the room; I can still see the uneaten yogurt out of the corner of my eye, but I don't want it – I don't want anything but Mason.

It doesn't seem to matter that my body just woke from a 10-hour rest, my broken heart longs for the relief of sleep. As my breathing grows deeper, my mind circulates through my many thoughts – *I put myself out there the other night. I did my best to remind him of what we used to have. I replayed our past. I brought up our intimate details. I quoted our song – but after all that, he still chose Jamie.*

* * *

A sliver of sun shines in through a crack in the curtains. After sleeping away yesterday, I tossed and turned most of last night. Still not wanting to get out of bed, I shudder at the recollection of Dr. Murray's words, "If you face the temptation to stay in bed, find something to fill your time. Engross yourself with any activity that will help keep your mind off the pain." I groan loudly, taking advantage of our empty dorm room to express myself. There is really only one thing to do on a Sunday morning – go to church. I awkwardly acknowledge that after two plus years on this campus, I still don't have a nearby church I can call home, so I roll out of bed and trudge over to my desk.

Flipping open my laptop, I glare at my uneaten yogurt from yesterday that is starting to smell. Angrily, I grab the container, fling open my dorm door, stomp into the hall, and throw the yogurt into the large trashcan. Experiencing another surge of fury over Mason's new status, I storm back into my room and slam the door behind me, immediately regretting my decision as I consider some of the girls down the hall who are probably cursing the noise right now. My laptop screen floods the dark room with light, and I quickly exit out of the Facebook page that has crushed my hopes and dreams for a happy future. Trying to control my emotions, I open a new window and begin searching for contemporary churches in the area.

Driving the short distance to the nearest city in Virginia, I find a parking spot in the crowded lot. I close my car door, pausing only briefly before walking apprehensively to the front entrance of Y Church. The information on the church's website revealed that this non-denominational church is a congregation of young adults who are discovering the truth that "Why" is more important than "How" in reference to church and God – hence the name. As I enter the building, a warm welcome startles me from my thoughts. "Good morning!" announces a young woman who looks about 27 years old. Returning her greeting with a smile, I walk past the welcome team and cringe at her words – it is not a good morning.

I make my way down the winding hallway to the auditorium where contemporary Christian music fills the bustling space. I sit at the end of the row in the back of the room. Many people smile in my direction, and the crowd looks friendly. Thankfully, no one bombards me with greetings or questions about my personal life, which I skeptically assume would have been their feeble attempt to dig deeper into the reason I am here. After a couple of minutes to myself, the background music begins to fade as the band fills the stage.

The worship is good; the contemporary tunes share words of truth that I need to meditate on. When the band leaves the stage, I take a seat and prop my Bible, along with my journal, on my lap, preparing to take notes as the pastor shares his message for today. After digging in my purse for a pen, I lift my gaze just as the pastor reaches the podium, and even though my view from the back of the auditorium is a bit fuzzy, my eyes widen at the young, attractive man on the stage.

"Good morning, glad you all could make it this morning," the man says with a striking smile. "My name is Kurt, and I am the head pastor here at Y Church." My eyes adjust to Kurt's attractive features; dark eyes, tan skin, brown hair parted and slicked back in a suave manner. His button down shirt presses against his muscular frame, and although his upper half gives off the tone of professionalism, his jeans allude to his casual side.

Kurt's voice brings me back to reality, "Please turn to Jeremiah chapter 29." I flip open my Bible at his request and secretly wonder how any woman in the congregation is able to focus on the sermon. However, as he lays the foundation for the passage, I am quickly impressed by his ability to utilize phrases that irrevocably focus my attention on God, despite his distracting features. "Follow along with me as I read Jeremiah 29 verse 11, a verse that I believe will help connect you to Christ as some of you face current or future difficulties." Following his instructions, I run my finger down the page to the appointed verse, and as each word is spoken, I flinch at the undeniable truth that the verse reveals; providing uncanny personal relevance to my current circumstances.

"…For I know the plans I have for you," declares the Lord, "plans to prosper you and not to harm you, plans to give you hope and a future."

The rest of the sermon is a deluge of truth coming straight from this verse and offering tangible application in my life. I manage to make it to the end of the message without shedding a tear, although I find this feat to be unequivocally difficult. As I close my Bible and journal, I recognize that the notes I copied from the sermon will be a point of reference during many of the heartbreaks I will undoubtedly face in the near future. I take a deep breath and rise from my chair. Preparing to exit the auditorium, I surprise myself when I turn in the opposite direction and meander up the isle toward Kurt.

As I draw closer, my heart begins to thud loudly in my chest. I didn't have any intentions of speaking to the pastor after the message today, but given the significance of the information shared from the pulpit and my peaked interest in a man who is undeniably attractive, I close the distance between the church leader and me. "Hi," I greet as I extend my hand to shake Kurt's hand, "I'm Tessa, and I just wanted to thank you for your message today; it's exactly what I needed to hear."

Kurt takes my hand in his and shakes it firmly. "Glad to hear it," he replies. "I don't think I have seen you before, Tessa. Is this your first visit?"

"Yes," I respond sheepishly. Looking into his dark eyes, I feel my face begin to flush. In an attempt to cover up my obvious attraction, I continue, "I'm in my third year at Callan University, which is only about 20 minutes away. I was recruited to play volleyball there, and unfortunately, the sport demands most of my weekends, so I am unable to attend a Sunday morning service regularly." I shift my weight, hoping that my internal reaction to his presence is not evident on my face.

"Oh, volleyball huh?" He says. "My wife played a little bit

in high school…" – his wife. Dumbfounded, I sweep my hair over my shoulder and sneak a nonchalant glance at his titanium wedding band - how could I have missed this? He continues with a few words, but my ears hear nothing as I reflect on the strange feeling of sorrow filling my heart – as if I ever had a chance to begin with. I offer another quick thank-you for his sermon, then head for the door. Turning quickly away from the married man who momentarily caught my attention, my face twists in dismay as I recognize that Kurt is the first man I have been attracted to since Mason broke-up with me. It is odd that my heart felt a sharp pain at the mention of Kurt's wife, and now I am left grappling with my resurfaced pain associated with disappointments in love, almost as if I have discovered Mason's relationship with Jamie all over again. Escaping from the warm building, I huddle against cold mid-day air as I dash through the parking lot to my car. Opening the car door, I fling myself inside, slam the door shut, and drop my forehead onto my steering wheel – *what was I thinking?*

Merging into the traffic exiting the church, I don't care that yelling at an unseen presence in my car might cause nearby drivers to think I'm a lunatic. I yell at God anyway, desperate to verbalize the confusing thoughts and tormenting pain coursing through me. "I just don't understand what you are doing to me! You wake me up at the crack of dawn. You remind me of Dr. Murray's words. You lead me to a church that shares the perfect sermon. You allow me to be attracted to the pastor. Then you send me reeling at the mention of his WIFE? What are you doing to me, God? Jeremiah 29:11 says '…plans to prosper me, not to harm me,' this certainly cannot be what you had in mind!" Shaking my head in dismay, I continue, "God, why has Mason moved on from me – and why can't I move on from him? He has Jamie, and you know I want him, but I can't have him! And the first guy that I find attractive happens to be married! How is this giving me hope and a future? Why couldn't Kurt have been single, why couldn't we have fallen in love, allowing me to completely forget about the pain Mason has caused?"

Keeping my eyes on the road, I sag in my seat, accepting defeat as I soften my prayer. "What does it matter, anyway? Kurt is a pastor – and there is no chance I would ever date a pastor, fall in love with a pastor, or marry a pastor – it was over before I even knew he was married. Besides, how would the church respond to me being a pastor's wife? This goes beyond the pain that Pastor Max caused – my past has permanently scarred me - I could never be a role model in the church."

As my car winds through the back roads leading to campus, I am sad that I can never return to Y Church – not because of the mission statements or how the service was conducted, but because I can't face the pain that will resurface when I listen to another one of Kurt's sermons. However, I know that today's message was the perfect prescription for my current predicament, and although I clearly don't have any answers, the notes I took will carry me through the next couple of weeks until I am back at home with my family for Christmas, experiencing the comfort and love that Fair Havens Church offers.

chapter eighteen

(December, 2009)

"Hi honey," my mom greets from the back door as I lug my large suitcase across the carport, "I'm so glad your home for the holidays – this Christmas is going to be a great one!" Her smile is impossible to ignore, and although I can't bring myself to match her buoyancy, I admit that I am happy to be home.

"Thanks mom," I respond. I rest my suitcase at the bottom of the stairs just as my dad flies past my mom. "Dad!" I exclaim, "whoa, you startled me! Hey, aren't you supposed to be at work? It's Saturday morning…"

My father bounds down the stairs and gives me a warm hug before taking my luggage out of my hands. "I decided to go into the office after you got here – I was just too eager to see my daughter arrive home for the holidays!" he punctuates every word with enthusiasm. As my dad lifts the suitcase up the stairs and through the back door, I smile at how I am obviously loved.

My mother waves me in, and I feel a weight lift off my shoulders as I close the back door, leaving behind the cold winter air. My dad takes my luggage upstairs while my mom disappears into the kitchen still chatting away to me; however, I pause for a moment and lean my head against the door. I didn't know how badly I needed to be in the comfort of my home until this moment, where the familiarity of my surroundings seem to wrap me in a blanket of relief, and the smell of my mom's stew combined with the pine needles from our Christmas tree floods my thoughts with happy childhood memories.

"Tess?" my mom questions. I open my eyes and see her head poking around the corner, a look of concern etched on her face. "Are you okay, sweetie?"

I lift my head and offer a faint smile, "I'm fine mom – just glad to be home."

I follow my mom into the kitchen, and Chantel skips down the hall at the sound of my voice. Mom pours me a cup of coffee, and we sit on our worn but comfortable couch beside the decorated tree ready to talk the morning away. Dad interrupts our conversation shortly after taking my luggage up to my room to say goodbye, kissing my forehead and telling me how happy he is to have me home for almost a month. I enjoy the morning with my sister and mom, laughing and sharing details of our lives, conveniently avoiding the topic of Mason, and I find myself relaxing with the distraction of good coffee and great conversation.

"So, Tess…" Chantel starts. I can tell she is slightly hesitant to share whatever is on her mind, so she takes a sip from her mug before continuing. "I met this guy," she pauses for a moment, to read my body language. I quickly raise an eyebrow and smile at her, knowing that my sorrow toward being single shouldn't place a wedge between my little sister and me. Having witnessed my forced grin, she continues, "His name is Zander, and he is 6'6", with curly, dirty blond hair. He plays the piano and is studying aviation science - so he has his own plane! And although we just met, he promised to take me flying – isn't that so cool?" I smile and nod, hoping that my excited little sister doesn't see right through my forced delight.

"That's great, Chantel," I respond, and I really do mean it. Our family has watched a steady stream of suitors over the past five years. However, Chantel has never been in a serious relationship before, and I not only envy her genuine elation for what could develop between her and Zander, but also her naïve approach to falling in love. I get up to refill my coffee mug in an effort to hide my face from Chantel and change the subject.

* * *

After dinner, my family gathers in the T.V. room to watch our favorite Christmas film, *It's a Wonderful Life*. This annual tradition always moves me to tears toward the end of the film. Not only does George Bailey, the main character, discover true happiness in the midst of a terrible situation, but he realizes that God is not irrelevant, especially when we call out to him for help. Fighting the lump in my throat as the credits roll, I know that my raw emotions don't need any encouragement. I say a quick goodnight through my Kleenex, recognizing my need for some prayer time. I am grateful that my family doesn't bother to question my motives as I slip upstairs and prepare for bed.

I huddle under my fluffy duvet, turn off the lamp on my nightstand, and allow the darkness to engulf me. Shivering against the cold sheets, I turn my thoughts once again to the series of events witnessed in the movie, and just as George Bailey called out to God, I silently do the same.

Lord, thank you that I am home with family. I am blessed to have so many people who love me and who are willing to help me through my struggles. And thank you for reminding me that you carry me through difficult times. Right now God, I need you to carry me. I don't want to hurt Chantel's feelings about Zander - she should be able to talk about the guy she is falling for without me hindering her happiness. Although I don't want to be reminded of Mason, I know that every time I am, it leads me crawling back to you, desperate to find some answers. So God, this is my prayer − as I go through this holiday, surrounded by my loving and caring family, please remind me more of what I do have, instead of what I don't have. I pray that you will use the busyness of each day to distract me from Mason. God, I'm desperate to move on. Help me. Amen.

* * *

My mom's cell phone rings from her bedroom across the hall, jolting me from sleep. I squint one eye open, glancing at my alarm clock. It's only 8 am, and since I came home for the holidays almost a week ago, I haven't been awake before 10. Groaning, I curse the fact that my mom sleeps with earplugs, while turning up her cell phone volume to high. The ring tone stops abruptly, and her muted voice seeping through my cracked door tells me that my mom has answered the call. Rolling over in bed, I hear an elated cheer come from across the hall, and I immediately know that I will not be going back to sleep – this is the call we've been waiting for.

"Amber's going into labor," my mother squeals while bouncing into my room. I slowly swing my legs over the bed as she darts out of sight into Chantel's bedroom, "Quick, pack a bag – we are leaving in 30 minutes!" she announces to both of us. Although the abrupt wake-up call has me rubbing my eyes, hoping the action will remove any signs of grogginess, I can't help but smile at my mother's overwhelming excitement – she is undeniably eager to meet her first grandchild.

Sucking in a deep breath, I hustle out of bed, brush my teeth, change out of my pajamas, grab an overnight bag, and shove in a few random items hoping that I will have enough to wear over the course of our visit in Georgia. Unsure of the amount of time we will actually be staying with Shane and Amber, I poke my head into my parents' room, and I am immediately taken aback as I stare into the framed photo of me and Mason perched on my mom's nightstand. The sight of Mason's smile makes me feel as if I have been punched in the stomach. Thankfully, my mother is too distracted with her own packing to notice my reaction. I shake my head, clear my throat, and try to appear calm. "Mom, how many outfits would you suggest we pack?"

Without even looking up, my mom answers, "Pack for a week,

but I doubt we will stay more than five days. Today's the 17th, and we plan to be back before Christmas Eve." I nod, although I know she can't see me. Fighting the urge to look at the happy image of Mason and me, I return to my room, and resolve that now is not the time to address the issue with my parents – it will have to wait.

Within a half an hour, our bags are packed, and the van is backing out of the carport. Chantel and I are sprawled across the back two benches, enjoying the space as we snicker at our mom's exasperated comments and questions. "You packed the camera, right?" she asks my dad. Shifting into drive, my father reassures her that he has packed everything necessary, and I watch my mom begin to relax as I settle in for the long 13 hour trip.

* * *

The flickering lights in the cement cave cast faint shadows across the ramps, and although my mother is eager to park the van in the first available spot, my father shows appropriate concern for a potential parking ticket.

"You missed another spot, right there – we could have fit there!" my mother half yells. She has been antsy since Shane called to announce that Amber had delivered. Shane explained that both mommy and baby are healthy, and it was probably best that we were still hours away from the hospital considering Amber's need to rest and the hospital's medical procedures for the baby.

"Look, love," my dad calmly motions to the back corner of the third story lot, "this spot will suffice, and we only lost about a minute finding it." As he cranks the steering wheel and shifts into park, he adds one last comment to my mother, "You need to relax a little – you're too high strung..." However, my dad is unable to finish the sentence before my mom grabs the camera case at her feet and flings open the car door – I doubt she heard a word my dad just said.

Navigating through the parking garage and into the hospital proves to be a whirlwind of my mother's frantic questions and barking orders. At each turn she flings her gaze in every direction, looking for signs and not hesitating to flag down a passing nurse or doctor to confirm directions to Amber's hospital room. My mother proves her remarkable ability to multitask as she requests that my father call Shane to tell him that we have arrived and encourages both me and Chantel to speed up, all the while reading signs and weaving down several halls to locate the Labor and Delivery Unit. My mother has always been headstrong, but Chantel and I glance at each other, admitting with our eyes that our mother is in rare form.

Eventually finding the correct corridor, my family and I speed walk down the long hall revealing row upon row of numbered doors. As we near room 632, I begin to sweat from the queasy feeling of unease developing in my stomach. My family doesn't seem to notice, but I slow my pace, hanging back as an uneasy perspiration forms on my forehead. *What is wrong with me? I have got to get a grip, this is a happy day. I get to meet my niece for the first time, and congratulate Amber and Shane on becoming parents – so why am I so hesitant?*

Thoughts of my miscarriage and the mishap fill my mind, and it takes all the optimism I can muster to smother them. I silently tell myself that this baby was born to a happily married couple - not to two teenagers who got drunk and made a poor decision, or because a girl oblivious to her surroundings was taken advantage of in the dark hours of an after-party. I repeat my convincing thoughts one more time before I reach for the door handle. My family is already inside, and I can hear my mother's coos and the congratulatory remarks from my father. My family has yet to realize that I am not in the room with them, so I take a moment to slow my breathing as I collect my emotions in the stillness of the empty hallway.

Here goes nothing.

I push open the door, and as the scene in front of me reveals itself inch by inch, time slows almost to halt. The picture captured in the room is like a scene from a movie. The images before me are filled with happy smiles, tears in my mothers' eyes, and the proud look of love and adoration that only new parents can project. Out of the corner of my eye, I see a nurse shuffle from one machine to the next, checking monitors to make sure that my sister is progressing well – the ease in her gaze confirms that Amber is just fine. Chantel is facing the opposite wall with her back to me, and I can tell by the poise of her body that she is cradling our niece. She slowly turns in my direction, having just realized that the creak of the door announced a new arrival.

As Chantel meets my eyes, she asks, "Look, Tess – isn't she perfect?" My captivated younger sister gently lowers one arm so the angle of her embrace reveals the beautiful face of the baby I was somehow nervous to meet only moments ago. A small yawn escapes from my niece as I absentmindedly let go of the door and hear it click shut behind me. The image of her flawless features framed by a small pink cap and bleached white blanket washes away all of my worry and fear, and I walk slowly to her side in awe.

"Meet Marley Fletcher," Amber says, exuding pride, exhaustion, and unfathomable love at the mention of her daughter's name. In a split second, I am dizzy with bewilderment from the overwhelming sense of love I feel for this baby girl.

* * *

After two hours of passing Marley from one elated family member to the next, my father stretches his arms and with a yawn of his own, he announces that maybe we should go back to Amber and Shane's house to get some rest. Shane offers to go back with us, not only to show some hospitality, but also to let Sadie out and get some much needed rest himself. Reflecting on the sorrow that fills my heart at the idea of leaving Marley for a night, I quickly offer to stay at the hospital.

"If that's okay with you?" I add hastily, turning to Amber and silently praying that she won't have a problem with it.

"Yeah, that's fine," Amber replies, "just as long as you know that I am going to sleep and you're only option for a bed is that chair in the corner which extends into a narrow, five foot long cot." I nod in agreement, confident that I won't get any rest tonight anyway - not when I could spend the night lost in the beautiful features of Marley's precious face.

After discussing plans for the following day, I settle down in the chair, reclining at an angle where I can still see Marley's face while comfortably cradling her in my arms. I pat her tiny little bum and somewhat startle myself at the normalcy of the action − as if my body has always been familiar with the gentle rhythm of a mother. Marley's tiny hand extends above her head, and I place my index finger into her palm as she closes her petite fingers around it. Somehow, holding this precious bundle doesn't send me spiraling in pain over losing my own child. I know that God has a plan for my future, and that a child didn't fit into that picture. Now, in this exact moment, I can't even fathom why I would have felt anything but love for this little one as my eyes become heavy with exhaustion.

What seems like moments later, Marley's soft cries startle me awake, and I blink a couple of times, not aware that I drifted off. I look up at the clock on the wall and calculate that she still has about 20 minutes till her feeding. Sneaking a brief glance at Amber who is sound asleep in the hospital bed, I conclude that I should take Marley into the hallway to avoid waking Amber until it's necessary.

Just as the door closes behind me, Marley's cries grow louder in the abandoned corridor, and I lift her up so that her head is resting on my shoulder while patting her back. "Shhh, baby girl don't cry, let's let mommy sleep for a little longer." However desperate my tone, Marley's whimpers persist. So, as my last resort I try singing. Ironically, the song that comes to mind seems to be shockingly appropriate, *"Don't worry about a thing, cause everything little thing is gunna be alright…"* As I continue from the chorus to the verses of my favorite Bob Marley song, I consider the words and the relevance they have for my own situation.

* * *

It's the morning after Christmas, and I wake up just before 11 am, still recovering from the late night hours with Marley and the long drive home from Georgia. Christmas morning with my parents and Chantel was perfect. We took our time exchanging gifts as we usually do every Christmas morning, reveling in the simplicity of being with one another while making each series of events memorable; the stockings, Christmas breakfast, swaying to Christmas tunes, and opening one present at a time, so every member of the family can be a part of the joy and gratitude that each new gift brings.

"Good morning, hun," my dad greets me as I stumble into the kitchen, the bright mid-morning light causing me to squint. "Well, you look like you could use one of my very own, specially made lattes!" My dad throws two thumbs up in my direction before sidling over to his new espresso machine that my mother gave him for Christmas. "If you would just grab your mug from the cupboard, I'll start this baby up!"

With a shake of my head, I half snicker at my dad's annoying cheer. When I open the cupboard door, the image of the picture taped on the inside of the cupboard wipes the smile completely off my face – Mason, again. The sudden churn of emotion gripping my insides sends me reeling. Amongst a few other pictures of family members – both immediate and extended – here is a yet another picture of Mason and me. This photo is of us at the beach during the first summer that we dated. While splashing around in the waves, Mason came up behind me and gently tackled me to the sandy surface. Just as we both fell to the soft, wet sand, a wave pummeled us and the expressions captured on both of our faces reflect pleasant surprise and unexplainable happiness. My heart tightens at the memory, and I close the cupboard door slowly. "Here Dad," I say as I place the mug on the counter, speaking above the sound of the espresso machine that is rumbling to life. "I'll be right back."

While struggling to keep my emotions from visibly marking my face, I climb the steps to my parents' bedroom where I know I will find my mother. As I enter the room, my mom, who has just exited the shower, is toweling dry her newly dyed hair. At the sound of my intrusion, she tightens the knot to her bathrobe and turns to me. "Hi sweetie," she greets, but her smile fades to confusion as she witnesses the sullen look on my face.

"Mom," I whimper, "I can't handle the pictures that are all around the house. It seems like everywhere I turn, I see Mason's face, and I am so desperate to move on." Pointing with an accusatory finger at the framed picture on her nightstand, I continue, "This one, the photo taped to the inside of the kitchen cupboard…even the collage of high school pictures on my massive bulletin board in my room – they all have to go." With my final remark, I break down in tears. Admitting that our house should be free of all traces of my ex confirms once and for all that he will never return.

As I fall to my knees at the side of my parents' bed and bury my face in their comforter, my mother comes up behind me and gently places her hand on my back. "I'm sorry, Tess," she whispers. "Your father and I should have been more sensitive. To be honest, we didn't realize these pictures would cause you pain."

My shoulders shake as my tears spill onto the pattern of my parents' bedspread, the wet drops beginning to form splotchy pools of darkened color. Eventually I reduce my sobbing to silent tears. "I know we have already had Christmas," I mumble. "But is it too late to ask for one more present?"

"Not at all, what would you like?"

I heave a sigh, knowing that this moment was coming and dreading it. "I want my room remodeled. Everything in that room reminds me of Mason; his face in the collage, the gifts he has given me, the sticker he taped on my nightstand, the stuffed animals tucked away in the corner that he enjoyed kicking around. All of it reminds me of his uncanny ability to frustrate me and make me laugh at the same time. He's no longer a part of my life, yet my bedroom is still filled with his presence." Wiping my face, I offer one last remark, "I just can't handle it anymore, mom. He's gone, and I want to move on too."

My mother nods, and the look of empathy in her eyes tells me that she is willing to do everything and anything in her power to help me move forward. "Of course I can do that Tessa," she assures me. "Why don't you go spend a day or two at Rachel's, and by the time you return, your room will be brand new."

chapter nineteen

(April, 2010)

The Hawks Nest is overflowing with university students. I add to the numbers as I weave through the crowded space, the base music pumping through the speakers and pounding in my ears. I decide that the back corner will be the best place to escape the volume and catch a good view of the step team's performance. The campus has been buzzing all day with the exciting spring activities scheduled for the evening. Once the step team performs, the cheerleading squad will be doing a dance routine, then the crowd will move outdoors to a big bonfire surrounded with games and activities led by the campus's fraternities and sororities.

Standing alone in the corner, I look around at the crowd. Rachel had asked me to come see her performance, then she promised we would participate in the many events around the bonfire afterward. The new song filling the room spurs a group of guys gathered in front of the speakers to dance. As their sagging pants and talented rhythm draws attention, I cheer with the crowd at their enthused movements. My eyes once again scan the multitude, then stop when I see Lucas slip in through the front door with a couple of other baseball players. I hold my breath, waiting to see Mason, but thankfully his face doesn't appear.

With a heave of relief, I glance down at my watch, realizing it was good that I arrived early. Although the step team's performance won't start for another several minutes, the room is already packed, and I am wondering if it can hold any more students without infringing on the sectioned off stage. My thoughts come to a screeching halt when I feel an unexpected tap on my shoulder. With a startled turn, I swivel to meet the familiar shaggy hair and goofy grin of Mason's roommate.

"Hi Lucas, you having fun tonight?" I raise one eyebrow, and tilt my head with a small grin.

"Yeah, this place is crowded," Lucas looks around the large room packed with people.

I glance at the group of baseball guys standing behind Lucas. "Where's Mason tonight?" I ask, but immediately regret this question when I consider the options and prepare myself for the answer. It's been six months since we've spoken, but I'm pretty sure I know how he fills his time.

"He left after practice today to stay the night with Jamie," he says, confirming my theory. "He's always skipping out on classes to visit her during the week," chuckles Lucas. "You know Tessa, I think you're a great girl – but Mason must really love Jamie."

My heart drops at his words. Mason really loved me – and although I know I ruined our relationship by breaking his trust, neither our break up nor our current circumstances can erase what we had. At this point, I don't care if my words will upset Lucas, or if Lucas will eventually share this conversation to Mason. "You know what, Lucas," I start, "I know I screwed up, but Mason really loved me. And yes, he has every right to move on with Jamie, but what we had was real and even he can't deny that." My face flushes with resentment, and at this point I am regretting my decision to move away from the speakers; I know if we were close to the thudding music, this conversation would not be possible.

Lucas's grin fades and he gives an awkward tug on his wrinkled t-shirt. "Yeah, but Mason wouldn't have sex with you – him and Jamie have sex all the time."

Pain rips through my heart, and I have to fight the desire to stomp out of the crowded hall. My chest sags slowly from the hurt, as if my heart is being compressed from Lucas's words; yet, deep down, I expected this to be true. Of course they're having sex. Mason shows no indication that he is following God, he has a gorgeous girlfriend, and he seems to be willing to sacrifice part of his education for her. However, the fighter in me wants to turn around and shout at Lucas - to tell him that sex isn't an accurate way to measure true love, but I don't. The step team begins their performance as the lights flash and the music pounds. My eyes are following their movements, yet I see nothing. My mind can't seem to focus on anything else but my depleted sense of self-worth. Between my miscarriage, my mishap, and my unrelenting love for Mason, I can't seem to find a reason why I even exist anymore.

* * *

My hand runs up the smooth wooden railing of the staircase as I make my slow ascent to my bedroom. Exhausted, I climb the steps slowly and consider, yet again, what Lucas shared with me the night before. I couldn't sleep much last night, thinking about Jamie and Mason together, and now that I am home for the weekend, I know what I have to do to get rid of Mason for good.

I open the door and once again take in the foreign surroundings of my newly decorated bedroom. The once green and yellow room, filled with items from my childhood and high school years, is now painted a blueish-gray color. The single bed pushed against the back corner has been replaced with a queen-sized bed arranged in the middle of the room, covered with a simple comforter and a display of white and orange throw pillows. The only other pieces of furniture include a white dresser with a framed mirror above it, a small stand supporting a modern piece of art angled in the far corner, and an adjacent bookcase displaying my high school trophies, metals, and several framed pictures of my family and friends. I place my small overnight bag in the corner of the room I am still getting used to. I know I asked my mom to remodel it in hopes that I would forget about Mason, but the truth is, his memory lives in my heart, and I will carry him wherever I go.

After dinner, I lock myself in my room, knowing what I need to do to solidify that my relationship with Mason is actually over. Honestly, the reason I asked my mom to remodel my room is because I struggle to do what I know needs to be done, but not this time. With renewed determination, I reach on my tip-toes to bring down the many boxes that line the top shelf of my closet. My mom informed me that she saved all the pictures from my past that were taken from my walls, kitchen cupboards, and picture frames. Sitting on top of my many childhood memories are the pictures that were banished months ago. But now, the time has come. I need to get rid of these pictures that only cause pain as I let go of my last shred of hope that Mason and I might eventually get back together. I don't even know who Mason is anymore; the only thing I do know is that he has moved on for good.

Setting aside an empty box for any pictures that involve Mason, I begin to sort them one by one. I toss in pictures of homecoming, prom, summer trips, pool parties, Christmas mornings, New Years Eve gatherings, and so much more. I throw in the many notes and paper flowers that he left on the windshield of my car. Taking out a personalized CD that Mason made for me, I run my finger down the list of songs, each one serving some sort of significance. An unexpected burst of anger surges past my sorrow as I look at the title of the song we were going to play for our first dance at our wedding. Now, Mason will more than likely marry Jamie. One thing hasn't changed about him; he has no intentions of wasting his time with a girl he couldn't marry. With a shake of my head, I place the CD into the box and pick up a stack of cards. I filter through them, but land on a Valentines card, and against my better judgment, I open it…

> *Dear Tessa,*
>
> *Happy Valentines Day. I'm not good with words, but I want you to know how much I love you. You are the best thing that has ever happened to me, and not a day goes by that I don't think of you. I love your smile, your laugh, your beautiful eyes, and your amazing personality. I can't wait to wake up beside you every morning. I love you.*
>
> *Mason*

These simple words evaporate my anger and leave me with my sorrow. I know that I will never have another relationship that will even come close to the love that Mason and I shared. After several minutes of crying, I eventually drop the card in the box. Ending my trip down memory lane, I tape the box shut and place it beside my bedroom door. I finally release myself from the locked room, emerging as if the air in the shrinking space was poisonous. Quietly racing to my car, I sit in the driver's seat, crack my window, and with a shaky hand, light a cigarette. I know I should be relying on God for strength, but somehow my emotions seem too overwhelming. As I sit in the quiet of my car, I lean my head back and close my eyes. After my second inhale, I shake my head, put out the cigarette and silently turn to God instead, praying for the strength to take that box to the dump the next day.

My Saturday morning passes as I fill my time, finding every excuse to avoid the daunting trip to the dump that I know is coming. Mrs. Hern has come over to spend the afternoon with my mom. With a pitcher of lemonade, an open back door, and a breeze that is gently flowing through our sun filled family room, the three of us make ourselves comfortable. Mrs. Hern asks many questions about my semester, how classes are going, and what's new on campus. We are all missing Rachel, who couldn't come home for the weekend, so I attempt to lift her mom's spirits by sharing the fun times Rachel and I have shared recently. We laugh the afternoon away, but eventually our time gets interrupted when my cell phone rings loudly from the kitchen.

I get up from the couch to grab it. "Oh, it's Rachel!" I turn the screen briefly to show Mrs. Hern before I answer, "Hi Rach, what's up?"

"Nothing really, at the baseball game right now." Rachel's voice hints toward her hesitation. "Tess, I'm actually calling to tell you some new stuff that just came up. Are you sitting down? It's about Mason…"

My stomach tightens at the sound of his name, and my mind races through all the worst possible scenarios. "Go ahead," I say. As my brow furrows, I watch the faces of both our mothers mimic my expression.

"Well, his coach got a report that Mason was missing a lot of his classes, and he has been temporarily suspended from the team." My jaw drops in unison with my heart. Baseball has been Mason's dream ever since I've known him, and my stomach churns, thinking this all could have been avoided if he had made some wiser decisions. Taking advantage of my silence, Rachel continues, "That's not all Tess. When Mason was visiting Jamie Thursday night, you know…" How could I forget, visions of the two of them have been skirting my conscious since Lucas shared that heart wrenching comment two nights earlier. "Well, he broke up with her that night."

I nearly drop the phone out of my hand. "What?" I half mumble, confusion clouds my mind, and I feel like I am going to be sick.

"Not just that." Rachel clears her throat, "He's at the game now, and while I was sitting with him in the bleachers, he shared all this with me, and he asked how you were doing."

My face contorts with a range of emotions. *He asked about me.* Not entirely sure how to handle my thoughts, I fall into the recliner, cover my face, and sob. Shocked by my reaction, my mom and Mrs. Hern surround me with love and comfort as I share the new information I have just learned. After an hour of working through my emotions with them, examining what has happened, and questioning many things, I know I need to be alone. In the stillness of my bedroom, I look down at the box of memories sitting beside my door, and I can only reach one conclusion; there is still hope, and with that, I decide to hang on to it for a bit longer.

* * *

While getting ready for a party at the softball house, I reflect on all that has happened in the past week. My emotions have certainly been conflicted since I received Rachel's call on Saturday, and the angst I have been feeling seems to grow with each passing day. Half expecting Mason to call or text, I have been keeping my phone close. Now it's Wednesday, and as I finish putting on my mascara in the mirror above our sink, I conclude that apart from not hearing from him, it's even stranger that I haven't seen him all week. Between his class schedule, meals in the cafeteria, and having the same circle of friends, we might have at least crossed paths. Thanks to our small campus, we have seen a lot of each other over the past few months, although we both avoid conversations. His last words echo in my memory every time we get around each other, and I know that he meant every word he yelled at me that night, communicating his desire to drop any connection that we may have had and move on. Hoping that he will eventually want to talk to me now that Jamie isn't in the picture, I send up a little prayer just as Rachel opens the door.

"Wow, you look good!" she says with a smile. She comes to stand beside me in the full length mirror, and we stare at our reflection for a moment. Looking at my concerned features, it's as if Rachel can read my mind. She slings one arm over my shoulder and tilts her head to the side, resting it against mine. Without sharing a word, my best friend knows my pain, and I consider my desperate need for both her encouragement and God's presence in my life.

The party is a hit and helps to distract me from my confusing emotions. Having sipped from the same bottle all night, I conclude that the last few mouthfuls of my luke-warm cider are not worth finishing. My desire to get drunk has yet to return since the night of the mishap, and I pour the remaining contents down the drain as I prepare to turn in for the night. Just as I leave the kitchen, a group of boys join the party, and my heart thumps in my chest as I see Mason's face in the middle of the crowd. He makes eye contact with me, but immediately drops his gaze to take a swig from his beer can. Rachel is already waiting outside to walk back to our dorm with me, but I know I need to speak to Mason despite my pounding heart and sweaty palms. Ignoring both the time lapse and severity of our last conversation, I meander to Mason's side and struggle to speak past the lump in my throat.

"Hi." I squeak. My voice is shaky, and I realize just how nervous I am in his presence. Mason acknowledges me with a side-glance. I can tell he isn't drunk, and that he's aware of my knowledge surrounding his current circumstances. "Listen Mason, I'm sorry about baseball and Jamie and…"

"Don't be. It's none of your concern," Mason interrupts.

I immediately look at the ground in response to his callous words. With another attempt I say, "I know it must be upsetting, but…"

Yet again, Mason interrupts, "Tessa, stop pretending that you care. You and I haven't spoken in six months, and I told you that I'm done with it all last time we spoke." Mason lifts his beer can to his lips with an air of indifference. His harsh words stab my heart and his condescending tone steals the air from my lungs. As my face falls with anguish, I take once last fleeting glance at him before leaving, but his face, staring straight ahead, is void of emotion. Taking a step forward, he joins the crowd as if I am a ghost standing there speechless beside him. For a moment I stare at his back and wonder how a relationship as wonderful as ours could have turned this bitter in the year since it ended.

* * *

I thrust a pair of shorts, a couple t-shirts, jeans and a few nice tops into an overnight bag. After I quickly zip up the bag, I check my laptop one more time for emails, then click it shut. I grab for my keys just as I hear the door to our dorm unlock and swing open. I cringe, then turn sheepishly to face my roommate.

"What are you doing?" Rachel stands in the doorframe, textbooks in hand and laptop case slung casually over one shoulder. My best friend takes in the scene that evidences my early weekend departure.

I know that sharing my plans would reveal just how pathetic I really am, but I accept that my actions demand an explanation. "I just can't take it anymore, Rach. I know it's Thursday and that I have classes tomorrow, but I need to go home." I stare at Rachel, who looks back at me as if I am a wounded animal. "You can't talk me out of it. Honestly, I barely made it through my classes today, and I can't risk running into Mason again. My heart can't handle this anymore, and I don't know how I am going to finish the year on campus with him."

Rachel quietly sets her things on her bed before turning to me. "Tess, he's not worth failing any of your courses. Exams are two weeks away. Are you gunna be okay missing classes tomorrow?"

I shrug my shoulders, then offer, "Well, if you can take notes during our morning class, I know I can get the PowerPoint from Katie for my afternoon class. I just have to get out of here, Rach. I'm sorry." My best friend gives me a hug goodbye while reassuring me she is always willing to help in any way she can, but that she still wants me to make wise decisions. I contemplate Rachel's words as I trudge down the hall toward my car. The irony is not lost on me because if I was capable of making wise decisions to begin with, I wouldn't be in this predicament.

* * *

"Hello?" I call to an empty house. Silence is my only answer, confirming that I'm alone. "Guess I should have called..." I say to no one. As I enter my room, I steal a glance at the box of Mason's memories sitting on the floor beside the door. Anger and pain hit me, and I turn to kick the box. I sling my overnight bag on the bed and collapse beside it, refusing to look at the box. Instead, I focus on the small hole in the ceiling above my bed. The image brings back the memory of the time I let my sisters re-shape my eyebrows. While lying on my bedroom floor, I focused my attention on this hole to distract me from the pain of the plucking. Amber worked on one brow while Chantel worked on the other, none of us considering the possible outcome that each side would be different. I chuckle as I remember standing in front of the mirror with a permanent, unintentional confused look on my face. My sisters and I had a good laugh about it, but in the end they helped me color in my eyebrows so I wouldn't look ridiculous in public. I shake my head and glance out of the window - the sun is beginning to set, so I roll off my bed wondering what has whisked my family away for the evening. My stomach slightly grumbles, but I ignore the need for food as I meander into the bathroom, undress, and start a hot bath. Remembering that I promised Rachel I would text her when I got home safely, I wrap myself in a towel and slip back into my room to grab my cell phone.

Hey Rach, I'm home. Thanks for being a good friend. Love you lots.

Returning to cut off the running water, I place my towel beside the tub and put my cell on top of it, knowing that I should have it by my side when Rachel texts back. I slip into the comfort of the hot bath and exhale slowly. Somehow, the pain that Mason has caused since we spoke at the party last night has extracted every last bit of hope, leaving me exhausted. I close my eyes and try to focus on the warmth of the bath. My phone buzzes, and I lean over the edge of the tub to dry my hands, then grab for my phone. Expecting to see Rachel's response, my heart lurches at sight on the screen – it's from Mason.

Tessa, I know I don't deserve your forgiveness for the way I acted last night, but I want to apologize anyway. I'm sorry for the way I've been lately – I honestly don't know who I am anymore. Sorry.

My cell phone quivers in my hand as I read the text message over and over. Hung over the side of the tub, I cradle my phone in my towel as a precious messenger of hope. In shock, I cover my face as I slip down into the water, releasing tears that have wanted to come all day. I don't know how long I cry, but my tears find an end, and in the stillness, I watch the ripple as a drop from the faucet breaks the glassy surface. I conclude that the warm water has reached its extent of comfort; it's time to emerge and face my fears regarding my response to Mason. After toweling dry, I empty the bath, grab my phone and return to my room. Slowly lowering myself to my bed, I open the text, read it one more time, then respond.

Mason, you hurt me. It's hard to explain all that I have gone through this past year since we broke up, but there are some things I need to tell you. What I have to say should be said face to face though, can we meet?

Mason's response confirms his willingness to meet, and before I know it, I'm in the car driving toward campus to meet Mason at a high school that is a convenient half-way point. While driving, I am in constant prayer that the conversation to come will happen according to God's will, but I know I can't ignore my desire for a future with Mason. As I park in the middle of the abandoned lot, I rub my hands together and bounce my knee out of nervous anticipation.

In my rear view mirror, I see his Blazer roll into sight. My heart starts beating faster and faster, to the point that I think it might be visibly thudding in my chest as Mason exits the blazer and opens my passenger side door. The first moment together is an awkward one. I know I called this meeting to explain how I've felt since the day we broke up, but now that it's time to speak my peace, I can't seem to produce any words. Thankfully, Mason speaks first as he tries to settle into my front seat, "Sorry I'm late. Jamie messaged me on Facebook right before I left – I guess I needed to tie up some loose ends."

My stomach clenches and without thinking I blurt, "What did she message you about?" Desperately hoping that Mason had not reneged on the break up right before meeting me, I hold my breath for his answer.

"She's just confused about why I broke up with her, and I had to explain that things weren't going the way I expected them to go." Mason shakes his head, then turns slowly to face me. His blue eyes are glistening with tears that he has yet to spill and the look of loneliness in his gaze is undeniable. In the moment our eyes meet, I consider the fact that he doesn't have family to talk to, his roommate is incapable of offering credible advice, and he doesn't have a relationship with God; he needs me.

"Mason, I…" I hesitate. As I lose myself in his familiar gaze, my desperation to pour out all my feelings and emotions press in on me. I want to tell him how much I love him, to fall into his arms, to be held by him. Overwhelmed with my desires, I look away and bite my quivering bottom lip.

Luckily, Mason takes control of the conversation before I say anything. He knows I asked him here to express my emotions, so I keep my thoughts in check, knowing my time will come. I patiently listen to him explain all that had happened in the last six months. He tells me that he fell for Jamie quickly, and that he was so happy to be moving on from me that he didn't think through all the changes he was making. His words sting, but I rest in the fact that his relationship with Jamie has ended, so I don't stop him from sharing his heart. He explains that she didn't believe in God, and that he associated God with me, so he put God in the past too.

"I just forgot about everything I knew to be true." Mason looks out of the window, silent for a moment before continuing. "It's weird, but about three months into our relationship, Jamie told me she loved me. I told her I loved her too, but something felt…different." He shrugs one shoulder, but avoids my eyes. "I went to see her one night last week, and she asked if we could finally have sex." My mind reels as he emphasizes the word *finally*. I try to make sense of what Lucas told me last week, but I don't interrupt. Mason drums his fingers on his knee, "I said yes, and just as we were about to, I couldn't do it. I couldn't stop thinking about my relationship with you, my relationship with God, my past and everything that happened…and it was like I finally snapped." Mason throws both of his hands up in defeat. "I told her that we had to break up, that I had gotten so far away from who I used to be, and that I had to try to fix it. I made a decision that night to work on my relationship with God, and then my coach found out that I had been skipping classes." From the corner of my eye, I can see his fists clench, "It just seems so unfair – I know I broke the rules, but it's not like I'm failing anything!" He shakes his head slowly, "Anyway, when I saw you on Wednesday, I was still really angry about it all. I took it out on you, and I shouldn't have - I'm sorry."

We sit in silence, and I swallow hard, trying to figure out the appropriate response to all that he just shared. There is so much to ask, but somehow my starting point doesn't surprise me. "So, you and Jamie weren't having sex?" I ask.

Mason rocks back in confusion, "No. Why did you think we were?"

My mouth opens then closes, then opens again. "Well," I finally say, "it's just that Lucas told me at the step team performance that you had gone to visit Jamie that night, and that you guys had sex all the time…" My face flushes with embarrassment, as if talking about Mason behind his back to his roommate has been a common occurrence.

Mason slowly nods his head, understanding dawning. "Oh yeah, Lucas and I had a talk in the locker room before I left. I basically hinted at the whole sex thing because I knew that's what Jamie wanted, but I didn't explain that we hadn't actually done it yet…"

Relief floods my heart at the news, and without thinking I blurt out, "Mason, I love you." I'm surprised at my words, but I continue, "The truth is, I've never stopped loving you. I've been through a lot this year, and I've learned a lot from God, but one thing is for sure, you have never left my heart." In the silence that follows, I push aside thoughts of the mishap, confident that if Mason found out, he would never forgive me. Although I feel like I'm withholding the truth, I just can't bring myself to share those horrible details and face Mason's rejection all over again. But one thing I know he needs to hear is how much I've grown spiritually since then.

Eventually, Mason breaks the silence, and I prepare myself for the worst, "Tessa, right now I need to get my life straight. Things are really screwed up for me…and I can't focus on anything else except getting my life back in order." I nod my head, wiping at a tear before it falls. "But I do need your friendship. I'm glad to hear that you've been learning a lot from God this past year, because that's where I need help the most." I look down at my lap and smile as a small tear slides down my face. Eventually, I meet his gaze and verbally agree to do everything I can to help him re-establish his relationship with Christ. We fall into deep conversation, and I reflect on how glad I am that Mason does need me; it may not be in the way I want him to need me, but he does need me.

Oblivious to the time, we comfortably settle ourselves into the familiarity of our friendship. My confession of love does not place an awkward wedge between us, and I am astounded at how easily our conversation comes. As dawn begins to lighten the sky, we both realize that it's time to head out. So he slips out of my car, and I give him a simple wave goodbye. I start up my car, but I am not ready to leave yet. Instead, I watch the Blazer pull away, and relief washes over me as lift up a short prayer of thanks to God for this small victory. It's been an agonizing six months, but I finally have Mason back as a friend.

chapter twenty

(May, 2010)

The knock on my dorm door produces a grin that spreads from ear to ear as I rush to answer it. Mason has been dropping by the past two weeks for Bible studies in between classes and exam studies. We are half way through exam week, and most of the campus will evacuate this weekend. Even though we are going back to the same town, I am enjoying my time with Mason as we explore the Bible together in my dorm room.

"Hi," I greet, trying my best to hide my elation, while painting my face with a simple smile.

"Hey, what's up?" Mason steps across the threshold, puts down his backpack, and settles in my desk chair. Rachel closes the closet door that was hiding her presence, startling Mason. "Oh, hey Rachel – I didn't know you were going to be around tonight." Rachel usually slips out to do some studying in the library while Mason and I meet, so Mason's response doesn't surprise me.

"Yeah, I only have one exam left, and I'm just reviewing vocab for it – I know most of what I need to know, so I figured you guys wouldn't be a distraction." She waves her hand in a nonchalant manner as if to say "carry-on and pretend I'm not here." Going to her desk, she slides into her chair with her back to us, cutting off the conversation.

Mason nods at her explanation while he reaches down to grab his Bible. I climb onto my bed beside my desk and we settle into the comfortable positions we claimed during the first time we met for a study. Leaning my back against the wall, I open my Bible and begin. "I thought we would pick up in Psalms, chapter 46."

"That sounds good," Mason replies while flipping to the passage. His eyes focus on the text, but I take advantage of his distraction to drink in his face. He lifts his gaze to indicate he has found the chapter, and I quickly avert my eyes; he knows I love him from my profession during our meeting in the high school parking lot, but he has not reciprocated those feelings, and I don't want to make my desperation obvious.

"Right, should we start?" I inquire. Mason looks back down at the page and nods. I begin to read in a hushed tone so that Rachel can still focus on her work, "Chapter 46, starting at verse one. 'God is our refuge and strength, an ever-present help in trouble'…" Reading through the passage, my focus remains on the first verse and the astounding truth it offers. I am reminded of all that I have gone through, and how God worked in my heart during those difficult times. I finish the passage with verse 11, "The Lord Almighty is with us; the God of Jacob is our fortress." Mason and I both remain silent for a moment as we absorb the impact of these verses.

Mason's tentative words break the silence, "I'm learning just how true this passage really is." He runs his finger down the lines, reviewing it one more time before continuing, "I haven't considered God much since I moved to South Carolina with Lucas this time last year, but with all that has happened in the past couple of weeks, I know that I need God's strength more than anything else to get me through my troubles."

We talk about the passage and the meaning it has in both of our lives. I tell Mason how this passage has proved to be true in my past when I struggled through despair. I'm glad that I am able to speak on the topic from experience, although Mason still has no idea what caused my lament, and thankfully he doesn't ask. Eventually we end the hour long meeting with a short prayer, in which I avoid voicing my litany of struggles. He packs up his Bible and thanks me for our meeting.

"Yeah, no problem – I've really enjoyed our studies these past couple of weeks. When are you leaving campus?" I ask.

"I have my last exam on Friday morning, then I'll pack everything up and head out Saturday sometime." Mason slips his arm into the other strap of his backpack, settles it in place, and opens the door.

"Wow," I say. "I'm impressed that you can pack everything in one day. As you can see, Rachel and I have already started…." I point to our emptying shelves, closets, and half packed boxes visible under our bed as evidence. Rachel turns at the sound of her name.

"Well, I guess I'll see you on Santa Monica in a few days," she says with a snicker, then waves goodbye. Mason chuckles and gives a short wave before closing the door on his way out. I get off the bed to put my Bible back on my bookshelf when I notice that Rachel is staring at me. "You know," she starts, "you have really grown in the last several months. I was listening to your study, and the depression you experienced over Mason must have really drawn you close to God." I nod, unwilling to explain that Mason was only half of the equation. Rachel looks down at her lap, "I've never gone through the pain that you've gone through, Tess. My life has been pretty easy, minus what our family went through with Pastor Max. But after listening to your Bible study with Mason, I wonder if I am going to need something difficult to happen in order for my relationship with God to deepen." She ends her observation with a contemplative look.

Reflecting on her statement, I offer, "Not everyone has to go through tragedies to deepen their relationship with Christ, Rach."

"Yeah, you're right," she says. "You know, I think it's time that I got my relationship with God straight. Next year I will be preparing for my career, and I need to focus on God as I plan my future. I spend too much time partying and drinking and not nearly enough time studying his word like you and Mason have been doing these past couple of weeks."

I smile at my best friend, understanding there is nothing that compares to the love Christ offers and wanting Rachel to experience that as well. "I would be glad to help you get on the right track, like I've been helping Mason."

Rachel nods, "I would like that." However, her small smile fades into a frown. "Tess, I do need to warn you to protect your heart when you're around Mason. You've been through too much to sink back into despair. It's obvious that Mason is happy being friends, but I sense that's all he wants."

I look to the door where Mason was just standing. I know Rachel is right, but it still hurts to hear it. "I'll protect my heart," I offer as an empty promise. It doesn't seem to matter whether Mason and I are not speaking to each other or if we are the best of friends; I love him, and I will never stop loving him.

* * *

My phone buzzes on my desk, and I move away from packing up boxes to answer it. "Hi Coach," I say into the speaker, "What's up?" Coach Greenly explains that she needs to call together a meeting before the team leaves campus after the final exam day tomorrow, and asks me to send a text message to the team about our meeting in the gym at 6 pm tonight. "Sure, I can do that," I respond, wondering what this emergency meeting could be about. However, I keep my questions to myself as I say goodbye and hang up. Since I am the sole captain for the team because Katie graduates in a week, I send out a mass text to all returning players. I revisit my packing while responding to my teammates' replies. Everyone except Destiny confirms they are coming, but that is no surprise, Destiny never replies to my team messages.

The team convenes in the back corner of the gym near Coach Greenly's office. Once we are all there, Coach Greenly joins us from her office with a thick folder in hand. However, most of us are distracted by the attractive male in his mid-thirties who is following behind her. The man is mixed race, and his beautiful complexion seems to highlight his dark eyes and excessively white smile. My brow furrows upon seeing him, trying to connect the dots before Coach Greenly makes her announcement.

"Thanks for coming on such short notice, girls," Coach Greenly announces as she approaches the group. "I actually called this meeting to tell you all that I will not be returning as your coach next year." My face falls with the news. Not only will I be losing my co-captain next year, I will also be losing my coach. Several of the girls offer their surprise either with a mumble of confusion or a look of shock. Coach Greenly briefly closes her eyes and puts up her hand to stop all the noise before continuing, "I know it's not ideal, and I'm sorry that the news came so late, but I wanted to have another coach in place before I made this announcement." She turns to the man, "So, with that said, this is Coach Mark Jameson, your new head coach." Coach Jameson flashes his bright smile at the group, and the girls all nod, their gaze showing grief for the change, but accepting that we have no other choice. I look around at the girl's scowls, but my eyes narrow as I catch the look on Destiny's face. She is not upset at all, unlike the rest of the team. Instead, she has a smile plastered across her freckled face and one eyebrow raised as she checks out our new coach from head to toe.

Coach Jameson brings my attention back to the issue at hand. "Girls, I know how difficult it is to lose a coach, and I'm sorry that you are faced with this news so close to your summer vacation." He turns to Coach Greenly, "But your coach has entrusted me with you all, and I will do everything in my power to produce just as much success, if not more, next season." I raise one eyebrow at his words, strongly disliking the vibes of pride and self-assurance he is exuding. Coach Greenly offers a quick thanks, then explains Coach Jameson's history, trying to affirm his qualifications for us, but I am left with a nervous pit in my stomach. Coach Greenly goes on to explain that she received a job offer from a division one team in Virginia, and none of the girls can deny that this is a big opportunity to advance her career. When she is finally done with her speech, she removes a stack of stapled packets from the folder and explains that, with the help of Coach Jameson, they have designed a work-out program for our summer to ensure we all keep in shape. She passes a packet to each athlete, and half the girls groan at the detailed exercises. As I examine the new activities listed in my packet, I am suspicious that Coach Jameson had more influence on the choices than Coach Greenly did. After a bit of discussion, Coach Greenly announces that it is time for us to introduce ourselves to our new coach. We go around the circle, offering our names, positions, and our upcoming year. The last player to introduce herself is Destiny, and I notice that she must have weaved her way slowly around the back of the group in order to position herself directly beside Coach Jameson.

"I'm Destiny," she greets, as she moves her hair to one side, exposing her bare neck, "I'm an outside hitter - yes, I know I'm short for an outside, but you haven't seen me jump," she adds flirtatiously. "I'm an upcoming senior," she throws in a small pout, as if to communicate her sorrow for only spending one season with Coach Jameson. At this point, the rest of the team figures that Destiny's introduction is finished, but she surprises us all when she continues, "We are really glad to have you with us for this next season. We are so sad that Coach Greenly is leaving, but we know that you will be an excellent replacement." She reaches out to shake his hand, and offers a seductive smile with her obvious flattery.

If my nose wasn't already turned up in response to Destiny's introduction, it definitely does when I watch Coach Jameson linger in the handshake, then offer a warm smile in return. I immediately wonder why a nicely built, attractive, young man is so eager to accept a position coaching a female team when most of his coaching experience has been with males. I shake my head slowly, and I know I may be reading into the situation more than the rest of the team, but the look in Coach Jameson's eye makes me uneasy.

chapter twenty one

(June, 2010 – July, 2010)

It's a week after my birthday, and the summer offers a sweet relief from all my semester studies. My family and Rachel planned a day at the beach for my 21st birthday; we soaked up the rays while lounging around in beach chairs and drinking hard cider. Even though it is now legal for me to drink, the thrill of getting drunk is lost, leaving me with the pleasant experience of relaxing with my family while enjoying an occasional beverage.

I slump up the stairs lethargically and throw my gym bag on the floor beside my bed. The hours of work in the Callan admissions office while I was at school adequately provide enough spending money throughout the school year. However, when I returned home I knew I needed a summer job to cover my present costs, so I started working at the front desk of our local fitness center. Considering the new work out plan Coach Jameson has implemented, I concluded that working at a gym would be a great incentive, so I work during the day, then exercise after my shift. Plopping down on my bed, I look out my window and revel in the fact that the sun is still shining brightly, even at 5:30 pm. I reach down to untie my shoes, preparing to slip into the shower, but the buzz of my phone in my gym bag stops me before I leave my room.

"Hey Rach, what's up?" I greet.

"Hey, so I just got invited to a party tonight in South Hermon," Rachel says. I roll my eyes thinking back to our conversation a month ago about spending less time partying and more time focusing on Christ. I prepare my answer, ready to hold Rachel accountable for her wish to follow God more closely, but she continues, "And I know that I would normally be up for a Wednesday night party to lift my spirits halfway through the week, but I'm done with parties."

My head tilts to the side and I smile, considering my best friend's commitment to her words, "Wow, Rach!" However, I don't get a chance to continue.

"But, I still want to do something to lift my spirits," she interrupts. "So, I went online and searched for college and career church services in the area, and there is one tonight at a church only 45 minutes away." Rachel's voice grows more animated with each new detail, "It starts at 7:30. I know it's short notice, but will you come with me? I can pick you up…"

I eagerly agree while Rachel shares some of the details from their website. However, I have to cut her off, assuring her that she can explain it all in the car. If I'm going to get ready and eat before we leave, then I have no time to chat on the phone. I hang up with a huge grin, excited for all this night has to offer.

* * *

It's Tuesday night, and although Rachel really enjoyed the service last week, she explained that she was busy and couldn't go this week. So, in an attempt to recruit someone to go with me, I corner my little sister in the kitchen and plead with her. "Chantel, this mid-week service is awesome – you have to come with me tomorrow and give it a try!" I say. Chantel is a homebody, and a large gathering of unfamiliar people can sometimes overwhelm her, so I take the next few minutes to emphasize the Biblical truth in the message instead of the crowd.

"Umm," Chantel pauses, contemplating my words. "Well, what time does it start?"

"7:30, and it ends at 9. It's only 45 minutes away, and I will drive." I raise both eyebrows, tilt my head to the side, and offer a pout. I can tell Chantel is seriously thinking about joining me, so I clasp my hands together in a plead-like fashion, just to show her how desperate I am for her company.

My little sister giggles at my gesture, "Okay, I'll go." She shakes her head, then her eyes widen, "Actually, I bet Zander would enjoy it as well. I'll call him and ask if he wants to go with us!" Chantel skips out of the kitchen to find her phone, and although I am excited that my sister has agreed to join me, my shoulders slump a little at the idea of inviting Zander. It's not that I don't like Zander, he is sarcastically funny – my kind of humor, and he shows obvious signs of his commitment to Christ, but now I am going to be a third wheel on an evening that I had planned. I straighten my shoulders and march out of the kitchen, making for my phone. If Chantel is going to invite Zander, then I am going to invite Mason. I consider that the evening has potential to exude signs of a double date, but the one thing that I am convinced will sway Mason's decision is that the trip is to a contemporary mid-week church service.

I pick up my phone from my bed and open our recent chat conversation. It may be a bit obsessive, but I often review the conversations that Mason and I have over text. Our friendship is so natural, and we usually text about funny or insignificant things throughout the week. If the conversation moves to a more serious topic, mostly surrounding God or a question about faith, then we will call each other. Thankful that our friendship has grown stronger over the summer, I text Mason about the service tomorrow night. I barley have time to sprawl out on my bed before my phone buzzes with his response. A smile sneaks across my face as I read his text communicating his willingness to tag along. I feel a quick flutter in my stomach as I excitedly text him back with the details.

* * *

The beat from a popular rap song pumps loudly through the speakers - the instrumental version without the lyrics keeps it appropriate for a church service. I glance at Mason on my left, who is taking in the flashing lights, thudding music, and mass of people as we enter the auditorium. The look on his face reveals how impressed he is, and the four of us amble through the crowd to seats in the far corner of the large room. While settling in our chairs, I reflect on the ride here and how easily Zander and Mason connected. There weren't any uncomfortable silences or awkward pauses in the car; instead, the conversation flowed easily and the topics of discussion were intriguing. The worship begins as we are called to stand, and my thoughts from the ride are interrupted as the band starts up.

"That really was a great service," Zander exclaims as we exit the church building. His dirty blond curls catch a small breeze, and I almost chuckle thinking that he must get more wind on his face then the rest of us, considering he towers over the crowd at 6'6". "Did you hear the guy on the keys? He's almost as good as me." We all laugh at his joke, and I watch Zander turn to catch Chantel's reaction. I know he is smitten with my younger sister, and I don't blame him – she's gorgeous. However, I love the way he shows little signs of how much he needs her, given that he is quick to cover up his infatuation with a sarcastic joke.

"Ice cream anyone?" I suggest nonchalantly, trying to hide my desperation for this night to continue. The group quickly agrees as we get in the car and unroll the windows. Chantel and Zander climb in the back, and while I adjust my rear view mirror, I am not surprised to see them settle into a comfortable cuddling position. I steal a glance at Mason, who is still unrolling his window on the passenger's side, and I contemplate his enthusiasm for an ice cream stop. *Is he just eager for something sweet to cool him off, or is he enjoying the night with me as much as I am with him?*

* * *

Anxiously checking my phone once again, I re-read Mason's text inviting me to his birthday celebration tonight. I can't believe that it is July already. The summer is flying by, filled with work, workouts, and the regular Sunday and Wednesday night services, but this is the first social event outside of church Mason and I have shared. I check the time again, wishing my co-worker would walk through the door and relieve me from my shift. My knee bounces as the minutes tick. I manage to say goodbye to a few sweaty members walking out of the gym before relief floods my face at the sight of my co-worker slipping in through the door. We exchange places at the front desk, I grab my purse, say a quick farewell, and dash to my car, eager to arrive home and get ready for Mason's birthday dinner.

I finish curling the last strand of my hair, check to make sure my make-up is perfectly in place, and filter through my closet for the ideal summer outfit. I pick out a few options and try them on in front of my full length mirror. Swiveling with each outfit to catch every angle, I finally decide on a grey and blue flower printed dress. The thin spaghetti straps on my shoulders reveal a bit of my nicely tanned back and chest, but I don't feel overdressed or scandalous in this outfit.

Pulling out of the driveway, I navigate the short distance to the most popular Mexican restaurant in town. Once I find a parking spot, I read Mason's latest text explaining that the group is inside. I walk through the front doors and slip my cell phone back in my purse as I scan the many tables. The volume coming from the back room is an indication to both the group's size and location. I turn the corner, and sure enough I find a long table filled with Mason's friends – mostly high school buddies who are back in town for the summer. I begin a quick scan down the table, looking for Mason, but halfway through my group inspection, a voice from behind startles me.

"Hey Tess – sorry, I just had to slip out to the bathroom. Have you been here long?" Mason's smile offers a warm welcome as I swivel to face him.

"No, I just got here. Happy birthday, by-the-way!" I hesitate slightly, but in that split second, I decide to take advantage of our encounter away from the group and give Mason a hug. Just as I lift my arm and prepare to move closer, Mason's eyes dart back to the table and he moves quickly to his seat.

Thanks - grab a seat wherever there's a free one," he says over his shoulder. I'm left standing there awkwardly alone, so I swing my purse from one shoulder to the next, trying to play off my desired hug as a need to shift the weight of my bag. Although I can feel my face flush from embarrassment, I know I have to face the group. I turn to scan the people again, thankful to find everyone distracted - looking at the menus and reaching for the bowls of chips and salsa spotting the table. My eyes stop when I see Lexi, I had no idea Mason's sister was going to join us tonight. To my surprise, Lexi's blue eyes, that shockingly resemble her brothers, are filled with sympathy. She must have witnessed my attempt to hug Mason and recognized how Mason quickly brushed it off as if he didn't notice.

Lexi smiles quickly to cover up her look of pity, then she pats the seat beside her, beckoning me to sit. I smile back and meander to the opposite side of the table, looking down at my feet the whole way hoping and praying that my red face will return to its tan color before I sit. "Hi Lexi, it's so good to see you again," I offer as I settle in beside her.

"How have you been, Tessa?" her question is voiced oddly. I wonder if her tone seems a bit distant, and consider it could be because I am no longer Mason's girlfriend, or maybe because she knows why we broke-up and is still feeling defensive for her brother's sake. Yet, the moment I lift my eyes, I see that her gaze is soft, and I feel like the scene she just witnessed moments ago has created compassion in her, as if she could see my longing for

Mason and hear the desire of my heart.

"I've been alright, thanks." I quickly grab for a menu and focus my attention on what I want to order rather than focusing on the interaction between Lexi and I that has communicated so much more than what we actually verbalized. Over the next hour, I have a chance to catch up with Mason's friends. I nod at all the right times, and smile with the group, yet I can't kick the sickening sense of rejection from the attempted hug. Toward the end of dinner, I push back my plate that is relatively untouched, and I grow quiet as the drinkers around me get louder. The waiters come out of the kitchen and place a sombrero on Mason's head while singing "Happy Birthday" in Spanish. Mason takes the tequila shot offered by the staff, but he cringes with the swallow. Most people around the table have just turned 21, and they are taking full advantage of their new privileges. At the other end of the table, I watch the guys order Mason a couple shots, but he slides them over to Braden who nods with acceptance while his surfer hair tosses back with each gulp. I have to chuckle at Braden's willingness to take those shots for Mason while sharing stories and entertaining the crowd, but my attention is mostly focused on Mason.

"Party at my place tonight!" Braden announces to the group. Obviously this party is a spontaneous drunken decision, but Braden is persistent. "Come on Mason, let's go man," he slurs.

Mason smiles and nods, but I can tell that he is not keen on making a night of it. "Okay, okay. I have to pay the bill, then we will leave." But Braden doesn't seem to hear him as he stands from the table, coercing the rest of the group to follow his lead. Everyone gets up except Lexi, Mason and me, but in the silence of the rapidly evacuated room, we quickly recognize there are not enough sober drivers in the group. Lexi jumps up and takes off after the guys, hoping to catch them before they squeal out of the parking lot. Mason and I sit for a moment, breathing in the stillness that surrounds us.

"You're not paying for everyone, are you?" I ask, breaking the silence.

"Yeah, my dad gave me money to go out tonight and bring a group of people with me." Mason shakes his head, "I wish he could have been here with us, but he had to leave earlier this week for another business trip. I guess he thought he would make up for that by offering to pay for everyone's food and alcohol." Mason speaks, but he never lifts his eyes up from the table to look at me.

I feel my heart sink. Mason has been surrounded by his friends all night, but I can tell he doesn't feel loved or valued. "Well," I start, hoping to pick up his spirits and reveal to him that he can count on me as a true friend, "I will pay for my own meal. Maybe I can save you enough money to go out and celebrate another time this week." I snicker, but Mason doesn't respond. Not wanting to leave the table, I rest my elbows on the surface and prop up my face. After a few moments, Mason looks up at me.

"Tessa, you're my only real friend," he says. I know I should be happy at his confession, but his emphasize on the word friend only confirms the fear that has been creeping into my optimism all evening; he doesn't want anything else but friendship – and that's not going to change. This realization draws my gaze to the table. He continues, "I'm so confused about my life and my future." He sighs, then goes on, "I don't think I can go back to Callan next year - all I have left there are parties to distract me from God and sorrow from my past experiences." I reflect on his statement. He could be referencing our break-up or his break-up with Jamie, but I imagine he's mostly referring to his suspension from the baseball team.

"I thought you were invited back on the team next semester?" I lift my head to ask, figuring baseball would help solve all of his problems.

"I am," Mason says, "but I feel empty inside, and I don't

think it's baseball that I need." He shakes his head, "I want to do something with my life, but I just don't know what. I haven't even declared a major yet, and I'm about to head into my final year of university." With a look of defeat, he shrugs his shoulders, "I know it might not be smart, but I was thinking about withdrawing from school and just going into the Army." He studies my face for a second, then asks, "What do you think?"

This is such a deep question that I take some time to filter through my thoughts before answering. Tonight has proven that Mason only wants to be friends; Rachel warned me of this, but there has always been that little flicker of hope. If he is no longer on campus, then we can remain friends, but I won't have to see his face everyday as a blinding reminder of my love for him. I know how much I will want to talk to him, either over the phone or through texts, but if he is training for the Army, then there really won't be time for that. I'm confident I will never stop loving him, but maybe if he isn't around all the time, we could stay friends - and maybe, just maybe, I would have a chance to fall out of love. I slide my elbows off the table and straighten in my seat. As much as I want to be around Mason all the time, being apart might be easier. So with a saddened determination, I offer my conclusion, "I think you should do it…"

chapter twenty two

(August, 2010 – October, 2010)

A crack of lightening illuminates the dark grey summer sky. It's mid-afternoon on my last day of summer; tomorrow I will return to Callan for my final year of university. As I pick up my cell phone to check the time, I let out a long sigh that is covered by a simultaneous boom of thunder. My mom, who is busy on her laptop in the recliner across the living room, is oblivious to my boredom. While I sprawl restlessly on the couch, I contemplate the many other ways I wish I were spending my last day of summer.

"Oh, wow!" my mom interrupts my thoughts as she frantically scrolls down her laptop balanced on her knees, her poise hinting at the possibility that my lazy afternoon might just get more exciting.

"What is it?" I ask, but my mom doesn't look up. I wait a second to see if she is going to answer my question, but her eyes dart across the laptop screen that is out of my view. "Mom, what's going on?" I ask again.

My mom steals a side glance at me, and for a split second I can tell she is wondering whether or not she can avoid the ensuing conversation, but after a moment of hesitation, she gives in. "Mason has just enrolled in my World Lit course…"

My brow furrows. "What? No way - last month at his birthday party he told me he was going to drop out of school and go into the Army. That can't be right – maybe it's another Mason Pierce."

My mom's eyes return to the laptop screen as she attempts to clear my confusion, "I thought that might be the case too, so I checked his file – his address, birthday, and middle name are all the same. It's definitely Mason…"

Mason and I have chatted a bit in the last month; a couple of texts here and there, an occasional phone call, and of course the interactions we have at church. However, he didn't mention that he would be returning to ECSU instead of pursing the Army. My heart hardens at the news, he had every opportunity to share this with me, and he didn't. Frustration surges through me as I pick up my cell phone from the cushion and stomp upstairs, while punching in Mason's number.

"Hello," he answers the phone just as I close my bedroom door, and I have to fight the temptation to slam it loudly in order to communicate my frustration.

"Hey Mason, hope I'm not interrupting anything," I start, forcing my voice to sound gentle. I move across my room while he assures me that he isn't busy. The thunder rattles my window, so I raise my voice a little, "My mom was just looking at her classes for this semester, and she said that you enrolled in her World Lit course. Are you going back to ECSU this year?"

It sounds like Mason fumbles the phone, but it could have been the weather reverberating through the ear piece. "Yeah, I was going to tell you," he says. "I just made the decision yesterday, so this is all kinda new for me too." He pauses, but I don't say anything. "I went to see a recruiter about joining the Army. Then, I had a talk with my dad and discovered that he is supposed to retire in December. I figured this would be a good opportunity to spend more time with him, so I decided to stay in town and go to ECSU instead. Besides, it's kinda stupid to drop out when I only have a year left, right?"

My heart gives a painful throb. Obviously, the expectation I had for the Army to remove Mason from my life will not become a reality. His training would have taken him far away and left him with barely any time to socialize over the phone – thus giving me no option but to break ties with him. Yet now, not only is he going to be close by, he is going to be taking my mom's course. Maybe this is God slowly removing Mason from my life, instead of ending everything with one Army order. "Tessa?" Mason's voice brings me back to our conversation.

"Yeah, this is probably a better option," I quickly reply, but my heart stings with my deceptive approval.

* * *

"Alright girls, gather in please," Coach Jameson signals the end of our intense practice. I slowly jog to the center of the court where I bend over to rest my hands on my knees while sucking in deep breaths. Pre-seasons have always been difficult, but my body has never experienced this level of pain before, and although I know all this exercise will push for team improvement, I secretly hold a grudge against our new coach for it.

"This was the last practice of our pre-season, and I'm happy with how things have gone," Coach Jameson says as I pick up my head and wipe the sweat from my face with the back of my hand. Glancing up at the clock on the scoreboard, I groan at the time. It doesn't seem fair that he has worked us this late considering tomorrow begins our first day of classes. I look around at the team. Most of the girls are still trying to catch their breath, but Coach Jameson is distracted as he shoots Destiny a quick smile that I wasn't supposed to see. My stomach turns in disgust at the exchange between Destiny and our coach. Returning his focus to the team he announces, "Let's bring it in." As a Christian school, all team practices are required to end with a prayer, but Coach Jameson has avoided leading that prayer time so far. "Anyone?" he asks, which is his way of asking who would like to pray for the team. One of the freshman recruits offers, and after she pants out a short prayer, the team disperses to the locker room.

"Tessa, can you stay behind please?" Coach Jamison asks.

With my back turned to him, I stop mid-stride and grimace – I know I am the captain of the team, and I can't avoid personal interactions with the coach, but it's hard to hide my dislike for him during our one-on-one conversations. I turn and force a smile as I dutifully approach his side. "As you know," he starts, "tomorrow night is our first match, and I am going to announce the co-captain." I raise my eyebrows and find that my faux smile fades into a genuine one as I consider that our senior, right-side hitter is the perfect fit for the position. Glad that Coach Jamison is willing to discuss this with me and consider my opinion, I open my mouth and begin to offer my thoughts, but he interrupts, "I've decided that Destiny will be the co-captain this season."

My face falls immediately, and I can feel my cheeks begin to flush. He didn't want my opinion, he wasn't seeking my thoughts – he simply made the decision without my input. "That's not a good idea!" I exclaim, completely throwing away any remnants of respect I may have had for my coach moments ago. "Destiny and I do not get along, and the team chemistry would really suffer if she stepped up into a leadership position." Although my body is physically exhausted from practice, I feel every aching muscle tense with anger as I read his facial features and predict his retort.

"Well, I see Destiny as a leader - she's been proactive in making me feel welcome and respecting my authority. Also, she's a talented athlete, her statistics these last three seasons are outstanding, and she has shown nothing but loyalty for my coaching philosophy," he shrugs his shoulders, revealing his lack of concern for my opinion. "When I discussed the position with her, she didn't have anything to say about you. In fact, she thanked me for the opportunity and promised to do everything in her power to uphold my vision for this season." His dark eyes narrow as he continues, "You on the other hand, are the one complaining." I open my mouth to argue, but he throws up a hand to stop me. "I've made my decision, Tessa," he states, matter-of-factly. "If you don't like it, you can step down from leadership."

My shoulders stiffen at his inconsiderate and unreasonable solution. If I step down from leadership, the team doesn't stand a chance this season. It's not that Destiny isn't a talented player – she is, but she shows zero concern for the betterment of the team, and her selfishness on the court is blatant. I purse my lips knowing that there is nothing I can do about this situation, and with determination, I offer a curt nod and say, "I won't be stepping down from leadership, so it looks like Destiny and I are just going to have to make this work." Without another word, I turn and leave the gym.

* * *

"Hi honey," my mom says as she answers my phone call. "How was your first morning of classes?"

I groan in response, "They were fine, but that's not why I called…"

However, before I can go on to share my frustration surrounding Destiny and Coach Jameson, I hear a familiar voice coming through my mom's phone, "See you tomorrow."

Shocked, I ask, "Is that Mason?"

My mom stumbles to respond, clearly trying to figure out the best way to explain the predicament. "Yes," she eventually manages to say, "he stuck around a few minutes after our first World Lit class to chat."

"Well, why will he see you tomorrow then?" I ask. "The World Lit class is a Monday, Wednesday, Friday course – is he taking two classes with you this semester?"

My mom quietly sighs, "No, he is coming over for lunch tomorrow." I can tell from her tone she had decided not to tell me about this, but as fate would have it, I found out anyway. "He has some questions about the study he is doing through the book of Proverbs, so he has asked to meet with me and your father. Oh, honey – I hope that's okay with you!"

Thankful that my mom can't see me, I hang my head in response. "No, it's fine – I'm glad he can go to you for help." My mom goes on to explain that he needs to discuss the chapters with people he trusts - people who share his theological approach to the text, but I can barely hear her. My mind can't seem to erase the painful conclusion that Mason would have come to me with these questions if I were around.

* * *

I grimace as my arms sting from Destiny's previous serve that I shanked out of play. Trying to shrug off my frustration, I readjust in my position on the back row. We are nearing the homecoming match, and uncharacteristic of this season, practice tonight has not gone well for me. Ever since Destiny became co-captain, the tension on the court has thickened, but surprisingly, this season has been my best yet. My statistics are soaring through the roof, and my confidence level has boosted tremendously, despite my dislike for our coach. Although I am proud of the way I have overcome the circumstances of this season, my progress is certainly not showing on the court tonight.

"Tessa, that's the third ball you've shanked tonight." Coach Jameson calls out from across the gym. "I don't want to see another one." I sarcastically throw a thumbs-up sign at him, then turn to roll my eyes.

One of the freshman jogs quickly over to my position to give me a high five and offer some encouraging words. I mumble a quick "thanks" while we get ready for the next serve. My face is contorted with disgust, even though I really appreciate the overall sense of support that our team exudes. On the other hand, I watch Destiny sneer from the opposite side of the net at my frustration. Unlike the rest of the team, it is obvious she is taking pride in targeting me and impressing Coach Jameson with her hard-driven, top-spin serves.

The practice comes to a close, and although my confidence is a bit shaken, my heart is overwhelmed with the encouragement that many of my teammates have given me throughout the night. Destiny spent most of practice rolling her eyes or frowning at the compliments that the other girls offered me, but as I walk to the huddle, I know I can't let her jealousy dampen my optimism. Like every other practice, Coach Jameson extends the opportunity for someone to pray, and for the first time, my heart wells up inside of my chest at his offer - before I can stop myself, I say, "I'll do it."

Instantly, my mind starts humming with adrenaline. As I go to bow my head, I have to fight the temptation to renege my offer. It seems hypocritical for me to pray – most girls on the team have known me as a drinker and partier from previous years. However, I refuse to let that stop me, I know I've changed, so I begin...

"Lord, thank you for this team. Tonight I have felt the overwhelming power of positive attitudes and undeserved praise from many of my teammates. Thank you that we can come together and lift each other up as we consider the value of our team chemistry. I pray that everyone will continue to show this positivity on the court, especially as we go into our homecoming match this weekend. Amen."

I end my prayer - short, sweet, and to the point. As I lift my eyes I catch Destiny's face and see the visible signs of hatred etched in her features. I turn to leave the gym with a shrug of my shoulders. After my prayer, I don't have room in my heart to reciprocate her emotions. Although I felt I had a terrible practice, I put it all behind me as I bounce to the locker room with my teammates in stride. The team giggles in the locker room as we share the many inside jokes we've developed so far this season. Destiny is strangely missing, but I'm glad that the tension she inevitably stirs is not lingering in the atmosphere. I throw on my sweats over my practice clothes, preparing to walk into the cold early October night air, and my gym bag swings at my side as a couple of girls follow me out of the locker room.

"Oh man," I say to the girls as we walk down the side hall of the gym toward our parked cars, "I feel like my legs might give out while driving back to the dorms." The girls laugh, "I'm so tired…"

"Tessa." Interrupted, I hear my name called from inside the gym as I pass the double doors. I stop mid-stride and frown, then wave the girls on without me. I turn slowly and lean through the double doors to see Destiny and Coach Jameson standing at center court. Destiny's hands are balanced on her tilted hips, and her freckled face is contorted into a look of loathing. "Can you come in here please?" Coach Jameson demands.

My heart begins to beat faster and faster as I close the small distance between me and my obviously distraught teammate and coach. "Uh, what's up?" I ask. "Something wrong?" My mind searches for what could have upset Destiny, but I quickly reach the conclusion that if anyone should be upset about practice tonight – it's me. I played terribly, and Destiny was clearly using everything in her power to take advantage of that as she targeted me throughout the practice.

Coach Jameson takes a step closer to me, as if protecting Destiny from my aggression – yet there is nothing attached to my demeanor that would even hint at an attack on my behalf. Confused, I cock my head while waiting for his words. "Destiny has just brought something very serious to my attention." My eyes dart to Destiny as she shifts her weight slightly behind Coach Jamison. "Destiny says that she felt your prayer was an obvious attack on her, and I think she is on to something…"

My jaw drops from shock, "What?" I cry out, "That's not true at all! I simply wanted to thank God for the positive attitudes on the team."

Destiny drops her hands from her hips and steps into view. "That's a lie!" She points an accusatory finger at me, then continues, "I heard all the compliments that the girls were giving you tonight. You played terribly – you expect me to believe that they just came up with those compliments on their own. I've known for a while how you try to coerce the team to following your lead!" she huffs. "I don't know what you've said about me behind my back, but your prayer tonight just goes to prove that you are forcing them to believe I'm the negative one on the team – that I'm the bad guy and that they shouldn't listen to me on the court." She steels a glance at Coach Jameson who is nodding in agreement, so she doesn't stop there. "I know I'm not the most positive person – but you didn't have to make that so obvious in your prayer, did you?" she spits out.

For a moment, I am stunned into silence by her harsh accusation, giving Coach Jameson time to leap to Destiny's defense. "You know, Tessa – this reminds me of our conversation when I told you that Destiny would be joining you as co-captain. Apparently I didn't make myself clear, you BOTH are the captains, and it really sounds like you haven't been fair to Destiny in her new position, even though you assured me that you could make it work between you two." I want to defend myself, but he doesn't give me a chance as he continues, "It seems that Destiny has done all that she can to take on the captain responsibilities, and that you have been dragging her down. So, with that said, I am going to ask you to step down from your captain position – I will reassign someone to the role before our homecoming match."

My mind is spinning out of control. *How dare he do this!* My eyes dart back and forth from Coach Jameson's disapproving glower to Destiny's slightly visible smirk – as if she has planned this all along. Unable to come up with even one cohesive thought to produce a sentence from it, I quickly decide that the meeting is over, turn to the door, and march out. However, in those few steps before I reach the exit, my thoughts become clear, so I turn and hurl my comments at Coach Jameson, "This is completely unfair!" I heatedly yell. "You have not asked for my opinion since the moment you took over the team. You have favored Destiny this whole time, and that is only because she has sucked up to you from the first day you met the team!" Thinking back to how Destiny reacted to Coach Jameson's appearance, I seethe with anger considering how she lured him into her web – and he fell for it! "And you know what," I continue, feeling my face burn with resentment, "Neither of you have the right to interpret my prayers! When I speak to God, he knows my heart – and he knows that everything I prayed tonight was completely genuine! If anyone is scheming behind a captain's back – it's you two behind mine!" Having felt that I said enough, I race out of the gym to my car. Slamming the door shut, I collapse in the driver's seat and finally release my hot tears of rage.

* * *

My phone buzzes in my backpack as I leave the cafeteria and walk to the admissions office for work. I fumble for it as I reach beneath my textbooks. A cold breeze blows through my hair just as I wrap my hand blindly around my phone; I shiver from the air indicating that an early winter is around the corner, but the text from Coach Jameson on my screen sends a deeper shiver down my spine …

Please meet me in my office in ten minutes.
– Coach Jameson.

I shudder as I think back to the heated conversation that took place in the gym last night. I shared the details with Rachel when I got back to the dorm, then I tossed and turned all night – replaying the scene over and over again in my dreams. Now, I am sure that I will be facing the consequences for my lack of control; however, I have no regrets – I prayed from my heart, and if that's what got me in trouble, Destiny and Coach Jameson deserved what I said. I suck in a deep breath, and redirect my route for the gym. Sending a quick text to the admissions counselor saying that I would not be in to work this afternoon, I wonder if I should stop by my dorm and pick up some work-out clothes. Almost positive I will be spending the afternoon running as a punishment for what I said last night, I walk the distance to Coach Jameson's office contemplating the agonizing exercise he will undoubtedly put me through.

Apprehensively, I approach the closed office door and knock. I hear mumbles coming from the office, but I can't make out the conversation that is taking place inside. "Come in," I hear Coach Jameson say. The door creaks open as I enter, and I reel a bit at the sight of the university's Athletic Director seated in the chair across the small room. "Please take a seat," Coach Jameson directs. As I move mindlessly toward the vacant chair, I immediately consider that having the Athletic Director here to reprimand me is a bit excessive. I know I probably shouldn't have yelled at my coach, but this is a bit much. I sit down and raise my gaze to Coach Jameson who is proudly perched behind the coach's desk that I wish still belonged to Coach Greenly. I barely keep my scowl at bay as I look into his arrogant, dark eyes. "Tessa," he begins, "I'm sure you recognize our Athletic Director..." *What a stupid thing to say, of course I recognize him – I've been here longer than you have!* However, instead of speaking my mind like I did last night, I respectfully turn to the Athletic Director and nod. "After sharing with him your actions from last night, we have come to the conclusion that it is best you be removed from the team, indefinitely." My heart drops to the pit of my stomach at his declaration, "You will need to turn in your jersey by the match this weekend – you're done here."

chapter twenty three

(October, 2010)

Ilift my gaze from my untouched food and scan the cafeteria again. With a slight groan of shame, I complain to Rachel across from me. "They are all whispering about me, I know it. Some are even pointing, Rach – and what's worse, they don't even know why I was kicked off the team."

Rachel slides a hand across the table to grasp my arm. "Tessa, most of the students on this campus know how committed you were to that team. I'm sure they're just wondering what happened – not assuming you did something terrible." I roll my eyes as my best friend continues, "Seriously, Coach Jameson is an idiot – anyone who comes into contact with him knows that! But if you want, I will gladly stand up and make an announcement to all the nearby gossipers clearing your name…" Rachel moves to stand, and in panic, I grab for her arm, keeping her in her seat. A silly grin appears on her face, letting me know she was just joking.

Giggling at her efforts, I scan the crowd with a bit more hope. I suppose Rachel is right, if anyone actually knows me, they will know this embarrassing situation is not my doing. After all, what ultimately got me removed from the team was a prayer; maybe I didn't handle things like I should have, but at this point in my life – I'm not going to let anyone misinterpret my relationship with Christ.

Forcing the smile to stay etched on my face, I shift in my seat to consider the line of students at the food bar who are willing to risk a second helping. However, my grin quickly fades as I spot Tripp ambling toward our table. My adrenaline begins to pump as I spin back around in my seat. We haven't spoken since Mason and I broke up, and although we have exchanged a half-friendly wave or two over the past couple years, I can't forget the way Tripp attacked Mason over the phone the dreadful night of our break-up. My eyes are riveted on Rachel, but Tripp's proximity keeps me from saying anything to her.

"Uh, hi Tessa," Tripp walks up beside the table and quietly greets me.

Rachel makes an abrupt decision. "I'm going to get another salad," she says as she slips from the table, leaving Tripp and me alone.

I can't quite bring myself to return Tripp's greeting, but I give him a small smile and meet his gaze for a brief moment to acknowledge his presence. Although his green eyes and masculine build attract many of the girls on campus, my stomach churns at the sight of him – his features offer a sickening reminder of the terrible decision I made two years ago. "Listen," he starts, "I'm sorry to hear about volleyball. This must be really difficult for you, what with homecoming tomorrow and your senior night right after fall break." I keep my gaze focused on my uneaten pile of rice, and with a nod, I gulp back tears. In the last 24 hours since getting kicked off the team, I have thought a lot about these two big, back-to-back events and how I am going to miss out on all that I tirelessly worked towards this season. But before I get too enveloped in my emotions, Tripp continues, "I watched a lot of your games, and although I don't know your new coach, I do know that he made a stupid decision – regardless of what led to it."

I half smile in response to his kind words. "Thanks," I mumble, but I can't lift my gaze to meet his. Out of the corner of my eye, I see Tripp move to walk away, then decide against it.

"One more thing," he adds. "I know that we haven't spoken since you and Mason broke up, but I don't want to be your biggest regret…"

At this, I manage to lift my gaze to his face. His concerned eyes reveal that his wish is sincere, but when I look at him, all I see is the mistake I made, and it reminds me of how desperately I miss Mason. Yet Tripp's comment resonates within me, and for a moment I contemplate his words. "You're not my biggest regret," I say, and it's the truth; he isn't – my mishap is.

Tripp nods, knowing that our conversation has come to a close. He saunters off as Rachel comes up behind me and squeezes my shoulder. I close my eyes for a moment, desperate to put aside thoughts of the mistake I made with Tripp and my mishap. Refusing to give in to my tears, I grab my fork and play with my food instead. "Rach," I say, "I'm so confused. Why would God let me be kicked off the team, especially when it was a prayer that got me in trouble in the first place?"

Rachel takes a seat beside me, sliding her untouched salad onto the table. I scoot over on my bench to make room for her as she moves to put one arm around my shoulder. "I don't know, Tessa," she offers, "but one thing I've learned in the last few months is that God is in control, and he has a plan." I nod, and she continues, "We might not know what that plan is, but God is trustworthy, we just have to rely on him."

Her words are so genuine that I can almost manage a smile considering how much she has grown spiritually in the last several months. She is no longer suggesting another party to lighten my mood, instead she is giving me advice to trust God – *Rachel has come a long way.* "However," she interrupts my thoughts, "I really can't give you any advice on how it feels to be unjustly kicked off a team…I've never been there before."

I drop my head back against her arm. "Yeah," I say as the spinning ceiling fans mesmerize me for a moment, "but I know who has…"

With slightly trembling hands, I leave the cafeteria and dial Mason. I don't know why I am so nervous to talk to him – maybe I'm worried that Mason will side with Coach Jameson and misinterpret my prayer as well. However, I know Mason has been studying the Bible with my parents every week, and I hope that his growing wisdom will help him respond sympathetically. My confidence builds while the phone rings, and as I walk toward the park, I also consider that aside from Rachel, Mason is my closest friend.

"Hey Tess!" Mason answers enthusiastically. But his exuberant tone changes the more I tell him about what happened. When I near the end of my story, explaining how I was wrongfully removed from the team, Mason offers his sincere condolences, and I'm thankful that he can empathize with my predicament. "I'm so sorry to hear all this," he offers. "I know how I felt when I was suspended from the baseball team because I was missing classes, even though I made the Deans list at the end of the semester – it really didn't seem fair."

"Yeah, I'm just so confused right now," I say, fiddling with a blade of grass as I sit cross-legged in the middle of the campus park, absorbing the warm sunshine. "My season was going so well. My stats were great. I was leading the team with confidence. I developed really great relationships with the new team members, and I even accepted Destiny's role as the co-captain, although I wasn't exactly happy about it." Sensing that the conversation is coming to an end, I get up from the grass and dust off my backside. I pause as my tingling legs regain some of the feeling that I had been slowly losing over the last 30-minute conversation. As I turn to grab for my backpack, I see Tripp crossing the park toward his dorm. Nausea builds quickly, and I avert my gaze. Feelings of guilt and self-hatred immediately rise, thanks to our conversation at lunch. "Ugh," I grunt into the phone. Although Mason doesn't know exactly how my emotions are currently being influenced, my posture slumps, and I throw my backpack onto my shoulder as I say, "I think I need to get outta town…"

* * *

"Well, it's all settled then," my mom says over the phone. "Tomorrow - you, Chantel, and I will drive to Canada for Thanksgiving. Chantel and I will drive back mid-week, and I will book your plane ticket so you can return on October 16th."

"Thanks mom," I say with overwhelming appreciation. I knew I needed to get away from campus, and when I realized that the annual weekend family trip for Canadian Thanksgiving was looming, I was surprisingly grateful that I was free from my volleyball responsibilities so that I could join them.

Distracted for a moment from my packing and phone conversation, I make a mental note to remind Rachel that I will be at the homecoming football game to watch her cheer. I quickly tell my mom the plans I have, sharing my excitement over the fact that they will be honoring the senior cheerleaders and football players at the game tomorrow.

"We will leave before the sun comes up on Sunday in order to get to the cottage for dinner," my mom says.

"That's fine, I'll just come home tomorrow night after the game," I reply. "I probably won't be home in time for dinner, but I can manage to get there before 7."

At the mention of my estimated time of arrival, my mom's tone changes. "Actually…" she begins slowly, "there is something else I should mention about tomorrow night." I raise one eyebrow as I press the phone closer to the side of my face. "Mason has started a college age Bible study group through Fair Havens Church, and tomorrow is his first night leading it. He didn't feel comfortable meeting at his dad's house, considering his dad will be around more after his retirement, so Mason has asked to run it at our house."

My heart tightens at the thought of seeing him again for the first time since mid-August, and I feel an unavoidable flutter in my stomach. It seems easier to keep our friendship contained if all we do is text and occasionally talk on the phone, but I know I can't suppress my love for him when we are face-to-face. I swallow hard and try to mask my emotions in my reply. "That's fine," I assure my mom. "I can attend too, right? Besides, it will be great to hear Mason lead his own Bible study." My mother agrees with me and hesitantly begins to tell me all about Mason's spiritual growth and vision for the college age students at our church. However, the pounding of my heart is drowning out my mother's words, as I confess to myself that my anticipation to see Mason again is winning over my need to get over him.

* * *

I hug Rachel one last time with my car door open beside me, the engine running, and my bags thrown in the back seat. "Seriously, Rach – the game today was great, you did amazing, and I'm so proud of your commitment to cheerleading!" After Rachel thanks me and wishes me a safe journey home and to Canada, I get into my car, close the door, take a deep breath, then drive away offering one more wave through the open window.

I spend most of my drive wondering what my welcome will be like. With lingering shame, I lift up many prayers to God surrounding my permanent removal from a team I care for and a sport I love. My phone buzzes from the cup holder in my center console, and I glance down at the screen to see who is calling.

My heart leaps into my throat when I see Mason's name. This is consistently my response when Mason calls unexpectedly, but I steady my voice as I answer, "Hello."

"Hey Tess," he greets. "Can I ask you to do me a huge favor?"

I smile, knowing that I am willing to do anything Mason needs me to do. "Sure, what's up?"

"Well I just got to your parents place, but I forgot to pick up the ice cream for the group. Your dad told me that you should be on the way home from Callan now, so I thought I would call and see if you could pick up a tub from the corner store on your way in?"

"Absolutely," I offer. "I should be driving through town in the next ten minutes – is vanilla okay?" Mason tells me that vanilla would be perfect, then he thanks me before we hang up. I can't seem to wipe the silly smile off my face from our quick chat - and the fact that I will be seeing him shortly doesn't help.

The bell to the small corner store rings as I step through the entrance. Around the corner I can hear some heated accusations flying from a distraught customer. Trying to avoid the altercation, I turn down the side aisle and make for the freezer section in the back. Opening the frosted door, a fresh burst of cold air hits me in the face, motivating me to lunge quickly for the tub of ice cream. Hoping to avoid the growing tension on the far aisle of the store, I dash to the counter and go to take out my debit card so I can pay quickly and leave. While sifting through my wallet, I can't help but to hear the raised voices, which causes my stomach to tighten.

"Sir, I am very sorry, but we don't carry that item anymore," the store manager apologizes.

"This is absolutely ridiculous!" the angry man retorts. "I have been coming here for years, and I don't even get a heads up – how inconsiderate can you be?"

"Please," the manager starts again, "if you could just follow me to the next aisle, I'm sure we can find something that would be a suitable substitute. It's just that we have been losing money with the downturn in the economy, and we can't afford to carry what you're looking for anymore."

I cringe as I listen to the customer bellow his disgust while I swipe my card and pray the receipt prints fast. My heart starts to quicken as I hear the grumbling behind me getting closer - I don't want to get caught up in the unnecessary fight that this angry customer is trying to stir. The lady behind the counter hands me the receipt, and I grab my bagged ice cream, quickly stepping away from the counter with my eyes glued to my feet; however, my escape is not speedy enough, and I nearly run into the man standing directly behind me. I look up to offer a quick apology before racing out of the door, but when we lock eyes, my heart freezes in my chest – I'm standing face-to-face with Max Gilliam. My mind floods with the memory of when I last saw him; a smug look plastered on his face while my family and I were getting thrown out of New Creations Church, our world crumbling down around us as we stood there in the rain.

* * *

Still trembling in the driver's seat of my car parked in my parent's driveway, my emotions are wrapped in many layers of anger, frustration, pain, and sorrow. My short drive home from the corner store was a complicated one, and I had to pray several times to get through the temptation to pull over at a gas station and buy a pack of cigarettes. It's been months since my last cigarette, and I couldn't bring myself to erase all my progress, but if there was ever a time I needed one – it's now.

A tap on my window startles me, and I look up into Mason's questioning eyes as he watches me visibly shake over my steering wheel.

I quickly look away – embarrassed that I am caught seething from my encounter with Max. The driver's door creeks open, and in my peripheral, I can see Mason crouch down beside me. For a moment, he doesn't say anything, and I squeeze my eyes shut, secretly knowing how eager I was to see him, but not expecting it to be in this way.

"Tess," he says quietly, "what's wrong?"

And at his words, I crumble. "I just saw Pastor Max at the store when I stopped in for the ice cream." Tears start streaming down my face, but Mason doesn't say anything, so my thoughts come pouring out all at once. "I couldn't believe it – I have dreamt of that moment for years! Would I punch him? Would I hurl the worst insults I could possibly think at him? Would I laugh at him because he was the one who lost the battle of getting us deported? But no, I couldn't do any of that. All I could do was stare at him. He cheerfully said, 'Hi!' to me, and when I didn't respond, he had the audacity to ask how my family was doing?"

Mason fiddles with a Bible in his hands, and I take a moment to wipe my face as I quickly surmise that is why he is alone in the dark on the driveway – this is the Bible he always keeps with him in the car. He must have slipped out to get it just after I pulled up. Mason speaks, "I'm sorry, Tess." Then he asks, "What did you say to him?"

At this question, my face falls shamefully into my hands. "I couldn't say anything, I honestly stood there dumbfounded at his words and how cheerful his greeting was - as if we were long lost friends. I just shook my head, then left the store." I stomp my foot out of anger on the baseboard of my car. "I've been waiting for that moment for years, Mason – to finally give him a piece of my mind for all he did to my family. I wanted to publicly shame him the same way he publicly shamed us, and when presented with the opportunity, I literally shrunk away like a little coward."

I fume in my seat, so angry with myself for the way I handled it, and so ashamed that I wasn't strong enough to carry out the plan that I had been plotting for years. I nearly startle when I feel a warm hand slide slowly around my shoulder, and I reel from shock as Mason gently pulls me toward his embrace. I don't remove my face from my hands, but immediately, my anger melts away as I realize this is the first time Mason has touched me since the night we broke-up. My world has been flipped upside-down in one split second, and in his warm embrace offering comfort and care, I know nothing else matters but this hug.

chapter twenty four

(October, 2010)

A small yawn escapes as I step out of my back door in the pre-dawn darkness. I shuffle down the back stairs to our van in the carport, and the humming engine combined with the smell of fresh October air starts to wake my senses. I hug my pillow close to my body as I rub at my eyes, deciding that I probably won't go back to sleep regardless of the fact that it's only 4 in the morning. I watch my mother shift around our bags in the trunk, but my eyes are quickly drawn to my little sister who is getting settled in the back seat.

The passenger's side door creeks open as I plop down in the front seat and look back at Chantel, revealing my annoyance with the slant of my squinted eyes. "Oh yeah," she says innocently, "I was wondering if I could take the back seat and get some sleep for the first half of the trip…" I turn back around in my seat and snicker, I can't bring myself to respond with anger when she exudes such palpable gentleness with her words. I hear her rummaging through the packed luggage that is piled in the two vacant captain chairs while she mumbles, "I'm going to listen to my iPod now – goodnight." Through the rear view mirror, I watch her yawn as she sticks the earphones in her ears then buries her face in her pillow, which she has used to make a bed out of the back seat. I look around for my mother, who must have rushed off to grab some last minute necessities before we pull out of the driveway and travel north to the Canadian border.

Waiting in the front seat, I prop my legs up on the dashboard and fiddle with the corner of my pillowcase huddled close to my body. With a shiver, I turn on the heat in the van, hoping that the engine has now adequately rumbled to life and can produce some warmth. As the heat pumps out of the vents, my breathing becomes steadier, and I take the few moments I have before my mom appears to sort through my emotions regarding all that has taken place in the past couple of days. My heart is conflicted; I feel anger and sorrow for getting kicked off the team, yet at the same time I am excited for this trip to visit my family in Canada that wouldn't have been possible if I was still playing volleyball. My heart throbs with disdain over Pastor Max and our encounter last night, yet I felt immediate peace the moment Mason slipped his arm around my shoulder. I let out a long sigh, then startle in my seat as the driver's door swings open.

"Oh gosh, you scared me!" I tell my mom as she climbs into the van with a big smile plastered across her face. It doesn't seem to matter how early in the morning it is, she is going to visit her siblings and parents, and that prospect brings her obvious joy every time the opportunity is presented.

She turns to face me, "We have everything? Are we ready to go?" I give her a short nod and grin as she shifts into reverse. "Chantel's already asleep, eh?"

"Yep," I say as my shoulders quake with my silent giggle. I glance back at my little sister who is sound asleep already, "I really wish Amber were here with us." I return my gaze to the road ahead as I consider the few short visits we have had with my older sister since she has been married. We chat on the phone often, and she constantly sends pictures and videos of Marley over Facebook, but these things never replace the time I desperately want to spend with them.

My mother sighs, "I wish she were here too. I talked with her last night on the phone before you got home, and she is having fun planning Marley's first birthday." I laugh, knowing that we are still roughly two months away from the big event. Amber's creativity for an event such as this begins long before the actual day arrives. However, I admit that my spirits rise every time the event is mentioned. "And you know what else," my mother adds, "she and Shane are talking about getting pregnant again!"

I share my excitement at the idea of having another little bundle of joy join the family, but my thoughts shift to the baby I lost years ago. I cringe at the specific words that send me spiraling; pregnant, miscarriage, rape…

"What's going on in that mind of yours, Tessa?" I hadn't realized that I had been silent for almost a minute. With a short shake of my head I look down at my lap. I know that I have grown closer to my mother over the years, and our relationship has really mended as I have matured; yet, I wonder if I am ready to share everything that's on my mind. I take a deep breath, knowing that I need to share my thoughts that have remained bottled up for far too long, but I sneak another quick glance back at Chantel, just to be sure she is actually asleep.

"I've made a lot of mistakes in my life, mom…" We both are quiet for a moment, and it seems this one short sentence bluntly communicates my regret. I break the silence with a voice slightly above a whisper, "The miscarriage, the reason why Mason broke up with me, and…" I gulp, "the mishap." Visions flood my memory, reminding me of all the reasons why I hate myself, and why I would imagine God hates me too. Thankfully my mom speaks, distracting me from my self-loathing.

"Tess, the amazing thing about the God we serve is that we can bring all our faults to him, and our sins are removed from us - as far as the East is from the West." I nod, and she continues, "You may have made mistakes in the past, but God forgives you, and he is a God full of grace, ready and desperate to invite you back into his loving arms, even when you are riddled with guilt from the past."

This truth is tangible, I have experienced it first hand; however, I am still quick to retort, "But I'm a terrible person.

I have done too many things, I have experienced too much – I mean, honestly mom, God might forgive me, but who is going to want to marry a person as used up as I am?" My face flushes, and I quickly find that the heat coursing through the vents is overwhelming. I reach out to turn down the temperature, feeling my face burn hot with emotion.

My mom speaks, and I notice the smile that was plastered across her face minutes ago has vanished. "God has a plan. Don't underestimate the work he can do in your life, Tessa. The man you will marry will be understanding when you share with him your past; and yes, you do need to tell him about the mishap. As difficult as that might be, it's unfair to go into a marriage with a secret as significant as this one." She slides her hands down the steering wheel, almost as if she has lost the will power to hold her arms up any longer. "Besides," she continues, "you'll face times where it will be important for him to know your heart, and you will need to talk about your past in a healthy manner." My throat tightens, and I know she is right. Yet, I consider my future - I love Mason, so it's hard to contemplate ever falling in love with another person. However, I know I could never tell Mason about my mishap - he would only blame me for my promiscuous ways that he is all too familiar with, thanks to the mistake I made with Tripp. I'm stuck. It seems that God has destined me to be alone forever, and ultimately I admit that I have earned my loneliness.

The clicking of the tires as we cross the bridge into a familiar part of town brings me out of my trance. We pass the corner store where I had my encounter with Pastor Max last night, and I suddenly realize that my mother was in bed early, preparing for the long trip ahead; I never had the chance to tell her what happened. So, leaving the conversation about my mishap behind, I surge forward with this new topic, "Mom, last night I ran into Pastor Max for the first time since he kicked us out of New Creations Church." I verbalize the emotions that marked my heart the night before, opening wounds that have not had enough time to heal, no matter how long ago the incident was. I share my unwillingness to forgive this man for how he shamed our family, and I quickly realize how angry I still am at myself for not following through with my plan to put Pastor Max in his place. "And what's worse," I continue, "he hasn't changed! Max was yelling at the store manager for some ridiculous reason. He was making a scene and showing no concern for the manager's emotions. He was mean, and angry, and lacking any kind of godly love – you cannot tell me that he is a man seeking after God."

My mother takes a deep breath. After all I just blurted out, I know she is torn as she ponders her response. "It's not our place to judge other people's hearts, Tess. God knows where Pastor Max is spiritually, and he will have to stand before our Savior one day and give account for all he has done." She shakes her head, "But our responsibility is to forgive."

Although I know she is right, I struggle with the concept. "I can't mom." I grip the sides of my seat as I vent. "I have tried, and I know it's what God calls me to do, but Pastor Max is the reason I can't trust anyone in the church. I over analyze the actions of the pastors I've met over the years, and I know that there is no way I could ever trust any of them whole-heartedly. Sometimes they don't raise their hands in worship when I think they should, other times they speak about certain subjects from the pulpit and I wonder if they practice what they preach at home. I know the reason I struggle to trust any pastor is because of Max, but my wounds are still too fresh – I can't bring myself to trust the church, no matter how great Fair Haven's has been to us."

"But look at your father, Tess." My mom doesn't skip a beat with her attempt to alter my perception. "He is a good man who loves the Lord. He is a pastor, and he proves to you every day how a pastor can be trusted."

"Yeah, but see how he was treated at New Creations Church. Dad is one-in-a million; he is a pastor who actually practices what he preaches, and yet he was still trampled on by Pastor Max. And people in our small, gossip centered town see Dad as the corrupt one – as the pastor who didn't honor God with his actions! How twisted is that?" All this talk about church leaders makes me think back to the one encounter that I had with Kurt - the young, attractive pastor from Y Church. I stitch my eyes closed as I consider the unsteady position I had placed myself in when I allowed my attraction for him to compel me. Apart from my negligence regarding his marital status, I flirted with the possibility of a future with a man who holds a position in a church – and that is something I have promised myself I would never entertain. A shudder runs up my spine, knowing that Kurt is the only man who has managed to turn my attention away from Mason, even if it was only for a few minutes. Then I remember the hug Mason and I shared last night, and my stomach flutters. "Anyway," I continue, "Mason talked me through some things last night – and the Bible study he led really helped me move past my encounter with Pastor Max."

"Oh," my mom reveals her obvious eagerness to change the subject. "Tell me all about it! I was fast asleep by the time the study ended."

A smile flickers across my face, but I mask it with an internal acknowledgement that it would not be wise to tell my mom about our hug last night. She has tried to protect my heart from any pain surrounding Mason, knowing my desire to move on, but not hearing the details that keep me deeply rooted in my love for him. "Mason did an excellent job!" I begin with what I hope looks like a nonchalant shrug. "It's weird, but it's almost like he's a natural, which I should have seen coming given the last several studies we did together. He led us through scripture while providing the perfect application to our lives. And a good crowd showed up last night, all of them needing to hear the truth that was shared." I tell my mother about the group discussions we had concerning the harsh realities faced in today's society. I share the conclusion we reached last night and how it held so much truth; in the midst of the sinful world we live in, God's word proves to be blatantly relevant in our 21st century, day-to-day activities.

My mother flashes a secretive smirk, hinting that there is something behind Mason's biblical teaching that I am unaware of. Immediately, I assume this smirk is due to the hours they have spent together in scripture with my dad - and I know that they have journeyed a long way since his first day in my mother's World Lit class earlier this semester. Yet, no matter how curious I am as to how these studies with my parents have progressed, I still refuse to ask about them. There is the slightest stab of pain in my chest at the thought of my parents meeting weekly with Mason, and I know it's because of my desire to be the one by Mason's side as he works through scripture.

Even so, my heart swells with the love and pride I have for Mason. "And the way he hugged me last night while I was crying over Pastor Max…" The words fly out of my mouth before I am able to stop myself. I grit my teeth wondering if this is going to be an item in our conversation that my mom brushes over without a blink of an eye. However, I see her head swivel in my direction the moment the words are out, and I know I cannot take back what I have just shared. My ears turn pink, and I shift uncomfortably in my seat, feeling her gaze on me and wondering exactly how long it will take for her to turn her attention back to the road. The silence screams at me, and I know she is waiting for me to speak. I bite my lower lip; *it's confession time,* "Last night was the first physical interaction we have shared since the night of our break-up…"

My mother slowly returns her gaze back to the highway that stretches out in front of us, indicating the endless hours we have ahead. Now that I have brought the subject up, I can't escape it.

Yet, there is a small part of me that is grateful for being remiss - my mom needs to know how I feel about Mason. "Well," she puckers her lips, and I can see her attempt to procure the ideal response. "How does that make you feel, Tess?"

I spill from the inside out, unable to hold back what I know my heart longs to say, "I love him mom - always have, always will." And with that simple profession, it's as if the floodgates to my soul have opened, and the power behind the rush of my emotions is too strong to barricade. Before I know it, four hours have passed and I haven't stopped pouring out my heart. Eventually, I reach behind the passenger's seat for the bottles of water my mother packed. I take a long swig to placate my throat; I have never in my life spoken to my mom for this long. However, it's as if our relationship has grown deeper with every passing minute, and the evidence is tangible. In the back of my mind, I wonder how I could have spent so many of my teenage years fighting with the woman who has just heard everything there is to know about my past and my relationship with Mason, yet still loves me despite it all. I twist the cap on my bottle, place it in the cup holder, and lean my head back. My eyes flutter closed and immediately I realize just how exhausted I am. It's as though sharing my heart and dissecting all the compartmentalized feelings I have been withholding has eased my mind and given me an eerie sense of peace.

I hear my mom reaching behind her seat, but my breathing is heavy, and although I feel a slight jerk of the van while my mom blindly searches for something, there isn't an ounce of energy left in me to help her. All of a sudden, the light-weight of a soft material spreads over my body, and my eyes slide open for a moment. Grateful for the blanket my mom has just placed over me, I fold my pillow under my head and recline my seat. Too tired to speak, I offer a faint smile as a thank you, and my mom smiles back, telling me that I should get some rest, and I treasure the unconditional look of love reflected in her brown eyes. She pats my shoulder, and before I know it, I have fallen into a deep sleep, basking in the release of guilt that my four-hour confession has yielded.

chapter twenty five

(October 15th, 2010)

Offering one last wave goodbye to my aunt, who has just dropped me off at the Buffalo airport, I saunter inside with my bag slung over my shoulder and my pillow hanging loosely by my side. Although there is a long wait to get through security, it passes quickly as I reflect on the amazing week I have just spent with my cousins, grandparents, aunts, and uncles. With an unremitting smile painted on my face, I unload my belongings on the security belt and make my way through the line. It's always a whirlwind of activity to get through security, but this time I have another reason to rush; I can't wait to call Mason and tell him about my week.

Having spent most of my time this past week talking incessantly about Mason with my cousins, I have to confess that I have been clinging to the hope that his hug has given me. His touch was tender and warm. There wasn't any hesitation in his embrace; instead, I felt like he knew how comforting that hug would be for both of us. Once I relaxed in his arms, my sobs that Pastor Max procured subsided, and I basked in the moment of intimacy that has been missing since the night Mason broke up with me.

"Miss, don't forget your pillow." I hear the security guard call for my attention, and I immediately blush, realizing that I have been collecting my things with a silly grin on my face, evidence of my distracted thoughts.

With a short lunge, I grab my pillow and thank the security guard, who is sneaking a side glance at me with one raised eyebrow, having witnessed my mystified state. Moving my feet so fast that I'm on the brink of a light jog, I race down the corridor to my gate. I check the screen one last time to confirm that I have reached my destination, I read *Flight 182 direct to Norfolk, Virginia (ORF)* on the screen above the currently empty help-desk. With an expression that I'm confident portrays my resolve, I settle in a seat far away from the other travelers, but still in view of the check-in counter. I take out my phone, thankful that the quick twenty minute trip from my aunt's house over the border to an American airport has given me mobile service for the first time since last Sunday. Quickly, I dial Mason, eager to hear his voice again and share all my stories. The phone rings numerous times, and I expect to be connected to his voice mail at any moment, but then the receiver picks up. I hear a muffled sound in the background, but no voice welcoming my call. "Mason?" I say into the speaker of my cell, "Hello, you there?"

After a few moments, his voice comes through the phone, and my tense muscles instantly relax. "Hey Tessa," he greets.

I try to act nonchalant; however, my anticipation to share with him the last week of my life is almost too overpowering, "What are you doing?" I force myself to sound aloof.

"Uh, nothing," he replies. *Is it just me, or does his tone sound defensive?*

My brow furrows ever so slightly, but I surge past my apprehension, "Oh, okay," I start, "Well, do you have a moment? I just had an awesome week with everyone in Canada, and I would love to tell you all about it! As soon as we crossed the border, we went straight to my grandparents for our Canadian Thanksgiving dinner…" I dive right into my story without waiting for his response, assuming that he does have a moment to spare, but my narrative comes to a screeching halt with his interruption.

"Tess, sorry but I can't talk right now. Can we talk another time?" His question stabs my chest, knocking the wind right out of me. His words aren't cruel, but it's what he doesn't say that hurts the most. He is doing something else, and whatever it is – it's more important than me.

"Yeah, of course," I choke, "I'll talk to you later…bye." And with an abrupt goodbye from his end, the line goes dead in unison with my heart. I place my phone on the chair beside me, slowly releasing the breath I've been holding. A teardrop darkens my pillow lying limply in my lap, and I feel another tear falling down my face. The reality of my tear stained pillow hits – how many times have I dampened this material with the tears that a life without Mason evokes? With the thought of my past lingering in my memory, I sit there in limbo, knowing that I need oxygen, but acknowledging how wonderful it would be if I were to never breathe again.

With quiet sobs, I reach again for my phone. I have internalized these feelings for too long, and I don't need to anymore. I dial my mom, knowing that she will understand given my recent four-hour confession.

"Hi honey," I hear her chirp through the phone, but I can't bring myself to respond. At this point my head is bent in my hands, and my bowed face is hidden by my long hair. A couple of sobs escape, and my mom knows - only one person could cause me to react this way. "Oh Tess – it's Mason isn't it?" I don't say anything - I can't say anything. For a while I sit there in silence, her sympathetic sigh offered as a condolence to my quiet sobs. I hesitate to admit what just happened on the phone between Mason and me. To admit it would mean that I have to accept that Mason dismissed me because of something else, maybe even someone else.

Eventually I speak, "I called him mom, I was so eager to tell him about my week. He cut me off and told me he couldn't talk, then hung up." I swipe at the tears as I glance up at a woman sauntering past me in search of her gate. By the time she is out of sight, I find myself falling to pieces all over again, "He didn't tell me why he couldn't talk, but whatever it was, obviously it was more important than me."

"Tessa, don't read too much into it, he's probably just busy and didn't mean to hurt you by saying goodbye so suddenly…"

"But you should have heard his tone mom, it was blunt and secretive, as if I was the last person he wanted to hear from. And it took him so long to answer too, he was obviously debating on whether or not to take my call."

"Well honey, he…" but her voice trails off. "Oh Tess, someone is knocking on the door. It's probably the neighbor coming over to discuss what should be done about our pine tree that fell on her fence during the last hurricane." I can tell she is torn, knowing she needs to answer the door, but not wanting to leave me in the depths of my despair without a shoulder to cry on.

With a quick wipe of my tears, I accept the need to hang up. "No worries, Mom," I assure her, exuding faux strength with my tone, "I am about to board my flight anyway. I will see you soon, okay? Remember the flight comes in at 11:00 tonight, Gate 3."

"Yes, I will be there, and I can't wait to see you," she says as I hear her shut the ever present laptop balancing on her knees, clank her cup of tea down on the coffee table and struggle to set the Lazy-boy out of the reclining position so she can make her way to the door. While still on the phone, I shake my head at how predictable my mother is. I know, far too well, the sound of determination in her steps, and can imagine the rolling of her eyes as she follows the knocking to its source. She undoubtedly feels frustration toward the fallen pine tree that is beyond her control. "Try not to dwell on this, honey. Just enjoy your flight. I love you," she rushes to say. I can hear the wooden door creak open just before she ends the call, but I miss the ensuing conversation about the tree that is causing tension between my family and our neighbors.

While I sit in silence, I glance at my watch; my flight doesn't leave for another hour. And although my cheeks are dry, my eyes are nowhere near it.

* * *

The hour in the airport, coupled with the time on the plane gave me ample time to consider my relationship with Mason. We were friends, and I had felt that Mason really crossed that barrier last week when he hugged me. However, I was wrong, and his lack of desire to speak to me on the phone was proof of it.

I cried most of the flight. The younger boy and his mom seated next to me shot perplexed looks in my direction the whole flight, but I didn't care what they thought as I used clumps of tissues to wipe my eyes and blow my nose. During the flight, I prayed a lot; which led me to this ultimate, heart-wrenching conclusion; my friendship with Mason is over. Everything is over.

The hope of his friendship will leave me wanting to call him at every turn in my life, but eventually Mason will get married to someone else. His wife will not want him talking to his ex-girlfriend. He will start a family, and how will he explain his relationship with me to his children? As I grab my bag from the overhead compartment, I shake my head at how pathetic it is for me to be clinging to a man that I love when he clearly doesn't love me back. Our comfortable friendship has given me false hope that there will be a future with him. I want to be his wife. I want to be the mother of his children. I want to wake up every day next to him. This is my heart's purest and most desperate desire, but his deliberation on the phone earlier this evening spoke loud and clear − I'm alone in my feelings, and that is why this friendship has to end. Tonight.

With renewed determination, I exit the plane. My mom, who will be at the end of the corridor to pick me up, is the perfect person to share my new insight with. I reflect on my need for her support as I consider my obvious desperation to end this chapter of my life, and move on to the next chapter that God has in store.

Thankfully our flight landed before 11:00, because the trip down the corridor seems unbearably long. Each step feels like agony, as if my feet are made of iron, carrying me to a destiny that I don't want, but can't escape – this decision solidifies in my heart that I will never love again.

I sweep my hair back behind my ear, and readjust my bag on my shoulder as I exit the secure area. With a quick glance around, I search for my mom but can't find her. Confused, I start to meander through the small crowd in case she is hidden off to one side. I soon conclude that my mother is running late – maybe she had to help the neighbor with the tree after all, causing her to lose track of time. I turn to find a seat at the gate where I can wait since I only brought a carry-on and don't have any luggage to claim. Now settled in a seat that gives me a perfect view to spot my mom once she arrives, a flight attendant holding a sign catches my eye, and I strain to read the familiar letters – it's my name. My face contorts, wondering why a female flight attendant with a plastic smile has a walkie-talkie in one hand and a small whiteboard with my name on it in the other.

My duffle bag falls from my shoulder and into my hand as I weave through the crowd to her side. "Uh, hi – I'm Tessa McRae," I say to the flight attendant.

"Oh yes, Tessa – I have a message for you." Her eyes dart toward her walkie-talkie, as if buying time in case any new information comes through the speakers for me. "Your mom was confused about the gate," she says. "Instead of meeting you here, she accidentally went to Concourse B – where travelers will emerge from Gate 30, and she would like you to meet her there."

Seriously, only my mom would be bold enough to get the airlines to direct me to where she was. I reminded her on the phone that it was Gate 3, but clearly the knock on the door distracted her. "Okay, thanks," I murmur, annoyed that this flight attendant still has an awkward look etched on her face. I head down the long hall wishing I was already in the car heading home. The number of people thins as I get closer to the arrival gate, and I wonder how my mom managed to find herself waiting at this desolate end of the terminal. I turn the last corner, my pillow in one hand and my duffle bag in the other. I pause to swivel in search of my mother, but what I find stops my heart. It's Mason.

I hear a thud beside me as my hands unconsciously release my luggage. Mason smiles shyly as he rises from the row of airport chairs with the most beautiful bouquet of flowers in his hand. My world turns in slow motion as I try to piece together the look on his face, the flowers in his hands, but most importantly, his presence here in this airport. But before I know it, he closes the space between us. With his free hand, he reaches for mine. I'm rendered speechless, not even sure what I would say if I had air in my lungs to speak.

"Tessa, this week has made me question what a life without you might look like. The truth is – I need you." My eyes search his face, desperate to hear the words that are on the tip of his tongue, "I love you, and I can't live without you."

Before I have time to say anything, he releases my hand and raises his to my cheek. Without a word, he holds me there for a moment wiping my tears with his thumb. Then, he kisses me. The most perfect and beautiful kiss I have ever had.

Wanting to disappear into the kiss forever, I open my eyes needing to confirm that this reality was my reality. Staring back at me are eyes filled with love, and my radiant response was a jumbled mess of smiles and tears. The moment I have been desperately waiting for has finally arrived. What I thought had ended – has just begun!

Mason takes me in his arms, and I can hear the plastic sleeve around the flowers crinkle as the bouquet presses against my back. My mind is so muddled, so confused. He was so short with me on the phone earlier tonight. How did he end up at the airport with flowers? I can barely speak, but I manage two words, "How? Why?"

In the solitude of this empty corridor, Mason doesn't let go of me, instead he speaks to me as I bury my tear stained face into the chest of the only man I have ever loved. His familiar scent offers the best welcome I could possibly imagine. "When you called earlier tonight, I was on my way to your parents' house to ask if I could pick you up from the airport. I wasn't sure if I should answer your call - you know I'm terrible at keeping secrets." I half laugh, half sob. He continues, "Your mom answered the door, and the look of shock on her face was priceless – I think she was expecting someone else. Anyway, she asked me to come in and we talked for over an hour. I told her all about how God has really been working in my life the last month, and how I felt like everything in my future was pointing to you – but I had to be sure that you still wanted to be with me, that you still loved me." I grin widely at his words, as if there was any question about my feelings for him. "Your mom prayed with me, and we both felt that this was God's plan. I thought your dad would be home too, but there was some big event going on at the church tonight, which was fine because in the end, we needed to be alone to talk about your…" I feel every inch of my body go stiff, "Well Tess, we talked about your mishap."

I don't dare to move from his embrace, but I recognize I can't speak either. *Is he mad? Does he blame me? Is he disgusted with me?* Mason pulls my face away from his chest. I look down - I can't bring myself to meet his gaze with all the shame and self-loathing coursing through me. Mason tips my chin up, and I risk a glance at his face. All I can see is forgiveness and grace in his eyes as he says, "I'm so sorry that happened to you, and I wish I could have been there to stop it, to help you through it, to do something…anything." At this, I become weak in the knees and fall helplessly into his embrace. I can't hold myself up anymore, but he can. The irony strikes me in this moment, he is my strength, and God knew I needed this strength. We stand there, holding each other while I cry with wonder at how God has worked things out so perfectly - Mason heard about my mishap, but I didn't have to be the one to tell him. God has so obviously prepared our hearts for this moment, and to have Mason hold me after knowing how low I've sunk is the most freeing feeling I have ever experienced. He loves me, despite my mishap.

My heart feels like it is going to explode with joy as I reach my arms tightly around Mason's body and cling to him, not ever wanting to let go. Mason laughs at this gesture, as if he knows my thoughts exactly. "Oh hey," he whispers, his lips are so close to my ear that his breathe tickles my skin in the most delightful way, "it's 11:11 – don't think I forgot."

We spend a few more minutes in this blissfully abandoned corridor, and it's not until people start to walk by that Mason hands me my flowers, and reaches down to grab my duffle bag. He glances around at the people rushing past, "And this is why I asked the flight attendant to send you to this end of the terminal." He smiles mischievously at me as he hands me my pillow. I tuck it under my arm, and my heart melts at his words – he planned all this – for me. Big tears of ecstasy have been rolling down my cheeks since the moment he came into view, but they begin all over again thanks to his determination to make this moment intimate and void of disruption.

With my beautiful flowers in one hand, my boyfriend leads me out of the airport. We walk in unison, facing the future before us with such rejuvenated elation that it almost hurts. I lean my head on Mason's shoulder, and I immediately know that I will not sleep tonight – I have never been more happy in my entire life – and I have God to thank for all of it.

epilogue

(December 17th, 2011)

That night, when Mason came to pick me up from the airport, was the best night of my life. Just as I had predicted, I barely got a wink of sleep. I called Rachel the moment Mason pulled out of the driveway. She was just as astonished as I was. I spent the next several months with my heart a flutter at the sight of the man I love, the man I was able to call my own.

I found out what prompted Mason to fall back in love with me. He had felt for a while that our friendship was something special, something that couldn't be replicated. He knew he could talk to me about anything, but the question was whether or not he could trust me again. He had to work through a lot, and he shared with me the steps that he took in prayer to get to the point where God allowed him to trust me again. God had also been working in my heart to become the woman that God wanted me to be.

Mason explained to me that he had been flipping through channels in September of 2010, the month before he asked me to be his girlfriend. He landed on *Dancing with the Stars*, not a show he would typically watch, but a former NFL player was performing. During the show, he spoke about his wife. He explained that he wanted to have his wife there at the performance, given that the art of dancing involves being in close proximity with another woman. He went on to describe his relationship with his wife; that his wife was his best friend, and the one who led him to the Lord. Mason told me that this was one of the first signs that really drew him back into considering a relationship with me. Mason saw so many parallels to this professional football player's story about his wife, and it started to get him thinking.

By the time Mason went to my house, knocked on the door, and stood face-to-face with my shocked mother, who had just hung up the phone with me, he had made the decision that everything in his future pointed to me. This gave my mom a great opportunity to explain how much God had changed my heart, and how God was constantly pruning me to be a woman who values a relationship with God above all else. Mason left my house that night ready to pick up his girlfriend from the airport; of course, I was exiting the plane planning to end our friendship given that my heart had endured all the pain it could possibly handle. Thankfully, God had a different plan.

Our relationship fell back into an easy rhythm, Mason and I were such good friends that a relationship was natural – we were meant to be together, but this time it was so much better than when we first dated. Roughly a month after we started dating again, Mason took me to look for an engagement ring. We didn't have any money, but Mason thought it would be wise for him to get an idea of what I was looking for. We did some looking around at first. Eventually, I saw it – the perfect ring. A beautiful, quarter carat, center diamond with side stones on a white gold band; it was exactly what I wanted. Mason turned to me and said, "It's beautiful – but right now, I can't afford it. I have to save up, and by the time I get the money, this ring will be probably be gone." My heart sank, but I knew that whatever we would find later would be just as beautiful. Ultimately, it's the fact that he wanted to put a ring on my finger and spend the rest of his life with me that mattered. However, I went home that night and dreamt about the ring anyway. I knew I would never see it again, but I was confident that I would want an engagement ring exactly like it.

The calendar year was coming to an end, and to celebrate all that 2010 had offered, my family threw a New Year's Eve party. The attire was somewhat formal, and I had friends and family there to celebrate the beginning of 2011, a year that I was confident would be even better than the previous one. We were watching the New Years Eve, New York Ball Drop on T.V., and it wasn't until we were a two minutes away from the new year that I realized my New Year's kiss wasn't in the same room. I frantically searched for him, and found him in the living room laid across the floor with his hand on his head; my parents watched from the kitchen, laughing. I thought I had missed an inside joke, but we didn't have time to discuss it, so I grabbed him, and ushered him into the T.V. room.

Immediately following the ball drop, my dad called the party together to make a toast. "To 2011, may you experience love and joy this year," he said. We toasted with a glass of champagne, and I expected the group to disperse; however, a second toast was called to attention. Mason turned to me, got down on one knee, and said, "I love you. I want to spend the rest of my life with you, will you marry me?" I burst into tears, unable to answer. Eventually, I squeaked out a barely audible "yes," then my fiancé placed the ring on my finger, stood up, and kissed me. It was perfect. It wasn't until I had managed to slow the flood of my joyful tears that I saw the ring – it was the one I had fallen in love with! He had gone back that day and purchased it without me knowing.

I was engaged to Mason Pierce, and I wish I could tell you that our relationship was flawless, that we didn't have any hiccups or bumps in the road, but our story could never go so smoothly, and a few months later I found myself struggling with the decision to end our engagement.

As we planned our future together, it was clear to both of us that God was leading Mason to pursue a degree in Physical Therapy. I sent off the paper work for him, eager to secure our future together. It wasn't until Mason returned from a church conference he had attended with my dad that I realized our future would be much different than what I had expected. Mason asked if we could talk privately. We sat down on the couch, and he told me that during the conference, God had called him into ministry. He explained that he wanted to be a pastor, and instead of pursuing a degree in Physical Therapy, that he was going to send in an application to a nearby seminary. I stared at him for a while with my mouth gapping. He knew how I felt about pastors, about being overly involved in a church, about my hesitations toward trusting the church. The horror of what he shared with me hit me hard, and I had a decision to make.

I tried to persuade Mason that what he had experienced at the conference was just an emotional encounter with God, that ministry was not our future. I explained that his application for Physical Therapy was currently being processed, and once he was accepted, he would see that PT was his future. I did everything in my power to change his mind, yet his response to me was, "I want to spend the rest of my life with you, but I'm going to obey God by pursuing a career in ministry, whether you follow me or not." The reality of this sentence pierced my heart. I wanted Mason to choose me, but at the same time, I understood his desire to place God's will above my own.

I cried for the next two days refusing to see or talk to Mason. I found myself staring down at my engagement ring, struggling with whether or not I was going to return it. I never wanted to be a pastor's wife; in fact, it was my biggest fear. *What was God doing?* I had finally got Mason back, and now he was going to be a pastor! So I prayed about it, and I concluded that if this is what God has planned for us, then I had to trust God enough to accept this role. In the end, I knew I couldn't do life without Mason, so I had to trust God that this was the future he had planned for us. So, with that in place - the wedding date was set, our future was in order, and our love grew stronger than ever.

* * *

I look down at the beautiful white silk clinging to my body. This wedding dress is gorgeous, custom designed to drop low in the back and hug my body at every curve. Alone in my bridal suite, I put my earrings in place; the last finishing touch before the ceremony begins, where I will commit myself to Mason for a life-time of all that God has planned.

I glance out of the window at the slightly grey sky, taking this solitary moment to reflect on all that has come together so perfectly. It's December 17th, the perfect day in the perfect month to get married. We rented a three-story beach house facing the ocean, and the ceremony was to take place in front of the big, beautiful bay windows that overlook the waves splashing magically on the sandy terrain.

With a smile, I thank God again for blessing me with such a great family and an amazing group of friends. My extended family drove down from Canada earlier in the week, excited to be there as Mason and I make a life-long commitment to each other. Rachel is my Maid of Honor, and she invited her new boyfriend to the wedding. They had met in church a few months earlier, and he has demonstrated his obvious commitment to the Lord in every thing he does. Amber and Chantel are standing as my two other bridesmaids, it's a small wedding party, but one that I'm confident supports me unconditionally. Their champagne colored dresses are custom made as well, which is ideal considering Amber had to make some alterations; she's pregnant again – another girl!

The door to my bridal suite swings wide open, and the most beautiful little flower girl waddles in yelling, "Auntie!" Picking Marley up, I swing her around in my arms a couple of times as she giggles repeatedly; music to my ears. We have just celebrated her second birthday, and she is adding new aspects to her endearing personality every day.

"You ready to do this?" Shane asks from the door, grinning as he watches his daughter's lively character illuminate my face.

Mason asked Shane to stand as one of his groomsmen. The task of determining groomsmen was a difficult one, but the ultimate decision came down to asking guys he knew would be in his life forever. I smile up at Shane and nod. Emerging slowly from the room, I see our wedding party standing at the foot of the most beautiful spiral staircase, dressed in colors of champagne and black; the perfect Christmas time, wedding ensemble.

The music plays as each couple makes their way up the stairs to where the crowd has gathered. My cue to start walking comes from Zander, who is singing the wedding procession and playing guitar. Although his main instrument is keys, he sounds amazing, and I know Chantel is sneaking side glances and grinning at him the whole time she walks the aisle. My heart thuds hard in my chest as I advance slowly, but confidently, up the staircase. I see my Dad standing at the top of the stairs, waiting to take my arm and walk me down the aisle, eventually giving me over to the most amazing guy I've ever known.

With each step I climb, I become more and more emotional. The last few years echo with every click of my heels against the hardwood. I've been through a lot, but God has been with me every step of the way, and now I get to commit myself to my best friend, the only guy I've ever loved, my soulmate. Before I know it, I'm standing at the top of the stairs, and as I slowly lift my tear-filled gaze, I meet the loving blue eyes of the man who is only moments away from becoming my husband.

discussion questions

Based on the storyline in this novel, there are many things that should be discussed. Whether you are using the following prompts as a part of your own personal reflection or you are meeting with a friend or in a small group, use these questions and verses to inspire more discussion.

Chapter 1:
Girls can often play the comparison game with their friends or peers. Why are we so focused on our flaws rather than our strengths?
> Psalm 139:14

Chapter 2:
In the dating world, we interact with many different personalities. How can we determine what qualities are worth pursuing in someone we might want to date?
> Proverbs 17:17

Chapter 3:
Sometimes our plans for the future get interrupted. When things don't go our way, how can we discover good in the midst of disappointment?
> Romans 8:18

Chapter 4:
Struggles and conflict within a family setting are things we all face at one point or another. How do you contribute to those problems, or how do you react when you feel frustrated about your family's circumstances or relationships?
> Psalm 34:14

Chapter 5:
When our lives move forward, there are many things to prepare for in relationships, education, or career choices. What factors should we examine when trying to determine the best direction for our future?

Ephesians 5:15-17

Chapter 6:
We are often placed in situations where our morals or ethical principles are tested. How can we put up parameters that will help us make wise decisions when temptation comes knocking?

1 Corinthians 10:13

Chapter 7:
When poor decisions are made, guilt will play on our conscience. Guilt and shame can lead us to keep secrets, so who can we share those secrets with in order to receive help while working through those difficult situations?

Proverbs 12:15

Chapter 8:
Some decisions we make will inevitably hurt others. Why is it important to own up to our choices rather than making excuses when we cause other people pain?

2 Corinthians 7:9-10

Chapter 9:
When our hearts are hurting, we often find ways to cope with the pain. In the midst of pain, how can we determine which coping mechanisms are healthy and which are not?

Philippians 4:6

Chapter 10:
Sometimes the bad can get worse. When we feel that our lives have fallen apart and there is no turning back, how do you escape when things are difficult; parties, food, unhealthy relationships,

unhelpful people? How can those escapes prove to be more destructive in your life?
> 1 Peter 5:8

Chapter 11:
There is evilness in this world that we can fall victim to, and we often wrongly blame ourselves. How can a victim recognize the real source of evil while dealing with self-hatred?
> Psalm 103:2-4

Chapter 12:
Rejections from our past have the tendency to feed into a depleted sense of self worth. What are some lies that need to be addressed from your past or childhood in order for you to clearly see your worth?
> Psalm 139:13

Chapter 13:
There are times when those around us judge us unfairly. What are some strategies that help us to work toward forgiving those who have wronged us?
> Colossians 3:13

Chapter 14:
Relationships from our past will often resurface bringing with them past conflicts. How can we respond to a past hurt in order to finally resolve it and put it in the past?
> Ephesians 4:32

Chapter 15:
We have all wrestled with fits of jealously at one point or another. What are some ways you can get past the jealousy you have for another person in a healthy manner?
> Philippians 2:3

Chapter 16:
Humanity is searching for answers. Although the world tries to offer some help, how does God provide the help we need as we are seeking answers?
Psalm 18:1-2

Chapter 17:
Even when we pursue all the right measures for comfort, we can still experience discouragement. In the midst of heartache and the feeling of defeat, what keeps you rooted in hope?
Jeremiah 29:11

Chapter 18:
It is so easy to focus on the negative, or what we don't have, rather than the positive, or what we do have. Where does your joy come from, or do you often find yourself overlooking the positives only to focus on the negatives that interrupt your joy?
Philippians 4:8

Chapter 19:
There are some seasons in life where we find ourselves on an emotional rollercoaster. In what ways do you deal with the highs and lows of life, and where do you find your strength?
Philippians 4:13

Chapter 20:
We have opportunities to pour into the lives of people around us, sometimes by using our personal experiences and other times by offering comfort. When you hang out with friends who are experiencing trials of their own, how do you tend to respond to their troubles?
Ecclesiastes 4:9-10

Chapter 21:
We can often perceive friendships to be deeper than they actually are. When you feel like you're not loved or valued in your friendships or other relationships, how do you determine what relationships

are worth keeping?
> Hebrews 10:24-25

Chapter 22:

Unfair decisions that are made without our input can frustrate us. When a person of authority goes over your head, what is your initial reaction and does that often cause more conflict?
> Titus 3:1-2

Chapter 23:

There are moments, maybe even seasons, where we have to grapple with regret. Have there been times where you have had to face your regret or a ghost from your past; and if so, what is the best way of dealing with the emotions evoked?
> Philippians 3:13 - 14

Chapter 24:

Gossip not only ruins reputations, but it is also destructive to the growth of individuals, especially when a difficult past is brought up. Have you ever judged people unfairly as a result of gossip, or have you ever been misjudged because of the rumors spread about you?
> James 3:5

Chapter 25:

Sometimes we focus on the right things, but for all the wrong reasons. When have you found your desires changing as a result of focusing on the right motives?
> Psalm 37:4

Epilogue:

There are times when there is no rhyme or reason to heartache, but occasionally it is revealed to us why we have had to endure such hardships. What heartaches have you had to endure, and where do you find your hope for healing?
> Jeremiah 30:17a

about the author

Tiffany Price and her husband Matt were led by God to pursue a 2-year missional opportunity in Manchester, U.K. where Tiffany penned her first romance novel, *Love's True Colors*. Following her undergrad years at Chowan University, Tiffany taught in a public high school in Durham, North Carolina. Currently studying through distance education at East Carolina University, Tiffany plans to use her masters in English to teach higher education as her career takes a shift in content and setting. Tiffany and Matt are relocating to Ann Arbor, Michigan to work with a church plant only a stone's throw away from Canada, where Tiffany was born and raised.